The House That Ate
the Hamptons

Also by James Brady

The Coldest War
Fashion Show
Nielsen's Children
Paris One
The Press Lord
Superchic
Designs
Holy Wars
Further Lane
Gin Lane

St. Martin's Press ❧ New York

The House That Ate
the Hamptons

A Novel of Lily Pond Lane

James Brady

THOMAS DUNNE BOOKS
An imprint of St. Martin's Press

Acknowledgments:

Women's fashions by Ungaro, Saint Laurent, and Giorgio Armani. Men's clothes by Henry Poole of Savile Row, J. Press, and L. L. Bean. Footwear by Church. Congressman Portofino's rug by Hair Club for Men. Mr. Glique's pruning shears by Hoffritz. Champagne by Dom Perignon, caviar by Petrossian, gin by Tanqueray.

Lady Alix's nipple ring by Cartier.

Her motor car by Aston-Martin.

Library of Congress Cataloging-in-Publication Data
Brady, James.
    The house that ate the Hamptons : a novel of Lily Pond Lane/ James Brady.—1st ed.
        p.   cm.
    ISBN 0-312-20558-9
    I. Title.
PS3552.R243H68   1999
813'.54—dc21   99-21749
                                                       CIP

First Edition: June 1999

10   9   8   7   6   5   4   3   2   I

This novel is for Sarah and Joe Konig.

———————————————————

It is dedicated to Kurt Vonnegut Jr., who, in defending the *actual* Sagaponack, played a most heroic role.

In Xanadu did Kubla Khan a stately
pleasure dome decree...

There are few secrets anymore.

And certainly not in the Hamptons, where gossip ranks slightly behind cocktails and just ahead of lawn care in our minuscule slice of the gross national product. So from the very start there was talk. No one believed they were putting up that big house on Sag Pond as a simple one-family residence for a mere millionaire from Texas. Murkier motives were suggested. Kurt Vonnegut Jr. threatened to leave town, and without meaning to do so became something of a local hero, kind of *our* Victor Laszlo, around whom a Resistance movement had begun to coalesce. George Plimpton spoke out. As did members of both the Meadow and the Maidstone clubs. Martha Stewart, as she was wont to do, kept her own counsel. As did Anthony Drexel Duke. Stillman the restaurateur sued but pensive Howard Stringer mulled the situation. In East Hampton, the Ladies Village Improvement Society got up a petition, while the more materialistic among us insisted there had to be *real* money behind all this, not just the lousy hundred million or so it was costing the

Texan. And a crusading New York politician with his eye on higher office (the White House? anything was possible) floated the possibility of subcommittee hearings.

Probably you know the place I mean. The mansion they were building out here last season, twice the size of the White House and believed to be the largest private dwelling ever in America.

If you have a place of your own "south of the highway," as the real estate boys say of the Hamptons' "better addresses," you may already have heard *too* much about it, both the house and the controversy it inspired: the vituperation, the lawsuits, the hurled insults, the holier-than-thou posturing, the rival architects whistled up as expert witnesses, the Sunday sermons about the sin of pride, the secessionist revolt mounted by local townsfolk, the cutting dead of people you'd known for years, the indignant editorials, the arrest for trespass of a neighbor who allegedly scaled a chain-link fence (Mr. Gildersleeve denied the charge. "I'm seventy-eight years old and have a replacement hip; I don't scale fences!"), the sound and the fury, all of it over a damned house being built for a man nobody knew.

And who was surely not one of *us.*

The name on the construction applications was that of wealthy oil wild-catter Chapman "Offshore" Wells. If this really was to be the Texan's place (and he was a bachelor!), was it intended as a monument to ego such as Ozymandias might have left behind? If not, then why was Wells building so large? And if not for himself, then for whom? For third parties unknown? And if Wells were just a front for someone, a foreign business associate, say, then who was *that*? As for just how swiftly, seemlessly, almost without notice, his various applications and permissions had slipped through the notoriously sticky local red tape, had both Southampton and East Hampton been caught napping? What happened to our zoning laws? If the towns weren't enforcing them, why not the county or Albany or the federal government? Had officials at every level been derelict in *their* duties? Or as the whispers grew louder, been *paid* to be derelict? In an enlightened age of instant communication, couldn't a mobilized and irate public opinion stop this dreadful building? After all, half the powerful public relations and advertising agency executives in Manhattan had second homes out here. And, most pointedly, why would anyone put up such an off-the-charts house in a fragile little beachfront hamlet like Sagaponack? Why build it at all and why build the damned thing *here*?

Even if you just rent in the Hamptons for the summer, or have a share with pals, or occasionally visit palmier, property-owning friends, or somehow end up on a Peggy Siegal PR list and get invited to the odd party or film screening, surely you've heard about the controversy. Maybe you've never even been to the East End of Long Island and "the Hamptons" doesn't mean anything to you, just another cliché from the columns like "Madonna," or "Donald Trump." But if you watch *60 Minutes* and read the papers, you know at least vaguely about the gargantuan mansion that threatened to spoil last summer and summers yet to come—the spread which whimsical locals, at first amused (and then appalled) by its sheer mass and vulgar pretensions, christened "Xanadu" (whether in tribute to Coleridge or to *Citizen Kane* wasn't quite clear). Others, just as appalled but less literary, dismissed it contemptibly as "that place."

The press, avid for precisely the right, quotable headline, labeled it "The House That Ate the Hamptons."

You'll probably recall (and if you don't, surely Graydon Carter will remind you), it was *Vanity Fair* that first used the line. The *New York Times* then took it up, on the front page, no less. *Time* and *Newsweek* weighed in. As did local television news and the radio call-in shows and *New York* magazine. Whatever it was called, the architectural monstrosity slowly rising before us was not only huge, and completely out of sync with its serene, rustic surround, it wasn't being put up by *us*. But by outsiders. A Texan, we were told at first, an oil man, and you know how *they* are. A Texan with connections in the Persian Gulf. Would that mean Arabs, as well? Arabs? You know how *they* are. Could it be a cult, millennium fruitcakes waiting for the spaceship? You don't have to be told about *them*. The house swiftly became a metaphor for everything we loved or hated in the Hamptons, and brought out in all of us (including myself, I regret to say) biases and spasms of xenophobia and chauvinism we didn't suspect we had. Wells's lawyers (he almost never appeared) claimed it was to be a private residence. But at that size? Surely it was meant to satisfy commercial ends. A think tank, a conference center, a corporate HQ, a . . . if Arabs were involved . . . harem? If you were a tree-hugger, you hated this house. If you loved slight, endangered, unspoilt Sagaponak, you hated it. If you had taste, you hated it. Mr. Vonnegut, our most respected local writer (well, with Joe Heller and Peter Maas), became so riled that, with a seemly eloquence which will surely outlive the controversy, he informed a protest meeting, "It will destroy Sagaponack for me, where I have lived and worked. So I'll be leaving. I think I can easily be spared."

He couldn't, of course. You don't just "spare" a neighbor like Vonnegut, lionized for the courage of his stand, and petitioned to stay. But that's what he said; it's what that bloody house did to good people. It turned them angry and suspicious, demanding to know who, if anyone, had been bought off, why the Architectural Review Board commissioners hadn't done their job, or why the Zoning Board of Appeals hadn't simply said "no." A few cooler heads suggested that, if we all shut up about it, the nightmare might just go away. It didn't.

Committees of protest were gotten up and "the best" people joined, many of them so self-oriented they spoke rarely even to their own children, so snob they spoke to no one else. People so private they would not have joined a committee called specifically into being to save their own lives. Or reduce the luxury tax on yachts and private jets. Or insulate the Maidstone and the Meadow clubs against being forced to accept for membership "just anyone." People joined the Sagaponack protest committees who never joined *anything*.

And they did what Hamptonites inevitably do in time of crisis: they organized lawn-party and cocktail fund-raisers.

Salman Rushdie, furtive, disguised and intermittently employing aliases while out here houseguesting (the fatwa for blasphemy had been lifted by Iran but freelance bounties remained in force), attended fund-raisers. That's how impassioned people became.

There were desultory attempts at manning picket lines, blocking concrete trucks and construction gangs from entering the property. But these were not terribly successful. It was one thing to join committees, compose letters to the editor, write checks; quite another to confront burly steamfitters or boilermakers eager to make a day's wage. Some of the more imaginative protesters sent their servants to represent them on the picket line. Others took their cue from wealthy men during the Civil War, who sent substitutes to fight so as to avoid soldiering, and hired people to parade about under a hot sun carrying placards in their names. In the end the placards were stacked in dim, cobwebbed corners and the picket lines simply whimpered out from sheer fatigue, as our protests came to an end.

And the work went on, frightening, noisy, disruptive, muddy in the wet days, dusty in the dry; the dynamiting and pile-driving, the riveting, the bulldozing, the low-gear grinding of big trucks, the drilling and the power saws, the pouring of cement, the welding of pipe, the entire enterprise as relentless and unstoppable as its own pile-drivers . . .

All spring, people said, there'd been the most gorgeous sunsets, much as happened following the eruption of Krakatoa long ago, when airborne dust particles filtered the sun's rays for more than a year into glorious rainbows.

That communal action was even attempted against it indicates how seriously the Hamptons took this absurdly vast house, towering there above the golden dunes that separated Sag Pond from the sea. It was an edifice so large, and so tall when completed, that it would be visible up and down the loveliest beach in America for miles. Rather like, wherever you are in Atlantic City, you cannot avoid seeing the famous Steel Pier, with its "diving horse" and other cheap attractions, whether or not you are in search of such diversion.

Since my people own a place in East Hampton, I became involved in the affair and ended up writing about it in my own magazine. But there's never space to include everything and the lawyers were uneasy about my being *too* candid.

And so, as briefly as I can, and as cogently, I'm going to try to set it down here, the whole story of the house sourly nicknamed "Xanadu," omitting very little and only changing a few names. I'll try not to be pious about it and bog down in ascribing motivation or drawing somber moral conclusions. For haven't we all, here in the Hamptons and indeed right across the country, had just about enough of that? Considering what happened to the President after he visited East Hampton last summer and stayed with the Spielbergs; and Kim and Alec Baldwin threw that swell, tented party; and Wasserstein the financier gave a $50,000-a-couple fund-raising dinner, and those wealthy gays on Ocean Avenue hosted him as well, bonding with and reassuring their guest, "Gay and lesbian people know about persecution, too, Mr. President."

Remember how Fauntleroy the Englishman, annoyed when the Secret Service told him for security reasons to stay away from his own windows while the President was next door with the gays, made his crude but gallant little gesture of protest. As Liz Smith reported in her column, "Cheered on by friends, the jovially plump Fauntleroy stripped naked, drained off a champagne cocktail, rammed a copy of the *Times* up his rear and set it on fire, before sprinting across the lawn to dive, smoking but only lightly charred, into his own pool."

Well, this story isn't about Fauntleroy aflame or the lovely Kim Basinger or the gays on Ocean Avenue. Or even about a disgraced President who, the instant he got back to Washington, issued sulky and grudging mea culpas, got himself a Bible, and began attending prayer breakfasts. There's been too much made of that already. So I'll cut directly to the story and set it down here as plainly and as accurately as I can.

Quite a yarn, I think you'll agree.

It's about a house, a grotesquely big house; a house going up on the rarefied shores of serpentine Sag Pond where it meanders between the ocean and Lily Pond and other classy lanes, lapping at various posh estates gloriously sited between East Hampton and Southampton, and thoughtlessly crossing several zoning jurisdictions as it wanders. Which was part of the problem.

Though *only* part.

t w o

*He might be anywhere from the Hindu Kush to
Arabia's Empty Quarter.*

My name is Beecher Stowe. Earlier this year while I was in Los Angeles doing
the piece for *Parade* magazine on Jay Leno and the *Tonight Show,* my father sent
me a few newspaper clippings about the vast Sag Pond house which had
people so upset. Skimming the stories, astonishing stats jumped out: a main
house with thirty bedrooms, larger than the White House or Hearst's San
Simeon or the new place that Bill Gates put up, as large even as the Biltmore
Estate in Asheville built a century ago by George Washington Vanderbilt.
There would be indoor and outdoor pools, a theater and a two-hundred-car
garage, a formal English garden of seventeen acres with an elaborate irrigation
scheme, horse barns and an indoor riding ring, seaplane mooring, chopper
pad, plus a large private zoo and aquarium (everything but Shamu the Whale),
the entire affair set on a sprawling oceanfront hundred acres which might be
nothing out West, but for the Hamptons is big. Really big.

"Thank God it's nowhere near us," my father noted dismissively in the margin, before going briskly on to more proximate concerns. There was an addi-

tional clip from the real estate section of the *New York Times*. An ad for another house on Further Lane in East Hampton quite close to our own, on the block for a modest $19.5 million. Disliking show, my father'd scribbled outrage in his distinctive hand: "As your mother might have said sarcastically, 'Ma fortune est faite!' And so is your eventual fortune made, Beecher, with real estate out here priced as insanely as this." My mother, who'd been French and a mannequin for Chanel, was long dead, but my father kept her alive in both our minds, and through his briefly scrawled quote, I could imagine her skeptically raised eyebrow.

In an accompanying letter he brought me up to date on East Hampton. Routine stuff, idle chat of no interest unless you lived here. Nothing at all about another of the neighbors, that marvelous filmmaker Samuel Glique, beyond a laconic "Played chess Tuesday with Glique."

There was little my father, the Admiral, had in common with Sammy Glique. And their few shared experiences most decidedly did not include teenage Asian concubines named Dixie Ng. Although as my father once remarked after a pleasant Tuesday evening over the chessboard with Glique, "That new girl of his, the one who fetches the ashtrays, is a stunner. The longest legs and cupid's-bow lips. And, oddly, a southern accent, suggesting the Creole, murmuring and syrupy." My father paused. "I wonder just what it is she and Glique . . . ?"

I took the old gentleman's question as rhetorical and offered no theories. In the established Wasp families we appreciate that some things are best left unsaid.

There are many strange and wonderful houses here in the Hamptons. One of them surely both strange and wonderful is located at 393 Lily Pond Lane in East Hampton, a house and grounds with private interior drives so long and sinuously winding, windrows of tall cedars masking the next curve, that speed bumps have been installed for safety. And the house itself? Well, that was built in the 1930s, inspired by the old Beverly Hills Hotel where Howard Hughes then kept a large cottage, replicated here to his specifications. Hughes was still (as far as we know) sane, romancing actresses (the cottage was *most* convenient), designing and flying fast planes (setting records as he did), and making popular movies at RKO. He was also running TWA, competing with Juan Trippe of Pan Am who had a jump on Hughes in the airline business and also in the matter of showcase houses, with a trophy place of his own on the East Hampton dunes. Perhaps the notion of deviling his rival Trippe played a role in Hughes's fixation on Lily Pond Lane. The story was that Hughes asked

Frank Lloyd Wright to put up the place but Mr. Wright told Hughes to go to blazes, that he worked from his own designs and, whatever the fee, did not ape "second-rate hacienda" architecture. So Hughes hired a local architect at an even higher price and got precisely what he wanted. It took two years to build and after that Hughes may have visited the house a half-dozen times when he was in the East. But that was about it. Because of its pink and green stucco ("Pepto-Bismol pink," said the snobs) and typically southern California look, so alien to the Hamptons, the place, the main house and four large, multi-bedroomed cottages, plus outbuildings, pool, stables, putting green, skeet range and grass court, became something of a white elephant which, over the years, passed into this one's hands and that one's.

It was in that house where every Tuesday evening my father, the Admiral, played speed chess with Sammy Glique.

Both men were passionate about chess and owned homes in East Hampton. Beyond that, as I mentioned, they had little or nothing in common. My father was a retired admiral who'd graduated from Annapolis and capped his active career as chief of Naval Intelligence, sort of our leading Cold War spy. A tall, athletic old Episcopalian (he'd stroked the crew at the Academy and still sculled our ponds and bays and paddled an ocean kayak), he had a big house and good bit of land along Further Lane, where he lived quite nicely (I, more modestly, had the gatehouse), tended to and provided for by a strapping and attractive Scandinavian woman named Inga, the precise nature of her services to my old man being such that I prefer not to elaborate. Inga lived for my father and tolerated me, and everyone else, just barely.

Sammy Glique made movies.

He was Brooklyn-born, a graduate of City College, scrawny, balding, unkempt, myopic, paranoid ("Of course I'm paranoid! I'm short and skinny, I wear bifocals, I'm losing my hair, and, need I mention it, I'll soon be fifty!"), and quirkily brilliant. At the moment he was being offered five million just for a screenplay. *More* if he'd agree to direct. The producers, oil Arabs who'd recently purchased a Hollywood studio, for exotic reasons only they might understand, wanted an updated and politically correct remake of *Elephant Walk*, the old Elizabeth Taylor chromo. In this one, the environmentally correct elephants rampage and take back their traditional turf from the colonialist planter. When Glique pointed out that was precisely what the elephants did in the earlier version, wrecking the planter's house in the doing, the chief Arab, a suave, dashing prince named Fatoosh, nodded. Yes, yes, he knew that;

he considered the original Hollywood picture to be an epic, but *his* elephants were to trample more people, especially white planters, and be considerably more "brusque" about their stampeding. All this to be done with wit and sophistication (even the trampling of planters, apparently), and accompanied by a rich, plummy musical score. "Family entertainment, my dear Glique, family entertainment," Prince Fatoosh said cheerfully, though at the same time, "an indictment of neocolonialism and celebration of the Third World."

"I assure you," Sammy marveled, "he actually said their elephants were to be more 'brusque.' My impression? They want *Springtime for Hitler* set in Ceylon."

Oh, yes, and Miss Taylor's role would be played by Sharon Stone. Sammy's meeting with Prince Fatoosh and associates had been pleasant but inconclusive. Five million was five million. And, when it came to elephants, Sammy could go either way. But Sharon Stone? Did he really want to write a flick for Sharon Stone? And with a story line as awful as this? Sammy dashed off a brief treatment of a dozen pages for a million flat (cash in advance) and sent it along to the Arabs. Right now, he was awaiting their critical assessment, but not anxiously so.

His real name was Samuel Glick, like the antihero of Budd Schulberg's novel of prewar Hollywood. It was that book, *What Makes Sammy Run?*, its enormous and immediate success, and its corrosive portrait of the industry, that caused Mr. Goldwyn to fire Budd from his job as a studio junior writer, and so exercised Louis B. Mayer that Mr. Mayer, a friend and fund-raiser for FDR, urged the government to deport young Schulberg. This despite Budd's being not only a native-born citizen, but a Dartmouth man.

As a boy, our Sammy knew nothing of Schulberg *or* his novel. That came later. But almost from birth he disliked his own name. How does a short, skinny sixteen-year-old named Sammy Glick pick up any girl, never mind shiksas? the boy complained. He became Sammy Glique, pronounced Gleek, and explained to people he was named for the French branch of his large, extended family. A few of the dimmer neighborhood girls who'd read naughty stories about Frenchmen and thought "Glique" exotic, were cajoled into necking with Sammy in the balcony of the Sheepshead Theatre. It was an early lesson for the young man that even a simple name change could pay off. How Glick became Glique legally and permanently was somewhat more complicated.

"I wanted to make movies. From City College on, I wanted. From childhood even, from P.S. 254 in Sheepshead Bay. Jewish children have heroes—why, we're not permitted? I had heroes. Not Sandy Koufax, not Mr. Justice Brandeis, not even Bernard Baruch, who, my father was reliably informed, was the smartest man in America, sitting on park benches thinking deeply, and subsequently telling President Roosevelt what to do. My idols were John Ford, Chaplin, Capra, Mack Sennett, Howard Hawks, Leni Riefenstahl. I know, I know, the Hitler thing. Listen, John Huston drank, Hitchcock was nasty to his leading ladies. D. W. Griffith, ask the NAACP about D. W. Griffith, all right? And Orson Welles? Don't get me started on Welles. None of them saints.

"Not to mention Jean Cocteau. During World War I—World War I! mind you—Cocteau served in the ambulance corps, wearing skirted uniforms made up for him by Poiret the designer, and had a male lover, a famous general. Not Poiret, Cocteau! Mother Cocteau gave young Jean a Kodak when he went off to the front. Did he snap photos of Verdun? Of historic battles? On the Marne or elsewhere? No, Cocteau got his delights in shooting pictures of naked Senegalese soldiers in their field showers. And his boyfriend, the general! Also a piece of work. One night a German zeppelin came over dropping bombs on the general's chateau. Down the stairs from the bedrooms they tumbled, all these gallant French officers headed for the wine cellars, and among them the general and young Cocteau, the latter in a frilly pink negligee! The Boches at the gates of Paris and Cocteau is wearing negligees and taking snapshots of naked soldiers showering. Does anyone today criticize his masterwork *Belle et la Bête* because of that? Of course not.

"In brief, these were my icons, these flawed geniuses my role models. I grew up worshiping them. I lived in movie houses, not being athletic. Besides, in the balcony, the girls. Ah! the girls. Sometimes they didn't wear bras; you got a feel. But I shouldn't start; even now, I get excited. In the Sheldon Theatre, Mr. Brown the manager, a Jewish gentleman himself, the name having been changed, of course, and better known as 'the Itch.' The movie house I assure you, not Mr. Brown, a fine man. His boy was in my class in public school. Sometimes, the Sheepshead Theatre. The Sheepshead had first-run films. Also an organ and free dishes, Friday night. They had a side door; you could sneak in. But not if the matron was watching. That matron, Nurse Ratched, believe me; a terror! But I risked facing even her, just to see the movies. I was the only boy at James Madison High with a subscription to *Variety*. At age fifteen I was reading Army Archerd. The motion picture industry was my destiny. I dreamed of becoming the new Irving Thalberg. Marrying actresses like

Norma Shearer. And dying young. I fasted and avoided suntan, all the better to look consumptive, coughing into a handkerchief like Camille, as I imagined the dying Thalberg might have done. But would Hollywood take seriously anyone named 'Glick'? Maybe studio people don't read. But they see treatments. And because of that troublemaker Schulberg, they knew about Sammy Glick. Even today, does 'Glick' get you past the receptionist at ICM? At William Morris? 'Glick' opens doors to Michael Eisner? To DreamWorks? Even there, Jewish gentlemen all, I believe there is a distaste for 'Glick.' So I changed it to 'Glique,' how the family spells it in France. I thought the spelling, the French pronunciation, gave a touch of class."

But if his name was such a burden, especially in the business where he would shape a career, why not change the name completely? To Jones. To Smith. To something Waspy, even something Irish as old-time Jewish boxers did?

Glique was a traditionalist. "There's a continuum, an homage to family. You don't just walk away from all that. Jews have roots, don't get me started on roots. To change my name to appear goyish, well, one just doesn't do such things. For shame, I say, even to consider it."

This logic ignored the reality that everyone else in his family, also Americans and Jews, spelled the name "Glick" and pronounced it that way as well, having their own ideas of tradition and continuums.

I'm not sure even now how Sammy and the Admiral first got together, but they'd been playing chess, according to their own, rigidly enforced "speed" rules, for a couple of years, and then afterward would sit over a quite good brandy or a single-malt scotch, briefly chatting about chess ("I've never liked the Rubinstein variation on the French Defense, have you?"), while my father, at Glique's urging, spun yarns of espionage, of the old days: of "the Great Game," as played out in years and centuries past by intelligence agents of the various powers, in dingy and perilous backwaters of Mittel Europa, of the Middle East, of Central Asia and along the fabled Silk Road from Cathay to Constantinople and thence to Venice and beyond. They never talked movies, about which my father knew nothing and Sammy knew too much. These pleasant evenings were usually held at Glique's house on Lily Pond Lane, about two miles from my old man's place.

Which was where I was heading now, to Further Lane, in late June of this past spring, to work on three magazine pieces I was writing for *Parade*, interviews I'd done over the period of a month and which I was hammering into shape for publication. The weather was good, my gatehouse sat pleasantly beckoning at the head of the gravel drive that led past the Admiral's house down to the dunes and ocean. So rather than stay in Manhattan and write, I packed my notes, calling ahead to alert my father. Only to get an irritatingly brief and not very helpful "The Admiral is traveling." That answering machine message in his own distinctive voice was undated and could have been weeks old, since he had little patience with left-messages, preferring signal lamps, carrier pigeons, coded entries in the personals columns of newspapers, invisible ink and page references to this or that obscure, out-of-print book (Holmes and Watson would have enjoyed Admiral Stowe). And aware of my father's peripatetic ways, he might be anywhere from the Hindu Kush to Arabia's Empty Quarter. Or even traversing, and not for the first time, the dusty, perilous trails of Uzbekistan through Bukhara and ancient Samarkand. Nor could I ask his whereabouts of Inga, whom I knew to be temporarily in Scandinavia on some sort of family crisis.

Well, I thought, I'll drive out to East Hampton anyway. The reported but as yet unwritten stories were about Oprah Winfrey, Senator Chafee of Rhode Island, and a pediatric nurse at Memorial Sloan-Kettering who dealt exclusively with little kids dying of cancer. I'd spend a couple of days trailing the nurse around the wards and the therapy centers and couldn't forget her remark, almost offhand yet so powerfully revealing, that "the little boys don't worry about being bald. They all wear baseball caps, anyway. The little girls all want wigs. They still want to be pretty." Little girls who knew they were dying but wanted to be pretty . . .

Just to put down those words sent shivers; I was leaving the writing of that one for last. That piece was going to be tough and might benefit from my being quiet and alone and able to concentrate.

You don't need to be told about the fragility of good intentions. How mistaken I was, so sure my own priorities were in order.

Nor did I yet suspect how my father, thousands of perilous miles away, would be drawn, and dramatically so, into the most dreadful of snares in the service of his country, over the apparently simple matter of yet another Hamptons mansion. After all, what affair was it of his, or mine, if a monstrosity of a house was rising along the beach in Sagaponack? How could that awful house possibly touch us, insulated as we were by a few miles, a little money, and an old Hamptons name?

Oh, but I was smug, forgetting what Donne taught us:

"No man is an island."

three

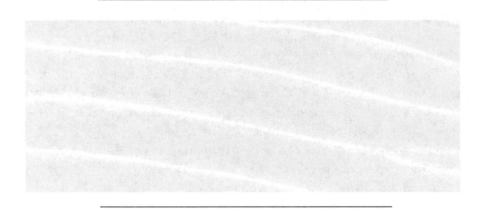

"For a poor, grieving widow, he puts in shitty faucets . . ."

A great thing about small towns is weekly papers like the *East Hampton Star*. After you get through the front page and read the letters column, all those impassioned arguments over trash collection and beach erosion and the inequities of the Zoning Board of Appeals, plus the familiar insults being swapped by the same compulsive correspondents (out here Alec Baldwin is one of our more tireless and eloquent letter writers), you feel once again very much at home. All those small, commonplace items convince you you've never been away:

Former Town Trustee Stuart Vorpahl was again challenging state law by bringing in a mess of fish well over the limits and purposely so, drawing down upon himself a summons, which Stuart coolly laughed off. He fished, he said, under the Dongan Patent, issued in 1686 by Royal Governor Thomas Dongan to reward East Hampton for remaining part of the Province of New York rather than joining Connecticut. Mr. Vorpahl claimed provincial law took precedence over current regulations, and compared himself to the famously independent "Fish Hooks" Mulford, an eighteenth-century East Hamptoner, who when visiting London captured a pickpocket by lining his trouser pockets with fish hooks.

Monsieur Bensimon's gorgeous young American wife had recently produced a child. Construction was underway on the Adelaide de Menil property. Barbara Goldsmith had a new book out and told an interviewer that between chapters, "I grab the pruning shears and attack the privet hedge." Mr. Brown was spending three million for landscaping alone, just for trees and grass, for God's sake! at his new spread on Further Lane. Billy Joel, his Elton John tour behind him, was preparing a solo trek of his own. Dr. Barondess and his wife, Linda, were understandably irritated by that ugly spec house built just east of their charming place. Leon Jaroff of Further Lane had a new meteor named for him. Seton Shanley had recovered from a bout of some sort and was again reading the Sunday lesson at the R.C. church. This summer's poison ivy crop was coming in more virulent than in years and gardening gloves were strongly recommended. Mr. Schulhof's house rebuilding on Egypt Lane was completed. A vandal had spun his tires in circles (turning doughnuts, as they put it locally) on a fairway of the Maidstone Club. Walter Isaacson, editor of *Time*, sold his place in Sag Harbor. An article recalled Edie Beale's (Little Edie, not her mother, Big Edie) famous remark, "Do you know, they can get you in East Hampton for wearing red shoes on a Thursday." Maureen Kirk, who was *never* seen wearing red shoes, was in residence for the long season. The A&P was again before the Town Planning Board with plans for a new supermarket on that piece of land where Jackie Bouvier learned to ride at the old Wolnough's Riding Academy. I actually knew most of these people (not riding master Wolnough or "Fish Hooks" Mulford, however).

On this occasion there was also a pungent essay by a man called Silverstone, who said that he'd been experiencing "down periods," and so for the first time in his life, had consulted a therapist, "who seemed disappointed to discover I'd had a happy childhood." But who concluded Silverstone suffered from low self-esteem and ought to have a hobby. Silverstone ended his little piece by saying he therefore bought a ship modeling kit and snapped right out of his funk. "I never even opened the box or made a ship model but I no longer suffer from low self-esteem."

By five that first evening, my own self-esteem in reasonably good shape, I pushed back from the IBM desktop and drove into East Hampton Village. *National Geographic* once called our Main Street the most beautiful in America. And I could believe it, even with traffic. I found a space and parked the Blazer down toward the post office, to walk back in the sun, enjoying the shop windows, the pretty girls clerking inside, the sleek people passing, the expensive cars, and being waved at by a guy in an ancient pickup, said hello to by Henry, the German who runs the Windmill Deli, and greeted by Ike, the old Marine gunny, who used to work in the movie house. Down the alleyway past Ralph Lauren's shop, the Blue Parrot was doing a nice cocktail hour business.

The Parrot is my favorite local dive. And the best-looking woman in the place was Michelle, a waitress with a couple of kids and a husband, a suntanned young fisherman who works on a dragger out of Montauk. They winter in Puerto Rico and come back here in April for another Hamptons "season," and seem to enjoy the best of both worlds. A housepainter I know was telling about the night he was stopped by the cops on DWI and when he got out of the car, he fell down.

"Nolo contendere," the painter had said as he crawled around David's Lane. The police always like a perp who admits guilt. And who knew the legalisms so he could make a plea. So they drove him home and took his car keys away and didn't charge him. But the near-miss helped the housepainter reform his ways and go dry. Which he is even today.

Newsweek had done a cover story that past week on the new beach season in the Hamptons and there was a swell photo of Martha Stewart. Lee, the owner of the Blue Parrot, had tacked it up on the wall near the phone, where they had a dust jacket from my book and two of Joe Heller's, and Christie Brinkley's autograph, a magazine cover photo of Billy Joel, another of Jimmy Buffet, stuff like that. Also tacked up, a newspaper clip that I'd missed and now paused to read, about rap mogul Puffy Combs having bought his rental house on Hedges Bank Drive, near Donna Karan's place, for $2.7 million. The clipping said that with the pool and hot tub, the house was "perfect for the kind of throbbing, all-night, limos-down-the-block, throw-the-girls-in-the-pool parties that neighbors will now just have to live with." Those clips and pix and scrawled signatures and such constituted a sort of Village wall of fame, and suggested without actually saying so that those mentioned regularly drank here. Not that the locals take it very seriously, but it titillates the tourists. Roland, who ran the Blue Parrot, briefed me on local events because I'd been away and was shamefully ignorant:

Sure, he said, local debate over "that house" on Sag Pond continued to simmer. But Vonnegut hadn't been in recently. "When he drops by for a cocktail people stand and sing a chorus of 'The Marseillaise.'" And not the barflies but the solid burghers, Roland said. "This probably sounds funny but it isn't to Kurt."

Wyseman Clagett the lawyer, already involved in the legal wrangling over Xanadu, had an additional scam. "High-speed hydrofoils from Montauk to Connecticut so gamblers can get to the Indian casinos faster." Since Clagett, who had a hideous facial tic, last tried to turn the Bridgehampton Raceway into a shopping mall, I thought I'd cast my vote against the ferries. "There's talk of a Si and Gar reunion concert. 'Save the Beaches' this time." But no one thought *that* would come off. Paul Simon lived here and played softball behind the A&P but he and Art rarely spoke. Maria Bartiromo, CNBC television's "Money Honey," reportedly was buying a place in nearby Water Mill. "And she'd be welcome here at the Parrot," Roland assured me, saying they were thinking of putting a photo of the Money Honey up there behind the bar along with Joe Heller's book jackets and Martha's *Newsweek* cover and Christie Brinkley's autograph.

Rex Magnifico, the magazine publisher, had totaled his Ferrari on Route 114 when he hit a deer. "It's okay," Roland said, "it's two years old." The Ferrari, he went on to clarify, not the deer. An archery open season to thin out the deer was being mulled. George Plimpton was telling people his Bastille Day fireworks show would be the most daring he'd ever staged. Sudsy, the antique dealer and weekly gossip columnist/cum restaurant critic, was writing this summer for the *Montauk Pioneer.* No salary. But then, think of the bylines, think of the free meals. Kate Capshaw, the actress married to Spielberg, had been in.

"Talk about 'honeys,'" Roland said, blissfully pursing his lips and mulling a blank patch of wall where perhaps a photo of Ms. Capshaw might fit in quite nicely.

When he was summoned to the kitchen by Kevin, the chef, over some culinary crisis, I sipped my Pacifico beer and looked along the bar. Dave Lucas, the Lawn Care King, was discussing Buddy Pontick's scheme for distilling a Hamptons label vodka from our local potatoes. Rinaldi was having a drink with Ingo, the engineer. I hadn't see Rinaldi for a time and bought a drink. Rinaldi did contractor work for spoiled rich people in the Hamptons. Or maybe that's redundant. Five years ago he was building split-levels in Dix Hills; today he was himself a millionaire with a place of his own out here, and the *New York Times* had, only slightly tongue-in-cheek, headlined a feature about him: CONTRACTOR TO THE STARS. But everything had its price.

"She calls me at home." He was complaining now about a high-profile Southampton client. "She gets my kids on the phone. She tells them, 'Your father is ruining my life. I'm a poor, bereaved widow, and your father is ruining my life.'"

How was he doing that? I asked Rinaldi.

"I put in a new bathroom for her. She don't like the faucets. She says if her dear husband was still alive, I never would have insulted him with faucets like that."

"And are they bad faucets?"

"Faucets are faucets. I'll change them. Put in new ones, no charge. Better ones, worse ones. No charge. Whatever she wants. But she likes to complain. Gets my wife on the phone. 'Your husband isn't there? He's in New York; count on it. Ruining my life and chasing bimbos. He's supposed to be doing my faucets. You don't know where he is; I don't know. Your children, do they know? Their father don't consider me, he don't consider them. Orphans is how he treats them. Me, a helpless widow with a faucet problem. Romancing bimbos. No concern for your children, for my bathroom. If my late husband was still alive . . .'"

"Wow!" I said. Rinaldi was always good value.

"She asks my wife if we were married in the church. My wife says, yes, of course we got married in the church, he's Italian. 'There! He spits in God's face, and for a poor, grieving widow he puts in shitty faucets.'"

Ingo, who'd heard these stories before, announced he was off to Pakistan to build a railroad. "If it's anywhere up near the Khyber Pass," Rinaldi warned, "watch out for them bastards. I seen movies about what they do up there. Tyrone Power in *King of the Khyber Rifles* . . ."

Attempting to reestablish an engineer's authority and to shut up Rinaldi, Ingo revealed trade secrets, "These days, railroad ties are precast concrete. No more creosote-soaked hardwood. No longer do they—"

"I'm just telling you, Ingo, watch out for them bastards."

Down the bar Gilbert, the portfolio manager, was nervous about the market and thinking of selling off his alpaca herd. Osvaldo, the dominant male, was acting up, suspected of killing a rival. Gilbert was having an autopsy done by Tufts. If only hornets would stop eating his wine grapes. Mellish, who had small tolerance for alpacas *or* grape-eating hornets, called out to me. He's a contributing editor for *Forbes* and knows everything. When I asked how he was, Rinaldi interrupted.

"He was in Australia. That's where they got wombats."

Mellish gave Rinaldi a scowl and started to tell me about diving on the Barrier Reef.

"They got worm farms, too," Rinaldi put in. "Thirty feet long some of them worms. Hey, Mellish, are them the ones if you step on you're dead?"

"The ones you step on are crustaceans. Only three inches in diameter but there's no known antidote for the poison that they—"

"But the wombats? They're okay? They eat the thirty-foot worms?"

Mellish turned to me, his back pointedly toward Rinaldi. "You dive right off the reef and down to fifty, sixty feet, the water's bright as noon. And all about you the most amazing variety of . . ."

Rinaldi ignored him.

"Up in the Khyber Pass, Ingo, watch out for them crustaceans, when you're laying them railroad ties; they're bastards, too. I don't know if they got wombats . . ."

Some women came in then, tall, attractive women with money, who parked fast, expensive cars outside, and were showing off nice Hamptons tans for this early in the season, proud of their suntans the way we all are in May and June. So I bought a round and we chatted them up. Considering it was Monday night, a pretty good crowd. Plus real estate salesmen. The season's new barmaid was kept occupied grinding up margaritas, and along the bar they were being consumed. The cold Pacifico beer was good, too. I hadn't gotten to the IGA grocery store yet and there was no food in the gatehouse and I didn't know what there might be in the kitchen of my father's house. So when Kelly Smith came in, I took her over to that new restaurant on the Montauk Highway, Peconic Coast, and we had dinner together. Kelly's tall and awfully good-looking and writes pieces from the Hamptons for the *New York Times.*

Two hours talking with Kelly and I knew most of what'd been happening since I was last here, fleshing out the weekly paper's and Roland's account. Even to the speaker at this week's Maidstone Club current affairs seminar (members and guests only), a Republican congressman named Portofino they were all talking about. Kelly had her own Jeep and drove off after coffee and I went home and was upstairs in bed before the eleven o'clock news. That's East Hampton in summer, for me at least. Raffish men and pretty women at the Blue Parrot; the more sophisticated hum of cocktail hour at the Maidstone Club yet to come. Two distinct worlds that met on occasion and sometimes shared a glass.

Nothing I'd heard tonight in East Hampton suggested that Sammy Glique would cross from his world to mine, would figure even marginally in my life. So he played chess with my father. The hell. You played tennis with a man. You played chess. You sat next to someone on an airplane or in a Broadway theater. You had a couple of beers. You walked away afterward. Beyond a chessboard, beyond both having a good address in the same rich, old Village, there could be nothing between a man like Glique and a man like Admiral Stowe.

That wasn't snobbery, or at least I hope it wasn't. Certainly not Wasp versus Jew. Or Old Money versus New. Simply the way things were in East Hampton.

I listened to Peggy Lee on a CD for a while but turned it off when she got to "Bye, Bye, Blackbird." When after a drink or two, especially if I'm alone, Peggy starts in slow and sobbing on "Blackbird," well . . .

From my bedroom you can hear the surf, and in between the crash of waves, the call of crickets from outside. I don't like crickets very much ("them bastards!" as Rinaldi might put it), clinging to cellar and garage walls in damp, dark places, and getting in the house on occasion; big, ugly, hopping things that squish when you swat them, but they sure sound fine in the night. Almost as wonderful as the ocean.

f o u r

*"The Northern Cheyenne senator who rode a Harley
and had a ponytail . . ."*

When I woke it was to sunlight and my first full day back in East Hampton in a new summer. I walked from the house down Old Beach Lane to the sand with the paper and a canvas chair slung across one shoulder, and sat there reading the ball scores and the editorials and how my mutual funds were doing and about Al Gore's prospects, and looking out through shades at the ocean. I'm always keen to see the menacing dorsal fin of a shark, and almost never do. Or a whale spouting. Sometimes we get porpoises along our beach. These, too, are rare. Last year, a green turtle. So I had to be satisfied with the ocean itself, quite flat with not much of a surf but awfully pretty, the green of the waves and the white foam, both set off against the tawny sand and a high blue sky. Fourth of July weekend was coming and there were quite a few people there already in the morning. Maybe three or four beach umbrellas and eighteen or twenty people counting kids. Quite a crowd on the beach in East Hampton is decidedly not like quite a crowd at Jones Beach. Some small boys were digging with plastic shovels and a grandfatherly fellow was attempting to show a little girl how to build a sand castle but every time he got a few hand-fuls of damp sand patted into place, she stepped on the "castle" and giggled happily, clapping her hands. I could see a career in demolition for this kid. The old grandpa seemed to enjoy it and just kept trying to put up sand castles while the little girl knocked them down. There were some older boys skim-ming a frisbee that a dog chased, barking but having fun, too, and a couple of teenage girls, one of them a real honey in what may have been the skimpiest thong of the young season to date.

I watched her over the top of my folded *Times* and wondered where Alix Dunraven was at times like these. It's how my mind works; I see a girl like that on the beach and I think about Her Ladyship. So I dove in and bodysurfed and flailed about for a bit and then toweled off. On my way back along Further Lane with the beach chair slung, I got a honk and it was Jesse Maine in his faded red Chevy pickup truck and he gave me a lift the rest of the way back to the house. I had him come in and gave him a cold Coke, the old Classic.

Jesse had a new enthusiasm, he said: archery.

"They reviving the art there on the reservation?" I inquired of Jesse, who, as you may know, is chief of the local Shinnecock tribe.

"Yeah, my idea. There's too many damned deer that people is wrecking their cars on. Getting killed themselves specially on Route 114 and Montauk Highway. But also it's keeping the sacred and traditional rituals vibrant and alive. People think casinos and cigarettes with no tax is all we Native Ameri-cans got. Ain't so. There's legends and ancient practices as well. UpIsland in Yaphank I found a Ukrainian woman name of VooVoo Vronsky. She makes bows on a lathe she got in the basement and teaches us poor Indians, and even white folks, how to shoot at targets. I got hold of her name through the archery website, Comanche Bowmen's Club dot com in Brooklyn."

"A Comanche archery website? In Brooklyn?"

"Yes, sir, and VooVoo's listed. She'll sell you a starter bow for seventy-five dollars and charges twenty-five an hour for lessons. Some bows go a lot higher. You buy the arrows at Caldor's, factory-made. Or at Sports Authority. VooVoo was in the Olympics, got a medal. I seen the medal, Beecher, so this ain't just talk."

Jesse admitted he was pretty good at the bow and arrow and a few of the others were catching on after just a few lessons. "Must be in the genes," he said, "when you can hit a fat raccoon in the head from forty yards at dusk with the light dying, and not spoil the pelt."

No, he hadn't seen the Admiral recently.

"I was in your daddy's house three days last fall doing a little carpentry, putting up bookcases in one of the bedrooms and replacing some banister dowels. His usual contractor, Mr. Uhll, was occupied and subcontracted me the work. Then I saw the Admiral a couple times this spring as I drove by in my pickup, out there whacking away at golf balls in the company of other rich Protestants on the fairways of the Maidstone. For a gentleman his age, he hits a long ball, Beecher. All in the leverage of being tall and having the slow backswing, I'd imagine."

I don't think Jesse'd ever played a round of golf in his life but he knew stuff like that. Amazing. And when curiosity got the best of me and I asked how he knew about slow backswings, Jesse said he'd picked it up watching the Golf Channel.

Then, not nosy but solicitous, a man who in his time had bent a rule, run afoul of law, the Shinnecock said, "Your daddy gone missing? Anything like that? Subpoenas served? Trouble, is there?"

I said no, just that I'd gotten a vague voice mail message. And with his housekeeper in Europe, I had no one to ask but neighbors like Jesse. The Admiral was traveling but hadn't said where and I didn't know when.

"Well, Beecher, it's spring and all that. The smell of manure in the fields and young women in heat. Men will roam, even solid men with roots, never mind lifelong sailors like your old daddy. And without suspicions nor libels being hinted at, not regarding a gentleman of his dignity, revered by his peers and the neighbors, in spring you never know, do you . . . ?"

"Spring ended a week ago, Jesse."

"There's echoes, Beecher, to be picked up by a sensitive ear like the Admiral's. Or my own," he conceded.

You rarely got anywhere nitpicking with Jesse. So I agreed that was so and Jesse promised to keep an eye out.

"The Pequots is observing an uneasy peace thus far in the year so I've got more leisure time than usual." The rival Pequot tribe was a particular irritant to Chief Maine and he never passed up an opportunity to blackguard them, not wishing as the saying goes, to spoil the Egyptians. For the moment his vision was focused on getting a tribal spokesperson in Washington, D.C., to push the cause of the smallish but proud Shinnecock nation in seeking federal designation as an official tribe. Plus the cash that might go with designation. And very specifically they needed a colorful figure to promote the Shinnecocks and trash the Pequots.

"What we ain't got is a lobbyist. A fellow like that lad from Colorado, Nighthorse Campbell, the Northern Cheyenne who somehow got himself elected senator and goes about on a big old Harley and sports a ponytail. I don't know how much of a senator ol' Nighthorse is, but he sure is a natural at getting on TV."

I told Jesse he probably could do that job himself, and splendidly, if the tribe could subsidize him in Washington. At which he turned thoughtful.

"No," he said at last, he didn't think he could swing it. "I got pelts drying and due to be tanned and commitments for carpentry, and regardless, there ain't no dough. Not for shuttle tickets and the cocktail parties you gotta throw for congressmen."

I secretly liked it that at the end of the twentieth century some Americans were still making decisions on the basis of tanning animal pelts. And doing carpentry. And not on spreadsheets and the Internet.

That afternoon my cleaning woman, Mary Sexton, phoned from the city. She reported what was in the mail and I told her what to send out. No word from Her Ladyship, from Alix Dunraven in London?

"No, sir."

Mary's voice softened. Just on that one word, "no." She knew what Alix meant to me, I guess. But Mary had her consolations:

"More damn-fool trouble with that MIR space station," she said with genuine satisfaction. "Whatever you think of Stalin, if he put up a space station, they would of gotten it right. If he had to send half the scientists to Siberia and shoot the rest in the basement of the Lubyanka. This bunch, what do they know about outer space or sending people to Siberia? Lot of amateurs." Her contempt for democracy was fierce. Then she said, the Irish brogue hardening once more, "Your government called. Some big noise in Washington . . ."

It was *her* government as well, I was tempted to say, but didn't. When your cleaning woman is Irish, a lapsed Catholic, and maybe the last Stalinist in the States, you don't get far arguing politics *or* religion. Let her clean the damned apartment and do the shirts, as she did, and without starch, and let it go at that. Besides, I'd had Mary for a couple of years now and couldn't conceive of doing without her. She was big, rawboned and of a certain age, ornery and wonderful.

"Oh? What'd he say?"

"To tell you your father has been out of touch and would you call them about it."

"Call whom?"

She gave me a name that meant nothing and a 202-224- number. That was Washington. And more than Washington, that was Capitol Hill. The United States Congress. I have that kind of mind; telephone numbers click in.

Why would a congressman's office want to know where my father was? He'd always been Department of the Navy, executive branch. Congress was, if not the enemy, the competition. And you know what they're like down there on the Hill these days, women and minorities and gays. And a Northern Cheyenne senator in a ponytail who rode Harleys. Not that there was anything wrong with any of them, even the women. But a career man like my father, spending his life in the intelligence establishment, he kept in touch. You were supposed to do that and you did it. The right people *always* knew how to reach an Admiral Stowe. The wrong people . . . ?

Well, now, that was another question, wasn't it.

I hoped Mary hadn't gotten into a dialectical argument with whoever called. They might not understand her Marxist views. I took the number from Mary and called it back. I recognized the congressman's name though not the aide answering on his behalf, swiftly said, "sorry," and hung up. I don't believe in leaving my name just for the sake of it. Journalists go looking for information, not trouble; the trouble tends to come along as a fringe benefit.

Any hour now, or one of these days, and it didn't really matter which, I was sure, my old man would be calling from someplace interesting. Or sending me messages in code. When you spend your professional life working the spy trade, you teach stuff like that to your kids. I grew up speaking foreign lingos, doing martial arts, and deciphering simple codes.

What was also interesting, intriguing even, was the identity of the congressman who'd placed the call about just where Admiral Stowe might be. I'd keep that one to myself for the time being.

five

Count Wigbold had several times set his dogs upon Glique.

When I picked up the phone, hoping it might be my father with some explanation of his absence, instead came the vaguely familiar voice, half bark, half insinuating whine, declaring, "It's Tuesday. Where's the Admiral?"

"Who's this?"

"The Admiral plays chess with me Tuesdays. We play speed chess. Fifteen seconds between moves, no more. Very strict on that. We have a clock."

"Oh, Mr. Glique. I'm the Admiral's son, Beecher Stowe."

"You don't play chess?"

"I know the blacks from the whites but, no, not the way you and my father . . ."

"Yes? So where is he? It's Tuesday."

"I know what day it is," I said, on the verge of saying more with a degree of asperity, but I was damned if I was going to tell Sammy Glique just where my father was. Even if I knew. And what was this all about? A congressman calling from Capitol Hill; Jesse Maine suggesting the Old Man might be in rut; and now an impatient Sammy Glique.

"He's traveling, Mr. Glique. I don't know just when he'll be back."

"Sammy. My name's Sammy. Everyone calls me Sammy, even people can't stand me call me Sammy, like we were together from public school. Like the Frank Merriwell-at-Yale stories."

"Okay then, Sammy. When I hear from him I'll tell him you—"

"You're sure you don't play?"

"No. Sorry."

"Not like the Admiral to travel on a Tuesday. Tuesdays we play speed chess, him and me, fifteen seconds between moves, on Lily Pond Lane."

"I know."

"Further Lane is okay, too. Nice little place your father has. But we play here. In the card room. That's what they call it. I hate cards. What is bridge? A bore. Gin Rummy, poof. The people owned the house before me, they played cards. Protestants, they were. I paid them top dollar for this place. One of the First Families. First Families don't play canasta; they don't play mah jongg. Bridge, they play bridge. A nice room. But not for cards. For speed chess, perfect. Miss Ng makes the tea, the coffee. She fetches little cakes that we should nibble, she lights a cigar, empties the ashtrays. That way we can concentrate on the game. On the fifteen-second clock. The quality of life matters, you know, whether it's making movies or playing chess. It's comfortable here on Lily Pond Lane."

"I'm sure," I said, visualizing Dixie Ng, her provocatively pursed lips, her long legs, a woman I'd seen only in photographs and on television, but about whom even my father was enthusiastic. Having Dixie as a live-in helper would make most places "comfortable," even if you were roughing it as more modest folks did here along Further Lane.

Sammy Glique had some difficulty in accepting the fact my father wasn't on Lily Pond Lane himself right now, playing chess.

"It beggars the imagination, to travel on Tuesdays when we always play—"

"Yes, well, I'll tell him you called, Mr. Glique."

"Sammy. They call me Sammy, even people think I'm a schmuck."

I wasn't one who thought that, not at all. Sammy Glique had made a dozen important American films, several more than important. He wrote, he directed, quite often he starred. His films were frequently nominated for Academy

Awards, for the writing, the directing, for best picture sometimes, for acting on the part of Glique himself; almost never did they *win* an Oscar.

"People out there don't like me," Glique shrugged. "You can't force them to vote in Beverly Hills 90210 for a guy lives on Central Park West 10024."

That was part of it. Sammy didn't suck up to the film establishment and didn't play golf. And he made and cast his movies in and around New York using actors from the Broadway stage. As far as the Coast was concerned, Elia Kazan was more popular. And they hated Kazan for ratting on the Hollywood Ten.

Which didn't mean Sammy was a folk hero in Manhattan, either. He was notorious for underpaying talent. They took the jobs anyway because a Sammy Glique picture would be "important," and it was worth sacrificing immediate gain for long-term advantage. Glique movies created "stars" and "stars" in their next roles made millions. And so actors put up with being paid badly, fobbed off with only two or three pages of script at a time, willing victims of Sammy's obsessive secrecy which left the leading players unsure where the story line was headed and why. Nor were Sammy's business partners overfond of the man. "You're allowed to put up the money," he told them. "And share in the profits, if any. That's all. You have no other rights and I make all decisions."

His backers were never permitted on the set, belatedly were informed of the title of the new movie, and only by accident would they learn who might be in the cast.

Glique had been married a number of times. The divorces were colorful and expensive. So Sammy stopped getting married and started moving in a pliant young woman for a year or so at a time. These young women were invariably beautiful, fans of his movies, recruited from the film schools of USC and UCLA, and half his age. And so long as they were with Glique, he was admirably monogamous, never cheating or playing around or even flirting with others. The sex? That, apparently, was satisfactory for both parties. Even when he was still getting divorced, no one ever said Sammy wasn't good value in bed, not even the wives. And when the girlfriends went off, as inevitably they did after worshipping at the shrine, the parting was genial; the girl had been provided for, often with a good job in the industry.

"Fringe benefits, like the dental plan or a 401K," Glique called these little perquisites, and didn't resent having to provide them.

Dixie Ng was his current friend. She was the one who'd so impressed my father, a man who didn't impress easily. Dixie was a nineteen-year-old sopho-more studying cinema arts at UCLA when Sammy came across her. Her fam-ily had a restaurant in New Orleans, one of the few fast food restaurants in that city of gourmands. "Uh Kentucky Fried Chicken franchise," Dixie would explain. "Y'all get tired uh moo goo gai pan aftah a while." She'd been living with Sammy for nearly a year now and stayed in touch with college courses by correspondence.

"Y'all'd be amazed how decent they ah about it," she freely conceded in that down-home Louisiana accent, "giving me three additional credits per se-mester spent with Mr. Glique. Tha dean himself approved: 'We give credits ta kids who intern summers in the mail room at MGM. Why not credits foh liv-ing with uh great director lak Glique?' They figure Ah'm learning on tha job. A real insider's view of tha industry, so t' speak."

She told all this to the *New York Times*, to Bernard Weinraub, southern accent and all, on the record and during an interview, explaining that while Glique pronounced her surname "Ning," she preferred two syllables, "Knee-ing." Check it on the Internet if you doubt me.

She and Glique were hardly alone at the house on Lily Pond Lane. For all his shyness, Glique enjoyed comfort, employing a staff supervised by the stern, demanding housekeeper, Mrs. Danvers. There was also an entourage, not large, but devoted, people who'd worked with Sammy for years, who dropped by and stayed: "Wolfie the producer"; Piano the banker, Lebanese and plumply shrewd, for some reason addressed as "Signor" Piano; and "Lars the cinematographer," a vast, handsome Scandinavian (with a touch of savage Lapp blood and the Finn's love of drink), who came inevitably with baggage (or "baggages," girlfriends). But why Lars? Why would the insecure Sammy tolerate a tall, handsome hunk like Lars on the premises? "A great cinematog-rapher, of course." Pause. "But in all of us, a voyeurism to which I freely ad-mit. The girls he brings? You should see them. *Animals!* Dixie can tell you. Tell them, Dixie."

"Lak Mr. Glique sez, they ah *animals!*"

It was not entirely clear if Dixie was for or against having such "animals" on site.

Wolfie was an exquisite woman of forty, gentle and caring, who co-produced all of Glique's films while also functioning as an intelligently indul-gent den mother. She had a last name but no one bothered with it. And she spent most of her waking hours reading scripts for possible Sammy projects.

Piano studied brokerage reports and was mostly silent. Lars had an unruly mane of blond hair going gray and a sparse English, the essential phrases of his craft: "lights . . . action . . . camera . . . lap dissolve . . ." and the like.

For the rest of it, Lars stayed with "Hi Ho!" which served him much as "Ciao" served the Italians, as "Hello . . . good-bye," or emotions in between. A limited vocabulary didn't seem to limit his social life and there were those who thought he ought to be a sitcom, *Lars and the Covergirls.* It was with such women, especially the American models, that Lars disclosed one additional bit of English, used as a seductive ice-breaker, a smooth euphemism for sexual congress:

"Make bouncy?"

This season there was an interim member of the coterie, George Plimpton. George's oral history of Truman Capote had done so well in the bookshops, he'd embarked on a similar book about Glique. Though George lived on a barge in East Hampton, up near the Devon Yacht Club, he was often on Lily Pond Lane, taping remarks and jotting notes.

Oh, yes, the fourth cottage, the one not being used by Wolfie, Lars (and the covergirls) or Signor Piano, had for a time been assigned to Senator D'Amato, an East Coast, far more respectable, version of professional houseguest Kato Kaelin.

"Why not?" Sammy responded defensively when asked. "We're both New Yorkers, born and bred. I'm a constituent, right? I shouldn't provide shelter from the sun, a nicely made bed, fresh towels and a washcloth, Ivory soap and Crest toothpaste, for a United States senator? And one with a desperate re-election campaign looming this fall? If not Geraldine Ferraro then Congress-man Schumer, a real putzhead that one. Though clever and well financed." But there'd been a recent falling-out, with Senator D'Amato abruptly departing. And despite the angst, Glique missed having him as a guest. "Such statesman, underpaid and with legislative burdens, deserve our gratitude."

But that story was cover; to intimates Sammy confessed the truth:

"Growing up in Sheepshead Bay, Brooklyn, I used to fantasize about Hyan-nis Port, the Kennedy compound, all those tall, handsome people who went to Harvard, and Mama Rose in her wicker chair, always smiling, smiling and nodding off. There I am in Brooklyn and is my mother smiling from the wicker chair and nodding off? Not likely; she's asking when am I going to stop already with the movies and get a job? While the Kennedys play touch football with shiksas (wearing no bras, mind you!), my mother is after me about jobs. Think of it up there in Hyannis Port: the power, the glamour, the girls, the straight teeth, the tousled hair. Do the Kennedy boys need Brylcreme? You're shitting me, just look at the hair. Do they have acne? You never saw such skin. And Rose Kennedy isn't nagging about jobs. No one counts the movies they see. And who drops by, joins the football game? Pierre Salinger, Frank Gifford, Art Buchwald, movie stars, even John Kenneth Galbraith! How dare I dream such dreams? Even now, with a compound of my own and a modest entourage, am I playing touch football?

"The nearest to the Kennedys I can come is Senator D'Amato." This said with a degree of resignation.

But if theirs was a congenial bunch (even D'Amato pro tem) within the confines of Sammy's property, relations with some of the neighbors along Lily Pond Lane were less amiable. Blame Sammy's pruning shears.

"Anal? Nothing to be ashamed about. I admit to being a little anal." Sammy was a tireless walker along the rural East Hampton roads and so anal that in his back pocket he carried a discreet pair of pruning shears, which he used, as he went along, to snip off an errant twig, a bit of privet hedge gone untrimmed, a rambling rose that had rambled. "You want the neighborhood to look nice. It should be neat; why else do we pay such prices if not for neat?"

His snipping had become so compulsive, he dropped by Bernie's Village Hardware on a regular basis to have his pruning shears sharpened. The trouble was, Lily Pond Lane preferred to trim its own hedges, its own rosebushes, its own errant twigs. Or leave the job to groundskeepers employed for the purpose. And not to busybody Glique.

"Nosy little bastard. Who gave him pruning rights to my privet?"

"With the best will in the world, I snip a little," he protested, "all for their benefit. And for the common weal. Sex? Yes, I admit it. I derive personal pleasure. But in this, I'm selfless. I ask nothing but nice shrubberies. To improve the neighborhood, to perform community service."

George T. Brodie was an irritant. His handsome grounds on Lily Pond Lane were east of Sammy's and as well tailored as the man himself, an international lawyer of enormous reputation and one noted for his exquisite manners and for never relaxing the dress code, once being described as "the only man in town to wear a homburg while washing his car."

It was on just such a morning when Mr. Brodie was washing his car (in his homburg), that he saw Sammy tiptoeing over the grassy edge of the property line to snip off an awkwardly drooping apple tree spray, and issued a polite but firm protest. One exchange led to another and a lawsuit was being discussed. Nor was the homburged Brodie Sammy's only antagonist when it came to pruning. Count Wigbold, treasurer of the local Beagle Club, whose ancestors returned the exiled Prince of Orange to the throne of Holland, had several times set his dogs on Glique. While Niblack Esbenshade, whose passion was leather bookbinding, and Mrs. Hamilton, instrumental in forming the first-ever Venezuelan women's polo team, were others along Lily Pond Lane who'd sent angry letters to the *East Hampton Star.*

I don't want you to think Sammy was at war with all the neighbors. Martha Stewart found Sammy "amusing." Mort Zuckerman never said a word. Too busy, one would think, running *U.S. News & World Report.* Jerry Della Femina had his own difficulties with the Village fathers. Nor did Lily Ponder William Clay Ford Jr. speak out, preoccupied as an owner of the Detroit Lions football team and recently anointed Ford Motor Co.'s chairman. There were even neighbors who quite liked Sammy and forgave him his pruning shears: Calvin Klein, Kummer the mathematician, Evariste Galois, twice amateur golfing champion of Long Island, and Colonel Burlingame, the biographer of Glubb Pasha, who was something of a crank himself, bombarding the *Times* regularly with letters urging that an elite camel corps be raised for light cavalry reconnaissance in the likelihood of a future war in the Persian Gulf.

Even Alec Baldwin wrote a letter, this one in tepid support of Glique as a fellow member of the Academy. But then, Alec Baldwin was always writing letters to the *Star.* Your heart rather went out to his poor wife, who bravely pretended to find her husband's letters to the editor persuasive, powerful and moving.

None of these reactions pro or con, dissuaded Sammy from his penchant for snipping as he strode. But of course he wasn't aware just who was about to arrive in the Village clutching a WANTED, PUBLIC ENEMY poster that bore Glique's name and face. Though, as occupied as he was, how could Sammy know?

Snip-snip, snip-snip, snip-snip.

s i x

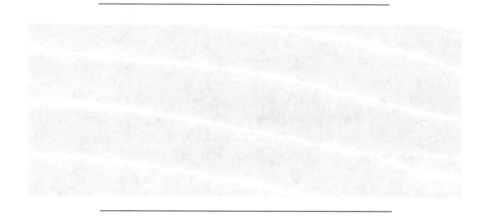

A congressman named Buzzy Portofino. He's
apparently all the rage.

Another call from Mary Sexton, her voice buoyant. "A message from Her Ladyship, Mr. Beecher. From London and lengthy."

I knew Alix would be corresponding in her usual cipher so Mary could fax it to me and with circumspection, via the File Box stationery shop on Newtown Lane here in East Hampton Village. I phoned to alert the File Box ladies and drove up to get it.

"Darling," Alix's communiqué began in code, "I enjoyed a cocktail at the Connaught and then dined and went dancing with your father the Admiral. Quel charmer. When I told him I was headed for New York on assignment for Mr. Murdoch, he scribbled the following message for you. Neither telephones nor E-mail were secure, he feared. 'There are enemies unknown, Lady Alix. One must be vigilant. And wily at the same time.' I told him, 'Admiral, my very sentiments. You can count on my being both vigilant and wily.' He seemed genuinely reassured, ordering another round of drys straight up, and said the following few words would inform you as to his whereabouts and indeed his intentions. Here is the message:

"'Book 231. Page 20. Sewers.'

"Does that make any sense? I assume it does. You and your father are both charmers, if I neglected to say so before.

"On another matter, are you acquainted with American congressman Buzzy Portofino? Even for your Parliament, what an extraordinary name! He's apparently all the current rage. I'm to pick his brains on behalf of my editors and get him to write a weekly letter from Washington for Mr. Murdoch and *The Times.* They say he's making a significant policy address at your dear old Maidstone Club."

There followed logistical information as to her travel arrangements and then some decidedly personal commentary regarding our last time together and how she missed me in some fevered detail, material I prefer not to broadcast here.

Having digested the faxed message, especially the randy parts, I went across the lawn to my father's house and into his library. There the books were arranged, hardcover or paperback, it didn't matter which, according to a mystifying numerical system all his own. Book number 231 was a tattered paperback put out in 1960 by Penguin Books Ltd. of Harmondsworth, Middlesex, a cheap (two shillings and sixpence) reprint of an old (1916) boy's adventure yarn by John Buchan.

I turned swiftly to page twenty, to a reference to "sewers":

"We have had our agents working in Persia and Mesopotamia for years—mostly young officers of the Indian Army. Now and then one disappears, and the sewers of Baghdad might tell a tale. But they find out many things, and they count the game worth the candle."

There was more after that, mostly dated, patriotic rubbish from the Great War of eighty years ago. I had the message my father intended that I have, thanks to his crude code. And to the vigilant and, yes, wily, Alix Dunraven, daughter of the twelfth Earl.

The book was called *Greenmantle* and though I'd never read it, it seemed a favorable omen that I'd heard Alix mention it as a childhood favorite of her own, having been raised by the Earl as something of a tomboy, since his late wife, her mother, had, in the Earl's vernacular, "foaled but the once, and that a filly."

So my aging father, with his international renown and great height, rendering disguise impossible, was en route to the most dangerous city in the world for an American officer. He surely knew the risks of treading on Saddam

Hussein's home turf, recalling for me "the sewers of Baghdad" and the "tales they might tell." But why go there? Formally retired, he traveled officially only on orders of the President or of his friend Bill Cohen, the Secretary of Defense. There must be vital reasons for the Admiral to be headed east, to Iraq and perhaps beyond.

And why was Rupert Murdoch dispatching Alix to America to "pick the brains" of Congressman Portofino? Who happened to be the very congressman whose office had, recently, called my Manhattan flat asking just where my father might be? Were there connections here between a rabble-rousing politician and my father? Coincidence? I don't believe in coincidence.

My pondering was interrupted by a call from Walter Anderson.

Anderson is the editor of *Parade* magazine and better informed than most people. But he had a nice way about his superiority, not rubbing your nose in it. With his senior writers, he was deferential, as if to say, "Now, you probably know a lot more about this than I do. But had you considered . . . ?"

"Beecher, it's Walter . . ."

I'd been writing the Oprah Winfrey piece, the part where she was saying modestly of her own very impressive acting, "You know, I don't make my living doing this."

"Hi, Walter. What's up?"

"Is this big house that has people so upset anywhere near you?"

"A few miles west of here. I haven't seen it yet. They say it's grotesque."

"There's talk the fellow building the place is just fronting for a rich oil Arab, to get around local prejudices and laws about foreign ownership. Could it be a story for *Parade*: New Money versus Old, the establishment resisting newcomers, a bias against foreigners?"

"Could be. The guy putting it up is Chapman Wells. He's the biggest wildcatter in Texas, and the most colorful, nicknamed 'Offshore,' and has the money. But he's hardly the kind of man you expect in the Hamptons. The South of France and tropical islands are more his sandbox. His outfit is Arabian–U.S. Oil, known as Arabus, and it's big. Big and important. And as a Dow Industrials component, a significant player on Wall Street. So he's got the right Arab connections. And there are already plenty of Arabs out here in the Hamptons and not all that popular. Buying up property, inflating prices already out of this world, big houses and undeveloped land both. Fast cars, fast blondes, throwing their money around, antagonizing the local bigots. Got a name for this particular Arab?"

"One of those odd, repetitive family names. A sheik named Sabah Sabah, something like that."

"Sabah al-Sabah al-Sabah?"

"That sounds close. You know these people?"

"I know the family. The Emir Sabah al-Sabah is the big noise of Kuwait. I know several of his sons. Went to college with one of them, Prince Bandar. Saw him again in the Gulf War."

"That's not the name. This one is named . . . Fatoosh. Is that the pronunciation?"

"Yes, Fatoosh. You got it right." The man who wanted Glique to make a movie starring Sharon Stone. And elephants. Brusque elephants.

"What's he like?"

"I've only met him at receptions, shaking hands, passing the diplomatic time of day. Handsome dog, smart as hell. Mother a Berlin film star and he was largely educated in German schools. Breeds thoroughbred horses. One of them ran in the money at the Belmont a few years ago. Bought a Hollywood studio. Back home in the Gulf teenagers think of him as a kind of rock star and ask for autographs. Older people consider him a bit flashy, unreliable. If he were portrayed in one of his own movies it would be by Antonio Banderas, someone like that. Or the young Omar Sharif. Very affable. But . . ."

"You sound unhappy," Anderson said, sensitive to mood and tone.

"I am. Fatoosh is a potential emir. Very ambitious. Almost everyone likes him. Except those who don't. There's something about him. A nasty edge . . . hot tempered with a mean streak. In the Gulf they're wary, very careful always to use his full title and honorific."

"And what's that?"

"His Serene Highness Prince Fatoosh the Malevolent."

Anderson digested that. "One thing more," he said, "a congressman named Portofino has his subcommittee investigating wealthy aliens buying up chunks of this country, people like Fatoosh. Portofino sounds like a populist demagogue after a headline, but he's scheduled to make a speech in the Hamptons. Maybe about this house they're all talking about. Could be there's no connection at all. Why don't you sniff around? I had the curious idea that out of all this, the big house, the Arabs, and Buzzy Portofino, there might conceivably be a story . . ."

When a magazine pays as well as *Parade* does and the editor suggests "there might be a story" somewhere, you tend to go along. I promised to look into it.

She was not just another
"rich man's toy."

The afternoon sun had begun its stately fall toward Hook Pond as golfers straggled in from the tough back nine, when I encountered bibliophile (and Maidstone Club librarian ex-officio) Cyril Pilaster in the bar and we agreed it might be a good idea to have a martini. The stemmed, wide-rimmed glasses that were all the rage last summer had just been set down before us when they began trembling and vibrating as the damnedest roar came through the open ocean-fronting windows of the club.

"By God! Someone's landing a chopper on the club beach, by God!"

All about the grand old barroom men were standing now, several tottering but by God! on their feet. Even Tony Duke, and you know how cool he is, was up and staring.

"Never seen that before," said Donald Kirk in amazement, the engine even louder.

"Nor I," Bryan Webb agreed. Webb was one of the keenest lawyers on Park Avenue, and impressed despite himself, sensibly knocked back a gin.

"By God!" Barney Leason called out, snapping his fingers for a waiter. "Fetch a refill here. I want to see this, by God!"

Not that there was much to see through the miniature sandstorm kicked up and sent whirling in every direction.

"Can't be a member," Chas. Mitchelmore remarked. "Not with foursomes still out on the course and lining up their putts, by God!"

The helicopter was a big one. You could tell even before its rotors slowed and the sandstorm thinned.

"By God! it's a big son of a bitch," a member murmured behind me, impressed despite himself. Cocktail hour at the Maidstone is not often distinguished by original thought or turn of phrase.

"It certainly is," I agreed, my own remarks as banal as any.

Out there on the beach, beyond the faded old cabanas, the chopper was at rest. Three crewmen now emerged, holding out helping hands to a tall young woman wearing shades but hatless, her dark brown hair pleasantly tousled by the wind, and clad in a leather flight jacket, slim tan slacks, and a white silk scarf knotted loosely about her longish throat. A very Amelia Earhart look. As I stared, she gracefully, nimbly, made her way down the aluminum ladder, followed swiftly by others, men, down to the sand. From this distance I had no idea who the men were. Besides, I was focusing on the woman, who looked awfully good. And quite tan. But perhaps that was makeup.

"Who the devil's that?" a member demanded.

"A woman, by God! It's a woman landed on the club beach!"

A woman, yes! I wanted to cry out. And what a woman! But why join in the general confusion?

"Who the hell are these people?" another shouted and then, suddenly aware these new arrivals might indeed *be* club members, he fell to mumbling, "All very well if they *belong*, I mean . . ."

"By God! they'd *better!*" the customarily gentle, soft-spoken Cy Pilaster offered. Poor Cy was already out of sorts about something else. Helicopters and women were simply added irritants.

The hatch secured and the crewmen back inside, the rotor was now turning as the wind again began to stir, and the chopper vanished into the enveloping sandstorm.

"But don't they have to file flight plans?" a trustee was asking of no one in particular and the entire club in general, "to say nothing of notifying the Maidstone? Using our beach and so on . . ."

"Well, yes," Stuyvesant Wainwright III said thoughtfully, "except that . . ."

"Damned women! by God!" somebody added helpfully.

It so happened that I'd recognized both the chopper *and* the woman who'd alighted from it but thought this was no time to say so, not with the membership in so considerable a stir. And so Pilaster and I had a second martini over which he told me what was really eating at him. Not helicopters or women. But Sammy Glique.

"I don't understand how your father puts up with him. Even at chess."

"The Admiral has his moments as well," I assured Pilaster.

"So do we all. But Glique? His peculiarities . . ." Pilaster hesitated, and then plunged ahead. "Recently he began collecting first editions. You know his enthusiasms. They wax, they wane. For a time there, rare books. Knowing of my interest, he called upon me this spring for an assistance I was only too willing to give."

"Yes?" I asked, not really caring but curious.

Cy Pilaster sipped at his cocktail, bracing himself perhaps. He was a thoroughgoing gentleman weighing the propriety of his words. Ought a man like Pilaster reveal what went on between him and Sammy Glique?

"You know how anal he can be . . ."

"Yes."

"Well, then, he asked me to bring my expertise to bear on the rather simple problem of cataloguing and arranging his books. There weren't that many, several hundred, many of them quite good. Others pretty worthless, foisted on the poor fellow by confidence men and swindlers. He'd had some fine teak bookcases built for his house, showed them off to me with considerable pride. So I set to work, utilizing a simple and universally accepted method of sorting the volumes by fiction and nonfiction, author and subject, and so on. Only to fall afoul of Glique's mania for symmetrical order!"

"You mean . . . ?"

"Glique threw out my system and rearranged every single book by the height of each volume!

"'Everything must fit!' he informed me.

"I guess I chuckled. 'But that isn't how one arranges good books, Glique,' I told him.

"'It is in *this* house!' he shouted, sensing a patronizing tone in my voice."

"How rotten for you," I told Pilaster. "There you were, helping out, and he—"

"Oh, it got worse, Beecher. Within moments we were rolling about on the floor of his library, books tossed this way and that, pages torn, bindings wrenched apart, two middle-aged men grappling and gouging, hurling insults in the most debased language. Both of us, I'm afraid, trashing books. I, in the end, as bad as Sammy Glique . . ."

I snapped my fingers for the waiter. Clearly, Cyril Pilaster could use another one following this account of an embarrassing interlude in an ordered and book-lined life.

I could use one myself, having recognized the big chopper that had so disconcerted hon. members. It belonged to billionaire Ronald O. Perelman, who owned the largest estate in East Hampton, and often ferried him back and forth between the Creeks, his magnificent spread on Georgica Pond, and Manhattan. I knew the sleekly impressive ship because, several years ago while still writing for *Newsweek*, I'd done a profile of Mr. Perelman, a rich man showing off his toys, and had been given a ride.

I also knew the young woman who stepped down from Perelman's magnificent helicopter at the elegantly faded cabanas of the Maidstone Club. And I knew her well enough to be sure she was not just another "rich man's toy."

Lady Alix Dunraven.

e i g h t

The first Italo-American president? It may have scared Cuomo but not this lad . . .

I was at the Maidstone to find Alix and, at the urging of my editor, to hear Congressman Buzzy Portofino. But knowing that Her Ladyship was supposed to be in his entourage, I'd determined to maintain a cool demeanor, letting others shoot off their mouths about Hon. Buzzy, branding the man a charlatan or hailing him as a political messiah. Club elders were permitted considerable latitude, whether denouncing politicians, women, or errant choppers. All very well for J. Harper Poor, a Maidstone member since World War I, to knock back a sherry (as he was now doing) and cry outrage at having airships disgorging "strange women" onto club grounds.

"In the War they didn't permit such flights!" he cried out. "Zeppelins bombed London, you know. That business didn't begin with Goering and the Stukas." Due to his great age, it was unclear just which war he meant; there'd been so many, and he shifted back and forth easily between them. I had no equivalent luxury of free, if irrational, speech, and just kept shut.

Members were already filing in for the seminar as I passed through, heading out for a breath of fresh sea air after having downed three martinis, my mind focused on Alix Dunraven rather than this Portofino. I made a turn and found myself on the parking lot. It was nice being in the night air. Cool, or coolish, the way early summer is out here. The surf banging against the sand not far away. Some nice cars pulling up with nice people getting out. Overhead, the first stars, while off in the west across the pond, you still caught the last glorious glints of sunset.

Just then, wheezing and lurching, a big blue pickup, the kind with a double-size cab and a huge flatbed in back, jerked to an uneasy halt on the club gravel where I was sobering up. The driver's side door opened and the driver, with a skeptical, slightly disappointed face that spelled "cop," stepped halfway out and looked up at me. I supposed for half a second that he might ask for ID. Instead:

"This is the Mainstone Club?"

From inside the cab came another voice. Less accusatory. A voice I'd heard on TV and radio. "*Maidstone!* The Maidstone Club."

"Yeah," I said, "it's the Maidstone Club."

Congressman Buzzy Portofino uncoiled his long legs and climbed out, a slender man in a shirt and tie that shouted "polyester" and a JCPenney navy suit, not very well cut. He wore a cheap thatched straw hat, of the sort "Felix Leiter" wore playing CIA second banana to Connery in James Bond flicks.

The hat, I assumed unkindly, was there to cover the . . . well, the infamous Portofino rug.

"You're Stowe, the reporter. I've seen you before. On *Meet the Press*," he said, surprise sneaking into his voice.

"Yes, and you must be Representative Portofino."

I'd never been on *Meet the Press* in my life. Tim Russert has his favorites. But why quibble?

He nodded. "I didn't think they'd send out reporters from New York."

"They didn't," I said, slightly emphasizing the word "they."

"But then . . . ?"

I gave him a break.

"I have a house here. I belong to the Maidstone."

"Oh." After an instant. "You're Admiral Stowe's son."

I nodded but said nothing more, enjoying putting him off, if only marginally. But if he wondered why I was here, I, too, was curious about him.

"I thought you arrived in that chopper landing on the beach."

"There are no free rides in politics. Or in life; there's always a quid pro quo. Mr. Perelman was flying out and two of my subcommittee staff and a couple of reporters went along. I prefer not to be personally beholden to anyone. So I drove, as I do whenever practicable."

Another staffer now emerged from the cramped backseat and dove into the flatbed for an attaché case. The big pickup was still idling. Didn't sound bad at all, not now. Sounded pretty good, in fact. And the tires, oversize and new, were Michelins. Sure, the truck looked like hell and sounded lousy. Don't get it washed, lose a hubcap or two on purpose, drill a few holes in the muffler . . . That's how you make a first-rate, reliable vehicle look and sound like a used car lot's "economy special."

My estimation of Congressman Portofino went up. This was a shrewder fellow than the neurotic rabble-rouser jealous enemies portrayed.

He and his men walked past me and went inside. Then, half turning, Portofino called out, "You coming to the talk?"

"Wouldn't miss it," I said, as he strode through the club doors without waiting to hear my answer. To me, sobering up out here in the lovely summer dusk, Buzzy didn't sound at all like a nut case.

Which still left two questions unanswered: Why had Buzzy Portofino's Capitol Hill office placed a call trying to track down my father? Anything to do with my old man's travels?

And more to the point, just where was Her Ladyship?

If America had a new idol as summer began, granted that he was an acquired taste, it may have been Portofino. He'd been for five years just about the most effective U.S. attorney anywhere and in New York's high profile Southern District. He prosecuted anybody: fellow Italo-Americans, Jews, Irish, blacks, whites, Asians, Muslims, even the occasional erring Wasp. "An equal opportunity prosecutor," *Time* called him. If you stole paper clips from the office, cheated on your wife, or double-parked, you were meat. "Shut-the-Gates-o'-Mercy-Portofino," *New York* magazine tabbed him. His first marquee case, the prosecution under RICO (Racketeer-Influenced and Criminal Organizations) was of the notorious "Philly Nose," a senior colleague of Don Finooche, and he just went on from there. You couldn't scare Buzzy, couldn't bribe him, couldn't sweet-talk or suborn the man. He didn't cut deals or cut corners and was suspected of every virtue but humanity. Ambitious? Compared to Portofino, Julius Caesar lacked ambition.

For almost three terms now he'd distinguished himself amid the nonentities of the House of Representatives and was again running for reelection in a safe Staten Island seat. The only question: how high would he next set his sights? New York's mayor? Governor of the state? Challenging for Pat Moynihan's Senate seat if Pat retired as some said he might? The White House? The idea of being the first Italo-American president may have scared Cuomo but not this lad. Only Rudy Giuliani loomed as a possible roadblock to Buzzy, just as young, just as ambitious. As a congressman, Portofino's fame was notarized early when he hosted *Saturday Night Live* and made cameo appearances on *Seinfeld*. In recent months he'd been shaking hands in Iowa (where the first caucuses would be held) and New Hampshire (site of the first primaries). The Republican party already had him short-listed to deliver the keynote address at the next presidential nominating convention. And if the convention deadlocked, well, who could say . . . ? He was the brightest, shiniest crusader around since Eliot Ness. Or Tom Dewey. Or Hoover before he wigged out.

Buzzy's Capitol Hill power base was the House Alien & Sedition subcommittee, long flaccid and underfunded with a tired, listless staff, but which under his chairmanship had become as thrusting and vigorous an investigative body as existed in Washington. You'd think the House Un-American Activities Committee, Torquemada, and Joe McCarthy had all come back to life. He probed everyone: the White House, the Supreme Court, even the Ways and Means Committee. Before long, the simple greeting "I am Congressman Buzzy Portofino, Republican, New York, chairman of the Alien and Sedition subcommittee," was sufficient to strike terror into the most calloused of bureaucrats. "He doesn't hold hearings," a crooked bureaucrat complained, "he conducts Inquisitions."

His fatal flaw? He knew how good he was and rubbed your nose in it. Oh, yeah, and his rug. Buzzy Portofino, a lean, craggy fellow, and except for a few tics, not unattractive, was cursed with the worst wig I'd ever seen. If Hair Club for Men had a poster boy, it might have been Buzzy.

Because he had a token opponent in this next congressional election, Buzzy was in need of an issue to keep him on the front pages. And he thought maybe he'd found it. No worthy rival? All right then, Buzzy would take the high road; he would run against sin.

And start in the Hamptons.

Since virtue came naturally to Buzzy, the notion of campaigning against sin made sense. He was so straitlaced and pious his wife, an attractive young actress, had left him for a career of her own, a regular gig on the new *Hollywood Squares* (she's to the upper left of Whoopi Goldberg). Interviewed by Liz Smith, Ms. Portofino said:

"Buzzy's the most decent, admirable, worthy man I know. In all candor, a saint! But he went direct from the seminary to law school to the FBI to U.S. attorney. Talk about a monastic existence. It was okay that he knelt to pray by our bed each night. But for forty-five minutes? And aloud? Forgiving them their trespasses. And naming each trespasser and reciting his rap sheet? This is foreplay? Give me a break!"

Although a Roman Catholic, Buzzy Portofino's heroes, his role models, were of various faiths and most notable for their ferocity. Zealous, uncomfortable men: the "little friar" Martin Luther, who suffered from piles; Oliver Cromwell, decapitated after his death and his head carried about on a pike for the peasants to spit at; John Brown and Savonarola, the former having been hanged and the latter burned at the stake.

In ways, Buzzy's idols might remind one of Sammy Glique's admiration for Hitchcock and Welles and D. W. Griffith. Inarguably talented people whom the contractor Rinaldi might quite accurately have characterized as "those bastards!"

n i n e

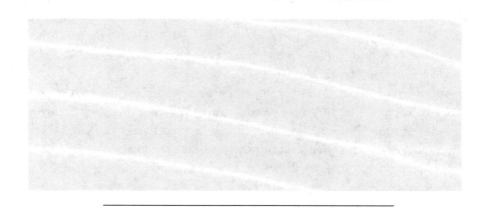

"Of all the Ten Commandments, only one sin qualifies for two mentions."

"I say, Beecher! They told me I'd find you out here regarding the sunset and contemplating your navel. Oh, but it's super to see you after so long . . ."

Since all this was accompanied by her throwing herself into my arms and kissing me full on the mouth, I don't really need to inform you that Her Ladyship, Alix Dunraven, had finally, and gloriously, appeared on the scene.

She'd traded in her aviatrix togs for a sort of Diane von Furstenberg little wrap dress, an updated and clearly pricy version in a wispy blue-green silk that not only set off her suntan, but sensually skimmed those long, lovely, and subtle curves, and at a length that gave good value to her legs.

"I saw you jump out of Perelman's chopper. Where've you been since? I—"

"All in due time, darling. There's a story or several to be told. But not here, not now." She glanced at the gold Cartier tank watch on her slender wrist. "I don't want to miss the latest rants of 'a future American president,' do you?"

"And that's what he is?"

"He thinks large. Chooses his audience. Since I'm a Brit, he rattles on in terms of Clive of India, of Cecil Rhodes. Or Marlborough and various Churchills. To say nothing of Henry V, Pitt the Younger, and Guy Fawkes.

"And then he launches into the most absurd nonsense. A conundrum, really, who keeps you wondering just which he is, demagogue or statesman. But, come inside, you'll hear for yourself," she said, grabbing me and tugging me along, not at all reluctantly, I assure you.

Buzzy Portofino was introduced to the Maidstone Club's forum on current affairs as a "man in the news" (previous speakers included Federal Reserve Bank chairmen, Jimmy Stewart, a Supreme Court justice, Tiger Woods, and Bill Gates), by a senior member, too senior, perhaps, of the speakers' committee.

"Congressman Positano," he began, almost accurately, "is a most distinguished member of the House. His committee assignments include that of chairman of the Alien and Sedition subcommittee, where he has done excellent work protecting our country against aliens and, well, sedition. And against immigrants from the Third World who, well, I needn't go on . . .

"Previously, Congressman Policastro had served, and nobly, as an assistant United States attorney, as an agent of the FBI, and . . . (vague pause) . . . in other distinguished posts.

"It is my great privilege and high honor to introduce our speaker of the evening, Congressman Buddy Fortunato."

There was considerable applause, the audience sensitive to the difficulty elderly Wasps have with names ending in vowels.

Buzzy, somewhat nettled about his introduction, tossed off a few cordial remarks about the beauty of the setting, the proximity of the ocean, the aristocratic committee, and this famous old club itself.

"Now, to the issues," he said, blathering on for a time about aliens, taxes, capital punishment, no parole, and in a bow to purely local concerns, a brief, throwaway reference to Offshore Wells's overblown house going up on Sag Pond, suggesting creation of a national Zoning Board of Appeals to give relief in such egregious cases. Which drew nods and a decent smatter of applause.

Then, so swiftly as to be jarring, he launched into an offensive against . . . lust!

"Of all the Ten Commandments, crucial to our Judeo-Christian-Islamic tradition, only one sin qualifies for two mentions. As Moses, fatigued and bent under their enormous weight, carried down the stone tablets from

Mount Sinai and read them to the multitudes in the desert, only one evil was cited twice."

As Buzzy paused, Alix tugged at my sleeve.

"You just know it won't be sloth," she whispered.

Being a Protestant, I wasn't sufficiently sure to pontificate, to stick out my neck. That "Judeo-Christian-Islamic" business bothered me. Were Jews and Episcopalians, to say nothing of Muslims, guilty of the same wickedness? I wished my father were here. He was always first rate on such matters, making distinctions and drawing conclusions.

So, in response to Alix's remark, I said: "Yes, I'm sure. But let's just listen."

"Right-oh."

Buzzy went on, his voice starting low and building in resonance as he went:

"If my remarks discomfort any in this cultured audience, in this splendid room, I offer apology in advance. But long ago, first in the seminary and later the FBI, I learned that to impress your listener with the gravity of the affair, you spoke out in candor and directly. In other words, to delve into the vernacular, you call a spade . . . *a bloody shovel!*"

"Here, here," one of the older members called out, jolted from his doze by the vigor of Buzzy's remarks.

"Oh, well done," Alix murmured. She did enjoy a melodrama.

The Congressman's voice fell, seeking the lower registers. Then, even more effectively in the hush, he went on:

"My subcommittee's area of competence is that of legislation regarding aliens and sedition. I shall this evening paraphrase Hemingway, who early in his career was covering a minor war in the Middle East and in reference to official corruption, reported in a cable to his newspaper:

"'Bismarck said all men in the Balkans who tuck their shirts into their trousers are crooks. The shirts of the peasants of course hang outside. When I found Hamid Bey in his Istanbul office, his shirt was tucked in, for he was dressed in a gray business suit.'

"Hemingway's attitude toward aliens," the Congressman somewhat illogically summed up, "is mine as well."

There was a deal of applause and a few cheers over that, which left me befuddled, the membership of the Maidstone all with their shirts firmly tucked in.

"Clever of Bismarck to have figured that out," Alix said. "About shirts tucked in. And doubly clever of young Hemingway to have recalled it." Buzzy paused only until the room fell silent.

"As for sedition, that's quite another matter. And one on which I intend to say a few words this evening. As I suggested in my opening remarks, the topic of my talk is sin. Not the sin of aliens, shirts in or shirts out, but sin on the part of Americans. Famous, influential, sophisticated, wealthy Americans."

Pause.

"Including a few who live here *among* you."

You could hear a communal breath being inhaled in shock. Men glanced furtively at each other. Would names be named? Would the individual turn out to be a member of the Maidstone? Someone in this very room?

Buzzy continued:

"Man errs. None of us is perfect. But occasionally one is confronted by sin so blatant that we must cry out in protest. You'll recall my remarks several years ago concerning the highly publicized relationship of Ellen DeGeneres and Anne Heche."

A murmur ran through the crowded room.

". . . which occasioned criticism of me as a narrow-minded prig. No matter. Whatever the personal cost, I believe in speaking out on principle. What famous actresses do in private does not concern me; when they kiss and pet in public, I will tut-tut and wag my head, regardless of provoking editorials in the *New York Times.*"

There were several, "Hear, hears!" at this, the *Times* being seen as dangerously liberal at the Maidstone. Buzzy resumed:

"As for the miscreant I denounce here today, his villainies are of such dimension as to demand response. Right here in East Hampton, this . . . voluptuary dallies openly with young women. And without benefit of clergy!"

Buzzy now paused again. Too lengthily for one member who, rather tipsily, called out, "What sin was mentioned twice? Eh?"

Buzzy was ripping and snorting now.

"A famous filmmaker, Samuel Glique, formerly known as Sammy Glick! And what may *he* be up to there on Lily Pond Lane? I ask you, what vile practices, what sins, mortal and venial both, are being committed or at the very least, tolerated, not a mile from this very room?"

We all leaned forward at that, I guess, desperate to know. Congressman Portofino did not disappoint, did not keep us waiting:

"And once your committee's invitation arrived, I understood what I had to do. I came to East Hampton to present myself personally at his gate and confront the man. Demand his comments. Perhaps Sammy Glique has a case. If so, I want to hear it. There'll be no shilly-shallying. This is why I have come to the Hamptons. Is Mr. Glique or is he not promoting the following:

"Lust! Fornication! Adultery! No-fault divorce! Indecent exposure! Sexual aids! X-rated videotapes! *Playboy* magazine! Hot tubs! Four-letter words! Pierced body parts! Nude bathing! Bikini waxings! See-through fabrics! Sex education! Federal funds for Viagra! Vibrators! Condom advertising on TV! Garter belts and push-up bras! Tattoos . . . !"

Somewhere toward the rear an overexcited member dropped his old-fashioned and as it shattered, Buzzy Portofino broke off, his voice falling.

"I could go on with this appalling catalogue in the most explicit of detail . . ."

There were few cries of protest I could discern. Though certainly that curled lip on Prince Bibesco suggested displeasure. Stuyvesant Wainwright, I think it was, who'd been a congressman himself, called out "Rubbish!" at one point (Stuyvy never did have much tolerance for humbug) and someone else, Dimsdale or Donnie Kirk, I believe, shouted, "Show this fellow the door!" Most members, however, seemed thrilled despite themselves, and applauded in hopes he would, indeed, continue. Chas. Mitchelmore was taking notes. By my side, Alix whispered:

"He usually does another thirty minutes. Astonishing, the variety of sins at his fingertips."

"It certainly is impressive," I agreed. But would he really trespass on Lily Pond Lane and tackle Glique?

In the end the Congressman called for questions (oddly, fewer questions about sin were posed than about Offshore Wells's house on Sag Pond, which might or might not have surprised Buzzy, and perhaps planted a seed in his mind), and ended with a rousing call for a nationwide boycott of Glique films, and a solemn pledge by members of the Maidstone Club never to accept such a man for membership. In considerable agitation, eyes darting this way and that, his face reddened, the absurd rug slightly askew, Buzzy cried:

"Who among you shall cast the first blackball?"

It was either Johnny Cannister or Aristide "Kip" Montgomery who was first on his feet enthusiastically asserting willingness to do so.

And being cheered on for his courage.

Given Portofino's talent for rabble-rousing, I was only surprised there were no calls for tar and feathers.

t e n

"He paid everything in cash. Credit cards
leave footprints."

Housing arrangements, Alix explained, had of course been made. Rooms at the 1770 House had been reserved for the members of Portofino's doughty little band, and the few journalists tagging along.

"Of course," I agreed. But we weren't going to need those rooms, were we.

"Of course not, darling."

I'd expected the answer but it thrilled me to hear her say so, that she'd be staying at my place.

"Is there luggage?"

"Yes, but we can have it fetched in the morning. You can send a man."

"Yes," I said, "I'll send a man."

That I didn't have "a man" was well known to both of us. But when you haven't seen a woman you love for some time, you observe the rubrics, you go along.

The night was still young and since we'd not eaten, we drove up into town and got a table at Peconic Coast and had a bottle of Robert Mondavi's

Cabernet '94 and a paillard and salad. "My, but that's mellow," Alix said, approving of the Mondavi.

Yes, isn't it, I started to say, but didn't. Instead:

"I've missed you, Alix."

She was like the Queen on her birthday, parceling out grace and favor to commoners and the lesser nobles, assuring me:

"And I you, Beecher. All these months . . ."

I'd kept up with the gossip columns and knew she'd not been idle. Neither in London nor on the Continent. There'd been reports, from Paris and Monte and the Islands. She was quite tan, as well, for so early in the summer. People said of Alix that she . . .

"This Portofino," I asked, not wanting to dwell morbidly on events over which I'd no control, "what do you make of that performance tonight? A bit odd, or is that his usual drill?"

"Oh, I've been with him less than a week. He varies his act according to the audience. But, yes, he's passionate, sincere, or seems to be, and zealous. Also, a trifle loopy. The more earnest of the Old Testament prophets come to mind, the ones in hair shirts, scourging themselves. Or your popular American icon, the chap in the song, 'John Brown's body lies a-moldering in the grave, John Brown's body lies a-mold—'"

"Yes, yes, I see," I said hurriedly, as several diners stopped eating to see who it was bursting into song. "But not a fake?" I pressed on, "Not just another poseur?"

"I don't think so. Mad, but constructively so. Like all outsize figures, a bit weird, perhaps. Mr. Murdoch is extraordinarily shrewd about such things and senses he's a comer. He wants the British to know about him. That's my task, to sign him up for a weekly column from America. So far, I see a narrow agenda, but very, very focused. You have to admire his convictions even as you disagree . . ."

Stalin and Hitler, I thought, they too were focused. So was Mao. I didn't say so. She'd trailed Buzzy Portofino for a week, talked with his people, listened to his oratory. I'd pretty much ignored him until now; had just met him for the first time.

"In any event," she went on, "there are always salutory lessons to be learned, are there not? I mean, look at me."

"I am."

"Bless you, Beecher," she said, taking my near hand and kissing it lightly, "but you know what I mean. How unfocused I am, not at all single-minded and ruthless in furthering my career, in getting ahead. I could be, like you, so much more calculating and—"

"But you're fine," I broke in impulsively, and meaning it. "A big job in Fleet Street on *The Times* is hardly to be—"

"Oh, KRM has been awfully decent. He—"

"KRM?"

"Rupert. That's how he signs his memos. Keith Rupert Murdoch in initial letters."

Oh, now she was getting memos from press lords. As you know, I tend to become arch, as I did now in remarking:

"I'm sure Mr. Murdoch appreciates the job you're—"

"Quite," she cut me off, sniffing out the stuffiness to which she knew I was prone, "but I've been taking notes, reading a biography of Clare Boothe, the playwright who married Mr. Luce of *Time*. After her first marriage was dissolved she worked briefly for Condé Nast, the man himself as well as the company, writing captions for *Vogue* and ending as a columnist for *Vanity Fair*. Whilst, cleverly apportioning her alimony, becoming one of Manhattan's more celebrated hostesses. And when she set up as a freelance, she'd have her secretary call this famous editor or that and ask him to cocktails. The chap was usually delighted to be asked. Only to realize on arrival, he was the sole guest, and to be informed by his hostess that, having time on her hands, 'it might be fun to dash off some articles for his little magazine . . .'"

Mmm, I thought.

"That's the sort of calculation I must say I admire. And it won her Mr. Luce eventually, as well."

"I thought Pamela Harriman was your role model. The world-famous courtesan. Irresistible to men of influence and power, whatever their age."

"As indeed she was for a time. Imagine, becoming your country's ambassador to France and then just toppling over dead at the Ritz. *Quel beau geste!* The Crillon wouldn't have done nearly as well. And on her way to swim laps. But eventually I dropped that idea. Being a courtesan carries burdens: hanging about with a variety of chaps without much choice in just who takes you to bed. So much classier being able to pick and choose, don't y'know."

"There is that," I conceded.

She then gave me a fuller account of her evening with my father in London, cocktails at the Connaught followed by dinner at Harry's Bar, both at his expense, then off to Annabel's for dancing, her club in Berkeley Square, with the Admiral her guest.

"One odd thing, however. Whenever it was time to settle up, there was no simple tossing of plastic onto the plate. He'd pull out the most astonishing roll of big bills and peel off a few. With anyone but your old Dad, I would have found that rum indeed, and suspected unlaundered drug money, or trying to make an impression. In London, but for the newspaper or a taxi, you never see anyone paying cash. Admiral Stowe paid cash for the lot!"

I had the explanation. "Whenever he travels, he carries at least ten thousand in each of several major currencies: U.S. dollars, British pounds, German marks, both French and Swiss francs, Russian rubles, Indian rupees, pesetas, Japanese yen, lire, kroner and the like. Cash doesn't leave footprints. Every credit card transaction goes into a computer somewhere. And wherever there's a computer, there's a hacker. The Admiral doesn't choose to leave behind a printed and time-dated record of precisely where he's been and when."

"So that's it," she said, "devilishly clever. Worthy of our old chum Monsieur Poirot, don't you think?"

"I certainly do," I said, recalling in silent amusement my father's other, security-driven eccentricities, such as the sewing into the waistband of his jockey shorts gold coins of one ounce pure gold, 99 fine, gold being of value in certain Third World regions where the most respected currencies had no worth whatsoever. Airport metal detectors eventually put an end to this, and he moved on to the concealment, also in his shorts, of a soft glove-leather pouch filled with small, one carat or less, uncut diamonds of the first water. Meanwhile, Alix was cataloguing the Admiral's virtues:

"He does dance well, Beecher. Better than you, actually," she said candidly. "And between sets we had the most fascinating lit'ry conversation. I'd been into the bubbly and was rattling on about my childhood enthusiasms for Lord Tweedsmuir, or as he earlier was, John Buchan, and his yarns for boys. The Admiral shared my enthusiasm for Buchan but couldn't abide Thomas Hardy so we moved on to which was our favorite Brontë sister." Then, incapable of stifling curiosity further, she asked, "Just what was the message I forwarded to you? I mean, if we're not talking 'eyes only' or 'preservation of the realm.'"

"He gave me a reference to a book you know quite well. And which provided a clue to where he's headed."

"Which is?"

"Not sure if I should tell you that," I said. Not for lack of trusting her. But suppose someone knew Alix shared our secret, wouldn't she be at risk?

She pouted prettily but briefly, knowing just how to handle me, as we smoked another cigarette. And she knew if I trusted anyone in the world, it was she. So why fence?

"John Buchan's *Greenmantle.*"

"Oh, wizard!" Alix enthused, "but he'd seemed so casual in chatting about Buchan. I had no idea he—"

"That's the Admiral. Poker-faced. Doesn't give much."

She didn't seem the slightest surprised she'd wheedled it out of me. Clearly, I was *not* my father.

Then, enthusiast that she was, Alix was off: "I'd wager that just like Dick Hannay and Sandy Arbuthnot, the Master of Clanroyden, your old Dad's off to the East. Stopping over for a bit of sport at Constantinople and then on to Damascus or Baghdad. It was at Con while attempting to foil the Kaiser's devilish plots that Hannay first came across the Companions of the Rosy Hours, but then, you probably know that."

So much for my vaunted circumspection, my prudently sealed lips. But I hadn't read the damned book. Just who might be "Hannay" and "the Master of Something" and "the Companions of the Rosy . . ." whatever?

Clearly she assumed my father had been so charmed by her enthusiasm for Buchan's novels that he'd impishly used one to convey a message. Yes, he had a photographic memory; clearly part of his uncanny success at speed chess that so impressed Glique, but had he literally memorized every page of his several thousand volumes? Of course not. He chose one book before the trip began and carried along a copy. So that once he provided the book's number, 231, and I found it to be *Greenmantle,* I knew that for the rest of this assignment, that would be our code book. I knew this; as did no one else, save perhaps Mr. Cohen, the Secretary of Defense.

An hour later Alix and I were sitting up in my bed on Further Lane. "I'm glad you're not at the 1770 House," I said. "This is where you belong, here with me."

"Could I do else?" she asked. The question, clearly, was rhetorical and I made no attempt at a snappy response.

"You know, Beecher," she said thoughtfully, "when I was in the bathroom there tidying up and such, I got to thinking about how long it's been between visits. And how basically decent you are."

"Oh?" I said, pleased but not sure where this was leading.

"Yes, I realize it's a small thing. But you always have a fresh toothbrush still pristine in its wrappings, there for an overnight guest."

"Well, I . . ."

"Very few chaps are anything like that considerate," she said firmly, her lovely jaw set.

Mmm, I thought. Was this information based on personal experience, overnight-guesting with "chaps"? Or something she'd heard?

But the really vital statistic for me was that she was wearing the gold nipple ring I'd sent her last October 25 to commemorate St. Crispin's Day, a date meaningful to her family, a Dunraven ancestor having fought with Harry the King at Agincourt and, regrettably, been sabered by the French. Being a Harvard man *and* an Episcopalian, I'd not gone lightly into this matter of nipple rings, mulling their propriety, consulting Tish Baldridge's book on contemporary mores, and in the end relying on the discretion and savoir-faire of Cartier's Ralph Destino, before making a selection. It had to be, Mr. Destino and I agreed, the right *sort* of nipple ring and nothing crass.

I was so pleased now to see her wearing my gift, I couldn't help stroking it. And since the dear girl was being so clever right now, making good use of the range of possibilities a king-size bed had to offer, it hardly seemed the time for chat. It was all quite wonderful, so pleasant in fact, that I very nearly was able to ignore how tan she was, even her breasts, with no pale strap marks anywhere, which meant she'd been bathing nude. Just whose was the yacht, whose the beach in the South of France, whose the private island in the Caribbean on which Lady Alix sported?

"Oh, darling!" she said now, or rather yelped. "That was smashing!"

It was, too, and hardly the moment for interrogations, so I just sort of yelped along with her as we moved.

e l e v e n

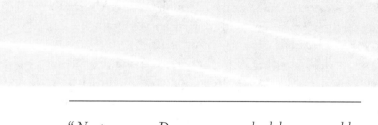

"Not even Devon can hold a candle
to your Hamptons."

I'd determined to be above brooding about her suntan and when in the morning I got back from Dreesen's with papers and their homemade doughnuts, I made coffee and poured some Tropicana home-style orange juice ("with juicy bits of orange"; I'm not much for reaming oranges), and gave Alix breakfast in bed.

"No one spoils me like you, Beecher," she said. "Absolutely no one. And so industrious. Like Samuel Pepys, 'up betimes and to market.' Squeezing fresh oranges as well . . ."

I smiled my thanks, not bothering to correct her, but leaning down to receive a very nice and somewhat extended kiss.

That's what I needed, that's why I fetched breakfast in bed.

So I undressed again and slid in beside her for a bit. Afterward, we lay there in the early sun brightening and warming us and the morning air. Then I said, "Swim?" and was delighted at her reaction, leaping up naked and dancing about a bit in youthful enthusiasm.

"That's another thing to adore about America. You wake to sunshine and dive into a gloriously warm, green ocean. I sometimes think God is still punishing England for the Protestant Reformation or sinking the Armada and all those good Catholic sailors. Cloud and chill, dank and drear, the way He's scanted us on sun and beaches."

With both of us being Protestants, I wasn't ready to assume God *was* a Catholic. I mean, Henry the Eighth had a good deal to answer for, but lousy beaches? She smiled at me so winningly, I concluded this was hardly the moment for theological disputation, even if I was pretty sure God (Catholic or Protestant) wasn't *that* petty.

Alix checked in with Congressman Portofino's press secretary. His daybook was slim and tonight there was a fund-raiser at Ron Perelman's spread. That Perelman was a Democrat and Buzzy a Republican didn't seem to matter. In the Hamptons, your wealth counted more than your politics. The PR man promised to brief Her Ladyship tomorrow.

"Super," she said, "I was afraid I might have to spend the day slaving away."

You might wonder about Alix's dedication to the journalist's trade. But I made no criticisms. After all, Rupert Murdoch paid her salary and I prefer not to meddle. Instead, I said I'd pack a lunch if she got the towels.

"Darling," she said, knowing how I liked it when she spoke French, "you're so *sportif.*"

In deference to members of the Maidstone Club, Alix wore a proper swimsuit, abbreviated but sufficient, covering the vital statistics and other parts, and we had a glorious day. The water wasn't cold and there was enough surf that you could ride the waves, yet without being bounced against the bottom or curled. The sun? You needed sunblock. I used the 15 power, Alix the 8. But then, she had a protective layer already. And just where the hell had she . . . ?

Men I barely knew came by to say hello. It didn't seem greatly to bother Her Ladyship.

"Chaps always do that. No harm to it, is there? Just being genial."

"I'm sure."

"This is lovely, Beecher. Not even Devon can hold a candle to your Hamptons. And as for the Channel . . ."

That evening we had drinks at the Blue Parrot. Billy Joel was there. Everyone out here liked Billy; he cared about the important, local things, like striped bass regulations. With him were a few of the Baymen, Arnold Leo and some others. Billy might have played a little piano except the Parrot management had sent off the battered old upright to be tuned.

"Then I'll have a margarita," Alix said, "and settle for the CDs."

Over our heads the big ceiling fans revolved sluggishly, stirring the air but not really cooling anything. It was okay. The windows were open, the Parrot being an indoor-outdoor bar, with the wooden floor painted a bright blue. I admired the long, old-fashioned surfboards, and the bullfight posters on the wall, checking on where the bulls had been raised, and just which matadors were on the card, and sipped a Pacifico beer. There were also old movie posters, quite faded, of cowboy actors I'd never heard. Zeke Clements? Had anyone ever heard of Zeke Clements? People came over to chat. Alix didn't object. There was a coating of margarita on her upper lip that looked fine. Like those milk commercials. Her Ladyship drew a good gate. Men, especially.

"What about this Portofino?" someone who worked for Ralph Lauren asked me. "Is this guy for real?"

There was a lot of that thanks to a front-page story in the *East Hampton Star.* People were choosing sides between the Congressman and Sammy Glique.

"The Maidstone Club in Buzzy's camp?" someone said.

"The Maidstone," I said stiffly, "keeps its own counsel."

What the hell did that mean? Even I couldn't say.

"Oh," the guy said, apparently satisfied.

We drank too much and closed the Parrot, then slept gloriously until, in the morning, breakfasting well on the patio, the phone rang.

There was a message from the Admiral, forwarded by Mary Sexton. He didn't know I was in East Hampton and was still communicating through Sutton Place and, ironically, via Mary, a known Marxist.

"Your father left a message on the answering machine. 'For whereabouts see 113.'"

That was all. I thanked Mary, and started across the lawn for my father's house, calling out as I went, "Alix."

She jumped up from the old Adirondack chair and hurried to catch up. Why should I rely on the discretion of my housekeeper but not that of a titled Englishwoman who was my lover and had proved her courage and resource in that showdown on the tennis court of Pam Phythian's place on Further Lane, when the bride left Fruity Metcalfe at the altar on Gin Lane, and how many other times over the past few years?

She slung her arm around my waist and I bent down to kiss her lightly on the throat.

"My dad's sent another message."

Inside the house I led her into the old library, a comfortable, lived-in room, with the antique globe and the cracked old leather armchair he habitually used, the library steps, the fireplace with a couple of Naval Academy oars hung above, and the opposite wall completely covered by books. "Since it's his system and not mine, I won't give away the starting point if you don't mind."

"Of course not, darling. Sir Richard Hannay himself could not have been more canny. And rightly so, considering the stakes . . ."

I had no idea what the stakes were, but didn't say so. Instead, I went directly to *Greenmantle.* "Hmmm, more references to 'heading east. Passing a big city the captain told me was Vienna.'"

"Hercule Poirot couldn't do it better than your old Dad!" Alix enthused. "Dear, dear Hercule, rattling along aboard the tatty old Orient Express. Brandies in the smoking car. Mysterious, veiled beauties. Monocled Mittel Europeans. English milords with sterling cigar cutters on their watch chains. White Russian émigrés muttering tsarist nonsense. Dusky chaps in turbans and brocaded robes. The lot of them headed for Con and the Bosporus and beyond it, the whole of Asia Minor. Oh, Beecher, I *knew* that the Admiral was marching in the very footsteps of Dick Hannay. I just knew it!"

I was less thrilled. The East, however one defined it, was a big place. But it still looked to me like Baghdad and a stroll into Saddam's lair. Had I been wrong not to respond to that phone call from Congressman Portofino's office on Capitol Hill? Maybe he'd been trying to warn off my father. And just what was the Admiral looking for and why?

Damn! How do you put a jigsaw together without pieces?

twelve

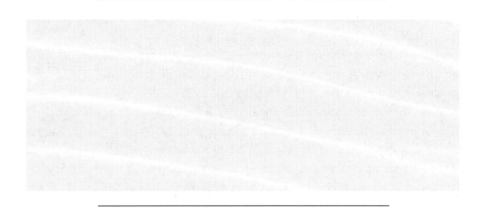

Newspapers carried sketches of her "strolling with lions borrowed from the zoo."

All this was very pleasant. And Her Ladyship a good deal more. The good weather held and the Hamptons had rarely been as splendid and welcoming. If you had to show a European visitor America at its very best, why not start here? The town fireworks had gone off gloriously on the Fourth. The surfcasters were bringing in the first striped bass off the beach and young girls in their swimsuits never looked better. Alix looked good, too. We had taken the papers and a couple of my old canvas beach chairs down to the water's edge and after a brisk swim were lying side by side on a big Dior beach towel smoking my cigarettes and drying in the sun.

"I'm dying to meet your father's chum, Mr. Glique. Everything the Congressman said about him at the Maidstone makes him sound a perfect poppet."

"Buzzy called him a voluptuary responsible for everything but acid rain and the ozone layer. Is that what makes 'poppets'?"

"Oh, poof! That's the usual hyperbole politicians spout. I've seen any number of his films and I'm sure your Mr. Glique is a charmer."

He was hardly "my" Mr. Glique but I didn't argue.

"You're a poppet as well, darling," she assured me, rolling over on the beach towel to brush her front against my back, always a pleasant affair, even if she was wearing her top. Then, having properly set me up, Alix did a little confiding of her own, counting on my largeness of spirit.

"You know, Beecher," she said, "I may have neglected to notify you I got engaged again."

I sat up so hurriedly that Alix recoiled despite herself, withdrawing to her half of the towel. It wasn't anger on my part, simply shock and not knowing just what to say since, really, what could one say?

"He's so well intentioned. So gallant. So hopeless. I couldn't resist. You know something about our political realities. And here was a chap attempting valiantly to reform the House of Commons whilst sitting in the Lords. Which I needn't tell you is virtually impossible. And not by browbeating chaps. Just giving good example and talking pious but admirable rot."

"Lord, no!" I cried, protest wrung from me physically. "You've not gone back to Fruity?"

"Oh, Beecher, you know me—*and* Fruity—better than that. No, this is a chap called Vyvyan Hardcastle, the seventh Marquess, and just one untimely death away from becoming hereditary Lord Great Chamberlain, who's the chap who walks backward down the aisle of the House of Lords as the Queen makes her way to the throne."

"Stout fellow," I murmured.

"Oh, quite. I knew you'd understand."

"Sure, it's how I am," I said, balancing good cheer and cynicism. "Now, what's the seventh Marquess up to that's all so valiant and hopeless?"

Before replying, perhaps sorting out her response, she smeared a dollop of sunblock over her nose and cheekbones, her thighs and belly, shoulders and arms, all of which looked awfully nice already, but which, with a lasciviously slick sheen of sunblock, well . . .

"Well, you know how they're totally juvenile in the Commons. Disgusting really. Superannuated schoolboys on a holiday. Childish pranks and japes."

I'd covered rough and tumble sessions of the House from the press gallery, so I had a vague idea, yes. But Alix pressed on, providing examples to convince me of Vyvyan Hardcastle's nobility of spirit.

"You know, of course, that poor John Prescott, the deputy prime minister, once worked as a barman on a Cunard liner? And so, whenever he gets up to make a statement, that beast Nicholas Soames cries out, 'Mine's a gin and tonic, Luigi!'"

I thought that actually was pretty good. But didn't say so. Instead, vaguely recalling having read some of this by Warren Hoge in the *New York Times*, "And doesn't Nick Soames also have a nickname?"

"Yes, 'Fatty.' They call him that all the time during debates."

"Well, then . . ."

"Granted," she said, "but what of the unfortunate Desmond Swayne, whose hair is rather unruly, being greeted with the barking of werewolves each time he rises to speak?"

I conceded that was unfortunate.

"And Patrick Nicholson," she went on, getting a head of steam now, "who once lost his license for drunk driving, and is invariably shouted down with cries of 'Taxi! Taxi!'? Or poor Mr. Hogg, who was Minister of Agriculture during the mad cow panic?"

"Oh, what do they do to Mr. Hogg?"

"Well, I realize this may confuse Americans, but when Hogg gets up, they all go 'Moo, moo!'"

The House of Commons is often called "the Mother of All Parliaments," and not for the first time, I wondered why.

"Anyway," Alix went on, "it's this nonsense that Vyvyan has sworn to do away with."

"Does he have a shot?"

She bit her lip, then shook her head.

"Of course not. Which is why I agreed to be his fiancée, at least for a while . . ."

I couldn't help myself. "You never get engaged to *me*, not even 'for a while,'" I blurted out, which I realized instantly wasn't very cool.

"Oh, don't pout, Beecher. You're far too good for that. With you, it's different."

"How?"

She looked pensive. "Well, you're one of those serious chaps. A desperado. With you an engagement wouldn't be simply a lark but a solemn vow. Now don't deny it, I *know* you, Beecher. Too many chaps rush into marriage, then a year later they're in the courts. I'm more the prudent, meditative type . . ."

I hadn't noticed but didn't say so and she went on.

"Yes, like my great-uncle Gavin, whom we all knew as 'Honks,' and was later Baron Faringdon. Do you know he took marriage so seriously that on the very eve of his wedding in 1927 he got eight two-gallon tins of petrol and poured it into the Thames, and set the river on fire?"

"No!"

"He did, y'know. The fire brigades had to come and everything."

"Was it that he dreaded getting married or was so thrilled about it?"

She chewed a lip. "Ma and Pa never said, y'know. Just that he tried to burn the Thames."

We went back in for another swim and then in the shallows tossed a beat-up old football with a trio of teenage boys, which gave me the opportunity to demonstrate to Her Ladyship how to throw a spiral, and when she finally got the knack of it, the three boys, already out of their minds in love with Alix, the thong bikini, and her accent, were shouting out, "Hey, Alix, toss it here!"

Winded from the football and back at the chairs where we toweled off again, she kissed me on the mouth, driving the teenagers mad with jealousy and unrequited passion, I was quite sure. "I love America, Beecher," she assured me. "Glorious sunshine. Playing footers on the beach with boys. Decent chaps like you not sulking that I got engaged again. And no one in your Congress barking like werewolves or shouting 'Luigi!' and ordering gins . . ."

Well, I conceded, not often. Though Senator D'Amato once sang "Old MacDonald."

When I phoned Sammy Glique from the house and explained that Her Ladyship admired his work, he said, of course, come over next morning. He wanted a firsthand account of Congressman Portofino's diatribe. There were aftershocks, of course, reporters calling, a TV crew arriving uninvited at his driveway (Wolfie shooed them away). It was all very upsetting. Perhaps we could stay for lunch? Did Her Ladyship possibly play chess?

Despite his attempt at sang-froid, Glique's performance on the phone was at the very least, an agitated one. As for Buzzy Portofino at the center of the maelstrom, he seemed to have gone to ground.

"Crumbs!" Alix said after talking to the 1770 House, "I thought I had them eating from my hand, fresh press releases on the hour. Now they say Buzzy's tied up. Hasn't confronted Glique as promised. Can't say just when he will, either. They'll get back to me. There were matters beyond my ability or need to comprehend there in the command post at the 1780 House . . ."

"1770 House."

". . . I'm sure, yes, where the Congressman receives shadowy couriers and haunts the Internet, makes mysterious inquiries and lays subtle plots. That sort of rot."

"You don't buy it?"

"Not a bit of it. Until forty-eight hours ago, I had the run of his camp. Buzzy and I were to dine every night while he was here. Now, all of a sudden, I'm, well—who was that woman who infected America years ago?"

"Typhoid Mary."

"Well, whoever it is, I find myself free for dinner, Beecher. I hope you don't feel like an afterthought, darling. I'd much rather be with you, as you're well aware.

"And besides," she said, chewing her lower lip in a manner I found sexually provocative, though perhaps it was just deep thought, "I'm not at all convinced he isn't up to something. That performance of his at the Maidstone had the smell of amateur theatricals. I think Buzzy, Congressman Portofino that is, may well be a more subtle, devious sort than he appears, and mayn't be hunting down your poor, lecherous Mr. Glique at all, but is after bigger prey."

The house on Sag Pond, for example? I wondered.

Her instincts on such matters were uncanny but at the moment, I was positively grateful to Portofino for leaving Alix to me. And not feeling at all like an afterthought. We dined at East Hampton Point on the outside deck where, over a champagne cocktail, Alix enlightened me about yet another of her heroines, a recent addition to the pantheon earlier occupied by Clare Boothe Luce and Pam Harriman. She had an entire *collection* of such people. Had I ever heard of "Isabella Stewart Gardner of Boston, born in 1840?"

Only the museum, I said, despite having gone to college nearby and knowing Boston reasonably well.

"Well, there was a wonderful book review in your *Times*. I have the cutting. Listen to this:

"When Gardner abandoned hope of motherhood at around 25, she also abandoned conventions . . . strolling with lions borrowed from the zoo . . . driving horses and cars at breakneck speed . . . smoking cigarettes. She had a pair of large diamonds mounted on springs and wore them, like antennae, in her hair. A passionate athlete and sports fan, she was seen at the symphony wearing a hatband inscribed, "Oh You Red Sox."'

"Are they a football side, Beecher?"

"No, the Red Sox play baseball. Formidable rivals of the Yankees."

"Oh. Well, Mrs. Gardner also had a dahlia named after her and a mountain peak somewhere, and discouraged houseguests by keeping them cold and hungry, explaining her frugality as essential to the preservation of capital."

I agreed Mrs. Gardner, too, was a poppet and called for a second round of champagne cocktails.

On the eleven o'clock local news we heard a brief item about our mysteriously elusive Buzzy:

"New York Congressman Buzzy Portofino was arrested for trespass this afternoon in Southampton. Police said the Congressman scaled the fence of a construction site of the huge house being built by oil tycoon Chapman 'Offshore' Wells. The house when completed will be larger than the White House and has stirred demands that building permits be rescinded. Security guards prevented the Congressman from conducting an inspection of the site and local police were called. He was given an appearance ticket and released. In a colorful sidebar, it was reported the security guards seemed to be Arabs armed with bows and arrows, not firearms, which are severely limited in the exclusive Village. Said Buzzy, 'Like General MacArthur, I shall return.' Mr. Wells could not be reached and his spokesperson Peggy Siegal had no comment, police said."

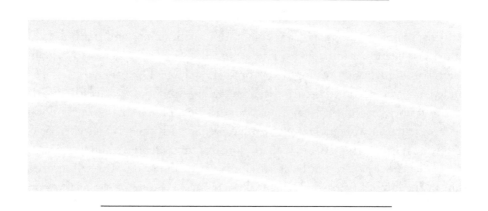

t h i r t e e n

"It's a German fella. From Mannheim.
Name of Speer."

Since Anderson had suggested a piece for the magazine and with the house back on the front pages, courtesy of Buzzy Portofino, I thought that in between champagne cocktails and making love with Her Ladyship, I'd better do a little legwork. A first stop was my boyhood chum and Suffolk County police detective pal Tom Knowles. Tom was my age yet still wore a Marine Corps crewcut, a hard man in a hard trade. So many people out here are "picturesque," Knowles was a pleasant change of pace. You got very little chi-chi out of Tom; he was as plain and essential as a primer coat of housepaint.

"It's hardly a police concern, Beech. The builders are entirely within the law. If some of the protesters get overexcited, like yesterday with Buzzy, maybe you'll have a trespassing bust. It's really in the hands of the Zoning Board of Appeals and the lawyers. But it's complicated. The property lines cross four jurisdictions, from Southampton Town into East Hampton Town, from Sagaponack Village to Wainscott Village. Suffolk County will have its say. Will the state get involved? You want good lawyers. Offshore Wells has Cadwalader,

Wickersham and Taft in Manhattan. They're tops in the field and have Wyseman Clagett as their local correspondent. The locals had been disorganized and bickering but they've finally got themselves some grown-up attorneys who didn't get their law degrees from correspondence school, Willkie, Farr. You seen the place yet?"

"No."

Tom shook his head, and he was a man not easily impressed.

"You gotta get down there and see for yourself, Beech. It looks like those old tintypes of the Panama Canal being dug, with cranes and big bulldozers and derricks and steam engines. Everything but Teddy Roosevelt in his campaign hat and laborers keeling over from yellow fever. The original house, Sag Lodge, is a wonderful old place that's pretty big itself but it's already dwarfed by the framework of the new house. Security people are living in the lodge; the construction workers are bused in every day with their ID checked at the gate. The framework of the new main house is three-quarters built, some of it still skeletal, but you've got to see it. Thirty bedrooms, a 1,500-gallon grease trap in the kitchen, squash courts, indoor tennis, a theater seating 165, pools indoors and out, two bowling alleys. And a microversion of the San Diego Zoo. For all I know, indoor skeet shooting . . ."

"These Arab guards. What was that all about?"

"Well, they're relatively new. At first Wells had Texas Rangers providing security."

"Actual Texas Rangers?"

"He's got some influence down there. But I think they were ex-Rangers. Or Rangers on leave, long, lean, leathery fellows in cowboy boots. Gradually they drifted off and were replaced by Arabs. Wells hasn't been around much recently, either. He does business all over the world. He's got more Persian Gulf exploration rights than the Saudis. What you see on the property these days except for the laborers is mostly Arabs. I guess these guys work for Wells whether he's here or over there. They've all got green cards."

"And this Arab friend of Wells, Prince Fatoosh?"

"Haven't met the gentleman yet. Some people think he's the real owner. But it's Wells's name on any paperwork I've seen."

"Is there a federal angle here? You mentioned the county and the state. No feds? Why isn't the Corps of Engineers wringing their hands about erosion and the beach?"

Tom paused. "I'd have thought they would be. But so far the feds are strictly hands off. Even the Corps of Engineers. Maybe because there hasn't been a hurricane yet this year. And since the Spielvogels sold their place, the beach erosion lobby's been very cool. Even Billy Rudin. But you're right; the zoning fight's been going on for eighteen months now with big names and muscle on both sides. You'd think someone would have some Washington leverage. But when it comes to the federal government, you've got me. Not a peep. You might ask around. Ben Bradlee usually knows more about what's going on in Washington than Washington does. And his own place isn't that far east of the construction site. Ben's probably pissed, too."

"Can I flash a press card and get on the property?"

"Worth a try. But he's been turning reporters away. Why not get out the canoe and paddle across Sag Pond. They may blow you out of the water but you'll get a look."

I hoisted my sixteen-foot Old Town Maine canoe atop the Blazer and called Jesse who met me at Sag Pond, where we slid the boat into the water. Even from across the pond more than a mile away you could see the cranes and the structural steelwork rising and hear the grind of motors and the pounding of pile drivers and the blasting caps and bustle of a big construction job underway, with tiny figures scrambling around the distant scaffolding like spiders. "My oh my," said Jesse happily. I think deep down he liked the idea of all this money being spent, all this construction. Anytime there was something this lavish underway, the potential for dubious profit was always there.

Swimming alongside our canoe as we paddled was a big snapping turtle hunting cygnets and ducklings. "Look at that bastard," Jesse said. "Turtle that size would take a man's foot right off at the ankle."

I bet it would, too.

We crossed the wide leg of Sag Pond without difficulty, a windless morning with flat water the way canoeists like it, and got close enough so you could see individual men's faces and hear ordinary conversation, not just the shouts. A wooden pier jutted out maybe a hundred and fifty feet into the pond, with power boats moored. Boy, it was a big operation. Couple of hundred men working in gangs. Tom Knowles was right. You had to see it. We started to move in closer but then there was some activity on the pier and a tall, spare gent wearing pristine white robes stepped forward with a bullhorn and called out in cultivated English, "Please stay away. This is a construction site. You could be in danger."

I shouted back, "Just sightseeing." And signaled Jesse to keep heading us in.

We got another warning and then the old boy in white pulled out a cell phone and said something into it that I couldn't hear. In about ten seconds one of the power boats started up and came out toward us, making a wide sweep, and stirring up a considerable wake. The canoe was set to rolling, damned near capsizing us. I thought of *Dr. No*, with the baddies chasing off James Bond and Honeychile.

"Okay, okay," I called. "We got the message."

Jesse spun the canoe about and we slid away, our boat rising and falling a foot or more in the wake.

"Not too hospitable, is they?" he remarked.

"No," I said. "But I didn't see any bows and arrows, did you?"

"Not a one."

Maybe since getting Buzzy arrested, they'd been told to cool it on weapons. Jesse drove back to Further Lane with me and helped me hose down the boat and rack it up in the garage.

"You know that crazy Howard Roark?" Jesse asked as we put the boat away.

"The architect? He's dead."

"Not so you'd notice. Old as hell. Lives up in Springs with that Russian woman wrote a book about him years ago. Got a house he built himself. Pretty nice house, too. I seen it. Not a nail in it and all local materials, the whole of it done by hand and shaped like Billy-be-damned, like nothing you ever seen before. Quirky. But it works. I enjoy just driving by and seeing it near where Jackson Pollock and Bill de Kooning lived among the rest of them local geniuses and whackjobs."

It was very East Hampton to have Jesse referring to people this famous as if they were familiars. Maybe they had been. Out here you either belonged, or you didn't.

But why Roark? Why now?

"I don't know much about architecture but they say this Roark was pretty good-sized caliber at one time," Jesse said.

"Biggest man in architecture since Frank Lloyd Wright," I agreed. "As big as Mies van der Rohe and bigger than I. M. Pei or Philip Johnson. Had a famous mantra: 'Function. Purity of line. Strength through mass.' Said you could boil down all architecture to those three principles." I cut myself off. Let Jesse tell me; he'd get to it in his own time, his own way.

Now Jesse did. "Anyway, I never heard him humming no mantras. But he's a strange duck and a fella that builds buildings and you're interested in this here building. Gotta be ninety if he's a day, tall, gaunt fella, still got all his hair, too. Redheaded, orange rind—colored more like it than red. Walks a lot. Chops wood. You see him at it chopping wood out there in the front yard. Likes to sing out loud while he chops. Hires out by the day on local construction jobs when he's in the mood or needs a buck. Broad-shouldered man like as if he left the coat hanger inside his shirt by mistake. Out there singing and talking to himself and chopping wood. Goes swimming in Three Mile Harbor off the terminal moraine the glacier left. Dives off the rocks and swims across, swims back. That's a fair swim, too, what with the currents and the boat traffic going through to Gardiner's Bay. Goes in the water in April and he's still at it in October, November. The Russian woman goes along, just sits on the rocks watching him swim, and waiting. Guarding his bathrobe. And that's another funny thing . . ."

"What's that?"

"Mr. Roark swims naked. Drops his terry cloth bathrobe and dives right in. Crazy old bastard. Gone senile, I reckon. Ninety years old but well hung, skinny-dipping in Three Mile Harbor."

"No," I said quietly, having read the Rand bio. "That's not senility. From the start, even before he was famous, he swam naked."

Boaters was where Howard Roark hung out. Not that he was a big drinker. A few beers. That was it. But he liked to swap yarns with the bubs, the locals, and complain. He was big for complaining, Jesse said. Which was why he thought I ought to go see Roark.

"When it gets to construction and architecture and such, he talks wild. That's when the complaining gets worse. He bitches about everything. About the builders, about the buildings their own selves. And he claims people is cheating him. They rip him off. This big job down here at Sag Pond they just chased us away from, he says that house was his idea first. That they stole the plans . . ."

"He says this out loud at Boaters? In front of people?"

"Yeah," Jesse said. "I heard it. Put it down to big talk and naught else. But when someone braces him on it, tells Roark he's talking crap, he don't get sore but just laughs at them. Invites them down to his house. Says he's got blueprints. Original drawings. Rendings . . ."

"Renderings."

"Yeah, stuff like that."

"Anyone ever check it out? Go look at his drawings?"

"Nah, Beecher. Them boys'll read a navigation chart for you and bring a boat through the channel in a nor'easter in the dark. None of them bubs up there at Boaters could read a blueprint anyhow. Nor a rendering or whatever."

He had something there. But then, neither could I.

"You want to go up there with me, Jesse? Go see Howard Roark one of these days?"

"Sure."

But first I wanted to talk to Ben Bradlee, by any standard the man who as editor of the *Washington Post* broke the Watergate story and brought down Nixon. Oh sure, Woodward and Carl Bernstein did the legwork. And brilliantly. But if a skeptical and intellectually tough Bradlee hadn't trusted them, and hadn't been able to sell publisher Kay Graham, the thing might never have happened. If any man understood government, Ben did.

"Use my cell phone," Jesse offered. That the Shinnecock Indians have cell phones sort of restores the faith in America that I lost at Wounded Knee. I took Jesse's phone and called Bradlee and got invited over. It's funny, we both worked for a time for the same company and I'd played softball with Ben in the Artists & Writers Game behind the A&P, yet as long as I'd known Bradlee, ever since I saw the *President's Men* movie, I don't visualize the genuine Ben but Jason Robards playing him. Odd, isn't it?

He and his wife, Sally Quinn, have a gorgeous place, a big old weathered cottage on West Drive Road just before it pinches out at the sandy margins of Georgica Pond. Ben is a tall, lean man with bad knees but very cool. As always. Gracious but controlled. Ben had been close to Jack Kennedy. He came back from Paris where he'd been working the same foreign correspondent beat that I later did, also for *Newsweek*, and there was Kennedy in the White House. A shame not to take advantage of such a situation, don't you think? Charlie Bartlett was Jack's best friend in the media, or so canny people said. Bradlee wasn't far behind.

Sally met me at the door and led me out to where Bradlee was lounging on a shaded porch. She was working at her PC on a piece for the *Washington Post* but she called in to someone in the kitchen and a girl brought me iced tea. Ben had one already and we sat there on the porch and talked.

Ironically, or perhaps not, this house the Bradlees owned, and had painstakingly restored, had long been owned by Jackie Kennedy's kinfolk, the Beales, who, to be polite about it, let the place run down. There was "Big

Edie" Beale and her daughter "Little Edie," both intelligent, charming, and, toward the end, odd. The Maysles brothers, who did the Rolling Stones film, did another documentary, called *Grey Gardens*, about this old cottage in Wainscott. Today it belonged on the cover of *Elle Décor* or *House & Garden*. But twenty years ago it was inhabited by the wacky Beales. As well as by a couple of hundred cats, lots of bugs, and just plain filth. When the Bradless bought it they say it took more than a year, just cleaning and fixing up and redecorating.

"What can I tell you?" Bradlee asked.

"This house Offshore Wells is building on Sag Pond."

Bradlee shook his head. "It's something. We're fortunate it isn't right next door. What can I tell you?"

I said that with all the litigation and protests, it puzzled me that Washington wasn't interested, not even the Corps of Engineers. "I know Wells is important but does he have *that* much juice?"

Ben looked at me for a bit. Then he said, "Foreign policy."

That was all. "Foreign policy."

He'd been a reporter; I was a reporter. I didn't feel embarrassed about asking.

"I don't understand."

I can't quote what Ben told me. Wouldn't be fair. He was retired. But he gave me the names of a couple of people I could call. They might know something. One of the sources did, of course. I promised not to quote him by name and he opened up:

"Offshore Wells's name is on the lease. But this is Arab dough. Important Arabs we'd like to keep friendly. Our relations with Islam are shaky enough already. Kuwait is one of the few friends we have in the region; Fatoosh is a son of the Emir, maybe a future emir himself. State doesn't give a shit if some rich people in the Hamptons don't like the shape or size of the house next door. State isn't going to piss off a hundred million Arabs, and maybe half of Islam, with all that delicious oil, just to mollify Kurt Vonnegut."

"So . . . ?"

"So, there'll be no Corps of Engineers beach erosion report. There'll be no environmental studies. There'll be no problem about the water table. There'll be no federal intervention with the local Zoning Board of Appeals. No amicus curiae briefs filed on behalf of anyone."

"Which means . . ."

"Which means this totally inappropriate, out of proportion, insanely megalomaniacal dwelling for a spoiled Arab prince named Fatoosh, is going to be built. Some rich Kuwaitis want the Taj Mahal for a sandbox, let 'em have it. Washington has its priorities and the Hamptons have theirs. Guess who wins that hand."

I hung up the phone with the fulfilled sense of one who suspects he's been told the truth for once. It's always good, I concluded, to deal with practical people and not with poets. The poetry is pleasant, as far as it goes, but the facts are more helpful.

It was smart to have gone first to Bradlee. If Roark the architect was as ga-ga as they all said he was, there was no hurry. He'd still be there, still be babbling. Now I made one additional stop, driving up to the Suffolk County office building in Riverhead to check out their bureau of recorded deeds, variances, easements. To see if there were Arab names, any Sabah al-Sabahs on the documents there along with Chapman Wells. Specifically if there was a Prince Fatoosh the Malevolent. The clerk was genial but not much help. The file on Chapman Wells's controversial house was sealed.

"You might file a Freedom of Information Act application," he reminded me.

"Yeah?" I said skeptically, "and hear back in October. Or maybe next year."

"Delays are possible," he conceded.

"What's the name of the architect of record?" I said. "Maybe if I go directly to him . . ."

The clerk shuffled a few papers. "Guess there's no secret about that. Want to take it down?"

I pulled out my notebook. "Go ahead."

"It's a German fella. From Mannheim. The street address's in German and I can't read it. I can read the name."

"Oh?"

"Name of Speer. A. Speer."

"Hitler's Speer?" I blurted out in astonishment.

The clerk shrugged.

"A nephew, a grandson?"

f o u r t e e n

"*La vie bohème. Barges on the Seine, cheese and red*

wine, chatting up old Hemingway at the Ritz . . ."

The good weather held. Glorious sun. Low humidity. A Chamber of Commerce morning. We were at Sammy's place just before ten and he was already impatiently pacing the gravel at the margin of Lily Pond Lane, darting suspicious glances this way and that, nervously scouting for ravening paparazzi or the morals squad, pruning shears jammed into his back pocket.

"I met the Queen once," he said, grabbing Alix's hand and pumping it. "I was there for a Royal Command Performance and we were all lined up to meet the Queen. Very nice. As an American and a frequent guest in your country, I steer clear of meddling in British politics, Lady Alix, but she has my vote. A truly decent person, you could see that. And with all of her troubles? Prince Philip, well, what can you say? A figure of considerable mystery, all the time, his hands behind his back . . ."

"Yes, I daresay," Alix responded vaguely, with one of those anglicisms that meant nothing and satisfied everyone.

Sammy got into the car with us for the drive to his house. Yet he had me stop twice, jumped out, shears in hand, to snip off an errant bit of hedge. Nerves? Or just a routine tic? After the second halt, I decided two could play at being annoying and said, "Your pal Cyril Pilaster and I were talking about your first editions the other night."

He turned arch. "Oh, a wonderful man. So fond of books, you wouldn't believe the love, a passion even. But some very strange ideas on their arrangement."

At the house, introductions were made. Signor Piano kissed Alix's hand. Just beyond where we chatted there was a large swimming pool with an amusement park's curved slide suitable for children. Lars and two covergirls were already sporting in the pool and waved damply. At least one of the covergirls was swimming topless. With Alix at my elbow, I made a positive point of looking away. Wolfie the producer lifted her shades and said hi from where she was comfortably stretched out on a lawn chaise marking up a script. Other lawn chairs were pulled up for us and a woman in severe black, lips pursed, her hair in an anachronistic bun, silently served tea.

"Mrs. Danvers, the housekeeper," Sammy whispered in explanation as she vanished back into the house. "Forever with the tea. Morning, noon, night we have tea. In summer, iced tea. She makes small concessions. The Chinese water torture? Compared to Mrs. Danvers with the tea, it's nothing. Here's Miss Ng, she'll tell you."

Dixie Ng was everything my father said; her southern accent the only jarring note. She was at least as tall as Alix, and sinuous, all long curves but without bulk, and not at all the Dragon Lady some had it. In part because she was so damned young, looked, despite everything, so innocent and open. What was she now, nineteen? At most. And she made the sweetest effort when meeting Alix to perform a sort of curtsy, very nearly pulling it off through sheer athletic grace.

"Well," said Sammy, when we'd all gotten our tea, "welcome to the armed camp. The 'gallant few' of the RAF, Custer at Little Big Horn, the Greeks at . . . where was it, Piano?"

"Thermopylae, I believe. Where the Persians in overwhelming strength defeated the Spartans in 480 B.C."

"Thank you, Signor," Sammy said, permitting a smile of pride in his banker's impressive fingertip knowledge. "But compared to me right now, the Alamo had whatsisname, the Mexican, just where they wanted him."

"Santa Anna. General Antonio López de Santa Anna," Signor Piano helped out. He was short, like Sammy, but plump, jolly, solid.

"All I need now to feel entirely trapped is for Oliver Stone to film *The Sammy Glique Story*. Ever since Buzzy Portofino's speech . . ."

Wolfie looked up from her script annotation. "Tell them about Woodward and Bernstein."

"You're right," Glique said, the usual bounce missing from his voice. "What with Charlie Osgood doing a poem on CBS and Larry King calling to get me on his show, and how many times has *he* been married? I almost forgot Woodward and Bernstein. First they bring down Nixon, now Glique? You wonder why I'm in therapy?"

I was impressed. Woodward and Bernstein covering Glique? And back together after all these years? Simon and Garfunkel held reunions more often than Woodstein.

"Well, they're here. Both of them," Glique said dejectedly when I expressed surprise.

Signor Piano tried to cheer his friend. You couldn't imagine Piano on the shrink's couch. "Now, now, Sammy. The *Washington Post*, a serious newspaper. Kay Graham, a delightful woman. It's not as if Geraldo set up shop on your front lawn."

Glique shrugged, beyond consolation. It was all too much. What had him really appalled was Buzzy's enthusiastic reception at the Maidstone Club.

"I mean, Portofino's Italian. A Catholic. And they cheered him? All those Wasps giving a standing 'O' to this guy, no disrespect intended, Stowe. Nor, of course, to Your Ladyship. But to me, that was a slap in the face. That the Maidstone doesn't want me as a member, fine. But to give this Congressman a platform to *slander* me? And to embarrass my houseguest the Senator?"

The club's choice of Wednesday night speakers was a notoriously random business and I didn't attempt to explain it. Though I had heard there was bad blood between Buzzy and D'Amato, two Italo-American New York Republicans jousting for advantage. Had Buzzy made his speech not to criticize Sammy but to maneuver Senator D'Amato into an awkward corner? Lars now got out of the swimming pool with one of the covergirls.

Sammy, distracted, called out in considerable alarm, "Dixie, a robe, a towel or something. Our guests . . ."

A robe was fetched and the covergirl put it on without protest. At least it seemed that way but since she was speaking Danish I really had no idea.

Glique shook his head. "That's all we need, foreigners in my personal pool swimming nude. What Portofino couldn't make of that! Think of the hearings, the Alien and Sedition subcommittee! Aliens in Glique's pool. *Naked* aliens! A shonda to the neighbors . . ."

"What's a shonda?" Alix whispered.

"A scandal, I think. In Yiddish or Hebrew, I'm not sure which."

"Oh."

She was an Oxford graduate with a double first who retained the spirit of intellectual inquiry.

Glique and his girlfriend gave us the quick tour of his grounds. In some ways, it reminded me of what I'd heard about Michael Jackson's place, childishly full of games and toys. Sammy, as if reading my mind, shrugged.

"When I was a little kid in Sheepshead Bay, what toys did I have? Did the Irish ask me to play stoopball? To join in their games? Never mind the Protestants. A Jew wearing glasses?"

You could begin to understand his fierce determination to play speed chess every Tuesday night with my father. In addition to the pool, there was a croquet lawn, basketball hoop, a badminton setup, volleyball, quoits, a trampoline, an archery target, and various balls scattered about the closely mown grass, the heart of which was a carefully groomed putting green with a rack of perhaps a dozen putters and sleeves of brand new Maxfli golf balls.

At lunch, with Dixie Ng presiding, Sammy seemed to be feeling marginally better about things.

"People jump to conclusions. Racial stereotypes. I'm Jewish; ergo I must be smart. Clever about money. Dixie is a mix of Chinese and—"

"Asian-American, Sammy, ah keep tellin' y'all."

"So, Asian-American. The political correctness, I should live so long . . . but you know how we typecast people psychologically. We expect from Dixie eggroll, bird's nest soup, General Ko's chicken, bean sprouts, and chopsticks . . ."

"But what y'all get," said Dixie, "is Cajun chicken, gumbo, frittered sweet potatoes, pone, jambalaya, 'n' knives 'n' forks." She pronounced "forks" as "fokes." To Alix she explained, "Ah'm from Loo-siana, Your Ladyship."

"Oh, you must know Paul Prudhomme? He's a great favorite of mine."

"Know him? Wha, we'all worship at his shrahn. Tha best restaurant in tha Vieux Carré. Ol' Paul's . . ."

How did Alix know things like this? I marveled silently. Somewhere close I could hear what sounded like a low-flying plane.

"Well," Sammy said, hating to be upstaged, "there are any number of excellent chefs who—"

Signor Piano looked up. "I think the paparazzi are about to join us, Sammy."

Glique panicked. The aircraft engine was much louder now.

"Don't look up! They enlarge the film. You can see even the pores. And if, God forbid, zits! Don't ask. Your face will be on the front page of the *Enquirer* next week. Worse, in the *Midnight Globe!* They . . ."

"Oh, crumbs!" Alix said.

"What, what?" Sammy asked in considerable agitation, fearing what he was about to hear, "are the covergirls naked again?" Alix cooled him off.

"I'm afraid it's for me, Mr. Glique. I'd forgotten all about it. I was supposed to be lunching at Ron Perelman's today. I told him I might drop by here en route. That's his chopper."

What the hell was this all about? Lunch with Perelman? Wasn't Ron married again . . . ?

Before I could voice my question, Mrs. Danvers in her black dress and sensible shoes emerged again from the house, heading for us.

"This must be bad news. Usually she's upstairs, peering through the curtains," Sammy explained, "always with the pursed, disapproving lips, if not the tea. You'll see."

"Mr. Glique, a phone call. Senator D'Amato."

"Oh, excuse me," Glique said, brightening. "I better get this. Surely, the Senator is calling to apologize. A gracious rapprochement, a gesture on his part. How thoughtful . . ."

Mrs. Danvers shook her head. "The Senator wasn't calling to speak with you. He left a message, telling you Congressman Portofino's speech is the talk of the Beltway. He specifically asked that you not, repeat *not,* call him back. The Senator said he's shocked to learn you and Ms. Ng are not even engaged. The Senator *won't* be visiting Lily Pond Lane again . . ."

Glique looked stricken. As if he'd been slapped. But said nothing.

Mrs. Danvers concluded, "And will you please send via UPS his dental floss? He left it in the cottage. *Overnight* UPS, he stipulated."

Glique shrugged helplessly. What had God against him? By now the helicopter had settled noisily onto the great lawn. When the rotor slowed and stopped, Alix ran over and called up her regrets to the pilot to be passed on to Mr. Perelman. The pilot, uniformed and in shades, nodded solemnly. And as they talked, a crewman leaning out of the hatch handed down a somewhat battered ten-speed bike. Then, behind the bike, a tall, spare, and rather elegantly rumpled figure dropped softly to the lawn, there to be briefly embraced and given air kisses by Her Ladyship.

"Does everyone know George Plimpton?" Sammy asked. And then, almost without pause, answered his own question. "Of course. Who in America does *not* know—"

"Hello, George," I said, sticking out a hand.

"Hallooo, Beecher," he responded, grabbing my hand in two fists and pumping it enthusiastically, as if playing host, "How good of you to come!"

I hadn't come anywhere, I started to say. I was here; *he* was the one who just arrived. And what was Alix doing giving air kisses? Glique cut me off.

"Look, already, two Harvard men, exchanging the password. And, already, with the secret handshake. Did we have passwords at City College? Secret handshakes? Well, maybe if you belonged to the Young Communist League. But at Harvard, in their white bucks and tweed jackets, smoking pipes, always the handshakes . . ."

Neither George nor I smoked pipes and when I glanced down, there wasn't a white buck in sight. But Plimpton had the floor. "I hitched a ride over, Sammy. Hope you don't mind my dropping in."

"No, why should I—?"

Alix didn't let him finish. "I told them to pass on my regrets to Mr. Perelman, explaining that my fiancé, Vyvyan Hardcastle, the seventh Marquess, was due in from London on the Concorde and I had to change for tea . . ."

"Tea? Tea?" Sammy repeated, "Dixie, for Her Ladyship, a little tea? Dixie, get Danvers back. You'll find her lurking behind the curtains. Finally someone wants tea and where is she? Usually, it's every thirty minutes, a new pot. Silver creamer, little cubes of sugar, God forbid we should use granulated . . ."

"It's true, ma'am, Miz Danvers 'n' tea, it's lak Lars 'n' tha covergirls."

"Hi Ho!" Lars shouted on hearing his name.

"I'll have some too," Plimpton said, unslinging his tape recorder and turning it on, "if it's Earl Grey."

"Are we being put on tape?" Signor Piano inquired pleasantly though prudently, being a banker.

"Oh absolutely," Plimpton said, "keep it humming all the time. Never know when you're going to pick up something useful for the oral history. I recall clearly that time at the *finca* when I was interviewing Papa Hemingway . . ."

The other covergirl had finally emerged from the pool, also quite naked. By now, Sammy didn't even bother to protest or call for robes. Lars and the girl shook hands with everyone, speaking something. Maybe Lapp.

Wolfie looked up from her script and shook her head.

"Sammy, the raw material is wonderful, but don't even think of turning all this into a motion picture; *no* one would believe it."

"Nice bike," I told Plimpton, having heard his Hemingway stories before and wanting to distract both of us from staring at the naked model.

"It's French. Peugeot sends over a new one every few years . . ."

"George used to live in France," Sammy put in proudly, "where he founded the *Paris Review*. A magazine, incidentally, largely ignored but which everyone should read. Dixie, for one, has a subscription . . ."

"Those were the salad days," Plimpton said heartily. "*La vie bohème.* Living on barges on the Seine. Chatting up old Hemingway at the Ritz. Writing novels. The cafés. The auteur theory. Reading the *Cahiers du Cinéma*. Did I ever tell you, Sammy, that when she was at Vassar, Jane Fonda was one of our summer interns? All these American college girls came over and worked for nothing. We sent them for cheese and red wine and tried to seduce them . . ."

"Oh, to think of it," Sammy said in wistful agitation. I believe he was seeing the comparative slimness of life at City College. Which was better, touch football with shiksas at the Kennedy compound? Or living on barges, and the *Paris Review* with Jane Fonda bringing in the cheese and red wine?

Sensing his pain, Dixie Ng moved to his side, leaning against him, a head taller than he was, an arm loosely around his waist, and kissed him lightly on the cheek.

"Darling, y'all ah an 'auteur theory' of yo' own. Didn't Truffaut once say so?"

"Godard," Sammy said quickly, "it was Godard said that . . ."

She kept right on going. "An' y'all got all tha college gals you need right here. An' red wine, besides. Who needs bahges in Paris?"

Her loyalty seemed to cheer him marginally and over lunch Sammy permitted his understandable resentment at Senator D'Amato to surface. Despite Plimpton's tape recorder. "I understand his discretion. But then to leave messages about his dental floss with Danvers. The Senator knows she despises me. Delights in having something to hold over me . . ."

He then went on to tell stories about his former friend D'Amato, not failing to include the well-known anecdote of the time in search of Baltic voting bloc support, the globe-trotting Senator strode up to the still-Communist border of Lithuania and informed the mystified border guard, "I demand to be permitted entry to Latvia!"

"Oh, I say, that is good," Alix applauded. "I wonder if Fatty Soames knows that one. Surely he'd use it in the Commons."

"If only I had something on Portofino," Glique said gloomily.

"Tell them about what Fatty calls out when that fellow gets up to speak who used to be a bartender for Cunard," I urged, always willing to liven up the table talk.

"Well, you see, there's an MP named Nicholas Soames, Fatty that is, and he . . ." Alix began.

I hoped Plimpton was getting it all down. A good oral history needs all the help it can get.

f i f t e e n

East Hampton had never been lovelier.

Or more fun . . .

When we got back to my house after Sammy's lunch, two strange cars were parked on the gravel, one decidedly flashy and empty, the other an olive drab sedan with government plates, idling and occupied. As Alix and I pulled up, a uniformed man with a holstered sidearm got out of the government car, snapped to attention and saluted.

"Ma'am, sir, I am looking for Mr. Beecher Stowe."

"I'm Stowe."

"I am Gunnery Sergeant Homer W. Tate, sir. United States Marine Corps. May I speak to you privately, sir."

He was looking toward Alix, which was understandable the way she looked and how she was checking out the unfamiliar uniform.

"Lady Alix has my complete trust, Gunny."

He hesitated a moment, squinting at a palm-size photo and then back at me. Evidently, I passed.

"It's a message from the Admiral, sir."

"In code?"

"Partially, sir. As ordered, there's nothing on paper. I've committed the message to memory. Shall I, uh . . . ?"

He was again looking at Alix. She gave him a winning smile.

"Go ahead, Gunny. Her Ladyship is well known to the Admiral. I'll take responsibility."

"Aye aye, sir. The message is as follows: 'Lift an ouzo to funster hot corner.' And there's a number of some sort."

"Mmm," I said.

He gave me what I knew to be a page number and then, "That's all there was, sir." The sergeant seemed to fear he'd disappointed me.

"That's fine, Gunny. Thank you."

Then he saluted us again, addressing Alix as "ma'am," and got back into the car. When he'd gone off, Alix said, "He was armed, Beecher. Is that customary with your Marines?"

"Signifies he's on official business."

"Oh."

Neither of us mentioned the sleek gray convertible still there unexplained in the driveway, a model I'd never seen before, low and fast, or surely looking that way.

Then Alix said, "And of course you understood the message."

"Yes. Except I'll have to look up the page cited."

"That reference to ouzo, that means Greece . . ."

". . . and Greece means that . . ."

". . . even as we speak the Admiral may be leaving Europe behind to enter Asia Minor . . ."

". . . where Islam rules and where . . ."

". . . Dick Hannay and . . ."

". . . that fellow Sandy . . ."

". . . Master of Clanroyden . . ."

I called a halt.

"Not fair, Alix."

"What isn't fair?"

"All you Brits have these glorious titles. Lord this. Lady that. Your daddy, the Earl. Fruity's being a Viscount. Sir Richard Hannay. And now Sandy, Master of Clanroyden."

"Well, your father's the Admiral, isn't he? Is that an inherited title? Upon his passing, will you become the Admir—?"

"Shut up. Let's go look up *Greenmantle.*"

"Well, I lose."

That threw me off. "You lose what, Alix?"

"A private wager. I'd bet myself you wouldn't be able to resist asking about the Aston-Martin. Are you sure you don't want to cast a practiced eye over it first?"

Well, yes, I did. But rather than be gauche, I'd waited until she brought it up.

"I phoned the Aston-Martin people yesterday whilst you were writing and they agreed to send out one of their new V12 Project Vantage concept vehicles for me to test-drive. I threw around outrageously presumptuous references to *The Times* of London and Rupert Murdoch and the like. They seemed terribly impressed. Odd, though, I asked for a car in British racing green and this one's sort of oyster gray . . ."

"Pity," I said.

Having admired Alix's borrowed car, and her cleverness, we pulled *Greenmantle* off the shelf and turned to the appropriate page.

"You're right," I said. "It's Constantinople, as it was then, and our friend Dick Hannay and someone named Peter . . ."

". . . Peter Pienaar, the great Boer hunter and guide. Reappears in several other of Buchan's novels . . ."

". . . are dealing with a sleazy gent named Signor Kaprasso at an establishment called . . ."

". . . the Garden House of Suliman the Red," Alix completed the thought. "Where they will shortly encounter, though I'm sure you've guessed this already, the 'Companions of the Rosy Hours' and witness their dance."

"Though hardly enjoying it," I said, reading rapidly down the rest of the page. "Listen to this: 'Cries broke from the hearers—cries of anger and lust and terror. I heard a woman sob, and Peter, who is as tough as any mortal, took tight hold of my arm. I now realized that these Companions of the Rosy Hours were the only thing in the world to fear . . .'"

I put down the book. "Just what the hell does that mean? That we're to avoid the Companions or somehow win them around to our side? And more vitally, just who are these lads?"

Alix for no reason whatsoever kissed me on the mouth. "That, my dear Beecher, is why you have to read this book."

"Listen, I'm falling behind on my own pieces. You fill me in tonight. I'll buy dinner."

"My, there's an offer."

She took a nap and then bathed and I hammered away all afternoon polishing the *Parade* piece about Oprah.

It was warm and with no moon so the stars showed and we got one of the sidewalk tables at Frank Duffy's place on Newtown Lane. For this night at least, they'd repealed political correctness and everyone was drinking cocktails and smoking. Or maybe it was just summer and East Hampton had never been lovelier. Or more fun. Even as she told me about her, "Companions of the Rosy Hours."

"They're dancers of a mad sort. Whirling dervishes. With a charismatic leader-cum-prophet who's also slightly mad but has the mysterious East mesmerized. Even Turkey is impressed. And beyond Turkey . . . all of Islam, a vast prairie just waiting for a grass fire to ignite it."

"But what does it mean in terms of my father's jaunting around the bazaars and sending coded messages via armed Marine couriers?"

Alix sipped at her martini, regarding me over the glass. "Beecher, it's a slim, entertaining book. Perhaps there's a real-life prophet Admiral Stowe seeks. If your father thinks enough of *Greenmantle* to use it to send messages from dangerous places, I think it's worth a quick read. Don't you?"

On rare occasions Alix grew terribly solemn. Now was one of those times. "Yes, Alix, I think it is."

"Good," she said briskly, and very matter of fact, "then let's have dinner. I'll make the coffee when we get back and sort of kiss you and flirt and such to keep you awake. The pages will just fly, don't you think . . . ?"

It was nearly one when I reached the final page. "Read that last bit aloud," Alix said sleepily. "It's such a grand finale."

"Sure," I said, having enjoyed the yarn but glad to be finished with it:

"'In the very front,' I read, "'now nearing the city ramparts, was one man. He was turbaned and rode like one possessed, and against the snow I caught the dark sheen of emerald. As he rode it seemed that the fleeing Turks were stricken still, and sank by the roadside with eyes strained after his unheeding figure . . .

"'Then I knew that the prophecy had been true, and that their prophet had not failed them. The long-looked-for revelation had come. Greenmantle had appeared at last to a waiting people.'"

As I closed the novel and put it down, Alix said, "Now, Beecher, don't you think you ought tell me about the 'funster'? And who or whatever the 'hot corner' might be?"

I took her up to bed then and lying there, pillows bunched up and the lights out so we could see the stars over the ocean beyond my windows, I talked of a boy I knew long ago at Dunster House at Harvard where he played third base for our house team, modeling his play on the hot-corner acrobatics of a major leaguer with a name curiously close to his own, Sal Bando of the Oakland Athletics.

"His own name is Bandar. At Harvard, very much one of us, a 'Dunster Funster,' though in real life a prince of the royal house of Kuwait, a son of the Emir. And just maybe, if I'm reading my father correctly, a clue to whatever's got Washington alarmed, roiling the Persian Gulf . . ."

"Gosh," said Alix. "Could your friend *be* the prophet? The 'long-looked-for revelation' his people await?"

I'd never thought of old Bando as prophet material, but I didn't say that. "We'd better ask him," I said instead.

"Where is he?" she asked, "and how do we get hold of him?"

Well, now, though I hadn't seen old Bando in person since the night before the Gulf War erupted, I knew exactly where he was and what he was doing.

But maybe, in telling Alix about Bandar, I'd better start with the last time we met.

"Well," I began, "If you've ever been to Kuwait, you probably know the Sceptre Club, atop the Ram Dass Tower . . ."

His sons, patronizing the casinos and attending to their mistresses . . .

"And you're quite sure about this, Beecher? He's really coming this time?" Bandar asked.

"I see the cables," I responded, bragging a bit but legitimately so, having a good source at our embassy.

The two of us, an American correspondent for *Newsweek* at the time, and an Arabian prince, were sitting over drinks on a July evening in Kuwait City waiting for a war to begin. The Sceptre Club overlooked the harbor, as sleek and comfortable a men's bar as you'd find anywhere east of '21.' This was the place where sheiks drank and the younger Kuwaiti royals such as Prince Bandar, the dips from the various embassies and consulates, and the bigger oil men out of Texas, Louisiana and California, plus the press boys, those few who could hold their liquor and be relied on to pay their tabs. A few women came here as guests, not members, of course. In Kuwait there were other establishments for that. As well as for pleasures not to be spoken of openly.

Yet on this evening the Sceptre was just about empty. Nothing to do with the Koran; Kuwaitis are famously relaxed when it comes to religious strictures on alcohol, though pious in most other things. Bando snapped his fingers and one of the club waiters hustled over.

"My Prince?"

"We'll have two more of these."

"Instantly, My Prince."

The Sceptre Club's servants were good, too. And faithful. A shooting war was about to start and the quality of service remained up to the Sceptre's rather stiff standards. Neither of the senior barmen had yet run off and there seemed the usual number of busboys hurrying and of waiters standing obsequiously about. Not even the Maidstone Club could boast a superior staff.

Outside, in the Kuwaiti streets, it was different; all was panic and chaos, flight and fear. A cosy little world was going bust and there was nothing to do about it but run. Yet here at the bar of the Sceptre Club, a sophisticated calm held. It was not considered chic in these precincts to be anything but cool. Suave men sipped their drinks and exchanged views. As Bandar and I did now.

"Those cables say just when, Beecher?"

"Tomorrow, the day after. Maybe the day after that. Washington's not sure. Except that he's coming."

Neither of us had to say who "he" was. The Iraqi despot Saddam Hussein had been growling his belligerence for weeks, issuing bloodthirsty threats and pledging, under Allah, to swallow Kuwait as just another province of the mother country, Iraq.

Prince Bandar nodded, subdued, very nearly solemn, not at all the devil-may-care playboy I knew, the fun-loving baseball player I'd known at college. But it was his country, wasn't it, that was about to go down.

At a few other tables men sat similarly over a glass, men in linen jackets from Savile Row, men in robes of gaudy stuff, heads close and murmuring. No high-stakes bridge tonight, no click of ivory dice for the bar bill, no evening clothes. Not tonight. It wasn't the Sceptre Club we both knew, loud and jolly, a boozy, laughing place. But then, it wasn't every week you got invaded. I wondered idly if it had been like this in Paris in the spring of 1940, just before the Germans came. You could hear ice cubes melting in the glasses it was so still, tense and moody, voices low and confidential, as the Sceptre Club waited to be Occupied.

But that was inside the club. Out there on the airport highway along which I'd been driven to meet Bando, and on all the roads to the port and docks, the last ships pulling away, well, that was something else again. That was sure something else. I'd never seen an evacuation before and not even the martinis could rinse it from memory.

"Just don't run anyone down," I'd told Abdul. "We don't need a lynch mob turning over the car."

"No, Mr. Stowe."

When I set out to meet the Prince it was only midafternoon with a high sun bouncing off anyplace flat or polished, a time of day when the streets should have been emptied as women dozed and children slouched in air-conditioned classrooms and men considered whether the slightest movement was worth the effort. Panic changed all that, the instinct for self-survival; war fever changed it. Abdul nudged the car forward through the auto traffic and the lorries and the occasional tank or armored car and the people with suitcases and shopping bags and burlap sacks. The people walking and lugging bundles were foreign laborers, Palestinians or Filipinos, the men and women who did the actual work in Kuwait. Why they were trying to get out, too, God knows. Could peonage under Saddam be much different than slaving under the Emir?

The whole chaotic, frightened, frenzied, confused and terrifying nightmare of the airport road reminded me of those opening scenes of *Lost Horizon,* with merchants and missionaries and soldiers and diplomats, all in an awful, scared mass of refugees, hurrying along with the peasants and hoping to get out. All we lacked was a cool British consul like "Conway," a smooth, collected Ronald Colman wielding a Webley .38 and shepherding his curious little flock aboard an old DC-3 for a flight to what they thought was asylum.

And turned out to be Shangri-La.

The car pushed slowly ahead, Abdul not sparing the horn.

My editor in New York, then Maynard Parker, had sent orders as precise as a shifting situation would allow. I was to hang in there until the Iraqi Republican Guards actually crossed the border, to be sure this wasn't just another feint in a war of nerves, not simply a little more sword-rattling by Saddam, and then to get out along with the Emir's government. That's what correspondents do, hang about and then, when the shooting starts, take a few notes and run like hell with everyone else.

"What about you, Bando?" I asked over our second drink.

"I'd like to stay and fight," said the Prince, "silly as that may sound considering the size and shape of our noble armed forces. Die gloriously and all that, outnumbered, doomed and gallant. Alas, Beech, it's but wishful thinking and nothing more. My father says, no, I have other chores for you."

Prince Bandar the Gentle was one of thirty-nine sons (his mother had been a Brit, quite beautiful, quite blonde) of the Emir Sabah al-Sabah al-Sabah, whose clan had ruled Kuwait since the time of Lawrence and the Turks and, episodically, long before that. He'd been sent off to an English public school at the age of six and on to Eton (he was the only boy with a subscription to *Sports Illustrated* and was consequently most popular every February when the swimsuit issue came out) and, still later, to Harvard, and was about as much an Arab as was George Plimpton, in whose *Paris Review* Bandar would eventually become an investor.

As one of thirty-nine sons, most of them senior to him, it was unlikely Bando would ever himself become emir, but he was a decent chap and being this low in the batting order didn't seem to bother him at all. He spoke instead of the literary life. A history of the Harvard-Yale game, perhaps.

"What sort of chores?" I inquired.

"Suffice it there are any number of treasures the Emir doesn't want falling into the clammy and avaricious grip of Saddam and his brigands. The oil we can't take with us, obviously, but there's other, more portable wealth. And since at least in theory, my brothers and I are not only trustworthy but canny, we've each been assigned this bauble or that, this sacred icon or other, and are pledged on our honor to get it across the border and to safety once Saddam huffs and puffs and blows our house down. And if we can't beat the bastards to the pass, bury the stuff in the desert with precise cross-references on the map, so we can come back later and retrieve it."

Not all thirty-nine sons had actually been given such an assignment; others being in London or Paris or Washington on family business or whipping up support for the regime, "or," as Bandar cheerfully admitted, "in the casinos of the South of France attending to their mistresses."

I emptied my glass and wondered about having another on grounds I might, after all, be making a dash for the Saudi Arabian border before the night was out. Aw, to hell.

"Boy! Another round here."

"At once, Mr. Stowe."

We toasted the war, toasted the peace, and then I said:

"So when the first Iraqi tank rolls into town and heads for the bar of the Sceptre Club, you're out of here with the Whisker of the Prophet or whatever it is, tucked securely away in your attaché case."

"Exactly, old boy," Bandar agreed, then dropping his voice. "In my case I've been assigned a holy totem known as the Rose Manteau, a pink cloak, a moth-eaten old relic but one of the Seven Pillars of Wisdom that give legitimacy to our Al-Sabah dynasty."

Then, abruptly, the Prince rose and went to the nearest window to look down on the city and its network of broad avenues leading to the sea or the open desert and its national highways outside the city limits where a good car could go 130.

"Anything?" I called to him in a conversational tone in the hush of the near-empty bar.

"Taillights, and plenty of them. An unending stream of red taillights. Headed south. Heading out. Ironic, isn't it?"

"What, that people are scared and running? Sounds pretty natural . . ."

"No, that it was so near here, between the Tigris and Euphrates, where both Jews and Christians believe it all began in that fabled old garden at Eden. And now . . ." The Prince lifted his hands in eloquently mute dismay.

We had one more round and arranged where to meet in Saudi Arabia when and if.

"You take care now, Beecher."

"You, too, Bando. You and the Rose Manteau both . . ."

We parted outside, a chauffeured Rolls taking the Prince to his father's palace; Abdul driving me to the American Embassy to catch up on the latest press room scuttlebutt. If the cables I'd sneaked a look at were accurate, and I believed they were, I'd soon have plenty to do other than concern myself with prophets and their sacred relics.

The Iraqi invasion began the next day.

seventeen

Brushing a few grains of cinnamon

sugar from her breast . . .

This was all very well, my war stories, her "boys' tales" shoved down a small girl's throat by a father who wanted a son and got Alix instead.

But when it came down to it, how much did I know or even suspect? Only that there was some vague link between the Admiral's mission and my old pal Bandar. Nothing beyond a single phone call to connect Buzzy Portofino here and the Admiral out there in Asia. Nor was I getting any closer to a look at this monstrous house Walter Anderson was curious about. I consoled myself that at least I knew how to contact Bandar the Gentle. Maybe that would be a start.

"Where?" Alix asked.

"He's an analyst for Charles Schwab. The petroleum futures market. He's a regular on CNBC, talking about oil prices."

None of the other questions were as easily answered.

I don't believe in brooding. I say to hell with it, and get out of the house. Go to the beach and check out the kids surfing and the birds working over the baitfish. Or amble across the golf course, pocketing the occasional lost ball (but only if no foursomes are in view). Or go up to Dreesen's on Newtown Lane for doughnuts and the papers. A brisk walk, the morning papers, a hot, fresh doughnut. You don't need therapists at one fifty an hour.

Which was why, just before seven, I untangled myself from Alix, who at that hour, and at other times, seemed all limbs, slender arms and legs splayed and entwined this way and that, her dark hair lightly strewn across two pillows. Being a man, I stood there for a moment, looking down at her; then, being a Harvard man, I tugged a discreet top sheet lightly across the graceful body I knew so well and with such pleasure.

The doughnut machine in the window was already spewing them. Raymond plucked out the best four, very hot and smelling sweet, and Jimmy took the money for them and the papers. Noel McStoy, who used to run the school, and Brad Marmon, the pharmacist, were perched on tall stools drinking coffee, while Rudy de Santi was butchering a nice cut of veal, and one of the Village cops read a paper he had absolutely no intention of buying, and it was all so routine. For all its "general store" look, Dreesen's was the local equivalent of Rick's place in *Casablanca;* everybody went there. This was what Portofino and certainly Offshore Wells didn't understand about East Hampton. That it wasn't all that glamorous a place, but homespun and simple stuff by which local people measured and chronicled their lives: the morning papers, doughnuts, the schools, the cop on the beat, the drugstore. Few of them knew any Arabian princes or were being investigated by Congress or had fathers mucking about in Asia Minor on orders of Defense Secretary Bill Cohen.

And absolutely none of them, I was reasonably certain, had a beautiful and titled Englishwoman back home asleep in his bed.

She was awake when I got back. Not dressed, of course; Alix didn't rush into things.

"You are a darling," she assured me sleepily. "Is there a cinnamon one in there? And our chum Jesse Maine called. I took it upon myself to invite him over later."

I'd chosen the cinnamon doughnut for myself. I gave it to her, of course, with the *Times* and a paper napkin to catch the crumbs, and went downstairs to make coffee. I wondered what Jesse wanted. When I got back Alix was propped up nicely in bed, wide awake by now, brushing a few grains of cinnamon sugar from her breast (inspiring me to do something silly but, to me, rather erotic, drawing from Alix a pleased little moan). There was a bit more related sport and then, remembering our situation, she said briskly:

"I've a super idea, Beecher. Here we have all these Arab princes somehow mixed up with your father and this mysterious house. With Sammy Glique being asked to write a movie for this other chap, not your chum, but the one they say is really building that awful house, mightn't we get Sammy to wangle an invitation to lunch? And take us along? I mean, if Fatoosh—whatever his full name is—is in residence."

"Fatoosh the Malevolent."

"Oh, I do love that. 'The Malevolent.' Wouldn't it be gorgeous to go through life being addressed by lackeys and mentioned in columns as the Malevolent."

As to her lunch idea, I said, "Might work," still uncertain, not having thought it through. But did I have a better idea? No.

"I knew you'd come up with a plan," she said generously.

When we phoned to broach the idea, Sammy readily agreed.

"Dixie, the Prince phoned his thanks when I sent him the film treatment. Do you have a number for Prince Fatoosh? If you can't find it under F try M for Malevolent."

It was actually under P for Prince. That hurdle cleared, it was the simplest of matters. And, mirabile dictu, Fatoosh *was* there at Wells's place!

"He says come for lunch," Glique phoned back to tell us. "I said we had guests. He said fine. Even when I told him Sharon Stone wasn't among them. Offered to send a helicopter for us but I said, no we'll sail over, we've got the yacht."

"You have a yacht? Why, that's swell. We can . . ."

His voice tightened, stressed for some reason.

"I don't have a yacht. It's expected of me, a man in my position. So embarrassing to say that I don't. I got nervous and just blurted out, 'yes, I have a yacht.' Why do I lie? A sense of my own inadequacy. But then, why do I need a house in the Hamptons? Miami Beach, that's where I wanted to buy. A nice condo. But my mother lives there. She'd be dropping by evenings. How could I explain . . . you know . . . Dixie, there in her dainties? And there'd be invitations to play mah jongg with her cronies. I don't need that. So I bought on Lily Pond Lane. John Drew used to live here, the tragedian. I saw a photo of his house dated 1901 and I thought, What could be bad, living next door to the spirit of John Drew? And no one to pester me about mah jongg. But instead, questions about yachts . . ."

"Never mind," I assured him. "We can charter."

Captain Bly and his fishing boat picked us up at Jerry Della Femina's marina in Three Mile Harbor. Jesse's pickup was there ahead of us. I wanted him for his familiarity with Sag Pond. "Hi, Your Ladyship. Hi, Beecher. This is Ms. VooVoo Vronsky, formerly of Kiev, my archery instructor."

VooVoo was a strapping blonde, very Xena the Warrior Princess, with a quiver of arrows and a polished bow slung over one broad shoulder and a single heavy braid hanging down her suntanned back, dressed in sandals, shorts and a tank top. Her handshake was a crusher but she had a nice, amiable smile.

"I bring my bow and some arrows, Jesse?"

Captain Bly had by now seen the quiver. "What the hell is this? I chartered for a run through the canal round to the ocean side of Sagaponack. Not Custer's Last Stand."

"No need, VooVoo," Jesse said, "just lunch with a prince of Araby."

The weather was perfect, the sea flat on the trip through Peconic Bay and the Shinnecock Canal and then back east past Southampton. Alix, Dixie and VooVoo sunbathed and rather prettily, though keeping their tops on, which disappointed Captain Bly considerably. He grew cheerier over the Coors beer. Signor Piano observed the horizon from a deck chair. Merchant bankers were like that. "Wolfie," Glique explained in an aside, "is reading scripts." To pass the time, I asked Glique idly if he ever ran across Budd Schulberg out here, the man who created the fictional Sammy Glick. I was surprised at the ferocity of his answer.

"Oh, sure, easy for Budd to play the innocent. That he never heard of me when he wrote the book. That I wasn't even born. True, but this unwarranted attack on generations of decent, hardworking Glicks? My father, a tailor on Seventh Avenue, did he ever screw his partners at the studio? Plagiarize the work of other writers? Seduce starlets? Make or break directors? I'm sure Mr. Schulberg began with purity of motive and the best of intentions. After all, a Dartmouth man; we who graduate public college, we expect nothing less from the Ivy League. Although he permitted these resentments of Louis B. Mayer, of the studios, to warp his judgment. But because of him, in Hollywood, my family's name is the mark of Cain."

"You ever discuss this with Schulberg?"

"We cross paths on occasion. But no. Personally, I take a dignified stance. I avert my gaze."

He paused. Then, "So, too, does Miss Ng. Don't you?"

"Always," Dixie assured me from where she lazed in the sun, "Ah, too, avert mah gaze."

Bly, sucking back a Coors at the wheel, ground his teeth. He liked it better when the girls went topless.

Alix, gleaming with sunblock, thought it might be helpful for Glique and Schulberg to air their differences. "You know, both of you talk it out for an article in *The Times*. The colloquy moderated by someone lit'ry, a Kenneth Tynan, say . . ."

"Ken Tynan's dead, Alix," I informed her.

"Oh, I say, bad luck, that! A wonderful critical sensibility. So very lucid."

"Wuz he evah married ta Kay Kendall?" Dixie asked, "Or wuz thet someone else?"

"I adored Kay Kendall!" Alix put in. "As a child I went to all her films . . ."

"No, wasn't it Rex Harrison she was married to?" I offered.

"He's dead as well, alas," Alix noted.

"There wah giants in tha land," Dixie remarked mournfully. "Tha *Cahiers du Cinema* is full of obituaries of auteurs who—"

"Well, we're not all dead," Sammy said in irritation, "and speaking of auteurs, how about Scorsese, Coppola, Bob Altman, Mel Brooks, Jim Cameron, Sydney Pollack, Kubrick, Woody Allen, Spielberg, Donen, me . . . though not," he put in hurriedly, "Tarantino. There, I draw the line."

Dixie nodded agreement.

"Sammy's very severe on thet boy. Severe!" She pronounced it in three syllables, "suh-vee-ah."

Jesse was rubbing suntan lotion into VooVoo's handsome back and shoulders as she made small, pleased, grateful noises and flexed, leaving the film chat to the rest of us.

Dixie was enjoying the shoptalk. Too often when she and Sammy were alone, the talk was of sex (which she certainly understood, the situation being what it was), or complaints about his mother, or of chess. Dixie tried, in bed, to get Sammy's mind off chess (and his mother), but no matter how industrious and clever she was, at some point Sammy would be up and pacing their bedroom, mulling the possibilities of the Four Knights' Variation of the English opening.

"Thar she is!" Captain Bly sounded off, "thar's our landfall."

The women leaped up bouncing from their sunbathing for a first view, delighting Bly, who also liked a good show of leg.

Jesse focused on neither the women nor the fast-approaching beach, beyond which you could see the towers and scaffolds of Offshore Wells's pleasure dome.

"What is it, Jesse?"

"Look."

I followed his arm. There, on the surface of the calm ocean waters, a trail of bubbles paralleled our course.

Our eyes met.

"Frogmen?" I said.

"Couldn't be nothing else. I think I'm going to like this Prince Fatoosh fella. The kind of boy you want to be on the right side of, Beecher."

Captain Bly's battered old fishing trawler was closing fast on the beach, the water going to shoal and getting greener and lovelier every second, bubbles or no bubbles . . .

e i g h t e e n

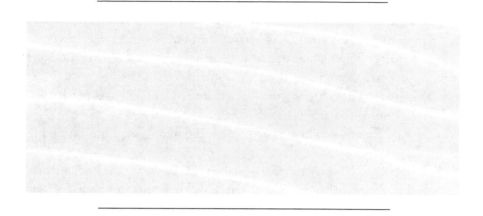

"Even to speak the name, the severest retribution.
Amputation and the lash . . ."

We anchored offshore just beyond the minimal surf and rowed in, using the rubber rafts, and strolled up the sunbaked golden beach to a wooden stair over the dunes that separated the ocean from Sag Pond. On the pond side the property, except for the muddied, cluttered, noisy construction site itself, was thickly treed, unspoiled, tranquil and impressive, featuring a cove with a surprisingly complex layout, helicopter pad, miniature drydock, corrugated ship-fitting shed, and power boats moored, plus the cranes and davits and compressed air pumps for scuba tanks, routine at such a place. Now a large welcoming party approached, led by a dozen decidedly Arabic-looking gents fitted out in burnoose and headdress and curled-toe shoes, armed with very ornate but nonetheless lethal-appearing crossbows.

"A traditional Kuwaiti weapon in our land," a smiling functionary, tall and ascetic, a court chamberlain of sorts, explained as we met and exchanged greetings. Jesse looked over at me; it was the fellow in white robes who'd chased off our canoe. Much pleasanter, now that we were invited guests. Behind me, I could hear VooVoo's grumbling.

"Hey, Jesse, they got bows and arrows, why not me? Ukrainian archery not so good enough?"

The court chamberlain, if that's what he was, clapped his hands smartly and led us along a smoothly mowed path, commenting as he went.

"I am Hassan Hassan, major-domo to His Serene Highness Prince Fatoosh. I regret that our host, Mr. Chapman Wells, has been called away. The Prince in his stead, bids you welcome. You need but ask and I shall attempt to do your bidding. Please do not address your needs to others; they are not all fluent in your tongue and may become confused."

So they were still pretending the place belonged to Wells and not Fatoosh. And were planning to keep us neatly reined in.

At my side Sammy was hissing at Dixie, his nodding head indicating Hassan Hassan:

"Remember *Lost Horizon*, the lama-in-chief, H. B. Warner, ushering Ronald Colman this way and that, hinting at secrets but revealing nothing. Uncanny, the resemblance!"

Flanking Hassan Hassan were an oddly matched pair, one lean gent with Asian features in a Western business suit, shirt and tie, right down to the wingtip black shoes, highly polished, and an enormous fellow in a jeweled turban, brocaded vest, and ballooning, diaphanous trousers, this one armed with a scimitar.

Hmmm, I thought, I've seen this pair before!

An elaborate picnic had been arranged on the long, gently sloping lawn that stretched from the water's edge to the historic old Sag Lodge and the scatter of massive structures being worked on beyond, with chefs and sous-chefs laboring away over spits and grills, and several lengthy tables laid with linen napery, silverware, Wedgwood china (with the Kuwaiti royal seal; nothing indicating ownership by Chappie Wells) and Waterford crystal.

Across that lawn now came a lone rider, on a high-stepping, impeccably gaited gray, a booted and jodhpured figure, slim and handsome, trotting toward us, followed by a handful of small Arab boys, racing, capering and tumbling in his magisterial wake.

"My Lord Fatoosh," Hassan murmured, bowing nearly double.

Fatoosh, looking down on all of us from a tooled and silvered saddle, his strong face suntanned, mustachioed (pencil-thin, you know the sort of thing I mean), his piercing eyes glinting in the sun, paused briefly and then, gracefully, dramatically dismounted in a single motion, to stand, boots gleaming, legs muscularly spread, fists on his hips. Small Arab boys kicked and punched at each other for the privilege of taking the reins, the losers howling and sobbing childish despair.

"Oh, I say!" said Her Ladyship, who doesn't impress easily.

While behind me I could hear Glique exhale: "My God, Rudolph Valentino in *The Sheik* didn't have such entrances."

"Hush, ma dahlin', don't fatigue yourself with tension," Dixie urged.

"Of course not. Why should I be tense?"

He was, of course.

And perhaps with reason, as the Prince greeted us with an energetic salutation, the equivalent of our three cheers or the British "hip, hip, hooray," except in German (a holdover from his school days?):

"Hochs! Hochs!"

"Oh my God," Sammy whispered, "not only an Arab but a Nazi, too." This was a side of his host not previously revealed in their film negotiations. But Fatoosh swiftly made things right; all glad-handing bonhomie, bowing to the men, kissing the women's hands, lingering marginally longer, it appeared to me, over Alix's. Then, looking up slowly into her face, pausing briefly, his smile even more winning.

Mmm, I thought, suspecting I was being silly. But I *do* hate pencil-thin mustaches, don't you?

"Such a gorgeous day," the Prince said after the introductions had been made, "a sin to waste the sun and sky. We shall lunch al fresco, eh?"

Sammy, the one of us who'd actually been here before, shrugged carelessly. "It's the company, not the table, that's what I always feel."

Being British, Alix "collected" old houses, and now pouted prettily: "Oh, I'd so hoped to see the old lodge, inside and out. I'm told it's magnificent."

"And it shall be again one day, My Lady," Fatoosh said smoothly. "For the moment, I regret, decorators are at work. Mr. Wells has been a dynamo of bustling activity. He even attempted to retain Martha Stewart herself, her practical hints for gracious living. Alas, she had prior commitments. One day soon I'll be proud to host a guided tour. But presently the place is a construction site. Scaffolding and plasterers, wet paint and exposed wiring, not at all suitable for honored guests."

There seemed to me a false note in all this. I had no interest in Sag Lodge whatever; my curiosity, journalistic and personal, focused on the big, new house being built. So why all this mumbo jumbo about the old lodge? What could he be hiding *there*?

But first, cocktails. And then a superb lunch. Over martinis Fatoosh proved himself hospitable, joshing with Sammy over details of their draft script, and trying, without avail, to get the filmmaker to agree to helming the actual remake of *Elephant Walk.* I was surprised at Sammy's firm refusals on this. More genially, Fatoosh asked about Miss Sharon Stone and if her recent marriage was going well, before moving along to explain to VooVoo the fine points of the Kuwaiti crossbow, discuss with Jesse the Native American question, and compliment Dixie on her English, having somehow gotten the notion she was a recent immigrant from Hong Kong and asking her opinion of the new regime. He and Signor Piano discussed Swiss banking and recent fluctuations in the dinar, the drachma and the Belgian franc. With Alix he chatted about race meetings they'd both attended at Epsom and Ascot, the stallion now servicing his prize mares, and various pleasure domes in London's West End; both he and she, it turned out, being members of Annabel's, with their own memories of HRH Princess Di.

"But he's a smasher, Beecher," she whispered to me when he'd turned to another of his guests. "Not at *all* malevolent."

Hassan Hassan hovered, ready at any instant to accommodate his master; the "odd couple" standing alertly behind Fatoosh, a sort of bodyguard, though the only weapon discernible between them was the taller man's scimitar, which he kept discreetly sheathed. Despite the continual clamor of construction work going on not half a mile off and the excavation dust raised, all was most pleasant until, over the freshly killed local venison (out-of-season exemptions had been issued to bow hunters to thin the exploding deer population) and a glorious marinated lamb studded with olives, the whole washed down with a lovely Chateau Petrus '82, I blew it.

Until that moment, Fatoosh was the perfect gentleman, the gallant, expansive host, the Arabian knight Hollywood might conjure up, and not at all the edgy princeling. Until I said:

"Tell me, Prince, your younger brother, Bandar. I wondered do you and he . . ."

Fatoosh had been so jolly. Suddenly, he went cold as tombs.

"Which Bandar?"

I understood his hesitation as to which "Bandar" I meant. After all, when there are thirty-nine sons, you run short of names, you repeat yourself. But I'd not anticipated righteous indignation.

"Bandar the Gentle. At college he and I were——"

Fatoosh leaped up snarling as his bodyguards tensed, the scimitar half drawn:

"That fellow's name is anathema in our family! And throughout the kingdom! The Emir (he bowed deeply in the general direction of the Persian Gulf), my father, will not have him mentioned. Even to speak the name calls for the severest retribution, and I do not omit amputation and the lash! My brother is in disgrace of the vilest sort."

"Amputation and the lash," Sammy murmured in considerable alarm, "think of it, Dixie."

I was too astonished by his fury to respond at all effectively. Alix sprang to my assistance.

"And quite right, I'm sure, Prince Fatoosh. My own family has had its share of black sheep. Orders go out and a footman turns portraits to the wall. My third cousin Reg has been turned to the wall for years; I haven't the foggiest what he looks like, beyond faded brown canvas backing and picture wire. My old Pa, the twelfth Earl, is quite firm on it. He'd certainly be in your camp when it comes to erring siblings. Death to the infidel! and all that."

Clearly, as usual, Alix had gone too far, especially with that "death to the infidel!" rubbish. But it was effective.

"It's jolly good of you to appreciate the position, Lady Alix. How painful such things are . . ."

Mollified, Fatoosh over the crème brûlées was all charm and flirtatiousness, after which he and Sammy disagreed, knowledgeably but politely, over which were the greatest westerns. Sammy, usually disputatious, was less than forceful in argument; I assume he had still in mind "amputation and the lash."

Then, abruptly, with a glance at his Cartier Santos watch, the Prince rose, bowed toward the ladies, urged Sammy to reconsider doing *Elephant Walk,* and clapped his hands for the court chamberlain.

I took a risk, getting in a final question as wire service reporters try to do with the President as he strides off across the White House lawn to the Marine chopper:

"Could Your Highness clarify just who owns this property? Who's building this new Versailles, you or Chappie Wells?"

Fatoosh smiled back at me, a narrow, joyless smile.

"Hassan," he called out, with new urgency, "please conduct my guests on a tour of the grounds." Hassan bowed while the pair of bodyguards departed with the Prince, once more mounted, trotting swiftly after his horse.

"Punjab and the Asp," I murmured when they were out of hearing.

"Who?" Alix asked.

"A couple of characters straight out of 'Little Orphan Annie,' a popular comic strip from childhood."

"Oh, but I saw the film!" Alix said, "with Albert Finney playing Annie's adoptive Uncle Warbucks, wasn't it?"

"Daddy Warbucks."

"Yes, well . . ." she said vaguely, not up to speed on the funny papers.

"Come," urged Hassan Hassan, very obviously steering us away from the new buildings, and back into the piney forests, "I'm sure you'll want to get to the animals."

Jesse Maine brightened at this. As a hunter, he was more into game than movies. Especially westerns.

"Animals? They got plenty deer out here. Red fox as well. I wonder what else . . ."

"Elephants," Sammy put in. "Fatoosh is putting in a zoo. He convinced Mr. Wells it's what every Hamptons house needs. As a child the Prince was taken by the hand to the San Diego Zoo and he's been a menagerie fanatic ever since. He likes how elephants sound in the night. When he lived in Africa and India he grew accustomed to the trumpeting; says it helps him sleep. Lions, as well. He has a pet lion. And black panthers on order, stalking, always stalking, silent and deadly. Water buffalo have been ordered. A regular Noah's Ark is planned. Sea lions and Flipper the dolphin. He told me all about it when we weren't discussing Sharon Stone."

"Elephants, well now," Jesse said, impressed, then asked, "VooVoo, any elephants in Kiev?"

"Only when the circus visited. The famous Moscow Circus. One of the most very splendidest circuses of the world. They have many elephants. Also dwarves . . ."

Glique looked at her.

"Also *dwarves* . . ." Sammy repeated thoughtfully, being, like Ingmar Bergman in his films, a great fan of dwarves.

"The largest dwarves in the world," VooVoo confirmed, "that's what the posters said. And true, for dwarves, tall, strapping fellows. Drinkers, as well, always at the vodka, bursting into song, the old Cossack dancing, and pursuing the women. My God, I could tell stories. You can be sure there was gypsy blood there. No woman was safe."

"But first," said the major-domo, gesturing toward a line of bull's eye targets, "a demonstration of traditional Bedouin archery. Led by Akbar the Hashimite, our country's finest archer and My Prince's chief of security, a passionate, brooding fellow, but faithful, I assure you, unto the death."

A small, slim, nimble Arab emerged, dark and saturnine, doing a sort of intricate dance step but very serious about it, his bow held high, followed by a dozen tribesmen in burnooses, trotting out while servants parceled out the drink. Hassan motioned us back, safely out of the way. Off went a first volley, the crossbow cords twanging powerfully. Every arrow hit, all but one in the circle.

"These lads is pretty fair," Jesse said.

"Corking!" Alix agreed. Signor Piano applauded, his soft, pudgy hands making almost no sound.

"When do we see the dwarves and elephants?" VooVoo inquired, snubbing the quality of the archery.

"First," said the chamberlain, smiling his delight, "the snakes. A starter collection of imported reptiles. When My Lord Fatoosh served the Emir as ambassador to Delhi he was quite taken with snakes. This shipment just arrived."

The snakes, dozens of them, were still penned in ventilated plexiglass carrying cases and not at all happy about it, hissing and showing fangs, licking out red tongues, occasionally throwing themselves against the transparent plastic, streaked sloppily with venom, as they expended their anger and energy, trying to get at us.

"A temporary snakepit is being dug. Eventually, there'll be a proper reptile house," Hassan explained. "We have to be sure of its placement. Not too much direct sun or exposure to the wind."

"Wow!" Sammy exclaimed. "A snakepit! It's like *Gunga Din*. The temple of gold. The thuggees of Kali. The regiment on the march, bagpipes skirling. The hills swarming with savage tribesmen. Cary Grant, Doug Fairbanks Jr., Victor McLaglen, and the British Empire at risk. 'Kill, kill, kill! For the love of Kali, *kill!*' Sam Jaffe, bugle in hand, skinny legs trembling. But can he alert the regiment? While below, the deadly pit, swarming with . . ."

We all crowded closer, peering through the Plexiglas. Asps, cobras, king cobras spitting their venom, native U.S. reptiles as well, rattlers and cotton-mouths and water moccasins, smallish snakes I didn't recognize. Larger ones I imagined were anacondas or boa constrictors. Tiny, colorfully ringed snakes you could be sure were deadly. Dixie, a girl from the bayous, was clearly intrigued. Signor Piano, more cautious, sheltered behind her. Jesse, of course, was pushing up against the Plexiglas.

"Look at them bastards, slithering this way and that, wriggling and carrying on. My God, I seen snakes before, but never in my life . . ."

"What do they eat?" Piano wondered.

"A reptile nutritionist is writing a diet," Hassan said. "For the moment, local field mice, chipmunks, live rabbits. They abound in Sagaponack."

"Live rabbits?" Signor Piano shuddered. "That's appalling."

"I dunno 'bout mice," Jesse remarked, appreciating the point of view of the snakes, "but there's lots of nourishment in a plump rabbit . . ."

VooVoo Vronsky chewed her lower lip. "We see few snakes in Kiev."

"When the Viceroy was still running India," Alix offered, "there were religious sects that deified reptiles, worshiped them as gods. But of course, those were exotic times: rajahs in revolt, the ritual of suttee, grieving young ranees burned alive on funeral pyres, the Sepoy Rebellion, chaps like Gandhi staging hunger strikes. Did you know Gandhi often slept with gorgeous young women to test himself, to prove his dedication to celibacy?"

"You're shitting me," Sammy said, unable to stop himself. "Please excuse my language, Lady Alix, I forget myself. But Gandhi and gorgeous young . . . ?"

Alix ignored him and continued. "As for snakes, they were ritually a part of the mix. They slithered this way and that, sinuous and suggestive, miming the erotic movements of dancing girls. They—"

"How does she know all this?" Sammy asked rhetorically. "Yes, ready to bite Cary Grant, even Doug Fairbanks Jr., that I accept. Gandhi having groupies. But erotic snakes?"

"Mr. Glique," Alix said blithely, "my great-grandpa on my mother's side *was* the Viceroy of India."

Sammy knew when he was out of his depth.

"Your Ladyship, forgive me. Being from Sheepshead Bay, who am I to question the close relatives of viceroys? Or Gandhi in bed with girls. It's just that I . . ."

Major-domo Hassan came to his rescue.

"Next, the high point of the Prince's collection, a herd of fully grown African elephants, an acquired taste on the part of My Lord Fatoosh from his diplomatic posting to the Congo."

We boarded a minifleet of Land Rovers to be transported to the far side of the lodge. It would have been a ten-minute stroll but I had the impression Hassan didn't want anyone wandering off and snooping about, getting close to the old lodge or the new buildings.

"There! Isn't it splendid?"

A large and apparently sturdy corral had been erected. There were no elephants.

"Mahout!" Hassan called, and a tiny, wiry chap, barefoot and wearing what seemed to be an adult diaper, trotted up.

"This is our keeper. He speaks no known language. But with elephants, he is extraordinarily clever."

The two jabbered back and forth a bit, mostly hand signs. There was something decidedly odd about all this. The setting was surely Indian. Or East Indian. The mahout as well. And yet . . .

"The elephants will arrive any day, a monsoon having delayed the ships. The mahout has trained several of these beasts to accept a howdah on their back. You know, the large baskets of reed and bamboo they attach to an elephant's back to carry passengers on a tiger hunt. Never before have African bull elephants been trained to carry howdahs. Indian elephants, yes. But not African, until now. Once they arrive, Mr. Glique, a brief ride? A novelty even for a man of your accomplishments, eh?"

"Well, I . . ." Sammy said, half torn, enjoying the invitation and its attendant flattery, but perhaps a bit cowed.

"Mahout! Display the howdah!" Hassan snapped out, smartly cracking his hands. Then, to Sammy:

"We'll alert you the moment the beasts get here. The first African elephant—borne howdah ride ever in this country. You, Mr. Glique, will make history."

It was then that I stepped up.

"I'm afraid that's impossible, Hassan. Mr. Glique suffers from a rare asthmatic allergy to elephants which . . ."

Our guided tour ended shortly thereafter and as soon as Sammy got me alone, he demanded explanations. He had every allergy *but* asthma, he wanted me to know. "And never in my life did I have an elephant ride! Think of the tales I could tell. I was very much looking forward to it . . ."

"Later. When we're back on Bly's boat," I hissed.

"Punjab" and "the Asp" were there at the dock, seeing us off, in company of Akbar the Hashimite, "faithful into the death," and his squad of bowmen. As Bly cast off, Punjab slowly drew his scimitar, held it up in a sort of salute. The Asp, more reserved, or chill, looked through us. I thought to myself I'd rather tackle Punjab, scimitar and all.

When we were a few hundred yards offshore and the bubbles from Fatoosh's frogmen had vanished, I gave Glique his explanation.

"There's a big difference between elephants, Sammy. Africans have bigger ears, for one thing."

"An elephant's an elephant. Who's to care from ears?"

I let him hyperventilate for a moment.

"I don't know just why Hassan or 'My Lord Fatoosh' wants you riding atop one of those elephants, Sammy. But I can tell you this. All circus elephants are Indian. And no African elephant would tolerate a howdah. They'll rend a man limb from limb with tusk and trunk simply for making eye contact. And then trample what's left of him into a sodden, pulpy mass. They weigh four tons and they're killers."

"Oh my God . . ."

"At the very least," I went on, "you'll undergo a terrible scare. *If* you live."

Glique went pale and staggered against the ship's rail.

"Sammy, y'all ought ta sit down, dahlin'," Dixie said, helping him to a hatch cover, sinuously rubbing against him in moral support.

"Let me know if I can be of assistance, Dixie," Alix offered. "I took a nurse's aide's course at the Hospital of St. Dismas, Martyr, and am always prepared with the old smelling salts . . ."

"Why, why?" Sammy wailed. "Importing elephants just to get me to write a movie for Sharon Stone? Trampling me into a sodden, pulpy mass?" No one responded and he went on. "Because I won't direct a lousy movie, I'll be rent with tusk and trunk? Louis B. Mayer never did such a thing. Not even Harry Cohn and you know what a bastard he was."

"Calm yourself, my dear Glique," Signor Piano quietly urged. Sammy paid no attention nor was he consoled.

I had no explanation to provide. I know a little about elephants. Much less about what motivated Fatoosh the Malevolent. Only that he seemed to be living up to his sobriquet and that Sammy Glique was being put most genuinely at risk. Merely for refusing to remake *Elephant Walk* with Sharon Stone? Was this possible? Was the charming Fatoosh *that* malevolent?

n i n e t e e n

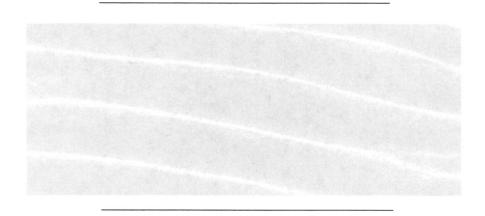

A road company version of . . .
Dr. Frankenstein's monster!

As Alix and I drove back from the marina to Further Lane, I said, "What do you make of all that?"

"Rum," she said firmly, "very rum indeed. There's a game afoot there at Sag Pond that's not at all *comme il faux*."

I was inclined to agree with Her Ladyship.

Sag Lodge out of bounds. No Chappie Wells. Not a Texan in view. Not an American of any persuasion except for the construction gangs. Clearly, in Sagaponack, "the East" was in charge. But there were no laws against that. Nor was it a story (not at this point) for *Parade*. Should I seek out Kurt Vonnegut and tell him what little I knew? Call on Buzzy Portofino and ask if there was any mutuality of interest here? In the end, except as a possible magazine article, was this damned house any business of mine at all?

No. Except that . . .

Back at our place I did what my father's latest message directed, placing a call to Charles Schwab in Manhattan. Prince Bandar the Gentle (known at the securities firm as Bandar Sabah) was out but I got his answering machine and left a message for him to call me in East Hampton. Then, out of sheer, cussed nosiness rather than professional curiosity, I phoned a friend on the Style section of the *Washington Post*, which may be the best style section in the country: were Woodward and Bernstein back together and working on a story in the Hamptons?

"Call you back," my pal said. And did, within the hour.

"No. Bob's been in East Hampton, probably gone by now, trailing Buzzy Portofino for a piece. And I'm told Carl's out there as well. But they're not working together."

"Then why is Bernstein . . . ?"

"A girl," he said. "There's a new girl."

Knowing Carl Bernstein, why hadn't that occurred to me? I put through a call to Glique.

"You can relax. Woodward and Bernstein have other meat. Woodward's working on a story about Congressman Portofino and Bernstein's got a girl out here somewhere. Maybe the Woodward piece will have a mention of Buzzy's Maidstone sermon on lust. Maybe including your love life. But that's hardly stop-press news, is it?"

Sammy sounded considerably more grateful than when I saved him from the elephants.

Entirely unlike her, Alix was up and about early next morning, phoning and then getting to the shower first and winding up the Aston-Martin, all this unseemly bustle in preparation for a renewed assault on Buzzy Portofino. I stood barefoot (and gingerly so) on the gravel and leaned in through the window to kiss her good-hunting. She looked awfully good there behind the wheel of a car seemingly custom-made for her.

"Just how long is the dealership giving you a freebie?"

"Don't ask, don't tell, isn't that what your military is forever urging the poofters? That's my attitude; if they don't send a chap to repossess, then they don't need it back quite yet."

"And the Congressman?"

"I intend to be very firm, Beecher. My editors in London weren't at all happy when I spoke with them this morning. 'Are we or aren't we doing a blinking deal with this wop?' They've put me absolutely on notice. Get his signature on a contract or fly back to London."

My face showed what I felt about that. So she turned round in the driver's seat and kissed me again.

"Darling, do have a little faith in my native cunning. See you anon . . ."

Alix spun the tires tearing up my gravel and then executed a lovely and entirely unnecessary gear shift into a racing turn before speeding out into a fortunately empty Further Lane, turning left for the 1770 House and a show-down with the Hon. Buzzy Portofino, R., N.Y.

Over a second cup of coffee I attempted to puzzle out just what was hap-pening: why was Bando in such hot water with his father the Emir? Why would Fatoosh want Sammy roughed up or even killed? I understood why they didn't want people snooping around the construction site of the giant new house. But why was old Sag Lodge being "decorated" and off-limits? Why the archers? I wasn't sure I bought that "private zoo" stuff. Clearly Wells was nothing but a front. But why did they *need* a "front"? Plenty of Arabs owned Hamptons estates. Why not Fatoosh? Why would the Admiral risk his neck in Baghdad? Nothing hung together. I'd almost finished shaving when the phone rang. It was Alix, her voice crackling with excitement.

"Beecher, momentous events are in train! Meet me instantly at your Maid-stone Club! The pro shop."

"Wha—?" I began. She was habitually so cool it took something extraordi-nary to get Alix worked up. But she cut off unspoken questions.

"There's been an attempt to assassinate Congressman Buzzy Portofino!"

The club parking lot was already dotted with police cars when I got there. Nothing yet on the car radio. Alix waved me down. Her Aston-Martin was parked by the practice tees. She seemed to have a uniformed policeman in tow and an escort of several young men from Buzzy's staff.

"What's all this now?" I hissed, not quite sure how much I was supposed to know. She already had the local cop charmed and he read off some notes to me:

"They found him in a sand trap just off the Hook Pond bridge between the fourth and fifth holes. An earlybird foursome came across him just after six. He'd been there several hours. Lost quite a bit of blood."

"Will he make it?"

"They think so. He's in the OR at Southampton Hospital. They're operat-ing, trying to get the arrow out."

"Arrow? *What* arrow?"

Alix looked narrowly at me. "Why, the arrow he was shot with, of course."

Buzzy Portofino shot with an arrow? What in hell . . . ?

"Morning, Beech," Tom Knowles said. "Hi, Your Ladyship. Seems like old times."

"Why, Inspector, how good it is to see you again," Alix said, remembering Tom from her first Hamptons summer and the Hannah Cutting murder, graciously promoting him now to "Inspector."

Knowles was on the case for Suffolk County homicide. Alix introduced him to Portofino's young men. One of them told Tom what they knew, that the Congressman had left their hotel well after midnight, apparently drove himself to the Maidstone, and was found this morning with an arrow through his throat. No, he had no idea if he was meeting anyone. Not that it meant anything, but there was an annotated copy in Buzzy's pocket of Rushdie's *Satanic Verses.* Detective Knowles's brow wrinkled on that.

"Oh?" He resumed taking notes, asked questions, took more notes, as controlled as ever. Now he flipped his notebook shut.

"Seen Jesse Maine around?" he asked me.

"Oh, come on, Tom. What is this, 'round up the usual Native American suspects'?"

"Jesse's got the tribe taking archery lessons, Beech. Just asked if you'd seen him."

I wasn't thinking of Jesse. I was remembering an archery demonstration yesterday after lunch at Sag Pond, the national archery champ of Kuwait and his Bedouin band. And thinking of a strapping Ukrainian woman with an Olympic medal for archery. And of a target set up on a lawn belonging to Sammy Glique, the embarrassed target himself of Portofino's campaign against lust.

We drove out in golf carts with Tom to the scene of the attack, a small courtesy extended by virtue of my being Tom's boyhood chum and Alix being, well, Alix.

If you've ever played Maidstone and have a tendency to hook a short iron on the approach, you know the bunker. It's deep and cut close to the green which itself is perhaps the most isolated on the entire twenty-seven-hole Maidstone course, nearly half a mile from the clubhouse, set into a curling arm of scummy Hook Pond, the home of swans, ducks, huge snapping turtles, fat old carp and catfish. Plus maybe fifty thousand lost golf balls.

"They found Portofino sprawled on the second cut of rough just outside the bunker and had the sense not to go tramping around in the sand. The only footprints in the trap appear to be those of the Congressman, staggering footsteps going in and then wildly careering steps trying to get out, with blood all the way back to the bridge. The arrow caught him in the throat while he was on the bridge approaching the bunker, but he got to the fringe before he collapsed. No one saw or heard a thing."

"What time was he hit?"

"The medical examiner'll have to tell us that. From the blood spilled, he'd been there a couple of hours."

"The arrow tell you anything?" I asked, still annoyed Jesse Maine was automatically a suspect.

"Not yet. But then, I'm hardly an expert on arrows," Tom said.

"They sell them a lot of places," I said, trying to make a case of sorts for Jesse. "Everywhere but the 7-Eleven. And those lads on Sag Pond at Xanadu, you know the security there carries bows."

"I've heard," Tom said dryly. "We'll check them out as well. We'll check everyone."

Alix and I drove over in separate cars to Southampton Hospital. One of Portofino's bright young men was pacing the lobby. She made the introductions.

"He'll make it okay," the staffer said. "But the arrow's too close to the jugular to pull out quite yet. They're trying to figure out just what to do and sort of working around it. He's awake. But on medication. I don't know what . . ."

He was nervous, talking too much. Couldn't blame him a hell of a lot. But when he led us up to Buzzy's room on Alix's pledge that we wouldn't stay, the Congressman noted for his oratory wasn't talking at all.

"Can't," the room nurse said in conspiratorial hush. "Pressure on the vocal cords."

Portofino was awake and propped up with pillows with the usual tubes and attachments in place, pale but looking like a routine postoperative patient pulling himself together. Except for . . .

"My," said Alix, "isn't that a novel effect, Buzzy. Can't say I've ever seen the like, neither here in your country nor at home. Isn't it like you to come up with something quite that clever."

And despite Her Ladyship's stab at being jolly, Buzzy's fevered eyes were locked on mine, seeing in my face what I dare not, out of good manners, say, that with an inch or so of chopped-off wooden arrow protruding boltlike from either side of his neck, Congressman Portofino resembled nothing more or less than a road-company version of Dr. Frankenstein's monster!

Alix, sensing his unease, wordlessly reached over now to pat Buzzy's hand, seeking to console him. His eyes swiveled now from my face to hers and was there rewarded with, for Alix, a weak smile.

I, too, remained mute. After all, what could one say when confronted by an effect this . . . unique?

twenty

"The voluptuous Princess Irina? Surely the Tsar had her whipped . . ."

In my car Alix was uncharacteristically silent. Then, as we rolled through Bridgehampton, she half-turned in her seat to look into my face.

"Beecher, promise me faithfully that if ever such a misfortune befalls me, that they tug out the arrow forthwith, even at the risk of losing the patient."

"Of course, darling," I said with appropriate solemnity.

"*So* thoughtful. You are a dear."

Sammy Glique, on our arrival, was anything but silent. "The police have been here, demanding to see my archery setup. At first, I was actually quite flattered that they'd seek assistance from a mere civilian in investigating an assassination attempt. Except that, as one of Buzzy's very public enemies, I find myself on a short list of suspects. Do you know anything about all of . . . ?"

"We've just come from Southampton Hospital, where, I am suddenly reminded, Beecher, we left my borrowed Aston-Martin in the parking lot . . ."

"We'll get it," I said.

". . . and where we saw the Congressman in his bed of pain."

"Alive," Sammy said. It was difficult to read into the one word hope or despair.

"Oh, he'll make it," Alix said, "though he does have the most extraordinary . . . well, best perhaps that I make no further comment."

Sammy looked from her to Dixie as if to inquire, What is she going *on* about?

"Hush, ma jambalaya," Dixie said, rubbing against him in affectionate consolation, "y'all jest tell 'em what happened with tha cops."

"Yes, yes," he said in some distraction. "Well, I took them down to where I have my targets set up, just the other side of the croquet lawn. 'See,' I assured them, 'all the arrows are tipped with suction cups. It's nothing but a child's set. Not dangerous at all.' With my eyesight? If they let me out alone with real arrows, I'd probably shoot Signor Piano. Or George Plimpton . . ."

Sammy chewed a lip. Then, "But when I showed them all my rubber-tipped arrows, they said, 'Yeah, but the real arrows. Where do you keep the real arrows?'

"Who am I? Saddam Hussein? Hiding biological weapons? Chemical weapons? Shooing away the UN inspectors? Suddenly I'm mixing up a nice batch of botulism and sprinkling anthrax in the Lexington Avenue subway?"

We attempted to calm him. Dixie rubbed against him a bit more. Signor Piano was there now as well, making small circular motions with his pudgy hands, as if to say, Well what is one to do? "Be at ease," he murmured.

"Oh, fine, easy for you to say, Piano. You haven't been accused of assassinations, of being Lee Harvey Oswald."

"Do you know the origin of the term 'assassin'?" Alix asked. "A Muslim Shiite sect in the time of the Crusades which conducted a campaign of murder intended to bring on a new millennium. The literal translation is 'hashish eater.'"

Glique's eyes widened. Was everyone mad? Cops scrutinizing rubber-tipped arrows? Congressmen shot? This one babbling on about hashish and the new millennium?

"Gather yourself, Sammy. The policeman asked questions. He leveled no charges," said Piano in a calming voice.

"Not yet," said Sammy dubiously. "They lull you into complacency and the next thing you know, you're indicted! They'll be back with warrants any hour now. With manacles. We better call Felder."

"Raoul Felder does your divorces," Signor Piano pointed out. "The Sullivan and Cromwell people do your contracts and other legal work."

"Plimpton's father had a big law firm. We could retain them, no?"

"Plimpton is inside repairing his tape recorder. Should I ask?"

Sammy shook his head. "No, the oral history comes first. Let George be at his endeavors. Give the case to Sullivan and Cromwell. There's a clever young woman there, a Ms. McKeon. Attractive, as well . . ."

"We could go upstairs 'n' lah down fo' a bit, honey," Dixie suggested, rubbing more urgently, and sensing how a mention of the "attractive" young lawyer was arousing Glique, "Don'tcha recall how y'all always feel bettah after uh little lah-down . . ."

"Well, yes. But at a time like this. Our guests . . ." he said, gesturing toward us.

"Not at all," Alix said swiftly, "we were just leaving." She hated to have a chap miss out on a good "lah-down" with a girl like Dixie.

"Right," I agreed, seeing her point.

But Glique wasn't having it. "No," he said, shaking his head angrily, "I'm too tense. Having policemen pawing over my bows and arrows. Trampling the croquet lawn. Sure, it's no secret. Congressman Portofino and I are not on the best of terms. But who am I to shoot members of Congress? My respect for Senator D'Amato is known to all. I could show you canceled checks to his re-election campaign. Despite our recent contretemps. And with rubber-tipped arrows at that?" he added in a stunning nonsequitur.

"There are always cabals and plots," Alix said murkily. "At Oxford I did a paper on the death of Rasputin. People blame Trotsky or Lenin but it was a conspiracy of nobles that brought Rasputin down."

Glique perked up a bit. "Oh? Then what happened to Buzzy, you think it was nobles?"

"Entirely possible. A political firebrand, a man of the people like Buzzy, it brings out the hostility of nobles every time . . ."

"We don't have nobles in this country, Alix," I reminded her.

"Of course you do. They don't have titles, or appear in the Almanach de Gotha. But nobles nonetheless, your power elite, bankers, Wall Street, in 'the groves of academe'—Yale, MIT, Harvard, Cal Tech—press lords, TV anchormen, Rockefellers, big-city mayors like Mr. Garibaldi and—"

"Giuliani," I murmured. She kept right on.

". . . your merchant princes . . ."

"Merchant princes, of course," Sammy said. "How could we have forgotten the merchant princes. Where was Stanley Marcus last night? Or Mr. Nordstrom? To say nothing of the Brooks Brothers . . . ?"

Dixie had stopped rubbing, a bit unsure of just who Rasputin might have been and what the nobles did. "Just who wuz Rasputin, Alix?" It was all the encouragement Her Ladyship needed.

"By 1916 the war was lost and revolution threatened," Alix began. "The Tsarina was telling the Tsar how to run the country, while Rasputin manipulated her. Alan Morehead has a splendid account of how the 'mad priest' reached conclusions: he took a steam bath, drank several bottles of madeira and went out dancing and wenching with noblewomen and/or gypsy girls, and in the morning he would announce, 'My will has prevailed,' and declare just which general to promote, which cabinet minister to sack, which trouble-maker to hang. And on this basis, the Tsarina would tell the Tsar what to do."

"Wow!" Sammy enthused, "to think of possessing such power. And wenching besides! With gypsy girls and noblewomen."

". . . and a good madeira," added Signor Piano, who enjoyed a small jest.

"But y'all said the nobles killed thet boy," Dixie protested.

"And so they did. It wasn't the proletariat, the so-called dark people. Not at all . . ."

"'The dark people?'" Sammy demanded. "Even then, they were racist?"

"The dark people were the ordinary folk. No, not they, not at all! It was aristocrats who bumped off Rasputin!"

We were all listening now. Alix told a good yarn, regardless of actual fact.

"On December twenty-nine, Prince Yusopov, who by-the-by was educated at Oxford and is still warmly recalled at high table, lured Rasputin to supper on the promise of introducing him to the voluptuous Princess Irina. Down in the cellar, Rasputin was fed poisoned cakes and madeira laced with cyanide. Then he demanded tea and asked Yusopov to play the guitar. Upstairs, listening to a phonograph playing 'Yankee Doodle,' the other conspirators waited for word of Rasputin's collapse. Rasputin had more madeira but did not collapse. Poor Yusopov went upstairs to ask what else he might do. The strain was considerable and Dr. Lazovert fainted. The Grand Duke Dmitri wanted to call off the whole business; Purishkevich was all for continuing. When Yusopov went back down with a revolver, Rasputin seemed drowsy. But another wine revived him and the rogue suggested a visit to the gypsy establishments, 'with God in mind.' Instead, Yusopov shot him and Rasputin fell backward onto a bearskin rug . . ."

"My God! What a visual," Sammy cried. "To fall on the wall-to-wall carpet, okay. But a bearskin *rug*! Didn't Jack Barrymore make a movie of all this?"

"Why, yes," Dixie said, "now Ah recall. It wuz in—"

Her Ladyship wasn't one to share a stage, and cut brusquely across the girl's filmography.

". . . except that one eye was twitching and, as Yusopov called for help, Rasputin leapt up with a ferocious roar and began to throttle poor Yusopov, tearing off an epaulet. In panic, the Prince rushed upstairs, with Rasputin, on all fours, coming in pursuit. There was a locked door but the mad priest burst through it into the snowy courtyard. Purishkevich fired two shots but missed. Then, biting his hand in despair, fired again and again. This time, the monster fell. Purishkevich kicked him in the head."

"What a scene," the filmmaker in Sammy enthused, "throttling the Prince, tearing off epaulets. Up the stairs on all fours! Biting one's hand in despair! Can you visualize it, Dixie?"

"Ah shoah can, Sammy. They say thet—"

"The conspirators bound the body in curtains," Alix said quickly, "and off they went to the Neva to toss it in. But in their stressed condition, they forgot the weights, and days later, when it washed up, Rasputin's lungs were filled with water, leading one to believe that he was still alive when dropped in the river . . ."

Glique shook his head in admiration. "Never in my life have I heard such a made-to-order screenplay. That lovely touch, forgetting the weights . . . so Hitchcock."

"I agree," said Her Ladyship, "except that Rasputin was so despised that the nobles pretty much got away with their crime. Yusopov was banished to his country estates in the south, Dmitri to Persia, and Purishkevich to the front."

"Oh, to have country estates in the south to be banished to," Sammy said. "And the voluptuous Princess Irina?" he inquired, always interested in such matters. "Surely the Tsar had her whipped . . ."

"Morehead doesn't say."

"Pity," Sammy said, his mind's eye feverishly seeing Irina brutally handled by booted Cossacks. George Plimpton chose that moment to emerge from Glique's house, recalcitrant tape recorder in hand.

"Hallo, everybody," he announced.

Her Ladyship wasn't quite through. "But then, doesn't history so often repeat itself. Recall if you will, Thomas à Becket in 1273. It was also nobles who did him in, at the behest of Henry II, right there in Canterbury Cathedral. Butchering the Archbishop on the high altar. As a Tory I hate to admit it but it again was nobles who—"

"See, George," Sammy said. "I'm in the clear on Buzzy. Her Ladyship says in these cases it's usually the nobles."

"I've got it working again," Plimpton said, ignoring his host but smiling, brandishing the tape recorder. "Hope I didn't miss anything worth taking down."

"Not a thing," I told him. Not wanting Alix to repeat herself, nor to upset a fellow Cantab.

twenty-one

"Cardinal O'Connor, a man of God. He visits the sick, buries the dead."

Early the next morning Lady Alix was at Southampton Hospital with the morning papers and hot, fresh doughnuts from Dreesen's, hand picked to be easily gummed; plumping up the pillows behind Buzzy Portofino and wondering where she ought to sit while reading to him. There was barely room for his bed and her at the same time, so crammed was the room with floral arrangements, mass cards, telegrams, brightly colored pictures of the Virgin, baskets of fruit and Whitman Sampler boxes of chocolates, from admirers in Staten Island and subscribers to the *National Review*. Buzzy didn't even like flowers (he found their perfume sweetly cloying) and was unable to eat. As for the mass cards, traditionally sent to console families of the dead, he was somewhat mystified. Had word gotten around Staten Island that his wounds were fatal?

And when Alix began to read from Page Six of the *Post*, the Congressman raised a cautionary hand. By now he had a Macintosh PowerBook on which he tapped out a message and held it up to Alix's gaze.

"I can hear normally. I can read. It's only my vocal cords that are damaged. I can't speak."

"Oh, but I so enjoy reading aloud. At Oxford I volunteered to read to old-age pensioners. And think of your poor eyes. Bad enough to lose the power of speech. If anything happened to your eyesight as well, I'd never forgive myself."

The Congressman was tolerant. He let her read away. After all, it was more pleasant having her here in the room than the loathsome Glique.

Yes, he'd been here. And in the middle of the night. What impudence! That offensive little man, patronizing him, inquiring about the bedpan, commiserating, whinily narrating the catalogue of his own woes. Here was Portofino with an arrow through his throat and Sammy Glique was rambling on about Rasputin and Thomas à Becket, about the Kennedy compound and touch football with shiksas.

But why? Portofino was a reasonably sure judge of human nature and yet Sammy's motivation was beyond him. The filmmaker attempted to explain:

"I know, I know. It's unlike me, turning the other cheek, after your speech at the Maidstone. So unfair, an appeal to the philistines. Why should I forgive? But then I had this intimation of my own mortality, torn apart and trampled into dust perhaps, just a day or so ago, by African elephants. With big ears! Rending and trampling. It was sort of . . . what's the word, a defining moment which . . . ?"

"An epiphany?" Congressman Portofino tapped out.

"That's it! An epiphany. Such as happened to Saul of Tarsus on the Damascus road. Thank you, sir. You see, not owning a yacht, I went on Captain Bly's fishing boat with Signor Piano to visit Prince Fatoosh and we had lunch, outdoors, the house being redecorated, but quite pleasant, I assure you. Except that Fatoosh refused to hear his brother's name spoken aloud. Amputation was threatened, amputation and the lash. A family dispute of some sort. All in the family, that's what I say. Jewish families? Don't get me started. But afterward, Fatoosh was yet again courteous. If only Sharon Stone would agree to make Fatoosh's movie, all would be ready. Yet even lacking a script, they already had snakes, oh my God, you never saw such snakes. Wriggling, their tongues flicking out. Oh, don't remind me. And as coming attractions, killer elephants with big ears . . . All this inspired me to reexamine my life, my very motives. So in the middle of a sleepless night, I found myself driving over here to solace you. Look . . ."

He held up a battered paperback.

". . . one of my favorite books. J. D. Salinger's collection, *Nine Stories.* Here, for you. My own copy . . ."

Buzzy Portofino was puzzled all over again. Salinger was hardly his favorite author. Another voluptuary, up there in New Hampshire seducing coeds.

"Here, Congressman, rest. The nation, whatever one's political orientation, needs you. Avoid stress. Husband your energies. A happy patient heals faster."

Buzzy started to yawn showily; thought better of it. Even a yawn might dislodge this damned arrow. By now Sammy had pulled up a chair and taken the laptop.

"Here, why should I strain your other senses, your ears. Let them rest. I'll type out Salinger's little story. Rest, Congressman, conserve your strength."

But before he could tap out the story's title, Buzzy snatched back the computer and rattled off a screed of his own.

"I can hear, for chrissake! I can read, I can hear, I just can't speak!"

Glique rolled his eyes. Talk about ingratitude . . . Wresting back the computer, Sammy typed:

"Don't you know your own religion? The corporal works of mercy? Visiting the sick, burying the dead. That's why I'm here, emulating your Cardinal O'Connor, a blessed man of God who visits the sick, buries the dead. As any decent Catholic would. Even a Jewish fellow like myself who—"

Buzzy snatched back the laptop.

"I'm not dead yet, Glique!" he typed.

Sammy took the PowerBook. A crude methodology was at work by now and instead of fighting, they just handed the computer back and forth, Glique patient and Portofino too weak for battle.

"Don't count chickens," Sammy wrote, wagging his head.

Morning brought solace to poor Buzzy. Glique gone, he'd slept, though fitfully, for some reason dreaming of elephants. Then came the gracious Lady Alix with doughnuts (he couldn't even gum) and the papers.

But why did all of them insist on reading to him, communicating by computer? In Buzzy's fevered mind there was already bubbling up the early, primitive outline of legislative relief, a federal law that protected hospital patients from well-meaning visitors. Bad enough to have Sammy Glique. But being a Roman Catholic (indeed, a Knight of Malta), Buzzy was also afflicted with visiting monsignori. And was beginning to realize that until you'd been prayed over by shifts of monsignors, you don't know about prayer.

Along with the eminent divines came a policeman, Detective Knowles of the Suffolk County force. What he wanted to know was why the Congressman was toting an annotated copy of *Satanic Verses* when he was attacked? Could there be a connection there, some sort of clue?

Thoroughly out of patience, and not wishing to compromise confidential matters, Buzzy fobbed off the cop with a bit of pious gibberish on the laptop:

"As an elected member of the Congress I have responsibilities to constituents of the entire political spectrum, regardless of racial, ethnic, gender, religious or socio-economic distinctions. The Islamic voter is ever in my thoughts."

Detective Knowles, who didn't believe a bit of it, went off shaking his head. Why would the victim conceivably shield the assailant?

Buzzy would soon confront greater trials. A supporter on Staten Island had begun busing in local people, forty at a time, to console their Congressman, much as on other days they were bused to Atlantic City to play the slots.

And would the Staten Islanders simply pay their respects? Not likely. Not when they could arrive with sweet rolls, potted houseplants, crayoned get-well cards from schoolchildren, homemade red wine, more mass cards, fresh pajamas, and copies of that day's *Staten Island Advance* and other newspapers.

"Buzzy Buses" were leaving Staten Island every hour for the 200-mile round-trip to the Hamptons.

twenty-two

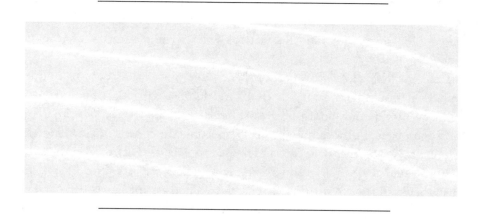

"Sorry, chaps, but I never get this right.
Who killed whom, Cain or Abel?"

Prince Bandar the Gentle returned my call.

"What are you doing analyzing the futures market? I thought by now you'd be home helping your old Pa run the country."

"If only, Beech. Don't you know? I'm in disgrace. Salman Rushdie is more popular."

He was speaking from his office on Wall Street.

"I know some of it," I told him. "Your brother Fatoosh gave us lunch the other day and when I asked about your health, good coat, clear tongue, he went ape. Wouldn't hear your name spoken in polite company."

"I'm the nearest thing to an untouchable," Bando said morosely.

"Well, cheer up. There's work to be done." I left it as vague as that, not trusting phone security. "Can Wall Street spare you for a few days to fly out here?"

"Of course," he said, brighter now. "The fact is I don't know all that much about oil futures and every time I go on CNBC, they issue clarifying statements."

Bando squared things with Schwab and caught the seaplane from the East

River. There were only two seats in Alix's demo Aston-Martin so we took my Blazer. The seaplane, its wheels down, was on the ground and taxiing toward the small whitewashed arrivals building of our local airstrip when we drove up.

"Alix, this is Prince Bandar the Gentle of Kuwait. Bando, Lady Alix Dunraven of England and Rupert Murdoch's media empire."

In the car I briefed him on the attack on Buzzy Portofino and my father's suspicions something dicey was happening in the Middle East. And about odd goings-on chez Fatoosh with monstrous buildings and a private zoo. Bandar's brow furrowed, taking me seriously.

"Your old Dad doesn't get the wind up easily," he admitted.

"But why am I telling you?" I said. "What do you think?"

Bandar gave a wary half glance at Her Ladyship. After all, she did work for Rupert Murdoch.

"Alix is the soul of discretion, Bando," I assured him, "and very much on our side."

"Of course," he said, half bowing to her from the backseat, "forgive me for—"

"Not at all, Prince. With chaps like you, Beecher and Dick Hannay, one knows how to play the game. For Oxford, England and Saint George! y'know."

"I do, y'know," Bandar replied solemnly. Clearly, there were vast distinctions between Kuwait and Great Britain. But Bando had been at Eton. And those were the formative years, weren't they? When he, half English, had also read Buchan's tales of Sir Richard Hannay and, like Alix, could recall them even today. The Arab Prince and the Earl's daughter understood each other.

Now, his flanks secure, Bandar began his story.

"Your Ladyship, my dear fellow, you wouldn't believe what's been happening. How an uneasy peace and the liberation of our small but precious country only mask turmoil and peril."

"Saddam? More threats?"

"That, too, of course. The 'Monster' is never sated. But more alarming, internal stresses which could fracture the domestic tranquillity."

I kept quiet. Let him tell his story.

"Even at peace, there are jealousies, conspiracy and betrayal. Our people tugged this way and that. The savage Taliban, with its cruel restrictions on women and modern life, appeals to certain conservative elements. In Algeria, open violence. In Afghanistan, bloody chaos. While that fellow Osama bin Laden crouches in his tent sending shivers up the global spine with terrorist plots. Is Kuwait next in this struggle between moderates and extremists? Saudi Arabia a nervous giant on one side, Iraq, still claiming us as a province, on the other. And within our borders, even our own family, vying one day to succeed my dear father, the Emir, this son and that, brother against brother, as biblical a tale as that of Cain and Abel. And as lethal."

Alix now interrupted for the first time.

"Sorry, chaps, but I never get this right. Who killed whom?"

"What?"

"Cain and Abel."

"Oh," said Bandar smoothly, his response as biblically sound as Reverend Falwell's, "Cain slew his brother. Jealousy. Cain thought their parents favored the boy . . ."

I got into it then.

"And Fatoosh believed the Emir favored others of his sons. Including . . . you?"

"Not at first. Fatoosh was an early favorite. And why not? Handsome, dashing, a judge of horseflesh, popular. Undeniably the most intelligent of any of the sons. Always. A true star, perhaps destined for greatness. But yet, there was . . . how do I define it, a flaw. It was first hinted at when he failed the entrance examinations for Eton and was packed off to a German prep instead. My father saw in some of us what he didn't in others. It's like your Oxford, Lady Alix, or our Harvard. An elite. With Fatoosh, well, perhaps the Emir discerned a dangerous edge . . ." Bandar paused, then, thoughtfully, "Do you know that of all the thirty-nine brothers Fatoosh was the only one of us who while still a teenager already employed a food taster?"

We absorbed that factoid in silence. Then:

"He's making movies, you know," I said.

"Yes, we own a film studio. For some of my brothers, this is a convenient excuse to visit Hollywood and cultivate blondes. Fatoosh is more serious about it. A fixation, or so I'm told. We don't speak . . ."

A fixation? I'd say, threatening poor Glique with trampling by elephants for not making his Sharon Stone flick.

We pulled into the driveway on Further Lane. It was time to ask Bando why he was in such bad odor. I didn't get the chance.

"But this is splendid, Beech. Just as I remember it from college visits. Your privet hedge taller perhaps." Then he saw Jesse Maine's pickup.

"You have visitors," he said, his voice cautiously lower, less casual.

"It's okay, Bando. They're friends."

Jesse and VooVoo Vronsky came around from the sunny patio where they'd been waiting for us.

"Beecher . . ."

"Jesse, I want you to meet a good friend, Prince Bandar the Gentle of Kuwait. Bando, this is Jesse Maine, Sachem and war chief of the Shinnecock Indian tribe. And his friend and mentor, the noted Russian Olympic archer, Madame Vronsky."

"Ukrainian!" VooVoo corrected me, not being fond of Russians.

Bandar was still a bit nervy, even as he exchanged pleasantries. What, I wondered, had he been about to tell Alix and me?

Her Ladyship came to the rescue.

"It's past noon. There's some DP on the ice. Anyone join me in a flute of champers?"

We all did, all except VooVoo.

"You got cold beer?" she said, guttural but smiling, not caring that in the Hamptons, champagne was clearly the beverage of the people.

Jesse shook his head in admiration as he slaked the first of the DP.

"That does cut the phlegm, Beecher." It also seemed to buoy his spirits. It wasn't like Jesse to sulk but he surely seemed unsettled.

Sensing the cause of his unease, I asked quietly, "Tom Knowles been around again, Jesse?"

"You got it, Beecher. Curious about where me and VooVoo was the night old Congressman got punctured. Thinking maybe us Native Americans was growing hostile."

"Tom knows better than that," I said. "He's got to check. Went over to Lily Pond Lane as well. Checked out Glique's bow and arrow set from the toy store. He's dropping by the Arabs at Sag Pond, too."

"Tom slap the cuffs on anybody yet?"

"He's as mystified as anyone, Jesse. Here, let me top off that glass."

"Beer is also good," said VooVoo. She liked it from the bottle, her muscular forearm lifting it to her lips, her pectorals flexing impressively.

"Well, Prince," Jesse said, "these old Hamptons is something in the high season, ain't they? And champagne's just the start of it."

He was cheering up now himself but sensed uneasiness on Bando's part and was trying to bridge gaps. I appreciated that, so I said, "Tell Prince Bandar about the problems you've got with the other local tribes."

"Well, it's much like what you got back there in those biblical lands by the Tigris and Euphrates, sir. We Shinnecocks are easy, amiable folks. Only they got another tribe, the Montauketts, that right now is anything but amiable. One gentleman claims to be chief; so does another fellow. But can they get federal recognition as an official Native American tribe so they can open casinos? So along comes an outfit called Dreamcatchers, which is a talisman to ward off evil spirits. Except that it's a real estate fella in Montauk thought it up. And they've got all variety of schemes and nostrums, anxious to assist 'lo, the poor Indian.'"

"But tell the Prince about the Pequots, Jesse. He's had similar difficulties with the Iraqis."

If there was one subject on which Jesse needed little prodding, it was the Pequots.

"The trouble goes back a ways, Prince, to when the Crown bestowed local rights to Mr. Lion Gardiner three hundred years ago. Back then most English thought all us Indians was the same. And simpletons. But not old Lion Gardiner, so our fellas asked Lion if he was pissed off at all Indians or just them pesky Pequots. Said Lion Gardiner, 'No, but only with such as had killed Englishmen.' Then Lion orated a statement precious to our people ever since:

"'If you kill the Pequots that come to you,' Mr. Gardiner announced, 'and send me their heads, then you shall have trade with us.'"

Jesse slammed a big hand on the table, "How 'bout them apples, Prince!"

He'd finally gotten Bandar feeling among friends.

"But it's just like the Gulf, Chief. Perhaps we ought to treat our enemies as did your admirable Mr. Gardiner."

VooVoo took a fresh Coors and Jesse, aware that the Prince was a guest, changed the subject from Native Americans so as not to bore him. "You see, Your Worship, it was only last year I met my first viscount. Right here, thanks to Lady Alix, and that got me accustomed to hanging out with the gentry, viscounts and such. But I can tell you it's mighty good to have an actual full-rigged prince among us like you and brother Fatoosh."

"Thank you," Bandar said politely. "And I'll take another Dom to that."

"Right-o!" Alix said, pleased things were going so well among total strangers.

"There is more beer?" VooVoo inquired.

t w e n t y - t h r e e

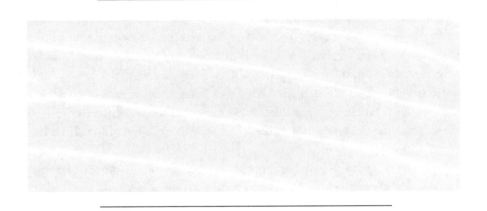

Alix permitted the high sun to burnish her tan closer
to perfection.

It was shortly before dawn the next morning when a ghastly and unsteady figure, as spectral as Banquo's ghost, dressed in hospital gown, disposable paper
slippers, and a purloined terry cloth robe, desperately clutching a laptop to his
chest, staggered from an Ocean Limo taxicab ("Best rates and service in the
Hamptons") to arrive at Sammy Glique's front door on Lily Pond Lane. He
hammered wordlessly for entry, then sagged exhausted against the highly polished and gleaming hardwood until a tall young woman of exotic appearance,
almost wearing something, came to the door.

"Wha, it's tha Congressman! Y'all okay, Congressman? Come in outa tha
night 'n' stay awhile. Jest set y'self down here 'n' make y'self at home. Y'all look
uh trifle peak-ed."

She helped their visitor to a straight-back chair in the large entrance hall. As
soon as he was seated, his shaky legs no longer the overriding concern, Buzzy
Portofino tapped out a message on the computer and held it up to Dixie.

"I'm confused. Lady Alix gave me her address. I thought this was where she was staying." Dixie, enunciating very precisely as people do with foreigners or the hard of hearing, said:

"No, suh. This here's Mr. Sammy Glique's place, numbah 393 Lily Pond Lane."

Oh my God, Portofino groaned inwardly. Both visitors had left an address on the cluttered night table of his hospital room; had he gone to the wrong one?

But then, could he be blamed for clouded judgment, besieged as he was by doctors bickering over his prognosis? They agreed the arrow could be removed without killing the patient but warned Buzzy he might never again *sound* the same; and to a politician, a recognizable voice was negotiable coin. And it wasn't simply the medical men. There was a constant stream of Staten Islanders arriving forty at a time aboard the Buzzy Buses and jostling one another for vantage points at the bedside, shoving pencils into his palsied hand for autographs.

After several exchanges on the laptop, when Buzzy finally grasped he was at the home of his arch enemy, the Congressman struggled to his feet and prepared to depart.

"Now, none uh thet, suh," Dixie said firmly. "Mr. Glique would have me on tha next plane ta tha Coast if Ah permitted uh Membuh uh Congress, 'n' one sorely injured, ta be turned away from his do'. May Ah serve y'all uh diet Dr Peppah o' somethin'?"

As Buzzy fell back heavily into his seat, Dixie made an effort to cheer the poor fellow.

"Mah," she said, "but thet's uh unique hookup they got theah on tha sides o' yo' throat. What'll medical science thank of next?"

"Thank you, but it's just my arrow," Buzzy tapped out.

Once Sammy was awakened and grasped the bizarre situation ("Buzzy Portofino here! On Lily Pond Lane? Sitting in my entry hall on a straight-back chair?"), he exploded into action, phoning me and Her Ladyship, waking Signor Piano and Wolfie ("Wolfie, do you know first aid? The changing of dressings? See to this poor man"), calling Lars at his cottage ("Lars, wake the covergirls! Is one by chance a registered nurse?") and sending Dixie on errands.

"Gruel! that's the thing for a patient unable to swallow solid food. Go yourself, Dixie. To Rudy at Dreesen's, his best gruel. See Rudy personally. Explain, the gruel must be the finest. No grit, nothing harsh on the Congressman's throat." Awakened by the comings and goings, Plimpton made his way up to the main house, wondering, once he grasped the situation, just how he could possibly take down an oral history from a chap who couldn't speak. Alix and I were there by eight, followed immediately by Jesse and VooVoo Vronsky, she full of enthusiasm for the Native American quality of life after having spent her first night on the reservation.

"With cigarettes so cheap. No tax. Marlboros even, a wonder to behold. The Shinnecocks, a fortunate people, I swear to God." Shown in to the patient, VooVoo fell swiftly to her knees and pulled off Buzzy's paper slippers, offering to massage his feet. "A brisk massage, the soles of the feet, that's where health begins."

"Heah's tha gruel," Dixie announced. "Rudy says tha finest gruel that Dreesen's stocked in yeahs."

"Gruel is vital," said Sammy. Then, fearing he might have offended VooVoo, on her knees, working away on both Portofino feet, "along with massage, of course. Who could argue? Both gruel and massage combined, naturally. Look at the Congressman's face. His color, already rosier. Even the arrow looks better."

Then, distracted, he turned back to Dixie.

"You went to town in your nightie? To Dreesen's? What must Rudy think, Dixie? Please remember, this is not southern California. There are Protestants here, and standards."

"Ah wuz in uh rush, dahling. Ah didn't think . . ."

Buzzy was tapping at his laptop with a new vigor. The gruel? The foot massage? Or Dixie in her nightie?

"What's he saying?"

Alix leaned over.

"He says, 'Don't you dare chastise this splendid young woman, you pornographer!' "

Sammy looked at me.

"Chastise? Chastise? I ask her to wear a robe in the village. In Dreesen's grocery. You'd have half-naked people buying gruel? Is this too much? This makes me a pornographer, that I uphold local community standards?"

"Hadn't we better get a doctor?" I suggested stiffly.

Sammy looked hurt but it was Buzzy who reacted even more forcefully, tapping out a message and shoving the computer at me:

"Those damned doctors are why I left! They want to pull out the arrow without regard to my vocal cords!"

By the time we had Buzzy comfortably ensconced in a ground floor sun-room swiftly transformed to a bed-sitting room ("He shouldn't climb stairs in his condition," Signor Piano suggested), Sammy and the Congressman had both calmed down. Vaguely recalled by Wolfie was the old Monty Woolley film, *The Man Who Came to Dinner*, about a man who broke his leg and stayed for months. "God forbids that happens to me," Sammy told her.

Secretly, he was pleased. Senator D'Amato's hasty flight had left an undeniable vacuum. And here, seemingly God-sent, came an even trendier Congressman! When he pointed this out to Piano, the signor quietly protested:

"But he's a fascist."

"A teeny bit fascist, I concede. But was D'Amato a member of the Socialist party? Another Norman Thomas?"

I called Tom Knowles to let him know. After all, Homicide was still on the case, and here was the victim a willing guest of one of the suspects and being ministered to by two others, Jesse and VooVoo Vronsky. When Tom arrived, he closeted himself with Portofino to be sure Buzzy understood the situation.

"He says he's not afraid," Tom told me, "tapped it out on the computer. Told me to stop harassing him or he'd complain to Speaker Gingrich. Grouchy sort."

Portofino's staffers were also here by now, fussing, making phone calls, getting telephonic second opinions from specialists who'd never even seen Buzzy's wound. Southampton Hospital, understandably nettled by patients who checked themselves out in the night, reluctantly agreed to send over their own man to check on the Congressman. But pledging not to yank the arrow without permission. There was also a request that someone—anyone!—call off the buses from Staten Island clogging the hospital driveway for a patient no longer there.

"I wish we could dress up that arrow a touch," Alix remarked "It looks so . . . stark . . ."

Glique had fallen into a philosophical mood. "Imagine, only last week, Senator D'Amato here as my guest. Gracing us with his presence. The table chitchat, fascinating. Then, a dispute, and off he went in a snit on the morning train. Only to phone later with insults via Mrs. Danvers. Now, totally unexpected, another distinguished member of Congress, Rep. Buzzy Portofino, R., N.Y., recovering from wounds in my own sunroom. One famous statesman departs; another arrives. Yes, there have been differences of opinion. But nothing personal. The bottom line? How can I as a citizen be anything but flattered? Not even the Kennedy compound could boast such a guest list. My mother would find it hard to believe, she of little faith . . ."

"Thet's how it goes, dahlin', don't it?" Dixie remarked dreamily. "Lak Doris Day used ta sang, 'Que sera, sera.'"

More down to earth, VooVoo Vronsky snapped, "A mother got to have faith! What the hell kind of mother you got, eh? What kind of mothers they got in this damned country?"

Signor Piano and Wolfie were exchanging ideas on how to make poor Portofino more comfortable when we left.

We'd set up Prince Bandar with a room and bath at the Maidstone Arms on Main Street but when we got back to Further Lane, there he was waiting in the driveway, pacing up and down impatiently next to a rented car.

"What happened? The room no good?" I asked.

"Quickly, Beech," Bandar said, "inside the house. You never know who's out there watching. And there are things best kept to ourselves."

There was no mistaking his urgency and I led us into the house. "I'll make coffee," Alix offered insincerely.

"No, please stay if you will, Lady Alix," Bandar said, apparently meaning it. "Your appreciation of the situation could be of enormous help."

Her Ladyship and I flopped into my wicker armchairs while Bando paced.

"I've received a message from sources favorable to me and opposed to Fatoosh. You'll recall, of course, the 'object' I was assigned to care for during the Gulf War?" Despite my assurances about Alix, he'd lapsed into a verbal shorthand.

"Bando, if you trust me, you can trust Lady Alix. Please, you needn't fence."

He smiled. "Forgive me, Your Ladyship. The 'object' is a relic revered by my people. It is called the Rose Manteau."

"I'm honored by your trust, Prince," Alix said. And he picked up his narrative.

"Well, as you may have surmised, in the confusion of battle I lost the overlays and map references to where I'd hidden it. Only to realize, after your army chased out the Iraqis, that I was unable to take back bearings and retrieve the Manteau. I was totally confounded."

Then, very agitated:

"So I've been branded at least an incompetent; at worst a traitor. Now it seems the sacred icon may have been found by people with no love for me. By those who—"

"Not Fatoosh!" I said, unable not to.

Bandar shook his head.

"Not yet. But of course you know that Chapman Wells is one of the few Americans still cozy with Baghdad. And at the same time maintains links to Fatoosh. This awful house in which they appear to be partners, for example. My information is that agents working for Wells are on the track of the Rose Manteau, or already have it . . ."

"But isn't there a taboo about something like that in the hands of an infidel?" I asked.

Bandar nodded.

"Which is where brother Fatoosh fits in so neatly. Offshore Wells could be trading the Manteau to Fatoosh in return for additional mineral and drilling rights, when and if Fatoosh succeeds my father as emir . . ."

"But why then this enormous house? He already has an existing Sag Lodge. Why irritate the neighbors, spend millions, and generate all this bad ink if his future lies either in making movies or ruling Kuwait, and not lazing about in the Hamptons?"

"There is a proverb of desert wisdom, Beecher. 'The arrogant man demands the most lavish tent in the oasis; the egotist, the finest in the entire desert; the megalomaniac, the grandest tent in all Arabia.'"

So Fatoosh was a megalomaniac, even by his own brother's testimony. I was thinking one step ahead now.

"My father the Admiral suspected *you* were the key. Told me to get hold of you. It's why I called Charles Schwab."

"So Admiral Stowe is on the same scent?"

"Could be," I said, being vague, not really knowing more. "But they'd have to get the Manteau into Fatoosh's hands. And he's here on Long Island, six thousand miles from home."

"Right," Bando agreed, "and guarded by one small detachment of Companions of the Rosy Hours."

"*Them* again?" I demanded impatiently. "Alix has me reading about them, my father warns me about them in code, and now you have detachments of them summering in the Hamptons. Just who the devil *are* they? Not in code or boys' stories but in real life?"

Bandar became, for him, almost solemn:

"Beecher, the Companions are brigands, fakirs and cutthroats of the very worst manner and sort. No more dangerous men exist on this planet. Compared to them, the Japanese Black Dragon Society and the Palermo Mafia are school-crossing guards. But along with being killers, they are by training the finest male dancers ever, in their crude, demonic way to be compared to Nijinsky, Astaire, and Gregory Hines."

"Oh?"

"Yes, but more to the point. For several centuries, rather like high priests permitted to enter the holy of holies, it has been the Companions of the Rosy Hours who stand guard over the most sacred talismans of our culture, such as—"

"The Rose Manteau you were assigned to protect . . ."

"*Precisely!* Whoever possesses the Manteau, and is of the royal blood of Sabah al-Sabah al-Sabah, has the sworn fealty of the Companions. And quite possibly the leverage to move Islam."

"So if it falls into Fatoosh's hands, they're his boys. But if you somehow recover it . . ."

"The Companions then become *my* faithful retainers."

The three of us took a break from all this heavy strategic thinking and went to the beach, picking up hero sandwiches at the Villa Italian shop across from the railroad station. Bando and I tossed an old tennis ball and Alix permitted the high sun to burnish her superb tan marginally closer to perfection. Glancing back to where she lay half asleep on an oversize beach towel, the sun examining her body, Bandar said:

"She's a honey, Beech. You're a most fortunate man."

"I think so," I agreed.

We resumed tossing the ball, and when Alix woke, teased her for indolence, at which she dashed for the water, challenging us to an ocean race. Which of course she won.

"It's buoyancy plus technique," she declared smugly. "I'd have swum competitively for Oxford had I not been fully occupied with coxing the varsity crew."

"Well," I said, "I came second, at least."

That didn't sit well with Bandar.

"A son of the desert isn't supposed to know how to swim. But you, with an admiral for a father, to lose to—"

Her Ladyship cut him off. "Rot! You lost fair and square, Prince. Dinner's on you."

When we got back from dinner at the Farmhouse, there was another message from my father. This time a reference in *Greenmantle* alerted us to a specific day of the week: Saturday.

What was that all about?

Bandar floated his theory. "Look, Beech, if my sources are correct that Wells or somebody has recovered the Rose Manteau, it could be en route to Fatoosh to exploit for his own malign ends. Now the Admiral gives us a day, this Saturday. Is he telling us that's when the relic gets here?"

"To be appropriately received, and concealed I'd wager, in Sag Lodge, which, I suggest," Alix said demurely, "isn't being redecorated at all. But has been prepared as some sort of holy sanctuary, guarded from infidels not only by the Companions of the Rosy Hours but by some *decidedly* unfriendly snakes."

Had we really stumbled on a link between my father's mission for the Pentagon and murky doings at Sag Pond? If so, and if we could derail Fatoosh's schemes in the Hamptons, the Admiral might then come home, mission accomplished. Which would be a relief to both of us.

Because I hadn't told Bando or Alix all of my old man's coded message: where he was heading after Baghdad. If there were an even more perilous place for Admiral Stowe, or any American spy, it was Bukhara, an ancient city in the grip of Osama bin Laden and the dreaded Taliban. I thought I'd better keep *that* alarming information to myself for the moment . . .

twenty-four

"Like some fierce old biblical prophet
out of the Old Testament . . ."

In all the excitement I'd never followed up on Jesse's cue and visited architect Howard Roark. Probably he was a crazy old man. But maybe he really did know something about Sag Pond. Alix and I drove up toward Louse Point.

"But just who is he and why is he important?" she asked.

I gave her a brief account, working mainly from my recollection of the Rand bio. How Roark refused commissions unless given a completely free hand. Not even the people putting up the money for the building had any say.

"He sounds an impressive chap. Though difficult," Alix said.

"Difficult? He was commissioned to build his dream project, a huge housing development in Manhattan, a job that would make him famous, and an assignment he would have killed to get, building good solid housing for thousands of middle-class Americans, along with creating jobs for a construction industry mired in the Great Depression. It was a win-win situation. Until the architectural dabblers on a public housing commission got involved and, without clearing it with Roark, had the contractors make some minor alterations to the original design on the first of the buildings to go up. Roark had stipulated an aesthetically clean facade with no columns at all, and here confronting him were pilasters and fluted doorframe columns of a Corinthian design. Roark flew into a rage. Demanded they restore the facade to its original design. 'Corinthian?' he raged. 'And fluted Corinthian at that? Why have columns at all? Doric or Ionic just possibly, but Corinthian, never!"

"What happened?" Alix asked.

"They caved in on the columns. Went back to his original design."

"So the crisis was ended," she said.

"Not bloody likely!" I responded, remembering Madame Rand's dramatic account in the bio. "There were the window boxes . . ."

"Oh, no," Alix said, "not window boxes."

"I kid you not," I said, "it's in the Rand book. When the public works people insisted that even city dwellers deserved to have flowers, defying Roark and his famous 'Function. Purity of line. Strength through mass,' Roark blew up the goddamned building. Just plain leveled it one night. Went out there with dynamite and a plunger, slugged the nightwatchman, climbed the fence and blew the building."

"Golly."

"He turned himself in the next morning, handed over the burglar tools, pleaded guilty to disturbing the peace, refused to retain counsel, said not a word in his own defense, and spent a year in jail. Lost his license to practice as well. He wasn't much more than thirty at the time, the most brilliant architect since Frank Lloyd Wright. And here he was, finished."

"And ended up here in East Hampton?"

"Well, this is just a summary. When the war came along the government needed men like Roark, no matter how difficult they were, and he did heroic work. Fell in love, as well, with an architecture critic named Dominique Francon. But it fell apart when Dominique went off with another man, a Hearst-like publisher named Gail Wynand who owned newspapers and magazines, and who hated Roark. If she really loved Howard, why marry his worst enemy? How *could* she? Dominique told Roark she wanted to determine his breaking point. Can you believe that? Anyway, Rand's biography swears it's what she said.

"After that Roark just sort of went downhill. When the Rand book came out there was a spasm of renewed interest but he wouldn't take advantage of it. Turned down commissions, set his creative demands so high no reasonable person would employ him. A genius, obviously. But also a royal pain in the ass. Who gradually dropped out of sight. Only this Rand woman continued to believe. Moved in with him, tried to take Dominique's place. But nothing worked anymore. In fact until I heard his name the other day, I assumed he had died."

We drove up to Roark's place in the piney woods on a side road leading to Louse Point. No name out front, just the road number. Down a long, winding dirt road here, suddenly, dramatically, was this absolutely terrific house of logs.

I slowed and stopped the car, and both of us just sat there, staring.

"That is *some* house," I said finally, lacking adjectives.

"Right-o!" Alix agreed, for once stilled.

We got out and went to the door. I'm no builder but it looked to me as if Jesse Maine had it right; it was put together without a single nail, the logs notched and fitted together—saddling, they call it—the solidity coming from the weight of one log atop and cut into the next. Yet the house didn't look heavy or homemade. It looked . . . , well, just as Jesse said, it looked great.

Madame Rand opened the door. Just the top half of it, one of those country doors where they check you out through the top half before letting you in the house. I thought that behind her in the half light I could see a shotgun leaning up against the wall. She was small but sturdy, a pugnacious and ugly woman, whose bright eyes were clear and focused, even without glasses. From the tanned, leathery look of her she might have been anywhere from sixty to a hundred in age, stronghanded as well, from the handshake grip she gave.

I told her who we were. "Here to see Mr. Roark if we can."

"He's swimming. Come back later," she said, her tone that of a throwaway line, her body language the same, leaning her thick forearms on the bottom half of the country door which she apparently had no intention of opening farther.

I recalled what Jesse told me.

"But you go with him when he swims, don't you? Guarding the bathrobe."

She realized I had something and looked more pointedly into my face. "Tell me what it's about."

We were still on the doorstep. Whatever her virtues, hospitality did not appear to be one of them.

I told her. The big house on Sag Pond Mr. Wells was building.

"Reporters," she said, contempt and resentment in her voice, "you people crucified him once. Leave the poor bastard alone."

I wasn't letting go that easy.

"He's been talking about the Wells house up at Boaters. Talking pretty freely. Offering to show people drawings he did for such a house . . ."

"Come on in," she said, "he's down getting the truck gassed."

"My, this is lovely," Alix said, turning on the charm. Except that it wasn't just charm. The house *was* lovely. Simple, comfortable, efficient, in harmony with the woods from which it had been carved. The windows, the door, a large skylight, all seemed cleverly wrought to permit the maximum of natural light to penetrate. Was there also artificial light? Not that I could see. What was semi-gloom from outside was joyful and bright. The main space seemed a combination of living room and kitchen, and Madame Rand now went to a large iron stove and stirred up a bed of coals under one of the circular oven-top grills. Coal? A wood fire? Whichever, a kettle was soon whistling cheerfully and we were given coffee. No tea had been offered nor had Alix asked. For a change she seemed a bit intimidated by this tough old woman.

The furniture was one with the house. Madame Rand saw me looking around at it.

"He built it all. Chairs, tables, fireplaces, shelves, closets, foundation, plumbing, wiring. Dug the well, installed a generator. We don't have town water, town electricity, town sewers. Or a phone. You want a man who can fend for himself, meet Howard Roark. All the construction gang bosses around here know 'Red' Roark. Even at his age, they need a solid man on a structural job, putting on a roof, climbing the high steel, building a chimney or a patio, they'll call Red. He gives them a good day's work, even now."

"And the Wells house in Sagaponack?" I asked.

She didn't answer right away. Seemed, in fact, on the verge of throwing us out.

"Look," I said, "this isn't just a magazine piece. There's odd business going on over there at Sag Pond. You know there is. That's what I'm trying to get to the heart of. Not Howard Roark."

She seemed to decide she could take a chance on us. But didn't say so. Just launched into it.

"That's typical of him," she said. "Claims to have designed a big house like it years ago and that Wells's architect simply . . ."

". . . stole his ideas?"

"Well, yes. Plenty of them stole from Howard. Rich, respected men. He was shunned and dead broke but had ideas worth stealing."

Madame Rand laughed, a harsh, chill laugh.

"You don't really find it funny at all, do you," I said.

She shook her head, a solid woman but with a vulnerability I didn't expect.

"Show him the cathedral at Chartres and Howard'll tell you the precise measurements of the rose window. He knows, to the millimeter. Because he *built* it! Chartres and its stained glass have been standing there in the Ile de France for eight hundred years and Howard Roark will swear on Bibles he did the original design."

Neither Alix nor I moved. Or did anything beyond breathing. She went on.

"Who knows? Maybe he did, crazy old man. In some other life he was French and a Catholic and he built cathedrals. But then again, the Fortress of Saints Peter and Paul on the River Neva in Petersburg, he did that one, too. The Sears Tower in Chicago. York Minster in England. And the Morro Castle in Havana harbor that the Spaniards erected three hundred years ago. And . . . well, I could go on. Only reason he doesn't claim the Parthenon is those damned Greek columns. Hates columns. Paranoid? He's the king of paranoia. He's a genius. And he's a wonderful old crazy."

She paused. Then went on. Talking about a man she clearly adored had melted reticence.

"I know more about him than anyone but Dominique, I suppose. I've been with him a hell of a lot longer. Not that he feels for me as he felt for her, I'm not saying that. She's a beauty and I'm, well . . . Then a couple of years ago he came across a photo of her and Gail, out there in Palm Springs. It was in *Architectural Digest.* I gave him a subscription because it wasn't really about architecture at all. But about money. He enjoyed looking at the pictures of the rich people who owned the big houses, making sarcastic remarks about their taste and how architects cheated them. And there they were, on a golf course, Dominique and Gail Wynand, sleek and well groomed and wealthy, posing with their best friends after a polite round of geriatric golf, all four of them looking their years but erect: Dominique and Gail and Dolores and Bob Hope."

She let that sink in and then said, "He was restless for days after that. Stalked about, talking to himself. Seeing Dominique again, with Bob Hope, it stirred something inside him. Maybe memories of when he was young and famous, and going to get rich as people like Hope. This isn't a man to go to pieces, believe me, but he wouldn't even pick up his banjo." She hesitated, then, "He's not simple. Just about the most complicated man ever. He told me once, and I have no reason for disbelief, that into every design he incorporated a flaw. On purpose! He put something in there that wouldn't work. Or would cause trouble later, long after the job was done.

"Now why would an architect as good as Roark do something self-destructive as that, d'you think?" she asked rhetorically. "Something as antithetical to everything he stood for, everything he was?"

I shook my head. Alix, again, remained mute.

"Because he suspected, he *knew* they were stealing his ideas. Putting their own names on them. It was his poison pill, you see, this single flaw that he knew about and could correct if and when he actually built the place. But that they, whoever *they* were, were ignorant of."

Alix and I looked at each other. But before we could speak, Madame Rand resumed, more emotional now:

"Leave him in peace, for God's sake. If he wants to boast a bit, brag over beers up there at Boaters, what harm does he do? They tell their fish stories; he talks of buildings he's built. Or would have done. An old man. Let him be . . ."

Alix looked at me and I got up. There was no profit in pursuing this. I thanked the old lady, taking her hand. So did Alix. Madame Rand showed us to the door, not pushing, just leading us out, a proud and furious old woman tending a flame.

As we drove slowly along the narrow, rutted dirt path in silence, still absorbing what we'd heard, from the opposite direction came the loud growl of a big klaxon horn, the kind of thing you find on tractor trailer trucks. Instinctively, I swerved onto the shoulder and halfway into the underbrush to let whoever it was through, when along came a battered pickup, with an orange-haired old man in overalls at the wheel, singing to himself and driving fast with a big fist on the klaxon horn, and we sat there watching as he passed.

"Funny," Alix said as I pulled back onto the rutted track and headed toward Old Stone Highway.

"Funny how?" I asked.

"The way she talked about him I expected him to look different. Like some fierce old biblical prophet out of the Old Testament, righteous and terrible in his wrath . . ."

"And?"

"Well, to me Howard Roark looked like a sweet old man, with a happy smile on his face. As if he got a kick out of driving fast on a dirt road, honking the horn, and singing at the top of his lungs."

You know, I might have put it differently, but on that, Alix was absolutely right. Maybe the old man was nuts; he didn't seem to be brooding about it. Not as happy as he sounded and the joy with which he sang:

"Oh Susannah, Oh don't you cry for me . . ."

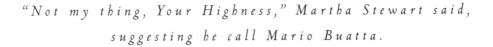

twenty-five

"Not my thing, Your Highness," Martha Stewart said,
suggesting he call Mario Buatta.

At number 393 Lily Pond Lane a florist's truck from Wittendale's arrived with a vast floral bouquet for Buzzy, an arrangement so elaborate as to have been equally at home gracing a wedding altar or a funeral casket. The card, addressed to Congressman Portofino, R., N.Y., read: "Buzzy, Hope your convalescence proceeding normally." And was signed, "With great affection."

Glique was taken aback. Even his ex-wives didn't write to him this coldly.

"You think the marriage isn't going all that well?" he asked Dixie.

Our council of war had convened in the richly appointed card room ("the chess room, please," begged Sammy) of Glique's house, our numbers now officially reinforced by Congressman Portofino, looking stronger with every hour but still silent and, in deference to his wounds, reclining (with laptop) on a wicker chaise.

Sammy found his silence soothing, having previously been through such angst with the talkative Senator D'Amato. Buzzy, ever curious, tapped out a question that had been eating at him:

"What really happened between you and D'Amato?"

Sammy pulled up a chair, eager to tell, though protesting insincerely, "I don't know just how candid I should be," until, at our urging, he recounted what had transpired:

"It was the morning after your speech at the Maidstone. The Senator was pacing the patio, folding and unfolding the *Times,* and rather agitated. Naturally, I made courteous inquiries. Had a Republican been indicted? Did Lars and the covergirls disturb his rest? Could I be of assistance?

"He broke off his pacing and stared at me. Then he began talking. You couldn't stop him. Flecks of foam at the corners of his mouth. The poor man, so many responsibilities, so many burdens. A difficult reelection campaign looming. Your heart went out . . .

"He honored me with his confidences, the two of us on the patio, as if we were equals. Like one of the Kennedy boys in conversation with Arthur Schlesinger. My mother would have been touched. The intimacy. He said to me, emotional and yet analytic:

"'Already we have Giuliani and me in the state. We need another Italo-American with political ambitions? Please. No disrespect intended, but New York Republicans can do without Buzzy Portofino. And so can Alphonse M. D'Amato. Bad enough we had Cuomo all those years. At least he was a Democrat. Yet here we have three New York Italians, all Republicans, all conservative, avid for the party's blessing. If Reagan was correct, if God really is a Republican, why must He impose Buzzy Portofino on me? Bad enough I have Rudy! Like Julius Caesar in the Forum, surrounded by Italians with daggers! Caesar had his Brutus, his Cassius. Me, I got the Mayor, and now Portofino! Here he arrives at the Maidstone Club, publicly assailing my host for lust. Don't you think in the voter's mind, this depravity rubs off on me? Even my mother phones, urging celibacy on me. So, I'm out of here!'

"I am not a callous person," Sammy went on. "I was hurt but I understood the man's dilemma. Without protest, I drove the Senator to the train, assisting him with his cardboard suitcase, his garment bag, the little beach bag with his shower clogs, his swimsuit from yesterday's swim. Heartbreaking, I tell you, his trunks still damp from my own pool. We had our differences. But to see this hardworking lawmaker returning to Washington in the heat and humidity of summer, with former Mayor Barry waiting there as well, it had me close to tears. On the platform we went from foot to foot, awkwardly, where once we enjoyed a casual intimacy. I attempted conversation.

"'Senator,' I said, seeking a positive note, 'this cardboard suitcase of yours. Innovation Luggage has a sale. All the brand names. American Tourister, Lark, Samsonite even. You could have a nice two-suiter, a three-suiter even, a man like you. Why the cardboard?'

"'Sammy,' he responded, always it was to him, 'Sammy,' the intimacy. Thrilling to me who dreamt of Kennedys, here I have a senator calling me Sammy.

"'Sammy,' he went on, 'the taxpayer, God bless him, sees his Senator carrying a cardboard suitcase and not Louis Vuitton or Gucci, and he says to himself, 'This is a man cautious with his own dough. Not one of those fellows feeding at the public trough, and screwing the people, y'know?'

"'Senator,' I said, deeply moved, 'I'm touched that you share with me your philosophies, your candor. Fine. But believe me, it's a crappy suitcase.'

"At that moment, as the train pulled in, it occurred to me, did Senator John C. Calhoun or Henry Clay experience such trials as now afflicted Senator D'Amato? Did Sam Ervin have a Buzzy Portofino? Why did I have to attack the poor man's suitcase? What came over me? I found it emotionally wrenching to release his hand as the 7:20 train to New York pulled out. I stood there peering down the right of way at the receding train for several contemplative moments. Did the nation deserve such men as Alfonse M. D'Amato? I know, I know, no one is perfect. There are accusations, allegations. But convictions? Not a one! No one can make that assertion of Senator D'Amato of whom I can say, even now, he was my friend . . ."

". . . 'n' people say Mr. Glique's not tha emotional type," Dixie said, clearly impressed, and wiping away a tear.

By now Congressman Portofino, having had sufficient sentiment, was tapping energetically, almost frenetically, on the laptop.

"Forget D'Amato. Let's get to the point! My subcommittee on Aliens and Sedition wants to know: these aliens, why are they in the Hamptons? What mischief are foreigners up to at Sag Pond? American congressmen being arrested for trespass. Being shot with arrows. The question now: how do we get in there and find out what's going on?"

I looked at Jesse. He was the local expert.

"It's a tough call, Beecher. I used to do a little poaching there in the old days. Slipped in and slipped out under cover of the dark. No more. Not since them Arabs took over. That place is bad medicine these days and no one knows shit about what goes on. Might be the Forbidden City in Tibet. Or even Pequot turf."

"But we've been there ourselves," Glique put in. "With Prince Fatoosh hosting a catered lunch. Met the mahout, seen the snakes, Sag Lodge, at a distance . . ."

"Precisely," Alix said. "At a distance!"

Oxonians were trained to make fine distinctions.

"How do we get a closer look? I asked.

"Martha Stewart," Alix said smartly.

"Martha Stewart?"

"Fatoosh said the place was in the hands of decorators. And didn't he express his admiration for Martha's household hints? He subscribes to her magazine, never misses her on the telly."

Dixie Ng added enthusiastic agreement:

"Remembah thet *Newsweek* cover story: 'She knows how; she does it now!' "

"Well, yes, but . . ."

Alix resumed.

"Isn't it at the very least feasible that he had Martha for lunch? Much as he did us. Except that in her case, he couldn't resist picking her brains on decorating schemes?"

Sammy thought this a good idea. "One of the few on Lily Pond Lane with a cheery wave, a genial 'hello,' that's Martha. Never a complaint over the hedges. If I trim here and there, well, she understands. Surely a woman of quality. Thackeray would have put her in a novel. Jane Austen, as well. Believe me, the stories you hear, the backbiting, the slanders, not true. Not a scintilla of—"

"Might we ask her over for a chat?" Alix inquired practically, cutting across the litany of Martha's virtues.

Buzzy Portofino was tapping away on the laptop.

"No," Sammy tapped back in petulant response, "I don't know if she's a Republican."

Snatching back the infernal machine Portofino responded angrily, "I can *hear*, you little satyr!

By some miracle of timing when Glique phoned, Ms. Stewart was neither writing, broadcasting, putting up preserves, fileting a salmon, fermenting grapes, insulating the attic, baking a shepherd's pie, cleaning pewter, or thatching a roof, and she was soon with us. I made the introductions and provided her with a somewhat expurgated version of what we were up to. And, yes, she *had* actually been inside Sag Lodge!

"Tea, Martha, and a nice platter of assorted Lu biscuits, perhaps?" Sammy asked. "My protégé, Miss Ng, makes a very nice mint tea. Mrs. Danvers, of course, her range of teas more extensive. Or perhaps a cooling fruit ade . . . ?"

"Later. Let's get swiftly to the business at hand."

My, she was brisk. But wasn't that what we wanted?

Glique was energetically signaling to Dixie. "The doilies. For Martha Stewart we put out doilies," he hissed.

"The point is, Martha," I said, "for complex reasons, it's vital for us to have some reasonably precise idea of the interior of Sag Lodge. The floor plan, the lights, where the stairs are located, whether there are alarm systems of one sort and another . . ."

"You mean, can I 'case the joint' for you?"

"Well, yes."

"Fetch drawing paper, a T-square and pencils," she ordered, without further question. And within minutes, working quickly, deftly, she'd limned out with architectural precision a floor plan of the ground floor of the old lodge and, shoving that sheet of drawing paper aside, had begun working on a similarly detailed second floor.

"She's extraordinary," Alix whispered. "Her ability to retain detail. Each and every—"

"I'll be damned," Jesse said, louder but equally deferential. While I wondered just why Glique would have a T-square and drawing paper immediately to hand.

Buzzy was ripping away at the old laptop, the protuberances on his neck bobbing and weaving in time with his racing fingers, but mesmerized by Ms. Stewart's bravura performance, no one seemed to notice.

When Martha finally pushed back from the card table, barely flushed, looking as crisp and fresh as when she first entered, her carefully faded jeans still uncreased, her brushed cotton white T-shirt pristine, her penny loafers gleaming, not a single slick bead of perspiration in evidence, we all gathered around her drawings.

"You must have trained as an architect, surely," I suggested, not flattering her a bit; simply stating the obvious.

Martha Stewart shook her head. "No, though a wonderful old man named Roark who *is* an architect, once gave me a fifteen-minute tutorial in blueprint drawing in his place at Louse Point." She paused. "I didn't bother to detail the wallpaper or the floor coverings," Martha said, almost apologetically. It was just about all she had left out.

Except . . .

It was Alix who raised the matter. I'd seen it; surely Jesse had. Maybe VooVoo, with her archer's keen eye.

"Ms. Stewart," Alix said, deferential but probing, "everything is so clear that I can easily picture it. All but this second drawing. Where there seem to be several missing rooms, an entire wing. Could you explain what might have been omitted?"

We all leaned forward. Martha gave Alix a tight smile.

"Very keen of you, Lady Alix, but I have no idea."

"But . . ."

Martha got up to walk away from the card table, then wheeled to face us. Her gaze was steady, her voice authoritative, her head thrown back. She knew just how impressive had been the virtuoso performance. No apology here, not a bit of it. Hers was the arrogance not of pride but of the expert at the top of her game.

"I assume it's those upstairs rooms, that wing, that you're interested in," she said, "and not the rest of Sagaponack Lodge. Well, I can't help you. Prince Fatoosh kept me on a short leash during the brief hour I was in the house."

"But, surely . . ." Congressman Portofino tapped out on the computer.

She ignored him.

"Certain rooms, the Prince said, were off-limits. Simply not ready to be seen, especially by professionals. Fatoosh did not wish that his simple country tastes be made sport of by critics, or be ridiculed in the pages of *W* or *Architectural Digest*. No state secrets, he assured me; not at all. The fixtures and fittings in those rooms just weren't up to his exacting standards. Or, indeed, mine."

"And did you accept this?" Alix asked.

"Did I believe it, no. Did I accept it, what choice had I? I assumed there was something, or someone, hidden in those rooms. A harem of young blondes. A private collection of erotica. Whips, branding irons and a medieval rack. A Mrs. Rochester, perhaps. None of my business, of course . . ."

"Mrs. Rochester?"

"Oh, Beecher," said Alix, "you must recall *Jane Eyre*. Mr. Rochester's first wife, mad and sequestered in the west wing. It's appalling that Harvard doesn't include the Brontë sisters in its required studies . . ."

"The *east* wing, I believe," Sammy interjected. "You remember, the fire? Oh, the humanity! Orson Welles gallantly dashing through the flames to save the crazy wife while Joan Fontaine wrings her hands. The east wing, I'm sure . . ."

"East wing, west wing," Martha Stewart said, "isn't it Sag Lodge we're discussing? If so, I'd talk to Mario Buatta."

"Who? Who? The man who runs Le Cirque?" Sammy asked. "What a restaurant! The plush chairs alone. The wine list. Dixie and I—"

"No, that's Sirio Maccioni," Prince Bandar, who knew the Manhattan restaurant scene, offered helpfully. "Buatta is . . ."

". . . a leading interior decorator," said Her Ladyship.

"They much prefer the term 'interior designer,'" said Martha.

Buzzy had been tapping away and now shoved his laptop at Martha. She took it, read his entry, and began to type out her response. We all leaned forward, trying to see what she was writing.

Furious, Buzzy grabbed back his computer. "I can *hear*, goddammit!" he wrote.

Martha remained cool, ignoring the outburst. "After I'd toured the house, all but the 'forbidden' wing, Prince Fatoosh asked if I'd take on the challenge of whipping his lodge into shape, suggesting I name a charity into which my fee might be paid.

"'Not my thing, Your Highness,' I informed him, courteous but cool. But if he wanted a really first-rate job done, he ought to talk to Buatta or one of the other leading people in the field. I scribbled Mario's phone number and suggested they chat. I was offered tea and Lu biscuits . . ."

"See, see?" Sammy said, nudging Dixie. "Tea and Lu biscuits. What did I say . . . ?"

". . . but declined and was returned to his chopper with the usual pleasantries, plus an armed guard curiously outfitted with elaborate bows and arrows, and flown back to Lily Pond Lane. The entire adventure occupied an hour and a half and that's about all that I know. And now . . ."

You had to admire her circumspection. Here was this architectural monstrosity going up literally within view, visible from her tasteful home on Lily Pond Lane, and she declined to issue aesthetic judgments. Instead, with a toss of her short blond hair and a cool smile for us (a brief handshake for her host Glique), Martha was briskly away.

Wow!

twenty-six

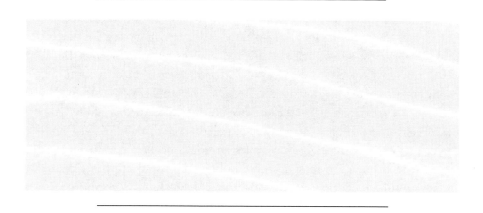

"No way he was going to refuse Paige Rense, editor of Architectural Digest."

Buatta was gracious but of little help beyond confirming and fleshing out Martha's testimony. Her Ladyship, who'd met Mario at various benefits and intimate London dinners, made the approach and reported back to us. Yes, the designer had spoken to the Prince, been flown out from Manhattan, toured the house (except for that same exasperating upstairs suite), been refreshed with tea (he was dieting and declined the biscuits), been offered a huge sum, and was teased with the possibility of future commissions when the new and immensely larger house was completed.

"I had to refuse," the designer told Alix.

But why? This was the work he did, Mario Buatta acknowledged, but:

"The Prince insisted on a confidentiality clause. Not a single detail of the work must appear in the shelter magazines. Not a line. Not in *House & Garden* or *House Beautiful* or *Better Homes*. Nor, above all, in *Architectural Digest*. There were, said Prince Fatoosh, security reasons . . .

"I told him I quite understood. But he must also appreciate there was no way I was going to refuse Paige Rense . . ."

"Who's that?" VooVoo asked now in an urgent whisper.

"The editor of *Architectural Digest*," Alix offered. "A formidable woman. It would take a foolhardy interior decorator to defy that one."

"Designer," Sammy politely corrected her, "I understand they prefer 'interior designer.'"

We were all of us (Bandar by now having been introduced and accepted as one of our doughty little band) pleasantly sprawled about in the sun of Glique's lawn in big old wicker chairs and chaises with overstuffed floral upholstery in bright green and pink sailcloth, enjoying cool drinks but getting absolutely nowhere. In the deep blue midmorning sky an old high-wing monoplane droned slowly overhead. Nice sound, that, one I've always enjoyed. So unlike the heavy throb of a big chopper or the whine of jet engines. The monoplane was making eighty-five miles an hour, maybe a hundred, tops, tugging heavily behind it a long advertising banner promoting the virtues of a moisturizing formula that would banish dry, itchy skin while exuding a scent irresistible to the opposite, or indeed *any* sex.

But as the old airplane droned on, drowsy as we, just where had Mario Buatta left us? At square one?

"Not at all," said the positive-thinking Prince Bandar. "Buatta confirms Martha Stewart's report. We know that one area of Fatoosh's headquarters is off-limits. Doesn't it suggest that whatever he's hiding, whatever he's plotting, it's got to be there?"

He looked at me over the others, cautioning against any mention of the Rose Manteau. No one picked up on it. I think we were all empty of ideas and dulled by the sun at this point. Signor Piano had given up the struggle entirely and was fast asleep. Dixie sipped a Diet Dr Pepper. Even the Congressman was subdued, the familiar computer lying fallow on his lap.

It was then that Her Ladyship noticed the concluding slogan on the airplane-towed advertisement.

"Be bold!? Be *bold!*" she now cried out aloud, "and why not? I'd say! Don't you say that as well, Beecher?"

Sunbaked, drowsily, I muttered, "Oh, yes, always."

Alix wasn't having any of that, I can tell you.

"Then," she said crisply, "enough of daydreaming and idle chat. It's time for action. To, as the advertisement counsels, *'be bold!'* But first, as Sir Richard Hannay might say, quoting old Maritz the Boer commando, 'We must a plan make.'"

"Sir Richard? Maritz the boor?" Sammy murmured, out of his depth. Dixie, sensing his frustration, rubbed her hip against him. "Hush, ma filé gumbo," she said quietly, "don't upset y'self."

"Not now, Dixie," Sammy said, shaking his head. "I'm too nervous."

"Richard Hannay, a major at the time but later a brigadier," Alix explained. "We've got to get on that mysterious property again and not take 'no' this time when it comes to penetrating the secrets of Sag Lodge. Come now, Beecher, and you, too, Prince. First-rate minds such as yours grow dull unless used. Surely Jesse Maine with his experience against the dreaded Pequot tribe can play a tactical role. And VooVoo, the greatest archer in Ukraine? To say nothing of canny Signor Piano who, when awake," she concluded rather lamely, "possesses most formidable powers of analysis."

Buzzy Portofino seized the moment to rattle off a rapid sentence on the laptop.

"Don't count me out of your plans," Alix read aloud, "I'm the only government official here."

"But your wounds, sir," Bandar protested.

The Congressman tapped out a rapid "Healing nicely, thank you, Prince."

I was thinking of reinforcements: Buzzy's corps of bright young men. Signor Piano and Sammy Glique weren't quite my idea of a landing force. But when I mentioned the subcommittee staff, Portofino shook his head so angrily, I feared he might injure himself with arrow ends.

"No," he typed out, "I won't ask young men who've not yet sired children to sail in harm's way."

"Oh," said a clearly insulted Glique, "and how many children have I sired? Dixie?"

"Not uh one Ah kin testify to, dahlin'. Not recently."

"There!" Glique cried out. But Portofino was tapping again.

"I'll represent Washington personally in this matter and happily so."

"Mah," Dixie said, "but he's uh game little fella, isn't he, Sammy?"

Glique shrugged.

"Easy for him, a bureaucrat with federal coverage, a generous medical/dental plan, a government pension. Death benefits if it comes to that, burial at Arlington, where JFK lies in honor. It's we civilians, paying into HMOs, who are truly at risk."

Portofino was tapping as fast as Sammy talked.

"Don't term me a bureaucrat, you fornicator! I'm a popularly elected member of Congress. 'Bureaucrats' are *appointed*, not elected."

Glique threw up both hands. "How smug, how facile these petty distinctions. On the very eve of battle, with all of us confronting our fates, the man stoops to nitpicking. We might as well have Budd Schulberg here, another fox among the chickens."

Wolfie looked up from her script. "Sammy, give it a rest with poor Budd. The man is eighty-five years old. He doesn't need this."

"Oh, and if Leopold and Loeb are eighty-five, we forgive them their trespasses as well?"

Dixie looked puzzled. "Leo Pole 'n who? Mo' fellas on yo' shit list, Sammy?"

We were spared another airing of Glique's suffering at the hands of Schulberg when a big pickup pulled noisily into sight and slid to a skidding halt on the lawn. Glique flinched visibly; a man who suffered if a neighbor's hedge went untrimmed did not enjoy seeing his turf torn up.

"Sorry about that, Sammy," Jesse Maine said as he climbed down from the passenger side, "but I'm teaching Madame Vronsky to drive a manual transmission and she has her little lapses. Over there in Ukraine they got wider roads, she tells me."

"I daresay," Alix said. Then, once again businesslike, "Jesse, we'll need your assistance. We're planning to mount a commando raid on Prince Fatoosh . . ."

"With all them snakes? And the frogmen? And Akbar with his crossbow? My, my." He seemed more impressed by our daring than our prudence.

"Well, yes. But think of them as Pequots. That ought to bring them down to size, don't you think?"

VooVoo was now out from behind the wheel.

"Crossbows is shit. You need a good longbow for accuracy. That's why in the Olympics they . . ."

Signor Piano was awake now. "Look here," he said, "Congressman Portofino's computer says he's going into combat. What's the man talking about? He's barely convalescent."

I shook my head. *Someone* had better introduce a little sanity to the discussion. And nominated myself:

"No one's planning a pitched battle. We're talking about sneaking into Sag Lodge to see what's going on. A reconnaissance, nothing more. If Fatoosh catches us at it, we'll simply accept appearance tickets for trespass."

They were all too worked up to listen.

"Well, the Congressman can't go. He's been shot once already."

That was the near-unanimous opinion. Even Plimpton's (he'd joined us now, having gotten his tape recorder going again). Buzzy's laptop was almost smoking, so swiftly did he counter the argument, and with what eloquent ferocity. It took the pragmatic Jesse to propose a solution.

"It's his arrow ends that worry me. He gets a hard rap on one of them, his jugular could go. Or his vocal cords . . ."

"Which is why the Congressman must remain here," Bandar agreed.

"Or . . ." said Jesse slowly, thoughtfully, as he came up with an idea, "if we could rig up some sort of device protecting his head and neck lest some sumbitch bump into him and dislodge the arrow?"

Piano had an inspiration. "Something rigid, a stout birdcage? One suitable for parrots or falcons or other powerful birds. Remove the bottom and set it upon his shoulders . . ."

"Bolted to a set of football shoulder pads from the sporting goods store," Jesse offered.

"Kind of a 'man in the iron mask' effect," Bandar said thoughtfully.

Plimpton liked the literary analogy. "I've always enjoyed Dumas, *père et fils,* and their novels. How about you, Congressman?"

Buzzy tapped a quick response on the laptop.

Plimpton, leaning over to read it, recoiled.

"Well, I'd no intention of offending you, Congressman. But I must speak frankly. In comparative lit at Harvard, we took a Dumas yarn anytime over a collection of short stories from de Maupassant. The full-blown novel always takes precedence over a 'casual,' as Harold Ross of the *New Yorker* called short stories."

"We still need reinforcements," Signor Piano put in. "Have you thought of simply going to the police?"

"My father would scalp me alive," I said without thinking. Then, to Jesse, "Sorry about that, Jesse. Just slipped out."

Alix, whom I was forever chiding for her blithely blatant use of racial and ethnic stereotypes, gave me a look. But not Jesse.

"Oh, hell, Beecher, you're practically an honorary Shinnecock. And besides, scalping was the MO of the Abenakis, not us. We beheaded fellas."

"But why not alert the police?" Piano persisted.

I tried to be patient, explaining the rules.

"The Great Game, Signor Piano, the intelligence rivalry among the major powers, has its rules—subtlety and stealth, confidentiality and nuance. It's not to be played out on the evening news or the front page of the *Times*. Far less on the desk blotter of your local police precinct. If Bandar or I or even the Congressman went to the authorities with the half-baked information we now possess, we might be compromising an operation of enormous delicacy. And, with the best of intentions, blowing the cover and endangering the lives of courageous men . . ."

"Such as Admiral Stowe," Sammy added, always ready to upstage Buzzy.

"One of tha all-time gents," Dixie said. "Ah can testify ta thet, havin' seen tha Admiral many uh night at tha ol' chessboard swappin' Ruy Lopez openin's with Sammy. Y'all can truly be proud, Mistuh Stowe, ta have uh daddy such as thet."

"I think we all feel that way, Dixie," said Her Ladyship, moving to make the matter unanimous. I thanked them all. For weren't they putting themselves at some, and perhaps considerable, risk, largely on my word? I got up.

"I have something to say. Since this entire operation may be sheer folly and quite risky, I owe you a fuller explanation of my father's situation before I ask anyone to accompany me to Sag Pond."

I had them now, everyone intent on my words.

"My father, the Admiral, is at this very moment in central Asia on behalf of his country. And I assure you he travels in harm's way. His destination, and he may be there already, is a center of Taliban zealotry and an exceedingly dangerous place for an American officer. It is west of Samarkand, in the famed and historic city of Bukhara!"

"Oh, no! Not Bukhara!" Sammy groaned, so agitated I feared he might be about to faint.

"Speak up, Glique!" Portofino ordered on the laptop. "What can Bukhara mean to Admiral Stowe?"

Glique turned, his face pale, slick with perspiration, looking much as his idol Thalberg might have looked in those final days, Norma Shearer at his bedside, brave but weeping silently, wondering if she should call Louis B. Mayer to announce the end.

Sammy mopped his face, pulling himself together. Then, his voice falling, he said very slowly, enunciating each syllable with unnatural precision:

"The . . . Bug . . . Pit!"

Only Dixie spoke, and not at all appropriately: "Theah wuz uh movie called *The Snake Pit* . . ."

"I can tell you this, Dixie," Alix said, seeing I was attempting to get my own emotions sorted out, and stepping in to assist, "The Bug Pit is the most dreadful of fates. For Admiral Stowe and indeed for a free world that revolves around the axis of central Asia with its vast oil reserves and Muslim passion. It was there, John Buchan wrote, that the loathsome Dominick Medina hoped to ignite a holy war."

Bandar was up now and pacing, distraught, wringing his hands. Buzzy sputtered, incapable of sound, his fingers laboring . . .

"Let me explain, Congressman," I said, pulling myself together. "Years ago a famous book called *The Silk Road* devoted an entire chapter to the Bug Pit and the tragic fate of Colonel Charles Stoddart and Captain Arthur Conolly, spelled with a single *n*, and two *l*'s."

"Please, Stowe," Glique said thoughtfully, "it is better not left to the loving son to recount the horror facing his own father."

Alix seconded Sammy's motion. I must have looked pretty shaken. Glique took up the tale:

"The provincial city of Bukhara was once the center of a powerful khanate, with a towering minaret built in 1127. Tallest minaret in the world, it is said. Very much like this house on Sag Pond, the largest private dwelling ever. But forgive me; I digress. The Admiral has often spoken of the place in his accounts over scotch of the Great Game. Stephen Kinzer of the *New York Times* has written eloquently. But it is Anatole Flon who is the customary source—"

"Get on with it, damn you!" Portofino pounded angrily at the keyboard.

Bandar attempted to cool the heated exchange.

"Congressman, in the East we have a saying. Before you carve the saddle of lamb, hone the knife, set the table. So too, in telling a story, it is better this way."

"Thank you, Prince," Sammy said, throwing Portofino a cutting glance. "As I was saying, this splendid minaret, not only a focus of religious faith, but on market days with its grisly aspects. Criminals would be led up its hundred steps . . . Kinzer puts the number at a hundred five—"

"Criminals? One hundred and five? That's a lot of criminals for one lousy market day," VooVoo said, impressed.

"Steps, not criminals," Sammy said. "Up they went, to the top, their crimes read off to the masses gathered below in anticipation. Then they were sewn into sacks. Burlap, I suppose, though neither Kinzer or Flon is quite clear—"

"It was burlap, Glique," Bando said, "I'm sure."

"Thank you, Prince. And then, once they were sewn up, off they went, tossed from the roof to cheers, crashing to their deaths on the stones below."

"Doesn't sound like much of a bug pit to me," Buzzy tapped.

"Not at all," Bando said. "The Bug Pit is infinitely more cruel . . ."

"Wow!" Dixie said, unable to remain silent, "Wuss than bein' sewn in burlap 'n' dropped on stones?"

Sammy patted her thigh soothingly and resumed:

"Adjacent to the mosque with its towering minaret is the ancient jail where Stoddart would meet his fate. He arrived in 1838 at a pivotal confrontation between the British Empire and Tsarist Russia for control of central Asia, hoping as Kinzer nicely puts it, 'to win the Emir's sympathy.' But did he? Not likely! The Emir Nasrullah, a 'deranged sadist' (Kinzer's words, not mine!), threw the Colonel into a filthy pit crawling with rodents and insects. And not content with that, arranged that a stone chute flushed fresh manure each day from the stables directly down into the pit atop the good Colonel, all the better to attract more and better vermin."

"Sammy, dahlin', y' can't be serious. Fresh hoss shit flushed down on tha Colonel?"

"I wish I weren't, Dixie. But there it was, every day, encouraging the swarming vermin. Appalling, inhuman, unsanitary besides, choose your adjective . . ."

"In the name of God, Glique!" Buzzy typed, "Get on with it!"

Sammy half bowed to the Congressman.

"I'm nearly there, sir. Two years after Stoddart began doing 'hard time,' there arrived another gallant officer. This was Conolly who'd come to save the unfortunate Colonel and mollify the Emir. But there were other motives. Listen to what's been written of his foolhardy gesture, that it 'may have been a result of depression at being jilted by his sweetheart.' "

Not even Jesse was immune to curiosity.

"Well, what happened? The Emir buy the deal?"

Bandar now stepped in, knowing the story well. "No, he threw Conolly into the Bug Pit alongside the Colonel."

"Two more years passed," Sammy said, "until on a June morning in 1842, the Emir being out of sorts, a touch of gas perhaps, the two men were led out into the square. As the historian writes, 'Filthy and half-starved, their bodies were covered with sores, their hair, beards and clothes alive with lice.'"

Glique knew the moviemaker's value of a dramatic pause.

"And then, to the cheers of the Bukhara mob, these two gallant officers were executed and their bodies buried under the square where they remain to this day, a popular attraction, and this may strike you as odd, especially for English tourists buying T-shirts and souvenirs."

"Well, I'll be goddamned," Jesse admitted, "if that don't beat the Pequots when it comes to being mean sons of bitches . . ."

VooVoo smiled her pleasure at being corroborated. "See, them bastids is the worstest we got."

"And how exactly did they execute them?" asked Alix, who believed that God was in the details. "Beheading, shooting, the garrote . . . ?"

"Well—" Sammy began.

"I think we can spare Beecher that," Bando interrupted, "in view of what his own father may be facing."

It was Buzzy who fetched us back from the nineteenth century to the present and to current dangers, with a fresh and stunning revelation. Typed out, of course, and at least for the moment, totally silencing Glique.

"This is all very well. But with Admiral Stowe thousands of miles away, I might remind all here that I am the only one of you who has an agent on the ground there at Sag Pond. About whom, for security reasons you'll surely appreciate, I will say nothing more."

"But you can't simply drop a line like that on us and leave it," I protested.

"Confidentiality and nuance, subtlety and stealth," Buzzy tapped out, mocking me. "All in due season," he continued, "all in due season."

Oh, but he was smug.

I just shut up but Sammy had reclaimed his tongue:

"An agent on the ground," he parroted in sarcastic tones. "That's better than a corner table at Le Cirque 2000. What I wouldn't give, Dixie, to have an agent on the ground. It's the current rage; all the best people have one."

The sarcasm didn't quite come off. Portofino issued no cutting retort on the laptop but just sat there grinning, arrow ends protruding impudently from his neck.

"Hush, ma dahlin' crawfish pie," Dixie murmured.

Sammy brightened marginally as the girl rubbed against him. Even that didn't deflate Buzzy, who knew he'd scored, and bathed us all in a wordless but complacent smile.

twenty-seven

"As darkness falls, George Plimpton sets off his fireworks at Boys Harbor."

For a manic twenty-four hours, we seriously considered this commando raid on Sag Pond. Though I knew it to be absurd, recalling as I did bloody accounts of Dieppe, and in the end, whatever my old man's difficulties, said, "No!" How could I lead this ragtag band into action against Punjab, the Asp, and the Rosy Companions?

The Children's Crusade set off to the Holy Land with brighter prospects.

Then to the rescue, entirely unknowing, came Chalmers Cooke's third wife Trish, and PR woman Peggy Siegal.

Prince Bandar and I had taken Alix to dinner at Estia in Amagansett (he had the quesadilla with shredded chicken and she and I Caesar salads with smoked salmon topping and the Monterey burgers) and then to the Blue Parrot for a nightcap at the bar where everyone was eating guacamole dip and drinking Corona or Pacifico beer.

"Odd cuisine for Long Island," Bando remarked. "All this Tex-Mex when you'd expect oysters, blueclaw crab, local duck and broiled lobster."

"There are many odd things this season," said Alix darkly. I was still growling over the Congressman's offhanded bombshell.

"'An agent on the ground'? Now what the deuce does that mean?"

Bando attempted to soothe my indignation.

"Didn't your detective pal Knowles say that they'd found a bloodstained copy of Salman Rushdie's *Satanic Verses* in Portofino's pocket, with annotations in Arabic?"

"Yes. And Tom said Buzzy sloughed it off as unimportant. That he was boning up as a service to Muslim constituents. Tom didn't buy that and apparently neither do you. You think that was from his man on the . . . ground?"

"Might be. And it may have been what lured him into the ambush."

"And," Her Ladyship swiftly leaped in to suggest, "it also suggests the possibility this so-called agent the Congressman has inside the enemy camp is playing a dual role. And may indeed have been a mole setting up Buzzy for entrapment. You'll recall, surely, how in *The Three Hostages* Richard Hannay cleverly contrived to smuggle Monsieur de la Tour du Pin into the very inner circles of that skewed rogue Dominick Medina."

"It's all *very* John le Carré," Bando admitted, drawing a briefly puzzled look from Alix.

"I'm sure you'll recall it was decidedly *not* le Carré, but John Buchan wrote *The Three Hostages*," she murmured, not giving quarter to anyone, even Old Etonians, when it came to boys' tales.

Over a second round of margaritas, we offered up and swiftly discarded stratagems for penetrating the stronghold at Sag Pond, and quite frankly not getting very far. There along the bar was Richard Ryan, whose boat had helped Her Ladyship and me save Royal Warrender during the hurricane two years ago. If only we might recruit Richard to our cause, a big, strapping fellow who knew boats, even if noisy outboards had deafened him in one ear. But those were the rules of the Great Game; you disseminated intelligence strictly on a "need to know" basis. Ron Perelman came in and he and Alix chatted. We all had another margarita and were about to go back to the house when that arch snob Trish Cooke joined us. She's blond and sleek, and if she didn't graduate from Radcliffe, she should have. You know the type . . .

"Can you imagine the gall of that towelhead?" she asked.

"What 'towelhead' is that, Trish?" I asked, and then rather showily introduced Her Ladyship and then Bando with all his various titles and honorifics.

"Oh, sorry," she said, dimpling an apologetic smile at Bandar, who'd long ago at Harvard shed his sensitivities about being a towelhead.

"Not at all," he said smoothly. "And what is it that my brother Fatoosh has done now?"

She did a second blush, not realizing the two were brothers. Once she recovered, Trish got to the point.

"I mean, building that bloody awful Sag Pond house and then inviting people for cocktails to toast the topping off."

That one lost both Bando *and* Lady Alix. I helped out.

"A traditional ceremony that construction gangs have when the tallest of the steelwork is finally in place. They 'top off' the work and put up a little Christmas tree or something and have a drink."

It turned out that, according to Trish Cooke, Prince Fatoosh and his good friend Offshore Wells were asking a choice list of Hamptonites to Sag Lodge Saturday night to celebrate the work's progress.

Saturday night? I for one perked up at that!

"He's retained that pushy Peggy Siegal to do the PR. She's circularizing both the Maidstone here and the Meadow Club in Southampton. No one who *counts* is going, of course," Trish said. "And a few of us plan to demonstrate out front. We're hoping to get Kurt Vonnegut. All the protesters in proper evening clothes and drinking Moët . . ." She thought this very funny and laughed, huskily.

"Oh," said Alix Dunraven, deftly going one up, "have they run short of Dom?"

As a member of the Maidstone who *hadn't* been invited, I permitted myself a brief petulance. But as soon as Ms. Cooke, thoroughly snooted about the champagne, had gone, I called over Joe Kazickas. He's in real estate and belongs to the Maidstone so he knows everything. "What's all this about a party at Sag Pond?"

True, Joe said sarcastically. "Your typical summer lawn party in the Hamptons: native dancing, archery contests, snake-handling, masks and costumes, badminton and miniature golf. It's Gatsby at West Egg without the bootleggers." But according to Joe, it looked as if good, old-fashioned Hamptons snobbery was going to save the day.

"People I've spoken to wouldn't be caught dead."

Mmm.

"What is it, Beecher?" Alix asked. She always knows when I'm thinking.

"Suppose *we* get ourselves invited? No need then to sneak in under cover of darkness. Get Sammy to call and set it up. As vain as he is, Fatoosh can't afford to throw a party with *nobody* there, can he?"

"Could work," Bandar said.

I borrowed the Blue Parrot cell phone. Sammy was delighted. He enjoyed a good party. "So does Miss Ng." And anything was preferable to actual hostilities. Then he halted in midsentence.

"Prince Bandar! How do we include *him*? Remember, the mere mention of his name, 'amputation and the lash'!"

"We'll think of something," I promised

Truth was, unless I got a belated invitation or Sammy could get us asked for cocktails Saturday night, we didn't have a clue just how we were going to pull off this caper. We conceived of half-baked schemes and as dizzily discarded them.

And then Alix mentioned George Plimpton. "He's jolly good company when not tape recording one. But *is* he one of us or not? Can one count on him?"

"Well, he does give you fair warning when he starts up the old tape," I protested, not wanting criticism of a Harvard man to go unchallenged. Even though George's oral history of the entire world was beginning to pall—

And then I stopped! So abruptly both Bandar and Alix regarded me with concern.

"Beecher, are you—"

"Saturday!" I shouted. "It's Saturday! When they bring in the Rose . . ."

Bandar started to shut me up until he saw my face.

"Yes, Beecher," he said quietly, having warned me off, "I'm listening."

"Our *distraction*. Saturday night, as darkness falls, George Plimpton sets off his annual Bastille Day fireworks to benefit Tony Duke's Boys Harbor. Get it, fireworks? Suddenly lighting up the night sky, turning night to day, startling the Arabs, and with sufficient noise to drown out a Puff Daddy pool party."

"By the Prophet!" Bando agreed. "I think you've got it!"

"And if we're there at Sag Lodge as *invited* guests . . ." Alix said.

". . . by nine," I picked up, "the dicing, gaming and wenching at full throttle, everyone drunk, when *BOOM!* The fireworks stun Fatoosh and his Rosy Companions and we nip into the house, cocktail glasses in hand, and sprint upstairs to the forbidden west wing!"

"Wasn't it east?" Alix asked.

In the morning I phoned Jesse. If we wangled our invitations, I still didn't like the idea of crossing picket lines. Especially those manned by my pals drinking champagne and numbering Kurt Vonnegut in his dinner jacket. So why not get there once again by sea . . . ?

"You and Captain Bly get along. Can you charter him for Saturday afternoon, back at the dock Sunday morning?"

"Sure, if the money's right."

"The money will be right."

Glique hadn't yet heard back from Fatoosh. But as we gathered on his lawn, it was evident Sammy had suffered an attack of nerves.

"Suppose I call William Morris and get Sharon Stone to meet Prince Fatoosh? She doesn't have to make the film. Just talk with him about it. Cross and uncross her legs a couple of times. Argue about points, gross versus net. Have her people call his people. No need for us to storm the beaches with John Wayne."

Buzzy tapped out, "Coward! Poltroon!" on his laptop and passed it around.

"Ha!" Sammy responded, jumping up to pace. Looking off toward the ocean, trying to be disdainful, but embarrassed in spite of himself.

"Will Sharon Stone cooperate?" I asked.

"No."

Congressman Portofino drew us back to the subject at hand. Typing rapidly, he wrote, "I have reason to believe Fatoosh and coconspirators are on the verge of a coup that could shift the balance of strategic power in the entire region."

"Here on Long Island?" Jesse asked, thinking perhaps of the Pequots.

Impatiently, Portofino shook his head, alarming us all. Dixie called out:

"Congressman, don't *do* thet! Y'all gonna dislodge yo' arrows!"

Annoyed at her concern, and attempting to rehabilitate his own image, Sammy said, "A man can dislodge arrows if he wishes, Dixie. I wouldn't concern myself." Airily, he regarded his own fingernails, above the squabbling.

Buzzy continued to type.

"It was why I agreed to that reckless assignation on the bridge that night. I felt myself getting close. Also why I attempted earlier to reach Admiral Stowe to coordinate operations. A sacred talisman was involved. Were the Admiral and my subcommittee seeking the same prize?"

Bandar and I exchanged anxious glances. How much did Congressman Portofino know about the Rose Manteau? If only I had some way to reach the

Admiral. Perhaps *he* could still make sense of the whole thing and guide our uncertain hands.

Lars the cinematographer chose this uneasy moment to emerge accompanied by covergirls.

"Hi Ho!" he called out. "Swim-swim, us?"

Only Plimpton took up the invitation. "Better get some of this down on the old tape recorder," he explained, following Lars through the hedge.

"He won't get much oral history over that din," Her Ladyship remarked, a bit pedantically, I thought.

"Hi Ho!" Lars shouted. "Hi Ho, indeed, old sport!" came Plimpton's distinctive voice in exuberant reply, amid the splashing and the laughter.

Oddly, the unseen pool party seemed to cheer Sammy. Maybe he'd finally succeeded in creating a facsimile of how it once had been at the Kennedy compound, when all the boys were still alive and all the girls were beautiful.

Just then Mrs. Danvers came out onto the lawn.

"Mr. Glique, a call from Peggy Siegal. Of course you're invited to Prince Fatoosh's party. How many guests can they expect?"

twenty-eight

"You play Peter Pan and I'll be Wendy, mother to all
the lost boys."

Following these momentous developments at 393 Lily Pond Lane, Her Ladyship and I again set out to track down Howard Roark, hero of *The Fountainhead*
and the man who'd tutored Martha Stewart in blueprint drawing. I had a wild
notion Roark might be our key to smuggling Prince Bandar into his brother's
party. The encounter was anything but banal.

Our first glimpse, just as in the opening scene of Madame Rand's book,
was of Roark standing on the edge of a huge boulder, the water far below him
reflecting not the depths but the sky above. The water seemed immovable, the
rock flowing. Alone, poised and naked, his body one of long straight lines and
angles, each curve broken into planes, a sculpted, mythic figure frozen briefly
in time, who hesitated for an instant, and then . . .

. . . Howard Roark laughed.

And dove with grace and power into Three Mile Harbor, deftly cutting
through the surface almost without a splash in what seemed to me a pretty styl-
ish half-gainer, and began a slow but steady and powerful crawl toward the op-

posite bank. While cross-legged atop the rock, Madame Rand sat placidly in the hot sun, her eyes following the architect as he swam, her strong, short fingers folding and folding again the terry robe he'd dropped just before his dive.

Alix and I had driven to Louse Point late that morning but when we found the place empty, the pickup truck gone as well, she said, "Now where is that rock he swims off? Mightn't he be there on a day like this?"

Might be. And was.

We got out of the car and scaled the rock ourselves. Madame Rand looked up. "Oh, it's you." She didn't seem enthusiastic.

It took Roark about ten minutes each way to swim the width of the harbor and when he came out of the water, shaking himself like a dog, drops flying, Madame Rand handed him a half-smoked cigar and relighted it, then held out his robe. But, his eyes on us, puffing out smoke, Roark didn't yet take it.

I told him our names and we each got a handshake. I'm not sure Alix had ever before shaken hands with a naked stranger but she handled it well. Not knowing quite how to open the bidding I remarked, "That's quite a swim. And we arrived just as you dove. Pretty impressive."

"It's a high dive at low tide," Madame Rand put in, "and scary. I'm forever expecting him to smash into the bottom."

"Little chance of that," Roark said. "I've been diving since I was a kid. Learned by diving into quarries."

How odd this all was, a couple of sailboats cruising silently past, the sun bouncing off the blue water, the four of us chatting casually, three dressed and one, an old fellow as tall as I was, puffing a cigar, streaming wet and stark naked.

"It's such a lovely vista here, and the water so inviting," Alix remarked. "I've quite the yen to just strip down myself and give it a go."

It seemed to me Roark's eyes brightened at that while Madame Rand ground her teeth. But before anyone could speak, or Alix undress, I decided that the niceties had been sufficiently addressed.

"Look," I said, getting right to it, "you're the sort of man for plain talk. It's no secret there's some variety of dirty work afoot at Sag Pond. We've been asked to cocktails by Prince Fatoosh and Chapman Wells Saturday night. It's our intention to try to find out just what they're up to at the lodge, Wells and Prince Fatoosh and the Arabs. You're a game fellow, Roark, and you've been there, worked there, know the lay of the land. There may be difficulties, even peril. I won't deny it. But Lady Alix here and several other friends, including women, have signed on. Can we count you among us? It would mean a good deal. And the stakes, about which I'm not free to elaborate right now, could be enormously high. My own father is playing a hand and at some risk to himself."

He didn't say anything for a moment and I thought I could see pain, perhaps fear in Madame Rand's homely face. Fear for him, not for herself. No one spoke, and I for one was holding my breath. As if mulling a considered response, Roark crouched, one big hand brushing the surface of the rock, as if gauging its density, the mineral content, the boulder a touchstone of sorts, and then, quietly and without getting up, he asked:

"What would be asked of me? How could I be of assistance?"

His reply was as much as I could expect. At least he hadn't turned us down flat. I spoke with the intensity I knew convincing him would take, explaining that we had to get Bandar on to the property as well, though with a price on his head we could hardly take him along as a guest. But if Roark, who knew the ground as well as anyone, could somehow smuggle Prince Bandar close to Sag Lodge, when the rest of us created a distraction as Plimpton's fireworks went off, well . . .

Roark asked a few more pointed questions that I attempted to answer. Then, unexpectedly and quite ignoring the fact that he was still naked, Howard Roark sprang to his feet to take my hand and pump it fiercely, before turning to Alix and bowing deeply in her direction.

"I'm your man, Stowe. And Your Ladyship. No one's trusted me with a responsible commission in years. Just tell me where we foregather and when."

"Howard," Madame Rand murmured, "your robe."

"Yes, yes," he said impatiently, reaching out a long arm.

As I drove off, feeling irrationally buoyed at our reinforcement, as if one eccentric ninety-year-old architect was going to tilt the scales, Alix leaned against me in the car. "You know, I think he knew we were going to ask him to join us. I think *she* knew. And why she tried to chase us off. Women in love are like that."

"In love, at their age?"

Alix looked at me. "Every so often, Beecher, you can be an awful boob."

"Yes, well . . ." I said, knowing how right she was.

Back at our house there were messages left and calls from here and there but except to call Bandar, I ignored them. When again might we have another peaceful afternoon? "Come on," I said, "the beach awaits."

"Yes, Beecher, let's."

It was another of those grand summer days when the sky has never been as high and filled with gulls and darting plovers nor the puffy clouds as white. The sun bakes down, but the world has been dehumidified and a slight breeze out of the north piles up the waves so they hesitate, just slightly, and then fall with a soft thud on the shelving beach and roll up richly foamed and smelling of brine, almost to your blanket, before they slide back to the deep.

"We don't have a true surf in the Gulf," Bandar remarked, already feeling quite at home here and qualified to comment.

"You're too far south," I said, not knowing what I was talking about.

"Rubbish!" Alix said, "think of Australia, how far south that is, and all those lovely bronzed young men on their surfboards. I've known jolly times there on Bondi Beach near Sydney."

Lovely bronzed young men? Jolly times? I didn't like that one bit. And tried to change the subject.

"This spring, April I'm told, a right whale and her calf were seen swimming slowly by this very beach. And, as you know, the right whale is decidedly endangered. To see one this close in East Hampton, well, it's quite . . ."

Bandar was clearly lost in thought, remembering St. Trop', perhaps, or someplace else he'd been happy before his exile, so I shut up and watched as teenage boys skimmed a frisbee and an old man collected shells. Very careful about it he was, taking only specimens he thought perfect and stowing them in a net bag slung over one old shoulder. That's me in another thirty years, I thought, collecting shells and working on my suntan and ogling teenage girls. A dog ran by, barking happily, splashing through the shallows. No dogs were permitted here. I've never seen this stretch of beach when there *wasn't* a dog. Closer to the Maidstone Club a volleyball game was going on, six a side instead of two, as they play in southern California. Well, the effete East. We three took a quick swim, no serious racing this time, and then retreated to the blankets to lie there drying and enjoying the hot sun.

An exotic family I'd seen before sported at the water's edge to our left, five adults and several children, all of them laughing and calling out loudly in French and intermittently kicking a soccer ball with bare feet.

"That's a handsome bunch," Bandar acknowledged.

"The French seem somehow to be made for beaches. Not at all like the perfidious English," Alix admitted.

The "wives," if that's what they were, had the slender-without-dieting look of European covergirls and couldn't have been much more than twenty but between them there were four children, quite small. Everyone was suntanned and happy, even the au pair or nanny, and they all wore the tiniest swimsuits, except for the nanny, the men's being little more than nylon jockstraps. The kids, two or three at most, helped the nanny build sand castles.

"The French are so cool," Her Ladyship remarked.

"Sensible, too," I said.

"Oh?"

"Yes, half the trouble at places like this is the husbands going off with the au pair girls. But these fellows marry the pretty girls and hire au pairs with thick ankles and short noses to watch the kids."

"Oh look, Beecher," Alix interrupted, "unless I'm terribly mistaken, we're about to have a major confrontation. That schoolgirl applying sunblock, the one sitting there topless . . ."

Bandar and I swiveled, dirty old men on the alert.

"What schoolgirl?"

"The redhead there."

She was only fifty yards to our right, close, too close to the cabanas of the Maidstone Club, and descending on her was one of the Maidstone's more ferocious arbiters of good taste, a blue-haired lady in a Lily Pulitzer floral print one-piece suit and beach sandals. When she reached the blanket where the redhead sat, her breasts pointed delightfully seaward, the arbiter began shaking a finger. You couldn't hear the words; you couldn't miss their meaning. The young redhead listened for a time and then, still very poised, got up, stretched, and slowly and very gracefully reattached her top.

"Oh, brava! Brava!" Alix called out quietly. "Very deftly done, both!"

"Both?" Bandar asked in confusion.

"Yes," said Her Ladyship, "the girl not debating the point but taking her time and giving you chaps a bit of a show. And the blue-haired lady doing what blue-haired ladies at clubs like the Maidstone are supposed to do. She defended the status quo ante."

"But she left the French girl alone? Who is also topless."

"That, too, demonstrates a keen appreciation of the world. American girls go topless to create a stir; French girls because it's their nature." She paused, then:

"We English are sort of in a muddle about the whole business . . ."

"Mmm," said Bando, whose mother was a Brit. And then we all went down to the ocean and dove in and swam for a while, both of us trying to get Alix to shed her top but not awfully convincing at it.

We dined that night at the Maidstone Club, just Her Ladyship and me. Not that we were alone, of course. Not in an East Hampton July. We wore evening clothes and drove over to the club at dusk in her borrowed Aston-Martin with the top down, which of course scored points with the fresh-faced Irish lads from Dublin or Trinity University they took on each summer to caddy and park cars, and members went out of their way to say hello. That was Alix, of course; I was hardly a club novelty and she looked smashing in a rose velvet long dress with silver beading by a designer I'd never heard of but by whom she swore: Badgley Mischka. We began with martinis in the bar amid the usual red-faced golfers boasting of their play, and their patient, nineteenth-hole wives. "They don't know how fortunate they are," Alix said, "only four hours for a round of golf. Cricket goes on all bloody day including tea." It was the usual Friday evening summer drill and out on the ocean side of the big old clubhouse down by the pool, they had an orchestra playing for dinner dancing. Alix's dress was slinky, held up, barely, with spaghetti straps. She felt wonderful in my arms and the music was of the sort even I danced to reasonably well. Which *was* a novelty.

"Stuff and nonsense!" she said. "You're a smashing dancer. So much better than . . . well, most chaps."

I hated it when she reminded me there *were* other chaps. But then again, she was here with me, wasn't she, and not with them. I held her a bit closer now and I knew she liked that, even without being told. With Alix, body language had always been fluent. There was a pretty good moon, lacking a day or two of being full, and beyond the pool and the orchestra and the cabanas out there across the narrow strand of beach you could see the waves coming in, the low surf metronomic, measured, and the moon glinting on the water all the way out as far as the night horizon where the black sky and the black Atlantic merged into one.

"Has there ever been anything this good?" I asked, exaggerating in typical Chamber of Commerce fashion, feeling my drink and pleased to be here. And with her.

"Well, actually, at Cap d'Antibes there's a terrace like this at the Hotel du Cap. They've nice music as well."

Mmm. Try to top that, Yank. So I didn't. Just asked, "Happy?"

"Oh yes, quite," she said. "You?"

I leaned down to kiss her on the mouth. Yes, I was happy. How could I not be? Yet, how unreal it all was. By this time tomorrow night we'd be at Sag Lodge, with a plan even I found difficult to explain or defend.

"Oh, bosh!" Alix scoffed when I expressed doubt. "Think of it as the Island of Lost Boys with Prince Fatoosh playing silly old incompetent Captain Hook and Jesse as the entire tribe of Indians and Mr. Glique as Tinker Bell, whilst you and Bando and darling Mr. Roark do star turns as Peter Pan . . ."

"And you?"

"I'll be Wendy, mother to all the lost boys."

And a super one at that, I'd wager, even if it was a bit difficult to think of Her Ladyship as maternal.

Dinner was on the terraces and even in July it can be chilly out there, especially if there's wind off the ocean. But it was a still night and dry and so that, too, was fine, and women went without wraps. Good omens? I hoped so. And on the strength of it, ordered a second bottle of a nice Saint-Estephe, a Chateau Meyney '93, to accompany the rare rack of lamb.

Alix touched the fresh glass to mine. "Eat, drink and be merry, for tomorrow . . ."

". . . we liberate the Lost Boys," I finished up.

"That's the spirit, Beecher Stowe. We'll have no long faces or gloomy outlooks here."

Cheered by her courage and with the orchestra returned from a break, we danced again and then repaired for a final time to the bar where we found Fillmore, a member of the club's bar committee. He was heir to a synthetic rayon fortune and had never worked a day in his life, so we permitted Fillmore to stand us a very decent port, over which he spent his time attempting to look down the front of Alix's dress. Young Bill Ford was there, who runs Ford Motor. He and Alix got into a knowledgeable discussion of famous British cars while young Ms. Ford and I listened. I don't know about her but I was impressed.

"What's significant," Alix was saying, "is how many of the truly grand marques are gone forever. I mean, it's splendid that your family's company owns Jaguar and Aston-Martin and are doing a good job with them. Just as BMW is running Rolls and Rover and even our dear, dashing little MGs. But recall how many of our cars have vanished: Allard and Morris and the Riley and Austin-Healey and Wolseley and Triumph. Remember the TR3?"

"Her Ladyship's grasp; she's astonishing," Mr. Ford informed me in an aside.

"Yes, I know."

As we left old Fillmore followed us to the door, wanting one final glimpse of her nipples, I guess.

"He's a poppet," she informed me as we waited for our car to be brought up. "I love randy old chaps who don't permit the burden of years to get in the way."

And I love it when Alix talks dirty. She drove as well if not better than I did and hadn't drunk as much so she took the wheel of the Aston-Martin and we sped home under a clouded moon. And when we got home and I'd put up the roof of the car against the morning's dew, we got undressed and went to bed and did something about it.

I didn't sleep right away but lay there for a time regarding the ceiling and thinking about my old man on the Silk Road to Bukhara. God, I hoped it was going to work out okay. Next to me, Alix moved lazily in her sleep. She was a strange, funny, gorgeous young woman from a distinguished family, the daughter of an earl, graduate of one of the great universities, and a representative of *The Times* of London. And she and I had been in and out of love for three years now. At least, *I* had been.

Or that was my take on it. And not beating it to death but only very happy that she was here.

Dawn. Uh-oh. I was up just after six and summer was hiding itself. There was no sun and a thin rain was falling. A real rain would cause Plimpton to postpone tonight's fireworks until next weekend and our entire scheme relied on there being fireworks. So I called George.

"Not a bit of it, old sport," he reassured me. "Clearing by noon, that's what I hear."

To be certain, I phoned Jesse. "The Weather Channel says clearing, Beech." When Alix finally woke and wandered sleepily into the kitchen and paused, frowning, as she regarded the rain running down our windows, I told her Jesse predicted clearing.

"Oh, good! There's a chap who knows his weather."

I made the coffee while she showered. When she came out, still dripping, toweling her hair but not anything else, leaving the rest of her shiny and slick, Alix asked what I thought she ought to wear.

"Well, right now, nothing."

So we went back to bed and tumbled about pleasantly, if damply, for a while and then she repeated the question, "I meant, for later. For D-day."

"Oh?" I said innocently, kissing her into silence but hardly discouraging her from doing other things besides talk.

t w e n t y - n i n e

"Sharks, electric eels, giant squid, manta rays. You never know with the ocean."

Were we being ridiculous? Was our scheme, this entire business absurd?

Of course.

Just as absurd as the reality that a renegade Saudi billionaire named bin Laden could be at this very moment sitting cross-legged on a rug somewhere in Asia spinning plots that had our FBI and CIA on high alert, the NYPD mobilized, U.S. embassies everywhere in a state of siege, my old Dad poking about Third World backwaters in disguise, American Cruise missiles blowing up aspirin factories in the Sudan, and flights of Stealth fighters roaring in to shoot hell out of a single, fly-blown goatskin tent in the mountains of the Hindu Kush.

Not to put too fine a point on it, but if we were nuts, and we probably were, then we were hardly alone.

Our rendezvous was at the marina of Three Mile Harbor. The rain was over, the sky clearing, higher and bluer, with sun now and steam rising from the wet roads and walks. Score one for Plimpton.

"I just *knew* it would clear," Alix told me, having her own experts. "Jesse and the Weather Channel, you can count on chaps like that."

Bly was to be there by two. Being Saturday the joggers came padding along Three Mile Harbor Road, pretty girls and slim young men sprinting and heavier runners laboring, and people with bad legs barely making a walker's pace. The fishermen were long up and about and the boaters as well. Saturdays out here at the harbor in summer are bustling and nice, really fine. Sammy Glique, nervy once more, wasn't so sure.

"We could turn back, y'know. Pay off Captain Bly and go back to Lily Pond Lane. A nice pool party of our very own. Dixie could call the Barefoot Contessa. A picnic on the lawn. We have white wine, French vintages. Also non-vintage for people who prefer. Who am I to impose my own tastes on others? Lars and the covergirls, calling out 'Hi Ho!' The girls topless, perhaps. They're adults; I say nothing. George Plimpton could preview tonight's fireworks . . ."

We'd considered black tie, in harmony with the protesters outside the gates, but decided that was a bit much. The women were in their summer dresses, the men tieless in linen or cotton jackets, but for Piano in a business suit. Sammy, very jumpy, rattled on, to no effect, breaking off only as Jesse arrived with the pickup truck, VooVoo Vronsky, and Congressman Portofino in black and white saddle shoes, gaudily striped broadcloth pajamas, and . . .

"Oh, my God!" I heard one of the passing joggers say as they helped Buzzy down from the pickup, the laptop computer nestled carefully in his arms, a vast birdcage enclosing his head and neck, bolted securely to football shoulder pads worn outside the pajama top. The cage was too bulky to fit inside the cab so they'd had to transport the convalescent in the truck bed.

"Careful, there," Jesse called. "Don't jar the goddamned thing."

VooVoo had a longbow slung over one shoulder and a quiver of arrows hung behind.

"For the archery contest. And just in case," she said ominously, "for them bastids. Crossbows is shit. If you don't believe a Ukrainian, ask the Olympic committee."

I was armed as well. When I tossed my old canvas golf bag with its rusty MacGregor irons into the Blazer, Alix had given me an arch look. "Well, now, isn't that clever, Beecher. If there's a lull in the proceedings, you can get in a few holes."

"I might," I said, ignoring the sarcasm. The miniature golf mentioned on the invitation gave me only a slim rationale for lugging a set of clubs. But listen, you hit somebody upside the head with a nine iron, you get his attention.

Wolfie was staying behind ("I have scripts to read") but she drove Piano to the dock. "Be careful, Signor," she cautioned him. "And watch out for Sammy. You know how reckless he gets when the blood is up."

Glique heard that. And secretly was pleased. Not five minutes before he'd been weaseling his way out. Now he was being accused of recklessness. Dixie went to him, sliding her youthful body against his and grinding a bit.

"Oh, dahlin'," she said, pointedly looking down at him, "y'all gettin' aroused befoh we even set sail?"

"Well . . ." he said modestly.

Lars came up in his own car, a Volvo. "Hi Ho!" he called out.

Glique, casting about for another excuse to stay home, swiftly forgot about becoming aroused.

"Lars, the covergirls. Is it wise to leave them alone on a Saturday in summer? There are so many renters out. Summer people. As much as I'd hate to miss out on our little cruise, perhaps I should stay behind . . ."

Then a second Swedish car pulled up, a Saab. The covergirls, this latest batch Americans, Kay and May. Or vice versa. Either way, they were minimally if attractively clad in pastel dresses.

"Oh," Sammy said, deflated.

You're either a fighter or you're not, have the instinct for this sort of craziness or you don't. Bandar had it. Sammy didn't; that was obvious. Did Dixie? Lars? VooVoo, for all her bellicose talk? Well, we'd soon find out. Alix had it. So did Jesse. So did I.

No great credit to me. Credit genes. Credit the Admiral. I knew that when you got into a fight, you went all out to win. Not to make a respectable showing. But to *win!* We were going to need determination to penetrate mysterious Sag Lodge, cobras or no cobras.

Portofino poked at me, breaking into my reverie and holding up his laptop. "Have the good grace to explain to Prince Fatoosh why I'm not properly dressed. Whatever mischief the man may be up to, I don't want him to think me rude." It didn't occur to him that in addition to the pajamas, I might have to explain the birdcage.

When Captain Bly hove into view we all set up a little cheer. I think it was less to welcome Bly than to dissipate our own doubts. But he took it as his due and gave us a blast of his foghorn in response. When he was secured to the dock, Congressman Portofino was helped aboard first.

"Now what in hell is that?" Bly asked, seeing Buzzy's birdcage.

"A protective device," I said. "The Congressman threw out his neck." I thought it best not to mention arrow attacks. Who knew how skittish a sober Bly might be? Later on, after we'd gotten some beer into him, well, that would be different. But as soon as Buzzy was settled into a fighting chair on the stern, strapped in for safety, one of those chairs charter boats use for hooking and landing billfish, he resumed tapping out directives on the old laptop.

"I assume everyone here is cleared by security. Eyes only, top secret, that sort of thing."

I nodded solemnly. "I'm quite sure, Congressman." My, but he was a stickler.

"Even Glique?" he tapped out.

"He was the first one vetted," I lied.

Since our little band included an Arab prince in exile, a Native American who made his living as a poacher, a Ukrainian archery champ, a British milady, the promiscuous Lars and two models, Sammy and his paramour, a Lebanese merchant banker addressed in Italian as "Signor," and a working journalist, Buzzy was taking a good deal on faith. And I don't even include Roark, a man who once blew up an entire housing project because he didn't like the window boxes.

"That fella in the birdcage," Bly whispered to Jesse and me, "what in hell's he typing on that machine?"

"He's a member of Congress. Working on legislation. Don't mind him, Captain."

"A member of the maritime committee, is he?"

"I wouldn't be surprised," I said, which seemed to impress Bly.

"Them sons-a-bitches," he muttered, but from then on kept his distance from Buzzy.

But then, of course, for all of Bly's ignorance, was I much better informed? There were things Portofino might know, with his demon subcommittee investigative staff, things about the Middle East which even now I can't reveal and didn't suspect then, about the Rose Manteau and its significance to global economies, the oil glut, Israeli-Palestinian peace talks, and possibly even a 10,000 on the Dow.

It was time to shove off. No Howard Roark, no Madame Rand, and most vitally, no Prince Bandar the Gentle. Second thoughts? No, the plan was for Roark and Bando to arrive overland, sneaking onto the property and then, when the fireworks went off, for a few of us to enter Sag Lodge and make our way upstairs to the forbidden wing. That was the plan; we weren't issuing warranties.

I nodded to Bly. "Okay, Captain. Let's go."

Glique interrupted my ponderings, "Why didn't we bring guns? For self-protection only, of course."

"The Ladies Village Improvement Society doesn't permit them," I explained.

"Don't you worry, friend Glique," VooVoo said. "I put an arrow through your right eye at a hundred meters if need be."

"No, no," Sammy said hurriedly, as Dixie hastened to intervene, thrusting her body between his and VooVoo's arrow, "not at all necessary. I promise you."

There was a flat sea and little wind and with the sun high in the sky, we now went into our pre-scripted relaxation mode. At top speed, Captain Bly could have gotten us off Sag Pond in a couple of hours. No rush, I wanted to hit the beach about six. And I wanted everyone relaxed. Bly didn't mind; he was being paid by the hour and not the nautical mile. Besides, he liked the look of Lars's covergirls and was hoping for a little sunbathing. "Hi Ho!" Lars called out.

Once we were through the Shinnecock Canal and out on the ocean with a cooling breeze, the sea kicked up. Not badly, just a swell and the wake of other boats. "I wish we could swim," Alix said. "It looks lovely."

Sammy didn't think so. "That's what pools are for. The ocean? Forget it. Sharks, electric eels, manta rays. You never know in the ocean. Dixie, don't sit on the rail. Killer whales. Giant squid. Surely you'll recall *Reap the Wild Wind.* Ray Milland, John Wayne, a giant squid and Paulette Goddard. Portuguese men-of-war, perhaps. Who knows? Piano, keep an eye out."

"Sammy, Ah've been swimmin' in bayous with cottonmouths and gatuhs. Don't y'all fret, honey."

No one was going topless and Bly scowled. What the hell kind of charter was this?

"Have a beer, Captain," I urged him.

"Good idea," he grunted.

There was an excellent snack catered by the Barefoot Contessa and now the

wicker hamper was laid open. Cold half chickens, shelled shrimp, lobster may-
onnaise, smoked salmon, a very decent pâté, Carr's water biscuits, salads and a
cheese platter. Two cases of wine, a chilled Moulin-à-Vent and a nice young
Graves '96, Haut la Croix, several cases of Coors and one of Evian. Signor Piano played sommelier, sniffing the corks, pouring the vintages. Bly's eyes
widened. All this but no topless girls? Except that the drink was better, he
might as well be taking out a party of beer-drinking Irishmen going after
mako.

"Beecher," Alix said, "will you do my shoulders, please."

After lunch some of us dozed off. The food, the sun, the wine, the smear-
ing on of sunblock. You tire easily. You dream of covergirls. You dream . . . of
Alix.

"Hey, wake up!" It was Captain Bly, kicking me.

"What?" I said grouchily, not fully alert.

"Crazy people, all of you. Bows and arrows. Men in birdcages. Anyway,
we're offshore of Sagaponack. Only four-thirty. You want to go in now or wait
a bit?"

"Wait till six."

The sooner we went ashore, the sooner we solved the mystery of Sag
Lodge, the sooner I might get my old man safely home. But he'd taught me
patience, timing; you couldn't rush things. We lay a mile offshore, close
enough to see trees and a tall antenna and the towers of buildings under construction but too far out to see individuals. We really had plenty of time to
kill. I tried to be patient and recalled my own advice—two or three hours of
cocktails, then, when darkness falls, when Plimpton sets off his fireworks . . .
Not much of a plan but it's the only plan we had.

Lars and the covergirls were still taking the sun, drinking wine. They had
their ways; I had mine. Signor Piano mopped his pale face with a silk square
and VooVoo was examining arrows closely, including this one as acceptable
and discarding another as not.

Buzzy Portofino remained mute. I mean, he wasn't even tapping out messages on the laptop. Though, inside the birdcage as he was, it was difficult to
read his expression, discern his mood. Had he suffered a relapse? After all,
this was his most extensive outing since being wounded. Perhaps he'd attempted too much. That's all we needed, Congressman Portofino expiring on
our hands.

It was at this moment that his computer began receiving a message. Buzzy, roused from drowsiness, sat up straight and bent over the screen, tapped out his own comment and held the screen up for me to see.

"It's all rubbish!" I said. "Some fool transmitting nonsense. Damned hackers!"

He snatched the computer back in elation to write:

"Shows how bright you are, Stowe. That's not rubbish. And it's not a hacker. That's my agent on the ground transmitting from behind enemy lines in official Alien and Sedition subcommittee code!"

thirty

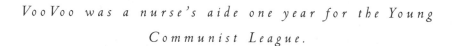

*VooVoo was a nurse's aide one year for the Young
Communist League.*

By now we were all awake, Alix looking even lovelier after her nap. It was nearly five and all around us, the fishing fleet headed back in, and along with them, small runabouts and fast cigarette boats, some towing water skiers, and, slower and more stately, sailboats large and small from the usual Saturday regatta. The sea was really getting up now with a breeze and another line of craft, including a handful of authentic yachts, floating gin palaces, leaving the harbors, heading out to party at sea with a distant, but clear and unobstructed, view of Plimpton's fireworks across there at Boys Harbor. One fleet returning, another setting out. Crisscrossing wakes, an afternoon chop, boating chaos, and cocktail hour combining to kick up a fuss.

I'd earlier agreed to indemnify Bly for any damage and, on his demand, now handed over a handwritten statement to that effect witnessed and, in fact, notarized by Signor Piano.

"I always take along my notary public stamp and pad," Piano explained shyly. "You never know when a document is called for." The little man didn't seem himself, though, and as he stowed away his notary's kit, he again mopped his round face.

Bly was to drop us on the beach and anchor overnight just over the horizon, returning at dawn to pick us up.

"Sure," he said. "I get it. Don't worry. I'll be there."

Sober, I wanted to say. And didn't. He was surly but he was a good skipper and this was a reliable boat and it might be our only way out. I didn't want to lose him to a wisecrack, didn't want to be on the beach tomorrow morning with Fatoosh and the Rosy Companions in hot pursuit, and no boat.

I was less patient with Buzzy Portofino. When I queried him, he turned back to the laptop.

"I regret," he typed out for me, "that security requires I not identify my agent to a civilian. And a journalist at that."

"Yeah, sure." The damnable part of it was we needed Buzzy, too. He controlled the "agent" in Fatoosh's camp; his was the laptop with which he kept in touch. Behind the bars of the birdcage I tried to see if he was enjoying himself. All I could tell for sure was that the wig was again askew.

Sammy, seeing Buzzy's wig, cheered up. But almost instantly sobered.

"Piano, you look terrible. Are there problems? Gas? What can I do? A Fernet Branca, perhaps?"

Signor Piano, it turned out, was seasick. The water all day had been so flat, the wind nonexistent, he'd felt perfectly fine until now.

"It's traffic. All those boats going by," Jesse suggested, "kicking up a wake."

"But we're anchored; aren't even moving," Sammy said. True, but Bly's boat was rising and falling in the chop.

"You better give him a bucket," Bly shouted from the wheel, where he was checking gauges and pushing control buttons. "We'll be moving again soon. Don't want puke on the deck. People slip and fall down. Smells up the place, too."

"Maybe we could wait until he feels himself again," Sammy suggested.

"Not if you want to be ashore by six," Bly said. "Make up your goddamned minds."

"Po' Signor," Dixie murmured.

As we got underway, the water really did kick up.

"Let's distract him," Alix said. "Get his mind off the ocean."

"That's thoughtful, Your Ladyship," Glique said. "You notice, it wasn't the

Congressman who came up with a sensible idea like that, but a foreigner. An Englishwoman."

"Distractions? Like what?" I asked. "Doesn't anyone have a seasick remedy?"

"Don't use that word!" Sammy hissed at me but it was too late. Poor Piano was retching again.

"The bucket!" Bly shouted. The mate shoved it at Piano, just below his nose. It was an old bait bucket and stank of tired, rotten chum. When Piano held it, he recoiled, retching anew. I wasn't sure it was quite the ticket for a queasy stomach.

"A distraction. What kind, I have no idea," Glique put in. "Anything to take his mind off, well, you know. Stowe, you're a writer. Do a reading. Recite. One of the sonnets. Piano! Stowe is going to tell a story. Take your mind off . . . Go ahead, Stowe."

Signor Piano groaned and then retched. I stepped back hurriedly; I guess we all did, not wanting to be splashed.

"That poor bastid," VooVoo said. "Where's the bucket? I was nurse's aide one year for the Young Communist League. Before Gorbachev."

I started talking, didn't matter what: "Piano, you know Scott Fitzgerald once wrote copy for an ad agency?"

The signor groaned, speech, apparently, beyond him. While I pressed ahead:

"Yes, and it's entirely possible that if he succeeded at it, he would have been another David Ogilvy. A Doyle, Dane, Bernbach. A Leo Burnett, and would never have written the great American novel."

Piano groaned. "I didn't know that," Sammy said. "So what happened?"

"He was fired."

"But why? Such a writer," Sammy said. "You'd think, for commercials, a natural."

"They put him on a chocolate account," I said. "Are you listening to this, Piano? I'm telling this story for your benefit."

He retched once more and we all, yet again, prudently stepped back.

"Did the story need to have food in it?" Glique protested.

"Look, then *you* tell a story. I'm doing my best."

"So go ahead. Tell us what happened," Glique said again, loving a good narrative. Even one with food.

"He turned in a piece of copy about the chocolate, Nestlé or Hershey or whatever, and got fired."

"So? What was the line? The line that turned Scott Fitzgerald to writing novels instead of ads?"

"'Rich and dark / Like the Aga Khan.'"

No one seemed to think it was very funny.

"Okay, okay. Someone else tell him a story." I don't beat my head against walls.

Bly shouted, "I see them bubbles again. Frogmen, like the last time. You want me to turn back? Or run them over? I could run them bastards down, y'know."

VooVoo dashed belligerently to the rail. "Show me. I'll give them bubbles, I'll give them frogmen!"

She had her longbow poised with a lethal-looking arrow notched and ready.

"Hi Ho!" Lars called out, shepherding the covergirls to the rail. It was the Viking in him; they enjoyed a little blood in the water.

"Hold on," Jesse cautioned. "Could be some local spearfisherman. Don't want to send an arrow through some poor clamdigger from Springs. I got enough grief already from the rednecks. Just empty Piano's slop bucket on top of them . . ."

Buzzy now resumed typing, very perturbed.

"What's he got now? Another message from his agent on the ground?"

Jesse took the laptop. "No, he says, 'Can someone give me a Kleenex? My nose is running.'"

"Piano is dying and he's worried about a runny nose," Glique said cuttingly.

"Here," VooVoo said expansively, slinging her longbow and whipping open the little door in the front of the birdcage, "Use my hankie. It's fresh from this morning. No snot. Almost clean."

She pushed it through the aperture and against Portofino's nose. He gave a loud, honking sound and she wiped vigorously.

"Nothing like a good blow," she said, retrieving her handkerchief and slamming the cage door shut again. "Clears the head, the mucus membranes. I was a nurse once, I told you, no?"

"A nurse's aide, you said," Glique protested.

"And who the hell are you, Dr. Schweitzer?"

Sammy looked hurt.

"She bites off my head, and for what? Am I questioning credentials? That's for the state boards. I was simply trying to clarify her medical background . . ."

Piano retched once more.

Having blown Buzzy's nose, VooVoo turned back to Signor Piano. "Here, Piano, the swill bucket. Keep holding that bastid right under your face. Believe me, I know such cases. One time in Kiev me and two garage mechanics took out a guy's appendix without anesthetic. The blood, you couldn't believe. The screaming. But a week later, up and about . . ."

Piano threw up again.

"Good, good, it settles the stomach. I tell you other operations I seen. Frostbite damage, you know, drunks fall asleep in the snow outside the bars. A lot of that in Kiev. Amputations. The flesh blackened and falling off . . ."

"Aaaagh!" Piano cried in agony.

"Do what she advises, Piano," Sammy hissed. "We don't want trouble with these people."

"Beach comin' up pretty soon," Bly called out. "Remind him to puke in the bucket . . ."

Hearing the expression, Piano again retched.

"Captain," Sammy pleaded. "The man has a sensitive stomach. Please . . ."

There was a pair of field glasses, 6x35, and I scanned the landing beach. "All clear so far," I said. Jesse had good eyes and he took a turn with the glasses and handed them back to Bly.

"Looks okay to me, Beech. Captain, you see anyone?"

"A goddamned lion! Is this crazy? Lions?" It occurred to me that even the phlegmatic Bly was beginning to sound surreal.

"Yes, we know about the lion, Captain. It's a pet," Alix said.

In the excitement over Piano and blowing Buzzy's nose, the frogmen were forgotten.

Jesse had armed himself with bow and quiver of arrows. "Be sure to check your windage, Jesse," VooVoo told him. "Goddamned wind, that's the enemy of the bowman. Blow a good shot right off the goddamned bull's-eye, you don't compensate. I tell all my students, watch the wind. Spit a few times for to gauge. Wind can be a bastid, I swear to Christ."

"Spit a few times," Sammy repeated. "I'll try to remember that when I'm out there in the backyard with my bow and arrow set. I'm always missing the bull's-eye."

I handed out golf irons, not bothering to issue instructions about windage. "Just swing hard," I suggested when people looked quizzical.

"Hi Ho!" said Lars, hefting a four iron. Seeing the beach coming up fast, Kay and May ran to the rail in their wispy minidresses. Bly watched. He wished he'd seen them two topless, how they bounced. A good leg show was okay, too . . .

"Beecher," Alix said, "do you really intend taking those golf clubs ashore? This is a cocktail party we're attending."

"For the miniature golf competition. Don't worry."

"Here, Jesse," Bly called out. "You and them fellers grab aholt of the Zodiac. The beach is shoaling up here and I don't want to go aground."

We were wrestling with the Zodiac and the outboard motor when Jesse looked up.

"Hear that?" he said.

"What?"

"There it is," he called out, excitement in his voice. "A big chopper, coming in fast."

I could see it now, too. Kay and May started to wave. They looked very nice waving. Captain Bly licked his lips.

Right on time, I thought. Just as my father said, Saturday. I was thinking that up there in that gleaming silver helicopter might be the sacred relic Bandar lost, and for which he'd been banished: the Rose Manteau, once more so close to hand. He and Roark would be somewhere nearby, close enough to see the chopper. Bando must be excited; he'd waited so long and searched so hard.

The chopper was big and shiny silver as it banked over the little cove where Bly was about to land us. May and Kay were still waving and Alix and Dixie had now joined in. I wondered if that's why the chopper was lower, and who could blame them? But it was only coming in to land, over there near Sag Lodge, with its suite of rooms no one had penetrated. Not even Martha Stewart.

As the chopper vanished over land, screened by trees, I looked at Alix.

"Did you see the lettering?"

"Did I not."

ARABUS OIL. The silver chopper, which might be carrying the most sacred relic in Arabia, belonged to Chapman Offshore Wells. Just a few weeks back he'd been on the cover of *Business Week* for his efforts to corner mineral rights in the Gulf. And had earlier been named Man of the Year by John Huey at *Fortune.*

"Hi Ho," called Lars.

As *Fortune*'s Man of the Year came in for a rendezvous with Fatoosh the Malevolent, who might shortly be in a position to barter those same mineral rights for the Rose Manteau and, perhaps, a throne.

thirty-one

There she was, dancing a sedate fox-trot . . .

"I'm going ashore, too," Signor Piano announced as we loaded one by one into the Zodiac. Jesse and I were holding it steady and fending it off slightly to keep from banging against Bly's boat as each of us in turn stepped down.

"Now, Piano, don't be rash," Glique said.

"Better death than mal de mer," the signor replied. I helped him into the smaller boat on unsteady legs.

"Thank you," he said.

"Nothing. Just didn't want to lose you overboard."

"No," he said, "I meant about trying to distract me. I rather liked that Scott Fitzgerald story."

"Oh."

Kay and May climbed in ahead of Lars who was bringing along a couple of bottles of Dom Pérignon.

"Hi Ho," he called out, holding one bottle above his head in greeting.

"Right you are," I told him, not knowing quite what else to say and wondering what help he and the covergirls were going to be in the inevitable confrontation with the forces of Fatoosh. As if reading my mind, the two girls quickly reached out helpful arms to guide poor Congressman Portofino, and his birdcage, into the Zodiac.

"That's well done," I said. "Keep an eye on him, one on each side. He'll need a hand."

Buzzy rapped out a snappy retort.

"What does he say?" I asked.

May (or Kay) read it off:

"'Just watch yourself, Stowe. Representative Portofino, R., N.Y., will do his duty, thank you very much.'"

"Okay," I said, snapping off a mock salute. Behind the bars of the cage you couldn't tell from the famous Buzzy grimace if he was happy or in pain.

By the time we slid up onto the beach and stepped out into the shallows, Bly was already pulling away, not bothering to wave or wish us luck. Buzzy's computer was rattling once more. He tapped out a message of his own:

"There'll be a welcoming committee shortly. Including a sedan chair."

What in hell? Was he receiving messages from his "agent on the ground"? When I asked he gave away nothing, only shook his head in irritation, the birdcage rattling with its little door swinging open, then slamming shut. It looked as if his nose was running again. Jesse came up. I told him there might be people headed this way.

"Okay, Beech. Now you better let me and VooVoo take the point. We got them bows and arrows and can move fast if there's trouble. I'll signal back if we see anyone."

"Sounds good. You, Kay, close the birdcage, please."

"I'm May. Does he need another Kleenex?"

But before we could set off, just as Buzzy predicted, here came the "welcoming committee," a dozen Arabs trotting up and bowing. Their leader beckoned Congressman Portofino to a waiting chair borne by four huskies. I left it to May to give Buzzy's nose a final wipe and then we were off. The chopper must have landed. You couldn't mistake the sound of its big engine, a sound that had faded to nothing.

We stepped out at a good pace, off the beach and into the woods. The sun was still very high but once we were among the trees, the visibility fell off a bit. Jesse and VooVoo, the athlete, moved quietly. Piano stumbled about and Kay and May, flanking Buzzy, tut-tutted aloud when branches whipped across or snagged his cage. Then Jesse came jogging back to us.

"Almost there. I can hear music." My hand tightened on the nine iron, just in case. Then, unexpectedly, there was this tall, orange-haired old man, in overalls and a carpenter's apron, shaking hands and laughing and slapping backs, palavering at a great rate with the Arabs. "I have my own ways," Howard Roark said, gripping my hand. "I drove over and talked my way in. The guards and these fellows know me from the construction gangs. Cocktails are already being served and your pal, who shall go nameless, is safely on the property and resting easy in a hidey-hole I worked up in the piney woods."

I made the introductions. Stuffed into the carpenter's apron were a dozen or so sticks of what looked to me like dynamite. Lars and the covergirls celebrated our reinforcement. "Hi Ho!" Lars said, and passed around the final bottle of Dom and we all had a swig. May (or Kay) thoughtfully opened Buzzy's birdcage door and held the bottle to his lips.

"My, but he's a gritty fellow, isn't he. Game as sand."

"I'll say," Kay (or May) agreed.

Roark had vanished, swiftly as he'd come, back into the forest. I looked at my watch. Just after six. Three hours to go. So much depended on George Plimpton, his fireworks, and his punctuality. You had faith in a Harvard man, of course, but there were so many variables. His watch could be off. Or the fuses damp. Full night was at nine and it would be then that George would ignite his pyrotechnics. You could count on Plimpton, I kept telling myself, count on Wasp precision.

Buzzy was typing again and one of the covergirls handed me the laptop.

"They're celebrating already. Do you hear the music?" his message read.

And what seemed to be laughter. Or could it be bawdy behavior? Would Buzzy's agent reveal himself? Was he an Arab? Maybe one of Offshore's Texans? So far, his intelligence had been spot-on accurate. But just who was he? And then we were there, out of the woods and onto the great lawn fronting mysterious Sag Lodge. And on a grand patio just beyond and elevated slightly above the vast lawn, there was indeed a party in progress, but too distant to discern yet just who was partying. If only we'd thought to bring binoculars. Or steal Bly's. Behind me there was a small commotion. When I wheeled to caution against alarming our escort, there was plumply elegant little Signor Piano, in his double-breasted pinstriped suit, his highly polished black wingtips from Church's slightly scuffed, but his face and color far more cheery, hissing at me and handing up a tiny, mother-of-pearl set of opera glasses.

"Here, Stowe, I never go anywhere without opera glasses. You never know, do you, when a last-minute ticket to La Scala is coming available. They're small but the lenses are excellent quality."

I thanked him warmly and handed up the glasses to Jesse, who surely had the keenest eyes.

"Mmm," Jesse Maine said. "That's queer."

"What? What?" Before Jesse could respond to me, there was another, louder commotion just to our rear. Distracted, I spun about to see Buzzy beckoning from his sedan chair, typing, and then shoving the laptop at me.

"I'll want those field glasses now, please. My agent may well be signaling me. And at considerable personal risk, I might remind you."

I looked at him. "They're opera glasses and you can't use them wearing that birdcage."

"Undo the shoulder bolts," he typed. "We can fit it back on after I've had a look."

As Dixie and Alix attempted to get the birdcage unfastened, I growled at Buzzy.

"Just be damned careful you don't alert them to our intentions. We don't want casualties, y'know."

The cage finally off his head, Buzzy typed a response.

"You've already got casualties, remember?" At which he motioned to his arrow wounds.

Jesse cleared his throat. "You have to admit, Beecher, the Congressman's got a point."

Buzzy stared for a time at the lodge and grounds, then at the messy confusion of the gigantic construction site beyond, with its half-finished buildings clearly visible, before finally handing the glasses back.

"Anything?" I asked.

He tapped out a response on the laptop:

"Hmm."

Very helpful. I got "Mmm" from Jesse and "Hmm" from Congressman Portofino. As the women reattached Buzzy's headwear, I focused the glasses and panned across the field below.

There were Japanese lanterns, festive hangings and elaborate trappings of various sorts, with urchins tossing paper streamers, long tables set with white linen and what seemed decent flatware and cutlery, dinnerware and crystal, the tables laden with what would turn out to be dishes of canapés, salads, finger foods, oysters and caviars. As well as with Kuwaiti specialties, delicious figs, coconut meat and succulent dates, hearts of palm and ripe persimmons, pitchers of warm goat's milk, and candied locust, an especial treat. Other tables offered bottles of wine from promising Long Island vintages, chosen by Fatoosh himself to encourage local vintners and earn neighborhood popularity. Even at a distance you could smell meats charring pungently on Weber grills burning mesquite charcoal, beyond which a lackey tapped a keg of Miller Lite and other small boys absentmindedly threw handfuls of confetti. All this to entertain and serve fewer than a hundred people, half of them in Kuwaiti dress, a dozen or so westerners, sporting stetsons and cowboy boots, and a mere handful of folk who looked, at least vaguely, as if they might belong in the Hamptons. To the left of Sag Lodge, a sports field with miniature golf and targets set up, beyond which a path led down to the marina with its small craft, all bright work and mahogany. To the right, the silver chopper belonging to Wells's petroleum consortium, hard by a blacktopped parking area with off-road ATVs, one Hummer, three Rollses, and a couple of trucks and run-of-the-mill stretch limos. Plus a few cars that might belong to guests.

A small orchestra, five or six men in brocaded livery (though oddly, barefoot), had set up on the patio, backed by a quartet of veiled women, quite fat. Servants passed around trays of drinks (their best clients were the Texans). Any number of men, including Prince Fatoosh the Malevolent, took turns dancing, some pairings of men dancing with men, plus a few more traditional couples, but all of them sedately, to a series of fox-trots. The affair was hardly the debauched orgy I'd half expected, but more reminiscent of a freshman mixer at a land grant college in the Midwest.

"Oh look, Beecher," Alix called out. "Isn't that our old acquaintance Wyseman Clagett? The fellow with the terrifying facial tic?"

"Indeed it is."

From here you could hear the music ("Smoke Gets in Your Eyes" and "Thanks for the Memories" were especial favorites) and also the laughter, some of it sounding forced. The orchestra's attention span seemed quite brief, for after some forty-five seconds of a fox-trot they lapsed into what I took to be a traditional Kuwaiti dirge, at which a woman of truly extraordinary girth (even fatter than the quartet) waddled out to ululate in the most horrible fashion. Then, with an encouraging pat on the buttocks from the orchestra leader, the singer waddled off, as another fox-trot started up.

It was my turn now to "Hmm" and "Mmm" a bit when Sammy, who'd come up to my side, poked me.

"Dixie wants to know when we're going to the party. She and the covergirls want to go to the powder room, you know, to freshen up."

What I really fretted about was that I hadn't yet seen Punjab and the Asp. The partyers were doing what partyers did; they were getting drunk. It made me uneasy that Punjab and the Asp were not among them: that twosome, sober, impressed me as more dangerous than a score of Bedouin and Texan drunks.

Buzzy had to have his say. "Sag Lodge," he tapped out. "My agent confirms the second floor is the sanctum sanctorum."

VooVoo cursed. "English is bad enough. Now you got to speak French, too?"

"It's Latin," I explained. "Means 'the holy of holies.'"

"Oh, them bastids," said VooVoo. "That's different."

The Rose Manteau? I wondered. Had Offshore Wells already delivered it into the hands of Fatoosh? Was the sacred treasure heavily guarded (Punjab? the Asp?) in that second-floor suite no one, not even Mario Buatta, had been allowed to penetrate? Was it *not* a topping off but the icon's arrival we were about to help the Malevolent celebrate with champagne and fox-trots?

t h i r t y - t w o

Fatoosh stared at Buzzy. "Just what is that on your head?"

Hassan Hassan hurried to meet us as we made our way across the lawn.

"So good of you to come, sir," he said, bowing to all of us but extending a flattering hand to Glique, whom he singled out as first in the pecking order of our little group. "May I offer you the hospitality for which My Lord Fatoosh is justly famed."

"Yes, yes, Hassan. Now, please, a bathroom? The ladies . . . a long sea voyage . . ."

Fatoosh, it turned out, was in a considerable snit. Not even the redoubtable Peggy Siegal and her publicity apparat had succeeded in attracting the membership of the Meadow and the Maidstone clubs. Should he instead have retained Howard Rubenstein, considered by many the alpha and omega of PR? Yes, Clagett was here, his face twitching, and accompanied by several decidedly classy attorneys from Cadwalader, Wickersham, imported from Manhattan for the occasion. There were a number of local tradesmen who wanted to maintain good relations with customers as wealthy as Wells and the Prince. And an assortment of the kind of Hamptonites who'd attend anything. Plus an almost famous local painter and his girlfriend, who moonlighted as a model. Others here for a free drink and a buffet. A couple in masks who enjoyed dressing up. People who just wanted to see the place. A minister and his wife who didn't want to give offense. Not, however, I noted with pleasure, that excellent fellow, Reverend Parker, the Methodist. Reverend Parker knew which parties to attend. As did Father Desmond, the Catholic. You didn't see the padre hustling canapés.

In the press corps, Alex Kuczynksi of the *Times*, a young woman from Page Six looking for a few names to drop, one TV crew from local news; a few other journalists.

You know, decidedly not the A list. Fatoosh's party, clearly, was a flop.

Dixie, having freshened up, quietly reported several bathrooms in use on the ground floor of Sag Lodge, but said access to the second floor was barred by Bedouins lounging on the stair. "Thaze uh dozen port-oh-pottys out back, as well, Mistuh Stowe."

I thanked her.

Neal Travis of the *New York Post*, hardly a public defender of Peggy Siegal, was sympathetic. "Can't blame Peggy. Organizing a party out here in high season? You need six weeks minimum. These boys gave Peggy five days. In five days you can't get Bianca Jagger; you can't even get Fran Lebowitz. Seen the construction site yet? Looks like the demolition derby . . ."

Fatoosh, attempting to maintain his cool, was genial with Portofino, still on the sedan chair. "Sorry, Congressman, not to have recognized you in that . . . whatever it is," and inquiring after the Congressman's health and regretting his "accident." And asked, in fact about his . . . ?

Buzzy, responding on the laptop, typed something and shoved it at Fatoosh who read and passed it back.

"Yes. A birdcage, of course. I should have realized."

Alix saved the situation by leading the Prince toward the dance floor.

"I do love a good fox-trot, Your Highness. One so rarely hears them these days. Which I think an enormous loss."

I got into conversation with a Texan at one of the bars. He was watching May and Kay dancing with Arabs and Dixie with a fellow cowboy.

"They ain't many women here," he informed me, "but what's here is prime."

I recognized several bartenders, locals hired for the evening. "Jesus, Mr. Stowe, there's more people outside picketing than they got here. What a waste. All this booze . . ."

"Who's on the picket line?" I asked.

"Rich people who hate this place like hell."

"Stowe, will Dixie be safe with that cowboy?" Sammy asked in some agitation. "You know how young she is. I have responsibilities. To UCLA, to her mother and father, acting as I do in loco parentis . . ."

Signor Piano had fully recovered. And, with Lars, seemed to be enjoying himself, both of them drinking champagne. "Hi Ho," said Lars. "Hi Ho," said Piano gamely. Hassan Hassan beamed his pleasure, desperately anxious to find *someone* having fun. Clearly, a failed party would reflect badly on *him*. On the dance floor another fox-trot ended and men hurried to Alix to fetch drinks, to light her Marlboro. Where had Fatoosh vanished? I caught a glimpse of Offshore Wells in a white cowboy hat and matching leather chaps. I guess that was his idea of a "costume" when you party in the Hamptons. The Asp had popped up tagging after Wells. Had it been he who flew in bearing the Rose Manteau? Or was it possible the damned thing wasn't here at all?

And how was my old man doing there in central Asia while I drank cocktails?

Eventually I worked my way onto the dance floor and reclaimed Her Ladyship. "You don't even like fox-trots," I complained.

"Just being genial, Beecher. Poor Fatoosh, no matter his sins, is as vulnerable as anyone else. My heart goes out to a chap who gives a party and no one comes."

She seemed to be working herself into a mood where she might again become engaged. "Now, Alix," I began.

"Don't concern yourself, darling. I've sworn off all that. Besides, I'm still affianced to the Marquess, aren't I? I meant to write *The Times*, announcing it was off. But with all the excitement, I've not had time."

Now they called for the archery competition.

VooVoo and Jesse Maine returned from the far lawn about twenty minutes later. "Longbows is the bestest," she assured us again. Jesse grinned his pride in her.

"Did you win?" Sammy asked.

"You shitting me?" she snarled. Akbar, the Kuwaiti champion, hadn't even entered. "He had no chance," VooVoo declared, showing around her winning medal. Jesse had a medal as well.

"Third place."

"I should have entered," Sammy said.

VooVoo and Jesse stepped out onto the dance floor for the next fox-trot, bows and quivers neatly slung, as Alix and I went into the miniature golf with a dozen others. She never played golf but came in fourth. A tough course; the sixth hole, the Old Red Mill, was bogey or worse for everyone. May (or Kay) took an eight there.

A cowboy grabbed at my arm. "Couple of us boys is getting out of here. You know a good bar in town?"

I recommended the Blue Parrot and assured him he could use my name with Roland.

"Thanks, pard."

By eight o'clock people were either drunk or drifting away. I'd put my nine iron down to dance and couldn't recall just where. There was a rack of croquet mallets handy and I resolved to grab one of those if need be. Where was Punjab? Upstairs with the holy relic, I'd bet. Very few people had bothered donning masks but one elegantly turned-out fellow in a "Ken Starr" rubber head, caught my eye.

"It's me, Bando," he hissed as I passed.

Howard Roark, I assumed, was lurking somewhere.

Eight-thirty. For the first time, the sun was so far down that the Japanese lanterns and other lights on the lawn and patio were starting to gleam in the deepening dusk.

Prince Fatoosh danced again, I was relieved to see, first with Dixie, then with another Arab gentleman, then with May (or Kay). I feared he was so frustrated by his treatment at the hands of Hamptons snobs, that he might in a tantrum just call off the party and celebrate privately, sending the rest of us packing, guests, barmen, servants, journalists. Even Wyseman Clagett who again seemed on the verge of attempting, grotesquely, horrifically, to eat his own ear.

Jesse had an idea.

"Me and VooVoo. When them fireworks blow, me and her can create a little ruckus."

"How're you going to do that?"

"You know we Native American fellers have our wiles and our ways. And if Madame Vronsky here saunters up to one of them sentries, why, you can't say what a wild Bedouin, who's on guard duty and don't get invited to cocktails, might end up doing. And eagerly so. A feller like that, he's the kind of boy you can talk into things. Specially a fine-looking woman like VooVoo."

But timing was everything. If, at the very instant the first of George Plimpton's pyrotechnics exploded in the night sky, startling and blinding the beholders, VooVoo and Jesse suddenly appeared firing arrows on Fatoosh's flanks, and Bando and Sammy and Signor Piano and myself, to say nothing of Lars and the covergirls, heavily armed with golf clubs and croquet mallets, also made unexpected sorties, why there was no telling what chaos might occur.

Even Buzzy was impressed.

"It could work," he tapped out.

A boy brought fresh cocktails and we all took one, except Buzzy. I slapped him on the back for being a good sport. But left off when he continued to write: "But I'm to be one of you. The subcommittee on Aliens and Sedition won't be deprived of prominent mention in the *Congressional Record,* for unmasking these rogues."

By now Jesse and VooVoo had vanished into the dusk.

"Is Plimpton *usually* punctual?" asked the man in the Ken Starr mask, obviously worried that we might be running late.

"A Harvard man?" I hissed back.

"Sorry."

Prince Fatoosh, looking tense, snapped his fingers, summoning the Asp, Hassan, Offshore Wells, and several other Texans and Kuwaitis, who gathered round, heads close together, Offshore's stetson bobbing energetically. I glanced at my watch. Were they about to unveil the Manteau? Any second now George would be letting loose. And he didn't just ease into the thing, tiptoeing around a theme, he liked a big opening, half a dozen rockets going up simultaneously to explode into the blackness. Plimpton always did think large . . .

Now I was the one getting nervous. My reveries were interrupted by the single most terrifying scream I'd ever heard.

"Aiiiyeeeee!"

"What the devil . . . ?"

Everyone on the patio, drunk or sober, oilmen and dancers and servants, was transfixed, all of us facing the lodge and looking upward. The orchestra, in mid—fox trot, dropped its instruments as they too looked up.

Toward the second floor! Toward what appeared from here to be a scantily dressed woman leaning out one of the windows and crying, "Snaaaakes! Snaaaaakes!"

It was Dixie Ng, who had apparently stumbled across the Malevolent's reptile collection. But wasn't Dixie supposed to be a snake handler? That upbringing in the bayous? No matter. Now, while she had them all distracted (the Arabs, not the snakes), was the time for us to move. Even if the fireworks hadn't begun, you seize the day, dammit!

Alix, for one, wasn't hesitating. I could see her sprinting through the startled dance floor crowd headlong for Sag Lodge. And if *she* was on the move . . .

"Come on, everyone," I ordered. "Come on, Signor. You, too, Sammy! Help the Congressman there, Kay, please . . ."

"May."

"Whatever," I said. "Just get his ass back up there on the sedan chair and make for the house. All of you. You, too, Lars. Come on, Bando! And hang on to your golf clubs! We're going in there with Alix and Dixie and take that damned lodge!"

"Right-o," Bandar responded, his Ken Starr mask still in place, leaping onto the patio just as, right then, the sky above exploded into brilliant, near-blinding light, and from afar came the delayed sound of half a dozen mortar shells lifting Plimpton's opening barrage of rockets into the night sky over Boys Harbor.

"By God, that man's punctual!" Bandar shouted, segueing into a half-forgotten but still undeniably thrilling, rollicking Harvard fight cheer:

"Resist fiercely, Fair Harvard! Deny them the ball!"

As, from the sedan chair in our wake, came the laughter of covergirls and Lars's happy shout: "Hi Ho!"

At which point, Howard Roark, until now so passive, strolled out of the woods, calmly lighted a stick of dynamite from his cigar and tossed it casually back over his shoulder into the forest bordering the great lawn.

Boom!

Not three seconds after, another *Boom!* Roark was tugging sticks from the carpenter's apron and setting them off, one after another. The cocktail party had by now pretty much fallen apart as Arabs and Texans, servants and singers milled about in confusion. I could see Offshore Wells cursing and dashing, this way and that. While Fatoosh, his handsome face reddened and frenzied, flailed about him with a riding crop, cuffing and pummeling anyone within reach, Arab, Texan or fat singer, and crying to the heavens in his own tongue. He knew about our Fourth of July; that we also celebrated Bastille Day in the Hamptons with fireworks had never occurred to him!

I looked over at Bandar. He'd jettisoned the Ken Starr mask and looked as happy as a pious Muslim who'd just seen Mecca. As for me, the whole affair suggested a Victor Herbert operetta, with Nelson Eddy and the Mounties galloping onstage to rescue Jeanette MacDonald.

On the patio, those who'd been staring up at Dixie Ng, crawling along the parapet, trailed by dozens of snakes, now turned to see coming at them, full tilt, a small mob of madmen, one of whom was tossing dynamite sticks, others brandishing golf clubs or croquet mallets. Above and behind them, Dixie was screaming again, bloodcurdling sounds.

Some snake handler, I thought indignantly.

Fatoosh and his crew weren't so much indignant as stunned. By now they'd seen us, seen Plimpton's fireworks, certainly seen Dixie and the snakes, been stunned by dynamite blasts, and witnessed the strange and horrifying sight of a man careering toward them with a birdcage on his head, brandishing a laptop computer. Just then, the first of the snakes had begun to slip from the parapet to fall, angry, spitting, and wriggling, among the drunks.

Chapman Wells, taller than the others, the stetson cocked rakishly on his head, looked about in alarm, and began edging toward the field where his chopper was tethered. If these lunatics disrupting Fatoosh's party were as menacing as they appeared, this was no time for Wells to find himself on the losing side. Better to have fought and run than never to fight again.

Except that Offshore had forgotten about Her Ladyship.

Alix was standing on a table now, waving one arm in my direction and crying, "Tally-ho, chaps. Yoicks! Yoicks!"

I waved back and gave her the response. "Yoicks, indeed!"

"Oh, well done, Beecher. Dixie found the treasure room. Up there, amidst the snakes."

The Asp was out on the parapet now in hot pursuit, edging his way toward Dixie from the rear, and lashing out with a foot at various snakes, more of which were dropping, angrily and heavily, on the heads and shoulders of Kuwaiti retainers and Texas oilmen on the patio below. Which led to oaths and lively stepping, I can tell you. But up there, the Asp had Dixie just about cornered at the angle of the parapet.

"Keep your filthy paws off that child, Asp!" Alix shouted. "Or you'll have UCLA down on you."

Behind me, Sammy added his voice.

"Just beware, you!" he called. "I've connections, y'know. Liz Smith and I talk all the time!"

But Dixie was not yet helpless. Dipping to one knee, and elegantly so, she reached out a swift and dexterous hand to grab one of the slithering reptiles by its tail and toss it deftly into the Asp's menacing face with its smugly chill grin. As the snake flew toward him, the Asp's mouth fell open and he stumbled, to fall screaming from the parapet, landing heavily on the bass player.

"Well done, Dixie!" Alix shouted.

"Hi Ho!"

I turned to see Lars and the covergirls, belaboring a Texan with a 55-degree wedge, a croquet mallet and a champagne bottle.

"Come on," Bandar shouted, "it's upstairs." He dashed for the front door with me on his heels.

By now Alix was clambering her way up the outside of the building, with Dixie's hand held down from the parapet to give her a lift. Good! I didn't like the idea of her being down here among the snakes.

Seeing Bando and me headed for the front door, Her Ladyship called out:

"Beecher, beware of the lion! He's inside the house."

I stopped in midstride. All I had was the nine iron.

"Where?"

"Dixie says roaming the upstairs hall."

"Oh." Bandar was through the front door and I hastened to catch up, as he whirled to shout:

"Hurry, Beecher, it's got to be the Rose Manteau!"

thirty-three

Punjab, near death, leaped to his feet and began,
powerfully, to choke Lars.

I don't mean to suggest this was Pickett's charge or the battle of the Little Bighorn; it wasn't. After all, when you have a plan of attack, no matter how nutty, with cowards and women and ninety-year-old men and a guy in a bird-cage, if the enemy is drinking cocktails, you usually win.

Bandar and I got up the stairs easily enough, dodging a couple of snakes slithering down a step at a time, bump bump bump, and elbowing one likely lad and his crossbow right over the banister, thwacking another with a golf club, and then encountering a reunited Alix and Dixie Ng in the long hallway.

"Swiftly, Beecher," Her Ladyship ordered. "I'll need your seersucker jacket. Poor Dixie, to think what's she's been through. I'm attempting to get the dear girl more suitably clad."

"How y'all, Prince, Mistuh Stowe. Ma, but we been havin' uh tahm up heah."

She seemed, though in her underwear, perfectly okay but I handed over my old Brooks Brothers jacket regardless. As she slipped into it, Bandar asked, trying to remain aloof but desperate to know:

"And, the locked room with the . . . uh, secrets. Just where might that be, Lady Alix?"

"Just along here, sir," she replied. "Past where that large chap is lying."

Punjab! And out of it, his turban slightly askew, the man himself, cockeyed, a freshly honed scimitar clutched uselessly in a hand the size of a catcher's mitt.

"I do hope he's going to be all right," Alix said, conveying marginal guilt. "I had to give him a knock."

"Look out!" Bandar shouted, leaping back as a brightly banded snake appeared from the other side of Punjab's prone body and slid quickly across his fat thighs toward us.

"Pshaw," Alix scoffed, "I'm sure that's but a harmless fruit snake, as Dixie will be able to confirm."

"No, ma'am, thet's uh king coral, jest about tha deadliest mid-size vip-ah theh is," said Dixie, briskly grabbing the snake by its tail and, with a vigorous snapping motion, cracking its back, before tossing it down the stairwell into discard. I certainly owed Dixie an apology for doubting her snake handling.

"Mmm," Her Ladyship said, "and I was quite sure from its markings—"

"Never mind that, Alix, where's this famous locked room?" I said, fully aware she knew absolutely nothing about snakes. But more concerned that until Bandar had the Rose Manteau in his possession, we were anything but safe. Fatoosh and his men had momentarily been panicked by fireworks and snakes and our wild assault, but the reality was they were armed and outnumbered us, and were on their own turf.

There was a bit of a scrimmage behind us on the stair and Bando and I both wheeled instinctively, ready to repel borders, but it was only Congressman Portofino with his laptop, supported vigorously on either flank by May and Kay.

"He's got a message for you," Kay (or May) called out. "Such an admirable man, so dedicated to the national interest."

"I'm sure," I said. "Let me see the message."

It was straightforward. "My agent on the island, for some reason, has broken off contact. I fear Fatoosh may have unmasked him. What a gallant fellow he was. I'm sure whatever the cruel barbarities suffered, that he maintained a discreet silence to the very end."

"Sorry," I said, "can't help you."

It was then that Buzzy saw the supine Punjab stretched out and grabbed the laptop from May (or Kay).

"*There's* my man," he tapped. "Can't you see that miniaturized radio transmitter in his turban? Is he dead? That bastard Fatoosh, I'll see that he's prosecuted under the organized crime statutes—RICO, that's the ticket! You get treble penalties, both prison terms and fines. You don't kill an agent of the subcommittee on Aliens and Sedition and walk away with impunity. Oh no."

"I don't think he'd dead, Buzzy." I said.

"No, not at all, Congressman," Alix put in. "I had to hit him reasonably hard, being he's so big. But I assure you, I had no idea there was a radio in his turban or that he was in your employ. Else I'd hardly have—"

"Mistuh Stowe! Prince! Theh's uh lie-un!"

There was indeed a lion. Padding toward us down the hallway.

"That damned room! Alix, Dixie! Which is it?" It wasn't the Rose Manteau we needed now but a door between us and being eaten.

"Hi Ho!"

It was Lars, coming up the staircase just behind the lion, which, alerted by his cheery greeting, turned now away from us, growling, to devour Lars instead of the rest of us.

"Well played, Lars!" Alix called out. "You've got the beast totally addled."

I was with her on that. There was a lot more of Lars to go around, when it came to being eaten. Outside on the patio I could hear shouts, curses, things being knocked over, and some badly off-key music as the dance orchestra attempted valiantly to restore a semblance of order, and if possible gaiety, to the scene. Had the forces of Fatoosh regained the initiative?

"Here, darling," Alix called out, "this is the room."

Finally!

The room to which Mario Buatta had been denied access unless he betrayed Paige Rense and *Architectural Digest.* As well as the room that might determine our fate, rehabilitate prodigal son Bandar, provide a key to my father's secret mission, mean war or peace in the Persian Gulf, and determine the price of gas at American pumps this summer.

Now that we were all inside, and for the moment safely away from the house lion, Kay and May helped Congressman Portofino to a large armchair while Bandar and I began a search.

"What is it we're looking for, actually?" Alix asked. "It would so help if we knew that."

"Ah'll say," Dixie agreed. She looked very nice in my jacket. I started to answer but before Bando could respond, we were distracted.

At one of the room's windows, the one through which Dixie had crawled to elude the snakes, pursued by the Asp, May (or Kay) shrieked, "Look, they're killing Signor Piano and Mr. Glique."

Alix moved swiftly to the window.

"Not killed as yet, Beecher, but pinioned by ruffians, Piano and Sammy both!"

Sure enough, we could see them in the light of Plimpton's star bursts, down on the patio amid the smashed fixtures and fittings, bound and being handled roughly by Fatoosh's thugs. But where was Jesse? And more to the point, VooVoo with her trusty bow? You'd think she'd be of some use with all her ferocious talk. What about Roark the dynamiter?

Portofino had been propped up and was typing rapidly as the Prince and I ransacked closets and bureaus. Where was the damned Rose Manteau? No difficulty finding snakes, plenty of them, and we kept having to fend them off, Dixie with her usual competence, May and Kay with panicked scurrying about and screams, as Alix continued to identify each species.

Inaccurately.

"Ah they still killing Sammy 'n' Signor Piano?" Dixie inquired, understandably perturbed.

Who could say? I dislike being the bearer of ill tidings and instead of replying, kept rummaging through cartons and crates. Then, a loud knocking on the door. Cautiously, I sidled over to stand just off center in case someone started shooting through it. "Yes?"

"Hi Ho!"

We let Lars in, considerably the worse for wear, even his cheery mantra less buoyant than usual.

"Lions no make bouncy, I swear to God."

"Well," Alix said, "I shouldn't think so, Lars. And a male at that?"

"#%@%*#@##," he cursed in Swedish, or Lapp, or so I presume, as Dixie began to bind up his claw marks. She wasn't very good at it but, given that we have very few lion attacks in the Hamptons, not a bad job.

"Beecher!" Prince Bandar shouted. "Here, in the closet, and on a wire coat hanger!"

"What? What?" I shouted back.

There was a dramatic pause. Then, quietly but with obvious emotion, Bandar the Gentle said, "Here, Beech. At last. The Rose Manteau . . ."

Stiffly, reverently, he did me the honor of handing me the sacred relic by the hook of the hanger.

"Gosh, Bando," I said, inhaling with emotion, and wondering as I inhaled, did I smell moth balls? There was a polybag draped from the wire hanger, the bag imprinted with the slogan "Texas's Cleanest Cleaners! No Dry Cleaner Dryer!" with a Houston street address, phone and fax numbers. I held it up for Bandar's benefit, pointing at the advertising slogans.

"Mmm," he said, "Typical. Texans would launder the Shroud of Turin if they got their hands on it."

But the amused smile faded quickly from his face, to be replaced with a solemn intensity as he took back the hanger. Clearly, it was a meaningful moment. But before he could remove the dry cleaner's slogans, he was interrupted.

There was a great roar, of pain or exultation you couldn't be sure, as Punjab, who until now had been unconscious and near death, at the sight of the sacred totem leaped to his feet and began powerfully to choke poor Lars, who just happened to be the closest, and didn't need this, having been already roughly treated by a lion. Portofino, in his easy chair, tapped out a brisk message and held it up to the enraged Punjab.

"Oh, he's one of us?" Punjab said, and dropped Lars. "Sorry, Congressman, didn't recognize you inside that birdcage."

I focused on Bando, who during the scrimmage all about him, had carefully lifted off the polybag.

"But that's really it? That's the Rose Manteau?"

Prince Bandar nodded, too overcome by emotion to speak.

thirty-four

"About Sharon Stone, Prince. I'm confident something can be worked out."

On the patio below, unaware of our triumphs, Signor Piano and Sammy Glique faced a Fatoosh back at the top of his malevolent form, waving and smiling, showing excellent teeth, as all about him the dancing and fluting and tambourining had resumed, accompanied by joyous wailing, rhythmic ululations, and the dervish whirl.

The only interruptions, an occasional snake being dispatched and the plaintive attempts to be heard of the captured, and decidedly more pliable, Glique.

"About Sharon Stone, Prince, and *Elephant Walk*, but of course! Why didn't I see it sooner? Sharon Stone and elephants! *Brusque* elephants! Talk about high concept! The thing reeks of Oscar. I'm confident something can be worked out contractually with Ms. Stone. My people will do lunch with her people. I'll be calling William Morris—"

"Silence, you worm!"

"Of course, of course. At times like this, who am I to interrupt? Signor

Piano and I are at your orders, sir. He, too, a great admirer of Ms. Stone and her film work. It would be our distinct pleasure to—"

"Search these spies for weapons," Fatoosh ordered, and when the guards sprang to their task, there were Sammy's pruning shears!

"Believe me, Prince," Glique said, oozing sincerity. "It's laughable to think of these as a weapon. Ask Piano, ask anyone. Count Wigbold could tell you. The local privet hedges, I snip as I go, trying to keep them neat. Privet gets out of hand if you don't keep up. And as anal as I am, well . . ."

"Shall I chop off this impudent fellow's head, Your Highness?" a small but menacing Bedouin inquired politely, running a thumb along the edge of his scimitar blade.

"Not yet."

Glique didn't like that "not yet," not one bit. He turned to chide Piano. "Enough talk, Signor. Don't you see the Prince has things on his mind? He hardly needs our endless prattle."

Piano, who had said absolutely nothing, nodded vigorous assent.

It was then that in the upper room we all stepped back to make way, as Bandar the Gentle stepped out onto the parapet above the patio, dramatically holding with fully outstretched arms above his head a cloak (still smelling slightly of moth balls) of roughly woven goat's wool, worn centuries before by a young man who came out of the Empty Quarter to become a prophet to his people.

"Behold!" Bandar called out in an ancient tongue, "I bring to you the Rose Manteau!"

At first, a total, stunned silence. Broken, jarringly, when a scimitar dropped with a clang to the patio, from the palsied hand of a gaping-mouthed courtier.

No one moved. Except to turn head and eyes upward. To the parapet. To where Bandar stood, frozen. Not even Fatoosh could avert his gaze. He, too, like the meanest of servants, stared up at Bandar and the rough cloak, more like a poncho than a true coat, held high above his head.

"And now," Bandar continued in measured tones of formal Arabic, "as required by Holy Law, and in your presence, I don the sacred cloak. Which according to legend can only be worn by a Prince of Sabah al-Sabah of the royal blood, whose shoulders are of the identical span of those of the holy shepherd-prophet himself."

Inside the upper room we were as crisply focused as the Kuwaitis below, all of us crammed together at the window, Alix and Dixie and the covergirls, Plimpton's pyrotechnics intermittently illuminating the dramatic scene below. Only Lars, badly used, hung back, gathering his strength, while the Congressman tapped out messages to someone, somewhere. Punjab, holier than thou, and having shaken off concussion, was telling his prayer beads. Oddly, I felt very calm. Bando was a Harvard man and it was inconceivable to me that this was all a mammoth bluff. He must *know* that the Rose Manteau would fit. Because if it didn't, that crowd down there, led by the Companions of the Rosy Hours, would tear him to pieces. And the rest of us along with him. Pious Kuwaitis don't take kindly to religious hoaxes that burlesque their most sacred relics.

Or, as Bando years before in my hearing told a scoffing, impudent fellow at Dunster House, "You don't dis the Prophet, Jack."

Not in the presence of the Companions of the Rosy Hours, in any event.

Need I say it? Of course the Rose Manteau was a perfect fit! Henry Poole of Savile Row with three fittings couldn't have done a better job. Balenciaga never cut a more perfect shoulder. Armani? Don't even ask.

But if we in the upper room exhaled in relief, the scene below was one of sheer chaos. The Companions of the Rosy Hours, as one might have anticipated, broke into wild, exultant gyrations; members of Fatoosh's personal bodyguard began fighting among themselves, this clique against that; the Asp, revived, sidled menacingly toward where Sammy and Signor Piano stood bound, a gleaming knife in one hand, while the drunken Texans seemed befuddled. Servants again passed around the cocktails and the band resumed playing the fox-trot, as the quartet of fat female singers returned to the stage. Howard Roark, a cigar in his mouth, the last of the dynamite still stuffed into his apron, mixed himself a cocktail.

Only Prince Fatoosh maintained a regal, if ferocious, dignity, still gazing upward, until, at last, his eyes met those of his hated younger brother Bandar, now victorious and garbed in the sacred cloak. At which instant, Fatoosh at last bowed his head in homage to the better man. And, in a touching gesture, called out in Arabic:

"There is but one first Prince of al-Sabah and heir to the Emir. It is my brother Bandar the Gentle. Whom I now salute and beg his blessing."

I could see Sammy nudge Piano.

"I told you, Signor. That Fatoosh, at bottom, a gentleman. Not one to hold grudges. Unlike certain senators I could name."

Piano, staring transfixed at the approaching Asp, shook his head.

"Sammy," he whispered urgently, "the knife . . ."

"Not to worry. He'll be cutting us free in a moment. They know where their bread is buttered."

It was just then that Jesse and VooVoo, bows drawn, arrows fixed, raced from the wood and across the lawn, up the stone steps to the patio, scattering the crowd, and bowling over the Asp so that his knife clattered harmlessly to the stone flagging, and drawing a bead on Fatoosh's royal torso.

"Oh, well done, Jesse!" Alix called out.

Fatoosh, who had already capitulated, called out to his retainers.

"Those two!" he shouted, staring at Glique and Signor Piano. "You know what to do!"

"So," said Piano sarcastically, "they know where their bread is buttered?"

But the knives sliced through ropes and not flesh as Fatoosh's men freed his prisoners.

Glique rubbed his chafed wrists. "This POW stuff, not a laughing matter. You begin to appreciate why Senator McCain does odd things on occasion, after what he went through."

I wanted to be down there but I was afraid that something might happen while I was on the stairs. I was still playing control freak, still trying to run this idiotic operation. It was then, in that moment of hesitation, that Alix shouted:

"Jesse! VooVoo! Look! That Offshore fellow! He's doing a bunk. And right behind him . . ."

That was how I saw VooVoo Vronsky slipping past Sag Lodge on the near side, pursuing Chappie Wells.

"Stay here!" I told them, and ran into the second-floor corridor, narrowly brushing by the lion, fortunately asleep. Then, down the broad, winding stair, kicking a small python out of the way and leaping over a good-size cobra, its hood spread, on the final step. The Hamptons didn't *use* to be this complicated.

Wells's flight crew had the big chopper wound up and ready to fly before he sprinted through the fringe of trees in his chaps and cowboy hat and hit the landing strip at full speed.

VooVoo sprinted close behind, her bow slung, the quiver of arrows bouncing lightly on her back. Could she fire accurately, panting from a long run? But she could, and did. She and Jesse, coming up on her heels, loosed a volley of arrows as the big chopper slowly rose and then, resembling a pin cushion, banked north, the high whine of its rotor fading, headed for Long Island Sound and New England beyond.

Back on the patio, the orchestra played, the fat ladies sang, the waiters with their cocktail trays moved again through the crowd, as Sammy and Signor Piano accepted congratulations for their escape. And the Companions of the Rosy Hours, in tribute to their new chief, broke into whirling, dizzying dance!

"You bastard!" I cried out at Offshore Wells, aware he couldn't hear me, but wanting to say it nonetheless. Was he still to get away legally with all this while good, decent men like Vonnegut were forced from their homes?

Well, yes, it appeared he was. As Jesse says, "Sometimes you eat the bear and sometimes the bear eats you." On the patio, Bandar, still sporting the Rose Manteau, and jauntily so, was handshaking his way through the guest list, embracing the Companions, who broke into even livelier dance. What was surprising, the dancers were being egged on by Fatoosh. But why would he play cheerleader? The vaunted Fatoosh charm? Of had the Malevolent still a hand to play?

Distracted, wondering how I could inform my father of our recovery of the Rose Manteau, I was only half listening when on the final beat of yet another wild, exultant Rosy Hour dance, I heard Fatoosh cry out in a curiously ecumenical mood:

"Well done, my lads, well done! Hochs! Hochs! And hip hip hooray!"

At which the Companions responded in kind:

"Okes! Okes! Eep eep ooray!"

thirty-five

"They pierce your tongue with a heavy iron hook.
Then make you dance the jitterbug."

If we thought all this put an end to the affair, we were pathetically mistaken.

For one thing, the house itself was uninhabitable. Snakes everywhere! We set up a command post on the patio by the light of Japanese lanterns, which provided a festive air suiting our mood. The summer night was warm enough, and we could tough it out here until dawn, feasting on canapés and swilling champers, awaiting Captain Bly. Of course we could have phoned for cars to fetch us. But I was reluctant to pass through even the tag ends of a picket line and have to issue explanations. Besides, wasn't this a romantic way to spend the night, under the summer stars with Alix, and then complete the round-trip by sea, a happy symmetry? Bandar, however, was uneasy.

"It's not like Fatoosh to take this all so well."

"Just being a jolly good sport?" Alix suggested.

Bandar shook his head.

"He's always been a sore loser. Blame it on being packed off at age twelve to a German gymnasium in the Black Forest that featured Wagner, the code duello, and cold baths."

"Oh, that is rum," Her Ladyship agreed. "One's formative years spent amidst trolls."

"And werewolves," Sammy put in, a devotee of movies starring Lon Chaney Jr. and Maria Ouspenskaya, "plus the essential sprig of wolfbane."

Chilling out over the Dom Pérignon, smug and secure, enjoying the sight of Fatoosh and the lads salaaming to My Lord Bandar, sporting the Rose Manteau, it should have nagged at me, what of Admiral Stowe over there in Indian country? Just how was my dear old Dad making out?

"Oh, I say, Beecher," said Her Ladyship, more agitated than at any time during the actual battle, "look at this. These are still desperate hours. Just consider what's come over the Congressman's laptop. Dire news from the Caspian."

Buzzy handed over the computer with a sorrowful look which I took to convey sympathy.

I read the message, read it a second time to be sure I wasn't hallucinating, and then, trying to stay calm, I gave them the gist of it aloud:

"My father! He's a captive of the Taliban. In the foothills of the Urals, somewhere north of Astrakhan!" I didn't dare, not even to myself, hazard a guess as to his precise location.

VooVoo Vronsky, of all of us, seemed the most deflated by the news. But then, she knew these people.

"They're sons-a-bastids, Mr. Stowe. The worstest. Worser even than the Afghan Taliban. Cruel and ruthless. Cut off your hand as soon as look on you. Two hands. The nose. Pierce your tongue with a heavy iron hook. Then make you dance the jitterbug. Imagine the pain, my friends. But don't get me started, please. Not for delicate ears, I swear to God, those bastids."

Jesse shuddered, and you know Jesse doesn't frighten. He must have been drawing parallels to the Pequots.

The actual e-mailed message was in English and certainly to the point:

"Admiral Stowe, the famous spy, is in our hands. Unless our demands are met, we start carving off parts of his body, without anesthesia, in sixty minutes. We demand freedom for Prince Fatoosh the Malevolent, to whom the Caspian Taliban swear allegiance. And we demand the return to *his* rightful possession the sacred totem, the Rose Manteau, now in your infidel hands and those of the arch-blasphemer, Bandar the Gentle. Reply at once. Our e-mail address is appended."

"But how do they know?" Sammy Glique wondered aloud. "Six thousand miles away and they know our every move in the Hamptons? It's like Katzenberg versus Eisner, I swear. Each with a spy in the other's camp. That's really scary."

Obviously, Fatoosh had gotten off an account of events before we shut him down. Bandar's handsome face communicated his agony. How could he surrender the totem which was his by every right? Yet could he permit my father to die by inches while we haggled by e-mail?

"But where is he?" Sammy asked. "Is it the Silk Road?"

"Yes," I said.

"He spoke often of the Silk Road, your father, over the brandy. After speed chess, you need a relaxing brandy. Otherwise, you toss, you turn, all night long. The ferocity of the game . . ."

Buzzy Portofino tapped out a question:

"What is this about silk roads? Your father! That's the concern."

"Not so loud, Congressman. Discretion, please. They're probably listening," Glique said, nodding meaningfully at the laptop.

Portofino was beside himself, "They can't *hear* through a computer, for God's sake!" he typed.

"Who's to say?" Sammy shrugged. "The high tech, the ingenuity . . . you can't put anything past them. Think of Bill Gates, wise beyond his years . . ."

"The Congressman's right," Alix conceded. "With Admiral Stowe undergoing interrogation and worse, the cruel reality of his situation must be our focus. Otherwise—"

"Otherwise," I broke in, "you'll recall what I told you the other day. About Bukhara. Its minaret. And . . . the Bug Pit."

"Tha Bug Peet?" Dixie repeated in considerable horror. "Them po' officuhs down there with tha hoss manooah 'n' tha vermin?"

"He could well be there," I acknowledged.

It was Bandar, gazing steadily into my eyes while trying to spare me unnecessary pain, who now spelled out that reality.

"Unless we cave in to their demands, release Fatoosh and hand over the Manteau, I fear that your father is a dead man."

Glique shuddered and Dixie sobbed into a Kleenex, while Jesse swore oaths in Shinnecock. It was at that instant that Portofino tapped out:

"The e-mail! A fresh message coming in!"

We rushed to where the Congressman sat, the computer cushioned in his lap. The message took no time to read:

"Dateline Bukhara. A quarter of your hour is up," it read. "The Admiral's trials will soon begin."

So it *was* Bukhara; it *was* the Bug Pit, and it was evident things hadn't changed all that much since Emir Nasrullah.

thirty-six

"With a cigarette and a smile up against a stone wall pocked with bullet holes . . ."

"Bando, is your cell phone working?"

"Yes, Beecher," he said, handing it to me. I punched in some numbers. It was Defense Secretary Bill Cohen who sent my old man on this job. And if the Pentagon sent him, maybe the Pentagon knew how we might get him back, even somewhat the worse for wear.

"The *New York Times* reported there's a carrier group off the Persian Gulf. How many miles as the crow flies to Bukhara, Bando?"

He began calculating the distance.

"That's the idea, Stowe," Sammy Glique applauded. "Go right in there with smart bombs and level the place!"

Her Ladyship was giving me one of those looks. I started to ask what was on her mind when the Pentagon switchboard picked up, surprising me with their efficiency. Except that—

"No one's there," Portofino announced on his laptop even before the Pentagon could. "I just realized. No one's in Washington. They're all en route to Myrtle Beach."

What we hadn't counted on! The mid-summer version of Hilton Head's Renaissance Weekend, the President and all of them, golf and meditation. Surely including Bill Cohen.

"They got radios, Beech. They got cell phones," Jesse pointed out.

I hit some more numbers. Yes, an officer smoothly assured me, my message would be brought to Secretary Cohen's attention. And promptly. What "promptly" meant on a summer's weekend in Myrtle Beach was not made clear. After eighteen holes and a cocktail?

"Not for me to say," Jesse put in, "but how about calling the cops? I don't know that Suffolk County got jurisdiction over there in Uzbekistan, but maybe they could call somebody."

"My father's assignments rate top security. He'd be cashiered if I mouthed it around."

"But the secret's out," Sammy protested with considerable heat, "they're cutting pieces off him."

I saw Glique's point. But before I could respond, Portofino interrupted, holding out to me his laptop: "Stowe, a message coming through direct from your father."

I grabbed the computer.

"Beecher," it said, "these fellows seem to know what they're doing. There's a pot of oil simmering here on the Bunsen burner, ready for cauterization. And they've been honing their swords on a proper whetstone. I've no worries of infection. As to the rest, well, see page 112. My warmest regards to your Alix and my love to you, son, as always." It was signed. "Father."

Glique shook his head.

"The courage, the dignity. Not for nothing do Wasps run things in America. I take off my hat. Yes, and gladly."

"What a darling, sending regards to me at a time like this," Alix said. "But what's on page 112?"

"I assume he thinks I'm back at the house, at his library."

"What, what?" Buzzy typed, feeling slighted, left out.

"My father and I; a code we use. He mentions a certain book and I—"

"Wait!" the Congressman typed, "another e-mail."

We again rushed to him. Once more, the message was brief:

"Beecher," it read, "give these damned fellows credit for knowing their trade. They're starting with the ring finger, where I wear my Annapolis class ring. Father."

"Oh, them bastids," VooVoo cursed. "Always with the ring finger, damn them."

"Sammy," Dixie whispered, "do y'all understand jus' what in hell's goin' on?"

"Sadly, yes, I do," he said, his thin face pale as Thalberg's.

I was as glum as Glique. And poor Bandar, the proximate cause of the Admiral's suffering, looked even more miserable. Yet clearly unwilling, even unable, to put his family's rule, and his country, at risk.

It was Her Ladyship who shook us brutally from our malaise.

"A sharp knife cuts two ways, y'know. You decent chaps, Beecher and you, as well, Prince, sportmanship and the old school tie. But recall that even Dick Hannay on desperate occasions took desperate measures. Think how he foxed von Stumm, pretending to support the German cause while intent on putting a spoke in old Kaiser's wheel."

She was right, of course. Both Bandar and I had been wringing our hands and playing the wimp. I, for one, felt rather ashamed. If the Admiral could withstand what was happening there at the Bug Pit, and if Alix wasn't ready to surrender, how could we? She saw the change in my face and went on:

"You have your trusty Swiss Army knife, Beecher, there are plenty of scimitars about, and I happen to possess a pair of cuticle scissors. Why don't we just have Prince Fatoosh trotted out here smartly, and take turns snipping away at his various vital parts, eh?"

"Lady Alix, please," Glique offered, "my pruning shears. At your disposal, by all means . . ."

"Why, how thoughtful," said Her Ladyship.

Why she carried cuticle scissors to lawn parties, I didn't attempt to guess, but Alix wasn't through. "An eye for an eye, a tooth for a tooth," she said smugly. "That's what I always say, don't you, Jesse?"

"I surely do," he responded. "One thing I've learned, and painfully, at the knee of the Pequots."

But Alix wasn't finished. "What's sauce for the goose, is sauce—"

"Okay, Alix. Get Fatoosh up here. But for God's sake, put a sock in it . . ."

"Oh, you are the cool one, Beecher. Whilst under the most extraordinary stress . . ."

Give her that; she knew how to lay it on.

By now, which said something about shifting loyalties in the East, Fatoosh's men had become Bandar's men and ferociously so, as they hustled up the Malevolent. Fatoosh remained defiant, snarling and cursing steadily. The more he cursed, the angrier his custodians became and they cuffed him solidly about the ears. Hassan Hassan, until an hour earlier My Lord Fatoosh's faithful lackey, cursed right back, and got in a few cuffs of his own.

"Filth of the oasis! Jackal slinking in darkness," Hassan cried, not neglecting to spit on his former lord as well.

"Traitor! Sweeper-up after camels! Offal of the great whore!" Fatoosh swore in riposte, earning himself another round of blows.

"We going to burn him up, the bastid?" VooVoo inquired eagerly.

The Kuwaitis who understood English began to jump up and down in glee, anticipating a royal scorching, as one of their number poked at the charcoal in the Weber grills, encouraging the flames.

"Cuticle scissors, pruning shears, or burning at the stake . . ." Sammy murmured, weighing the options.

"Y'all have uh preference, honey?" Dixie asked, not yet indicating where *her* vote might be cast.

It didn't take long. Bandar jabbered at his brother in their own tongue, informing the Malevolent of the gruesome things that were about to be done to him unless he called off his boys in Bukhara, busy dismembering the Admiral.

"I have no authority," Fatoosh declared in surly tones. "Those fellows keep their own counsel."

"Not so," Bandar responded. "The Companions inform me the Bukhara Taliban report directly to you. They said so themselves in their first message."

"Where do I start, Prince?" Alix now asked of Bando. "He's your brother. Is there a part of him he's especially fond of? If so, I'll simply start snipping there."

To illustrate her point, she waved the cuticle scissors about, just under Fatoosh's handsome, aquiline nose.

"The nostrils? Tender tissue there, I'd wager."

Fatoosh gave up then, sagging against the two huskies gripping his arms, and uttering a despairing cry which, if my Arabic still serves, came out to something like:

"Long, long life to the Emir Sabah al-Sabah al-Sabah, whose loins produced both contending princely brothers. May the Emir's gardens flow always with sweet water, reeking of rotting blossoms and the fresh, hot dung of camels, fertilizing a better, greener earth under the cruel sun. I yield to Bandar the Gentle . . ." and a bit more along those lines, all of which I attempted to translate.

At that, the Companions of the Rosy Hours broke again into whirling dance, as other Arabs in a rather charming little chant pledged their eternal loyalty to the Emir. And to his son Bandar the Gentle, togged out in the Rose Manteau and clearly a beneficiary of God's blessings. All this as the Companions continued to whirl, madly, dizzyingly, joined briefly by Bandar himself, who essayed a few prancing steps in his robes, to the Companions' delight and cheers from the others. Sammy, who admired the choreography of the late Busby Berkeley and loved pomp, shook his head in admiration, "That stuff about productive loins, rotting blossoms, and hot dung. Wow! That Arabia must be some place."

"Lak Malibu, honey," Dixie threw in, Malibu being approximately her idea of heaven.

"The *better* addresses only," said Sammy. "Recall the line 'Honi soit qui Malibu'? Not all of Malibu is—"

"More like Kiev, Glique," said VooVoo Vronsky. "Believe me, since we throw out them bastids, the Russians."

"Jest wheah is Kiev?" Dixie asked.

"No time for that now, Dixie," Alix reminded her, "those chaps at the Bug Pit still hold the Admiral."

It was Bandar who tapped out, with Buzzy's assistance, the message that just might save my father from the fate of Stoddart and Conolly.

"Forgive me, Congressman," he said, "but doing this directly in their tongue will save time."

"I quite understand," Buzzy tapped back, for once willing to take a back seat.

Bandar's message was addressed directly to those Companions of the Rosy Hours at the Bug Pit: "Your former chief Fatoosh has conceded to the better man, his royal brother Bandar the Gentle, and the Rose Manteau has proved a perfect fit. Please confirm receipt."

The message sent, Bando turned back to Alix: "Keep the scissors handy, Alix, in case Fatoosh is foolish enough even now to resist."

"Right you are, Prince."

There was a desperate moment when the laptop, about which we all now bunched, went blank.

"Oh damn, the batteries . . . ?"

"Can you ring them again?" I started to say, when Congressman Portofino exultantly lifted the computer in both hands and held it high for us to read:

"Our concern for Prince Fatoosh the Malevolent," Bando read off, translating into English as he went, "persuades us to accept conditions. We salute our new leader, Prince Bandar the Gentle, and agree to barter the famous spy Stowe for our Malevolent."

Pause. Then, "As is."

"That's it?" I asked, still tense.

Bandar looked into my face as, quietly, he said, "We've won, Beecher. We've won . . ."

Alix kissed me on the mouth as all about us the Companions of the Rosy Hours (*our* chapter) once again broke into madly whirling dance and behind me I could hear Sammy cry out in considerable exultation, "The end game! The end game!" While from Lars the cinematographer:

"Hi Ho!"

Three hours later, as we lazed on the patio at Sag Lodge, considerably more relaxed, came a call from the American legation in Baku. The Admiral was on the line, attended by a staff physician, safe if not entirely sound.

"Collateral damage," he reassured me over our speaker phone. "Not our way of doing things, I grant you. But the Taliban have their traditions. Anyway, nothing missing I can't do without."

What did that mean?

"Look at it this way, Beecher. Does a man my age really need three joints to *every* finger?"

I'd seen plenty in Bosnia and Algeria. I'd written a book about terrorism. But this was my old man. Didn't the Taliban know how essential fingers were to an oarsman?

"Those bloodthirsty—"

"Now, now, Beecher, by their lights, they were considerate. Mindful of infection, cauterizing with hot oil and a branding iron as they went along . . ."

Her Ladyship murmured, "That *is* thoughtful, you've got to admit. Infection is always the concern . . ."

Glique nodded amiable agreement. The Admiral would still be able to play speed chess. But just how adept would he be with his fifteen seconds tick-tick-ticking away? In speed chess, you took any edge you could get, that was

Sammy Glique's philosophy. A Queen's Gambit defense, for example. You wanted dexterity. Keeping it to himself, he wondered just how many of the Admiral's fingers had been edited.

Whatever shots they'd given him, the Old Man sounded different, wandering a bit, but wanting me to know what we'd accomplished:

"Washington couldn't afford to alienate the Middle East by siding with Kurt Vonnegut against the house at Sag Pond. But unofficially and behind the scenes, I was dispatched by the Secretary to discredit the Malevolent. If I could find a direct link between Fatoosh and the Taliban, and to Osama bin Laden, well then, our government could afford to dump Fatoosh without losing favor with our good friend the Emir."

Sammy shook his head. "It's pure Hitchcock. *North by Northwest*, with Cary Grant on Mount Rushmore, outfoxing James Mason . . ."

"Beecher," my father resumed, even fainter now, "d'you remember Frederick Bailey, a British agent who traveled in 1919 to Bukhara to win over the emir of that era to the anti-Bolshie cause?"

"The name. But not precisely just what—"

"During the Russian Civil War, the Bolsheviks had already dispatched fifteen secret agents of their own to the emir, and every one of them was captured by the emir and strangled."

"Golly," Alix said, while Sammy, so recently himself a prisoner, shuddered perceptibly.

"So in order to pass through the Red Army lines and reach the emir, Bailey volunteered to join the Reds as the sixteenth spy sent to Bukhara!"

"Stout fellow," Alix murmured, this Bailey decidedly her sort of chap.

But my father was going on. "Colonel Stoddart and Captain Conolly. Then Bailey. All of them at the Bug Pit . . ."

"Quite," I agreed. Where was this leading? Was the Admiral more severely damaged than he was letting on?

"I'd prefer to go out with a cigarette and a smile up against an old stone wall pocked with bullet holes. Just another inning in the Great Game. But not by torture. You can break anyone as perhaps they might have done to me at Bukhara."

Deeply moved, no one spoke. And then the Old Man said something which remains with me.

"Not a bad place to die, y'know, Bukhara, in the company of men like Stoddart and Conolly and Frederick Bailey . . ."

thirty-seven

Signor Piano was feeling queasy again
and went to sit down.

"As an interested party," Sammy remarked, trying to be casual, "might I inquire just how it was Dixie ended up behind enemy lines in her undies?"

Wisely, I thought, Dixie permitted Her Ladyship to provide the account of how they penetrated Sag Lodge and smuggled Dixie upstairs to the forbidden suite.

"Dixie and I went inside to freshen up. And though we went to the ladies' together, only I returned to the party. Dixie sort of undressed a trifle, and then casually strolled down the hallway to the stairs, where the guard was so startled he permitted her upstairs for a tour. Where, whilst he was distracted, she slipped the bolt on the snake containers and stood back.

"Meanwhile, I was flirting and dancing fox-trots and such, until nine P.M. when Mr. Plimpton's fireworks were to go off, and you, Beecher and Bando and Jesse, plus of course Congressman Portofino in his terrifying birdcage, would startle the foe with excursions and alarums of every sort . . ."

Once the snakes slithered out, stimulating an understandable chaos and confusion inside the lodge, the Asp appeared on the scene, and Dixie was swiftly out the window, screaming and pursued by snakes.

Attempting to be suave about all this, and reassuring himself, Sammy said airily, "Well, then, there's a rational explanation. And it *was* the Asp who fell out the window."

"Of course, dahlin'," Dixie assured him.

Once Lady Alix had scrambled up the wall and in through an upstairs window to join Dixie on the second floor, the Asp's colleague, Punjab, had made his entrance. Little did they know he was Congressman Portofino's "mole" inside the enemy camp.

"He was beeg, Ah could tell thet raht away," Dixie said.

"And you, you were . . . well, in your scanties," Sammy said.

It wasn't that which distracted the man, she responded. "It was tha snakes."

"Yes, the snakes," Her Ladyship said.

"Ah got ta say, they had thet po' fella Punjab, runnin' about," Dixie said, "tryin' ta corral 'em."

And that gave Alix the opportunity to slug Punjab from behind.

"Poor chap. And Fatoosh, for his part, so attentive and courteous. I felt almost guilty gulling both of them so."

"Oh?" I remarked.

"Nothing untoward," Alix assured me. "Just the usual cheek-to-cheek pleasantries of the fox-trot, calling me 'his dove . . . his little date palm . . . his succulent one,' and suggesting we might later enjoy the 'sipping of nectar . . . the perfume of persimmons . . .'"

"Wow!" Sammy said again, "these Arabs. The dialogue . . ."

Fatoosh, despite being in our custody, permitted himself a smile. Until:

"Whilst we're at it, Prince," Alix said sweetly, "and you're being so genial, why not unburden yourself on just who it was attempted to bump off the Hon. Buzzy Portofino?"

Fatoosh, whose night was not going well, shook himself in fatigued irritation. "Ah, perhaps the most deplorable aspect of the affair. And entirely the fault of Akbar the Hashimite."

"That chap who put on the archery exhibition?" she asked, relentless as prosecutor Starr.

"None other. At my instruction, he'd been playing a double game with the Hon. Buzzy, seeking to lure him into indiscretions. The annotated copy of Rushdie's foul volume being only one of a series of fake, but quite plausible, messages intended to compromise any subcommittee investigation into my dealings."

"Yes, yes," Alix said impatiently, "that's all very well. But who fired that arrow through Buzzy's throat and why?"

"Good for you," Glique applauded. "No need to be scrupulous, now that *he's* the Prisoner of Zenda."

"Nahs-lee say-ed," Dixie remarked, and Portofino tapped vigorously at his keyboard.

Fatoosh ignored them and went on. "It was Akbar's idea to rendezvous with Congressman Portofino on the golf course. Certain vital information was to be exchanged under cover of darkness, entirely bogus information on Akbar's side, of course. But . . ."

It was my turn to cross-examine. "But then why kill the man? If Akbar was handing over bogus dope, what was the point?"

Fatoosh launched into a reply.

"Akbar is a passionate fellow and was carried away. I indulge in moments of ferocity myself," he cheerfully conceded, "but political assassinations of U.S. congressmen are hardly to my taste. For Akbar, it was not sufficient to meet Portofino on the little bridge. Proud of his own stratagems, as well as his prowess with the deadly crossbow, and also being one of the most powerful swimmers in the Gulf, where few can swim at all, Akbar entered Hook Pond at an obscure turning in the lane, swimming to their meeting underwater using swim fins, a snorkle and mask. And armed with a medieval bow."

"But Buzzy was alone. He was cooperative. He made no threats, did he?"

Fatoosh gestured in annoyance.

"That's what is so damned irksome. Akbar behaved like, in your parlance, a cowboy. He free-lanced. Something happened, words were exchanged, and from the water, in irritation or in panic, we shall never know, he fired that single shot, hitting the Honorable Buzzy in the throat. Our plan was to *use* Portofino, not to kill the man . . ."

We all fell silent. Only the tap of Buzzy's keyboard punctuated the quiet.

Then, "What did Akbar say happened?" I asked.

Fatoosh shrugged. "We never had a chance to ask. He drowned in Hook Pond."

———

It took all of us a stunned moment to recover from that.

"In Hook Pond? With Akbar a powerful swimmer and Hook Pond barely five or six feet deep at best?"

Which it was. Silted over and scummy and full of golf balls. It took Jesse Maine to suggest what happened.

"He must of bogged down," said Jesse quietly.

Fatoosh nodded.

"We found him two days later when your police departed and the crime scene yellow tapes had been taken down. Went in by night with a couple of divers. Not fifty feet from where a wounded Buzzy was discovered, we found Akbar, his finned feet sunk into the muck up to his knees, the dead man, or what was left of him, standing quite erect, the top of his head inches beneath the surface."

"What was *left* of him?" a horrified Sammy inquired.

"Yes," said Fatoosh with appropriate solemnity, "he'd been eaten by snapping turtles!"

Glique groaned aloud while Signor Piano shook his great head in horror. "Turtles?" said Kay (or May), "those itty-bitty little things?"

"You can't be serious," Alix said.

"He is, Lady Alix," Jesse offered. "They talk of last frontiers. But you bog down in the duck and goose droppings at the bottom of a Hamptons pond with thousands of golf balls in there sort of cementing the crap, you're lucky if you drown quick, afore the turtles come. Some of them snapping turtles I've took out of Hook Pond or Lake Agawan, they'll run fifty, sixty pound. I've heard of hundred pounders. They'll take your foot off at the ankle. Pull down a near-grown cygnet, swallow a good-size carp. And a man bogged down? Why, they start eating the extremities and sort of chomp in toward the innards . . ."

"Them bastids," VooVoo weighed in, "they're sons-a-bitches, them bastids."

"We got 'em in tha bayous uz well, VooVoo. Big uz gatuhs," Dixie said.

Signor Piano was feeling queasy again and went to sit down.

t h i r t y - e i g h t

From within the dripping birdcage, hung
with seaweed, came a faint answer.

When shortly before ten next morning Bly nosed the fishing boat back into the town dock at Three Mile Harbor marina, there was a bit of a commotion on the dock beyond which a half-dozen yellow school buses idled. Now what was this all about?

Alix tugged at my elbow:

"Buzzy's been at the laptop for hours, and very confidential about it at that. I'd wager he's alerted people to his miraculous return."

As three monsignors and an auxiliary bishop in their robes and skullcaps led the way down the rickety old dock, flinging holy water piously about, and chanting a very nice (to my Protestant ear, at least) Te Deum, I suspected Her Ladyship had come up with the explanation. And when people disgorged from the school buses to rush down the ramp, arms filled with flowers or hands extended high to exhibit gilt-framed holy pictures and rosary beads, cheering and blessing themselves, I knew she had.

Congressman Portofino, still wearing his protective birdcage ("The seas might be rough," Bly had warned. "Better keep that thing on, you silly bastard"), was helped up by May and Kay from boat to dock, where he paused to accept a small bouquet sent via 1-800-FLOWERS by his wife, the accompanying card signed, "Fondly," before kneeling to kiss the bishop's ring. At which he then rose to greet his fans from Staten Island. Except that. . . .

"Careful, you sons-a-bitches!" Bly called out. "I don't want my goddamned boat damaged!"

It was too late. The faithful, caught up in their fervor, rushed down upon Buzzy, the monsignors, the auxiliary bishop and Kay and May, bowling the lot of them off the dock and into the greasy, shallow waters of Three Mile Harbor.

Jesse and Lars and I got them out easily enough, with most simply wading ashore up the boat-launching ramp, the holy clerics holding high their sopping skirts and not at all happy. But Buzzy had taken a knock and the birdcage was decidedly askew, draped with seaweed and kelp.

"Easy there," I warned. "That thing's about to fall off. Don't let it catch on his arrow."

Jesse took charge, with Sammy Glique hovering. "He's all right, isn't he?" Sammy asked uncertainly, not all that delighted he'd been so swiftly rescued.

"Jes' fahn," Dixie responded. "Excep', wheah's his laptop?"

It was gone, submerged in Three Mile Harbor.

From within the battered and loosely hanging birdcage with its fringe of dripping seaweed, came an answer, weak, hoarse, only marginally enunciated and difficult to catch, but an answer nonetheless:

"Get this damned thing off me!"

Buzzy Portofino speaks!

"My God," Sammy said, truly astonished, "there hasn't been anything like this since the talkies."

The lead monsignor, recognizing a miracle when he witnessed one, blessed himself. And Staten Islanders fell to their knees as a nun began leading them in a thanksgiving, telling their beads.

"Should we kneel as well?" Glique asked in a whisper. "I don't want to give offense."

"A slightly bowed head will do," Signor Piano suggested.

"Come on, Alix," I shouted, "that damned arrow could shift again." Richard Ryan was about to go bluefishing but we drafted him and his pickup hurriedly into service. "Southampton Hospital, Richard. And right away!"

As we sped west along Route 27, Buzzy and Alix sitting in back, with Alix holding the birdcage stable so it wouldn't dislodge the arrow, and deprive Buzzy of his voice all over again, she shouted happily at Richard above the roar of the engine:

"This is such sport, Richard. Brings back memories of the hurricane, when we stole your boat to save poor Mr. Warrender from cardiac arrest."

Richard, his cap squarely on his head, nodded grimly as we sped into Southampton. "Just hang on to that birdcage! The hospital has speed bumps!"

At the hospital they rushed the Congressman inside and we were finally able to relax. Richard drove us back to Further Lane where Alix immediately began peeling off her dress. "Darling, I'm desperately in need of a hot shower," she said as she stripped. "Better stand off at a distance. I smell rather ripe."

"You smell delicious," I lied.

"Beecher, you are sweet. But you, too, could use a comb and a brushup; why don't we sort of shower together? And sport about whilst we wash."

That evening when we dropped by the hospital, the doctors said when Buzzy was knocked into the harbor, it loosened the arrow remnant fractionally away from the vocal cords but no closer to the jugular. And once they'd given the Congressman a local and began delicately to probe, the truncated arrow slipped out rather easily. Could we see him? Well, he needs rest. . . .

Which I guess was why they had a Southampton cop in the corridor outside his third-floor room, keeping the Staten Islanders at bay. Inside the room, Buzzy was sitting propped up against pillows amid flowers.

"So odd to see you without your birdcage," Alix said. "I was becoming rather attached to it."

"But you look fine," I said, choosing the positive note.

"Thanks." And, despite the sore-throated growl, he sounded better, too. He'd made a decision, he told us.

"I don't want to pursue this matter further, Stowe. I'm going to recover, your father the Admiral got out okay, the good Prince got the holy poncho, Chapman Wells isn't going to take over the Gulf. And that fellow who shot me, well, he's history. Sleeping with the fishes. Right?"

"Not to put too precise a point on it," Alix responded, "but rather with the snapping turtles."

Portofino gave her a false half smile and went on. "So why create an international incident and compromise Admiral Stowe's mission or whatever legislation my own subcommittee may end up writing? As for Glique, what can I say? The man's a rogue. Poor Miss Ng, what she has to put up with . . ."

"And if people press you about the attempted assassination?"

"Well, 'I shot an arrow into the air. It fell to earth I know not where . . .' Won't that justify a verdict of 'misadventure?'"

"You've mellowed, Congressman," I said sarcastically. I know I shouldn't.

"Yes, I have," he agreed with an irritating complacency. "When you have higher motivations than lesser men, they impose on you the burden of generosity, of largeness of spirit . . ."

Her Ladyship had had just about enough of that.

"Well, now," she said briskly, "we at *The Times* of London, and I'm sure I speak for Mr. Murdoch as well, are certainly proud to have signed you as our special correspondent, and shall be awaiting with considerable interest your first dispatches from America, Congressman. I'll be off now, reporting to my chief. Ta ta."

"Yes, well . . ." he growled at us, one of those people who just don't know how to be gracious. I understood why his wife sent cards that read "Fondly." But as we exited, out in the hallway perhaps forty or fifty Staten Islanders still waited, saying prayers and munching on buttered buns. The monsignori, being more worldly sorts, had gone to wherever it is holy men go.

Alix paused to look back.

"I've been reading Holyrod's biography of Lytton Strachey, y'know . . ."

"Oh?"

"Yes, where the Bloomsbury gang goes to Rye to pay tribute to Henry James. Clive and Vanessa Bell and Keynes and Strachey and Virginia and Leonard Woolf. All of them, gone to see James. And they, too, were munching on buttered buns."

"Fancy that," I said.

thirty-nine

*"He's blown up places before and he'll
blow them up again."*

The headlines next morning screamed the news:

OFFSHORE WELLS FOUND ALIVE!

CHOPPER CRASHES ATOP INDIAN CASINO!

According to the press reports, Chappie Wells's chopper, damaged in some mystifying manner, had gotten itself across Long Island Sound to Connecticut and, looking for an open space to crash-land without killing anyone, pancaked to a more or less successful conclusion on the roof of a Pequot Indian reservation casino ornate as Versailles and the size of the Pentagon.

The Pequots, being paranoid, at first assumed it was an aerial attack by Donald Trump and other Atlantic City casino owners, jealous of their Connecticut successes.

A local highway cop was first man on the scene and, having surveyed the damage, radioed back to his headquarters. "All alive but injured. No fire. The pilot has arrow wounds. Also Mr. Chapman Wells. Not life threatening."

A highway police lieutenant received the message and turned to his leading sergeant.

"That Hanley is drinking again. I won't have a man on highway patrol with a bottle problem. Suspend him. I gave him a second chance and he's drunk. Arrow wounds? I won't have intoxicated highway patrolmen casting slurs at our good friends and Native American neighbors, the Pequots, as well as the state's biggest single employer. Arrow wounds? You shitting me?"

Now this was all very well, as far as it went. To tidy up things:

Fatoosh and the Taliban wouldn't be taking over the kingdom (amputation and the lash, restoring the chador, banning cocktails). Bandar was reconciled with his father the Emir and awarded a Gold Palm of the Seven Pillars of Wisdom. The Rose Manteau was appropriately gussied up by the Royal Dry Cleaner for display to the Kuwaiti faithful. Arabus Oil was no longer in a position to fix world oil prices. But thanks to Alan Greenspan and Treasury Secretary Rubin, things were handled so adroitly the Dow Industrials declined barely five and an eighth in the doing. While Offshore Wells himself faced charges of trespass and failure to file a correct flight plan.

But just where did that leave The House That Ate the Hamptons? Or poor, endangered Sagaponack?

Wells still held valid title to the land on Sag Pond and presumably could go ahead with the house. Just why he would was unclear; but we know that people do irrational things out of sheer cussedness, in the settling of scores. Months and years of legal wrangling and staggering costs loomed, all the while with the grotesque, half-completed monstrosity towering over the ponds and green lawns and golden dunes of Sagaponack. What options had local people? Few to none, it seemed.

It was in this mood, a blend of triumph and fretfulness, that I gave a small dinner at the Maidstone for Roark and Madame Rand as a gesture for the architect's gallant part in our little "raid" and to reintroduce this great and unjustly snubbed man to polite society. To my relief he appeared fully dressed in shirt and tie and a decent if fatigued navy business suit. No banjo. A summer storm was brewing up along the horizon and instead of sundowners on the club patio, we repaired to the library for drinks. Alix got Roark talking on the advantages of nude swimming (less drag, he said, and an overall tan), but as soon as I could politely, I broke in. "Tell me about Speer the younger and this awful house he designed," I urged over cocktails.

"He'd sought me out on the first or second of his visits," Roark began, "and I had him up to our log cabin. He was amused by its primitive nature but intrigued by the method used in building without nails. He talked about the house on Sag Pond. Said he'd protested that it was out of all proportion but was told there was no compromise: it must be huge! And it was this requirement of vast dimensions that led Wells to Herr Speer.

"'Your uncle would have understood,' Wells told this latest Speer. 'Didn't he and Hitler collaborate on plans for the largest buildings in the world? Places larger than St. Peter's in Rome? Concert halls to seat 300,000? Boulevards wider than the Champs Elysées? Everything on a vast scale? I want the biggest place in the Hamptons, the largest private house in the country.'"

I asked Roark, "Did he tell you much else about Hitler that his uncle recalled?"

Roark said, yes, he had. "And since all architects are mad, myself included, I was fascinated that it was a failed architect who nearly brought down the world."

According to Roark, the young Speer talked freely, calling on the memory of what his uncle told him:

"Hitler was pleasant enough, passing around little cakes, getting to his feet if a woman entered, but a fanatic on the subject of architecture. He disliked America but admired our architecture ('Radio City Music Hall, the Empire State Building, the Rose Bowl . . . why didn't German architects create such wonders?'). Uncle Albert was ordered to show Hitler every blueprint. Along with the specifications: the gauge of wiring, nature of the outlets, the plumbing. A new system of toilet bowl floats and valves particularly intrigued Hitler. He hung around Speer's studio, looking over Uncle's shoulder, the ultimate kibitzer. And ideas of his own? Mein Gott! Not only buildings but autobahns, ocean liners, factories, kitchen appliances. Was I aware several versions of the Volkswagen Beetle were personally drawn by Hitler? He drove Ferdinand Porsche nuts. At the Chancellery Hitler spent hours poring over the drawing boards, while Mussolini or even Krupp cooled his heels. Speer said his uncle had the sense that Hitler would happily have spent his life putting up one-family houses. Instead, since he lacked talent, he ended up demolishing things instead.

"'So there was no talent there?' I asked."

Roark, quoting the German, continued. "'None! Nothing beyond a passion for size and weight. Concrete, he loved concrete. Had a childish knack for sketching. The architecture schools were fully justified in rejecting this impudent fellow.'"

"But your uncle," I protested to Herr Speer right here in East Hampton, "studied under Tessenow, graduated with honors. How could he work for this madman?"

We all waited silently, even Alix. Said Roark, "Speer said his uncle put it this way: if you were a German architect in 1936, Hitler was a dream client. As Uncle Albert said, 'I have found my Mephistopheles.'"

Over dinner Roark discussed Chappie Wells's house. "I found myself," Roark said, "becoming fascinated by the insane vulgarity of its dimensions. If you were to build a lousy house, then make it truly lousy. Don't shilly-shally. If Wells wanted a 150-car garage, give him two hundred. The washing machines and dryers, industrial strength. A bowling alley? Put in two. Bedrooms? Why stop at twenty-five, put in three dozen. Bulletproof glass? Why not? Chimneys? Why not smokestacks? Wells knew nothing of building and cared less. And in young Speer he found his man, a Teutonic master, building higher, heavier, faster, wider, longer, thicker. I was caught up in the megalomania. If Speer asked my advice, I was mischievous and told him, 'Bigger! Make it even bigger!' He had no hint yet, nor did I, that there were Arabs behind it, a Prince Fatoosh, and all he cared about was having the biggest place in the Hamptons. Didn't matter what it looked like. I found the project so ludicrous, so monstrous I was mesmerized, drawn to it, ineluctably. Here I was, a back number from the woods, watching as they dug the foundation so deep the ocean came rushing in and huge pumps had to be kept going night and day. A construction boss recognized me and offered me work. I think he was doing me a favor but I leapt at the chance. If this was to be an historically, insanely awful building, in some perverse way I wanted a front-row seat."

And Speer, I asked, did he come back?

"Several times. I think he knew how bad it was going to be and didn't spend much time gazing upon it. He picked my brains on local matters: copper conduits, various types of reinforced concrete, the effect of saltwater on local pipes, new developments in lightning rods, even the new antimildew paints for a place this close to the ocean. Shop talk between architects. It must have puzzled the construction gangs to see 'Red' Roark, this crazy, washed-up old-timer, being questioned by the boss. And actually listened to."

It had begun to rain during dinner and when a nearby table was taken, the men still shaking water from their hair and the women excusing themselves to freshen up, Roark became agitated. Alix sensed his unease and chatted pleasantly. Roark was distracted only for a moment and then got up and started pacing the dining room, muttering to himself.

"The storm, the storm. How do you slow the storm?" Then, "Hurry, the wind is swift." Finally, "But can I be sure of the rods?"

Nick Gallery, a member of the Maidstone, looked up in alarm. But Madame Rand was equal to the occasion. In great dignity, and not patronizing him, she rose and took Roark's long arm.

"We must go. It is the storm. He is most sensitive to storms, to falling barometric pressures. The wind, the thunder, the sound and the fury. His inner ear . . ."

I had the giddy image of Dr. Frankenstein and his hunchback hurrying up the steps into the raging thunderstorm, harnessing lightning and creating life. Did the good doctor, too, have an "inner ear" sensitivity to falling barometric pressures, I wondered?

When I'd seen the highly excited Roark and Madame Rand to their pickup, I stood there briefly in the club doorway under the canopy, looking out at the night. The storm was picking up, heavier bursts of showery rain, some wind, and way off, the low rumble of thunder and the blink of distant lightning.

"Now what was that all about?" Alix inquired when I got back.

"Barometric pressure."

From then on, both the storm and events moved swiftly. By midnight Alix and I were in bed kissing, murmuring, enjoying a cigarette, listening to raindrops rattling on the glass, those little homey things one does on a stormy night in a snug house, when the phone rang. It was Detective Tom Knowles:

"You better get over here to Sag Pond, Beecher. He's way up there on the girders, baying at the moon, only there's no moon, and we can't get him down."

"Who?"

"Your pal Howard Roark, stark naked and climbing the structural steel in a thunderstorm."

"My God!"

"Says, stay away. That's he's blown up places before and he'll blow 'em up again."

"Well, he has y'know. What else?" I asked, trying to think.

The detective was understandably sarcastic: "Oh, the usual thing. Shouting and naked, dancing on the girders in the lightning. And, oh yeah, he's got a banjo up there and he's singing in between the shouts."

Tom didn't have to tell me what Roark was singing.

I told Her Ladyship what was happening as I pulled on a pair of shorts and climbed into Topsiders and an old navy sweatshirt. "Stay here and keep close to the phone," I ordered.

"You jest," she said, tugging on a T-shirt and scouting around for something to put on her bottom.

It was all so different at the construction site: no pickets, no Arabs, no major-domos, no Texas Rangers. Just excavations and half-built structures and a helluva summer rainstorm, one fire engine, a couple of local police cars, a volunteer ambulance, and a few pickup trucks. As we rolled to a stop next to the ambulance, a bolt of lightning exploded fairly close and in its light I could see Roark way up there on top of the steel skeleton and other men on the ground with flashlights, could see Tom Knowles coming toward us, slopping through the mud.

"The night watchman saw him come in over the fence and called 911. He's still up there. Him and his rope ladder, which he's got coiled up so we can't use it. Not that I'm climbing up there with him. Or sending anyone. The way this storm's boiling up, I give Roark about three more minutes and he's toast."

"Who's that out there?"

"Couple of cops, a fire chief, and Jesse Maine and a medicine man from the reservation. How the hell they knew about this I can't say. Heard the drumbeats, I guess. The medicine man is the one dancing."

I could see him, too, through the sheets of rain.

"Hello, Inspector," Alix said. "Rarely dull or predictable here in the Hamptons, isn't it?"

She was barefoot and wore shorts under the T-shirt, and her long, tanned legs were slick in the rain.

"One might say that," Tom said, mimicking her anglicisms and giving her legs a look.

Jesse Maine came toward us.

"It's a ripper of a storm, ain't it?" he inquired cheerfully. "These holy fellers, they like to dance in a good thunderstorm. Like it's heaven listening and answering back. Real loud, too," he added as a particularly powerful boomer shook the ground.

"Can you talk him down, Beech?" Tom asked me. "I don't like to ask, not with this lightning, but . . ."

"Hell, I dunno. I can try."

"Oh, well played, darling," Alix said enthusiastically. "No white feather for Beecher Stowe!"

Lightning scares me and I'm not ashamed to admit it. But how could I chicken out with Her Ladyship cheering me on? So, soaking wet and thoroughly miserable, I started walking toward the tallest wing of the vast house Howard Roark had chosen for his perch.

Beside me, and God bless him for it, walked Jesse Maine, war sachem and chief of the Shinnecocks, holding a big flashlight and talking low.

"Good man, Beecher. I hate lightning, too. But I can't let old medicine man know it. Let's just keep walking and hope to hell."

"Yeah."

At the base of the tower Jesse shone the light near vertically so I could see Roark.

"Mr. Roark. Howard, can I talk to you? It's Beecher Stowe."

"Oh, Susannah, oh don't you cry for me / I've come from Loosiana my true love for to see / It rained all day it rained all night, the weather it was dry / It was so hot I froze to death / Susannah don't you—"

"Mr. Roark, could you come down so we can talk? I think it might—"

"By damn!" Jesse shouted as the ground shook, bouncing us about a bit. "That was a pisser."

Thunder boomed almost continually now and the near-constant lightning so illuminated the scene we didn't really need the flash. Of course, the slashing noise of the wind-driven rain and thunder sort of drowned out Roark's song. But you can't have everything. I could barely hear the medicine man, who wasn't ten feet away, dancing and chanting, barechested in the rain. "Woo woo, woo woo."

"Mr. Roark," I called again. "Can I call Madame Rand for you? Get you a cold beer? Anything . . . ?"

Truth was I didn't have a clue how to get this nut off his perch and back down on the ground. But by now, it was swiftly becoming academic: the lightning had begun to hit the towering turrets of this vast homage to self. Boom! Boom! One by one the six separate towers at the corners of the main house exploded and collapsed with a bang and then a roar, structural steel, masonry, scaffolds, wood, stone, plaster, piping, conduit, wiring, down it all came in a noisy chaos of destruction. Boom! Boom! Boom! The lightning cracked and ripped and burst abruptly about us and three more turrets fell. Five down, one to go! By now, all I could see in the rain and wind, my eyes dazzled by alternating darkness and sudden light, was Roark up there high above us, clinging to the sixth and final surviving tower, the last of Xanadu . . .

It was then the most powerful lightning bolt of all struck, knocking Jesse, me and the medicine man right on our cans, and bouncing Howard Roark off into dizzying space.

f o r t y

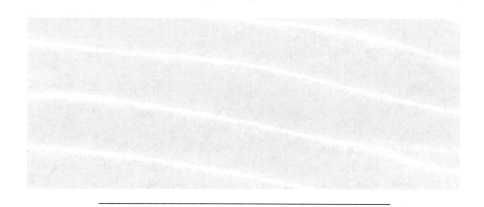

She curled up and closed her eyes, a child permitted
an excuse from school.

When I came to, which was a matter of seconds, Jesse and the medicine man were groaning but alive, and amid the flashes of blindingly brilliant white light I could no longer see the structural outlines of a huge building but only a tangle of charred and twisted wreckage, could smell the stench of burning wood and tar paper and stacks of shingle, of scorched earth. Lightning continued to hit, seemingly picking out with an uncanny intelligence the few substantial steel segments still tottering blackly above us.

Someone was standing over me, reaching out a hand to help me up. Tom Knowles? The ambulance driver?

"Sorry about that," said Howard Roark. He was naked but for a rope ladder draped around his shoulders as a sort of sacerdotal vestment. "Didn't mean for you fellers to get fried."

"Mr. Roark! You're alive."

"Sure, when the bolt hit I just let go of the steel and the rope sort of pendulumed me down. Got a couple of bumps on the way but rope won't conduct electricity, y'know."

"I hadn't realized that," I said, feeling stupid.

Oh, one other thing. His orange-rind hair had gone stark, staring white.

The insurance companies are still threatening to withhold payment to Chappie Wells and Arabus Oil but what happened's been officially put down as "an act of God."

The House That Ate the Hamptons is gone. Construction shut down and probably for good. A couple of thanksgiving services are being planned at local churches and the homeowners' protest committee has disbanded. Mr. Vonnegut allows as how he may not move to the North Fork. The Wells property is up for sale and will likely end up subdivided into a dozen or so nice four-acre parcels where ordinary rich people will build sensible houses, six or eight bedrooms, the hot tub, the pool, the tennis court, a modest three-car garage. You know, the normal, everyday sort of American home.

I don't know how many people know, or even suspect, that from the very start it was Howard Roark's intention to incinerate Xanadu, having "helped" build the place by very carefully installing faulty lightning rods that would attract the electricity but wouldn't discharge it harmlessly into the ground. They say when he heard a big storm was coming and getting close, he left us at dinner to sneak out there and be sure the rods still weren't properly grounded. From that moment on, what happened was inevitable. Or so they say. But you know how people talk out here. And no professional journalist is going to write a piece like that without better sources than hearsay.

Roark himself is keeping quiet about it and Madame Rand just smiles and takes him swimming and waits there with the terry robe until he comes back and lies down to dry in the sun. Then she relights his cigar and runs her thick, strong peasant fingers through his white hair.

Now that Lady Alix had Buzzy Portofino signed to a News Corp. (Murdoch) contract, she couldn't stall any longer and was going home to London the next day. So we went out for an evening on the town.

It was pushing five A.M. as we turned into Further Lane with an orange sky brightening low in the east, and the golf course of the Maidstone empty all around us and the skinny yellow flags drooping in the windless dawn, and Alix asleep beside me, when I saw the fox. Why had we stayed out so late, closed so many places? Because she was leaving, that's why. And I didn't want her to leave. Alix was going home. Leaving town. Her Ladyship was outta here! And I was losing her again. I felt sorry for myself for a few minutes. For more than a few minutes. And then . . .

The fox.

Well, how about that, a red fox on Further Lane, just trotting east along the blacktop about twenty, thirty yards ahead, not alarmed or hurrying things along at all. Didn't panic, just trotting east toward the rising sun. Going home after a night of hunting. Sleek-bellied and filled? Or still hungry? I liked it that with a fox you couldn't tell. They didn't send out press releases or buy classified ads. Had dignity, kept it to themselves. I slowed so as not to over-take him or frighten him into scampered flight behind the privet hedges. He turned his head once or twice, checking on me, making sure I wasn't tailgating. I think he found the Blazer nonthreatening, maybe even oddly supportive. It was a young animal, one that hadn't yet grown into its long legs, but with a nice, bushy tail. I followed his tail for another three or four hundred yards and then I was at the driveway to my father's place and my own house, wondering if I should wake Alix.

"Excuse me, Your Ladyship, but here's a red fox trotting along. Thought you might enjoy seeing it. We don't often get a fox along Further Lane, you see, and . . ."

Or maybe just send up the traditional British foxhunting cry of "Yoicks!" Which translates, in U.S. terms, to "There goes the son of a bitch!"

I decided against doing either. In her time, she'd probably seen more foxes than all of East Hampton. Besides, she looked so cute curled up there bare-foot with her shoes kicked off and a faded old sweatshirt of mine that said HARVARD tugged on over her filmy dress against the predawn chill that you get out here, even in summer. Which was quite okay. Perverse of me, I'm sure, but I liked having her wear my clothes so that afterward, when I wore them, they smelled of Alix.

The fox trotted a bit farther after I slowed and stopped, turning back one last time to be sure nothing had happened, that both the Chevy Blazer and I were still okay. Foxes out here in East Hampton are like that; they care. Satis-fied, he again turned east and resumed his purposeful trot toward the sun.

I pulled up our own graveled drive to the gatehouse and killed the engine and just sat there for a time looking down on her. Listening to her breathe. Watching over her. It was real summer now and quickly getting warm, and with the sun climbing slow, it was nice just sitting here with Alix, and nobody else around. Then a long way off there was a bicycle coming. Doc Whitmore, the tree surgeon, on that rickety bike nearly as old as he is, with the shopping basket up front so he can fetch home the groceries. Doc is about six-three and gaunt but cycles all year round and never wears socks. As a concession to winter, he adds a red down parka to his red baseball cap and bare ankles, but that's about it. Mittens, maybe, I can't remember. Doc went by pedaling slow but steady as always and gave me a wave. That was one of the great things about Further Lane, people like Doc waving and being waved back at. I suspect Alix appreciated stuff like that about this place, even in her sleep. Good women are instinctive that way and Alix was a good woman. It made me feel fine being here with her in front of my own house, Doc waving and the sun up and a fine day looming, all that on top of seeing a young fox trotting along and glancing back at me.

Isn't that what being in love feels like? *Jawohl*, Herr Doktor Freud, I think it is.

I'd known her three years now and we'd had some times together, hadn't we. Here on Further Lane with Hannah Cutting and Pam Phythian and Mr. Warrender. And down in Southampton along Gin Lane with Cowboy Dils at Tony Duke's old house. And over on Lily Pond Lane with Samuel Glique and the Congressman and Prince Bando and, of course, Jesse and the Shinnecocks. To say nothing of the snakes and George Plimpton's fireworks in the distance and Howard Roark up there naked in the rain with his banjo.

Mostly out here it wasn't that exciting, of course, regardless of what Alix told Tom Knowles, and given her breeding and Sloane Ranger connections, the Hamptons might long term be pretty boring for her. Especially out of season. Though Gordon Vorpahl promised to take her skating if she came out in winter when there was good ice. And a town trustee like Gordon, you could go to the bank on his word. Which in East Hampton was more important than anything. Your word. Except then didn't old Gordon go and have a heart attack and die while working in the pits for a pal at the car races? Why do good guys like Gordon have to go early like that? Damn!

Everything was a trade-off. With Her Ladyship's breeding and intelligence and beauty, I sensed she knew the time was coming when she would settle down with someone, somewhere. Would she be happier here with me on Further Lane or in the elegant precincts of London's West End and the South of

France dancing with "chaps" and the bustling excitements of Rupert Murdoch's great newspaper offices at Wapping Old Stairs? Maybe I ought to wake her now and just ask.

Then tell her about the young fox and Doc Whitmore pedaling past and how grand a morning this was along Further Lane, take her inside and help her pack and maybe even, one last time, "make bouncy."

A glorious place, the world, though a bit nutty. In the end I concluded we all, especially the best people, were a little nuts. Alix included. Except with her it was different. Sweeter and better and, well, I'd like to be more precise about all this, but with her Ladyship, there were vague wonders and joyful moments you couldn't help but enjoy, but which were somewhat difficult to define. Like Fatty Soames's "Make mine a gin and tonic, Luigi!"

She stirred now and woke, eyes blinking, dizzy with sleep.

"What time is it?"

"I don't know."

"Oh, good," she said, "then it's not too late."

And she closed her eyes and curled up to sleep again, a child excused from school and free to nap some more. I love watching Alix sleep.

Or, to be more precise, as Harvard teaches us to be, I love Alix.

She woke after a while. And we got her a limo into JFK and her BA flight to London. And she was gone.

A few days later the Aston-Martin people called about the borrowed car she'd carelessly forgotten to return, and which crouched gracefully on my driveway, dead still but as always looking to be going at speed. I gave them something of a song and dance and told them where they could pick it up.

Oh absolutely, I assured them, Lady Alix would be giving their new car a good write-up in *The Times* of London and in all the other important papers Mr. Murdoch owned. His TV stations, as well. A rave. That was a dead cert and they could rely on it.

For some reason Aston-Martin gullibly bought my nonsense, seemed quite pleased. Like me, I suspected, in their own way, they too were in love with her . . .